ON THE OTHER SIDE

OF THE SKY

©2021 Hugh Aitken Reviews Publishing

This is a work of fiction. Names, characters, places, brands, and incidents are either the product of the author's imagination or are written in respectful tribute to the lives of real characters and incidents featured in this story.

On the Other Side of the Sky

Hugh Ashton

ISBN-13: 978-1-912605-75-0

ISBN-10: 1-91-260575-9

Published by j-views Publishing, 2021

www.HughAshtonBooks.com

www.j-views.biz

publish@j-views.biz

j-views Publishing, 26 Lombard Street, Lichfield, WS13 6DR, UK

CONTENTS

DEDICATION

DEDICATED to my parents, who taught me that books were a constant source of joy and learning.

Also to the people of this "City of Philosophers", Lichfield, including the Lichfield Writers, who continue to display the qualities that led one of their most famous sons, Samuel Johnson, to describe their city in this way.

And to the memory of another famous Lichfeldian who appears in this book, Erasmus Darwin, grandfather of the more famous Charles, but in his day, England's leading poet, physician, botanist, and a famous inventor and member of the Lunar Society.

And on a more personal note, to my wife Yoshiko who has patiently struggled to understand my recent obsessions with alchemy, Rosicrucianism, and Kabbala.

Very special thanks to Vicky Yardley, who has acted as a constant and valuable source of inspiration, ideas, and corrections. This book would not be what it is now without her imagination and critical skills.

And to those who have helped me with research on those things about which I was pitifully ignorant. Any remaining ignorance and misunderstandings are my responsibility, not theirs.

GLOSSARY

IT OCCURS TO ME that I may have spent too long in the eighteenth century recently, and therefore expect every reader to be as familiar with the details of the characters and the setting as I am. For those who might be a little confused, here are the names and details of some of the historical elements of the story. More details are obviously available on the Internet.

Armonica, glass	Not a misprint, but a musical instrument invented by Benjamin Franklin, which produced tones through the friction of damp fingers on spinning glass bowls.
Boulton, Matthew	(1728 – 1809) Industrialist, a maker of "toys"(metal ornaments, etc.). Member of the Lunar Society.
Darwin, Erasmus	(1731–1802) Doctor, poet, scientist, inventor – a leader in all these, and the grandfather of Charles Darwin, whose theory of evolution he anticipated by several decades. Member of the Lunar Society.
Elementals	Earthly spirits described by the Rosicrucians with an affinity to one of the four traditional elements: Fire, Water, Earth and Air. Elementals have no souls.
Fae	Creatures who have made their way from another world/universe which has suffered a catastrophe. Similar to the Little People/ Good People/Fairies of folklore.
Fuseli, Henry	(1741 – 1825) Swiss-born painter, famous for his macabre and supernatural paintings, and his renditions of scenes from Shakespeare.
Gnomes	Earth Elementals, squat creatures, living underground, with the ability to move through solid earth, walls, etc.
Hugo Lombardi	(15?? – 16??) An obscure alchemical philosopher with an interest in Kabbala.

Glossary

Landgrave (Landgraf)	A title of nobility in the Holy Roman Empire, equivalent to a duke, and above a count (Graf).
Lunar Society	A group of scientific and technical minds in the English Midlands who met on nights of the full moon (for reasons of safety when travelling).
Rosicrucians	A secretive group of 17th and 18th century mystics who may be regarded as the forerunners of Masonic thought.
Salamanders	Fire Elementals, taking the form of a lizard or a beautiful human, living in fire.
Sans-culottes	The name given to members of the French Revolutionary mob – without the breeches of the upper classes (they wore trousers) hence their name (without breeches)
Soho	An area to the north of Birmingham where Boulton sited his manufactory.
Sylphs	Air Elementals, capable of flight through the air
Undines	Water Elementals, living in streams, rivers and lakes
Watt, James	(1736 – 1819) Engineer, and inventor of the condenser design of steam engine as well as numerous other improvements. Business partner with Matthew Boulton. Member of the Lunar Society.
Wedgwood, Josiah	(1730 – 1795) Industrialist and founder of the Wedgwood pottery brand. Member of the Lunar Society.
Wollstonecraft, Mary	(1759 – 1797) English writer, philosopher and advocate of women's rights. In love (unrequited) with Henry Fuseli.
Wright, Joseph	(1734 – 1797) Self-named "of Derby". One of England's foremost painters of the day. His painting of *An Experiment on a Bird in the Air Pump* forms a scene in this book.

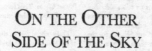

ON THE OTHER SIDE OF THE SKY

Being a Compleat and Accurate Account of the Most Singular Adventures of Miss Jane Machin of the County of Staffordshire

HUGH ASHTON
(Author of divers other Workes)

j-views Publishing, 26 Lombard St, Lichfield, WS13 6DR, UK
info@j-views.biz

OF FAERIE AND THEIR PROPERTIES

This Classe of Being some term the *Goode Folke*, though in truth they doe lacke most of those Qualities of Christian Men and Women. Others do call them *Sith* or in the Tongue of the Scots, *Daoine Sidhe*. Some term them as Demones or Fallen Angels, and some see them as the Survivors of an older and brutish Race of Men, who hyde from us through Feare. Still otheres term them *Fae*. The Doctors of our Schools for the most part do believe them to be a Race older than ours, neither Human nor Divine nor Hellish, with Powers such as we do not possess.

Faerie may make for themselves Dwellynges, the whych they term Palaces or *Brugh*, though they be no more than Holes in the Earthe. They are ruled by One they term their Kynge, who nonethelefs appeares to be possessed of no Majestie or Dygnitie, his Quality being the Possessor of a greater Strength than the others, whom he subjugates by Force.

It is also said by some that this Kynge may possess the Qualities and Attributes of all his Subjects, the latter only possessing a smalle Portion of the same.

Certes, they do lack the Power to distinguish Goode and Eville, and may often steale away small Infantes, claiming these unfortunates as their own. Some foolish Women have claim'd congress with these, even with their Kynge, and borne children. Such children are held by the foolish to have Powers like those of the Elementals as described below.

As to the home Landes of the Sith, though they inhabyt their Moundes and Holes in wylde and rugged places such as the Northern Mountaignes and Laykes, and the Hylles of Derby Shire, their true Home is held to be in the sixth Sphere above the Heavennes, that is to say the Primal Chaos. Thus some do name them as the People of the Other Side of the Skye.

These others, that is, the Subjectes of the Faerie, may be divided into four Classes or Categories, each Categorie in correspondence with the four Elements, thus:

Primus: *Earthe*, represented by the *Gnomes*, of a squat and brutish Forme, who have Power to move through solid Grounde and Walls of buildings.

Secondus: *Water*, inhabited by the *Undines*, of a smoothe and shining Appearance, who like Fysshe may exist and take their nourishment from beneath the Waves of Pondes, Rivers, and Oceans.

Tertius: *Ayre*, in which dwelle the *Sylphes*, of a tall and pleasing Forme, who may travel through the Ayre, though not as do Byrdes.

Quartus: *Fyre*, wherein the *Salamandres* have their being. In their human Forme, they are possess'd of great Beauty, but more commonly take the Shape of a loathsome Reptile.

These four Classes we may term *Elementals*, in reference to their attachment to the Elements. They bear little Relation to the Faerie, being Natives of our Worlde, but now unwillingly serve as Slaves of the Faerie.

De philosophia contra naturam Mundi,
Hugo Lombardi, York 1547

PART ONE

THE FAERIE CHILD
(1769)

The Beginning

"WHAT ARE YOU DOING, ABBIE?" Her mistress's voice came from the front room.

"Just putting out some of the stale bread and some water for the urchins, ma'am." She unlatched the back door and made her way through the gently falling light snow to the shed, where she would place the honey-spread bread and milk – she'd lied to Mrs Jowett about the contents of the dish as well as about the hedgehogs – carefully by the door.

Would he ever come back? she asked herself for the fifth night in succession. With long hair of a gloriously shining lustrous black, eyes that seemed to burn straight through her, and a voice that turned her insides to a liquid like the silver pools from a broken thermometer that she had once seen at Doctor Simmons', his memory refused to fade.

"You could be mine, little Abbie. You *should* be mine," he had said to her six nights earlier as he stepped out of the shed, before wordlessly taking the urchins' dish of bread and milk

from her unprotesting hands and starting to eat. Had he really been in the shed? She wasn't sure. The door hadn't opened,
she would swear to that. Had he simply stepped through the
wall as if it were no more than the early morning mist on the
meadow? Impossible. But there was no other explanation.

Still painfully aware of her emotional turmoil that night,
she bent to place the dish on the ground, and felt her wrist
gripped by a cold pale hand from behind. Another hand, with
long slender fingers, gently took the dish from her, and carried it out of her range of vision as the grip on her wrist was
released.

Startled, but unafraid, she turned to see her... Assailant?
Captor? Lover? All these seemed to be pitifully inadequate
and inaccurate, and yet all of these perfectly described him.
He was smiling as he took the bread from the dish and put it
in his mouth, licking the beads of honey from his fingers with
a long dark tongue that seemed to be forked like a serpent's,
while watching her

"Who... are... you..?" she asked, but not expecting a reply.

"Come, Abbie," he said, taking her wrist once more. How
did he know her name? He turned so that they both faced the
wall of the shed and took two steps forward, through the wall,
bringing Abbie with him. She had no choice in the matter.

The feeling of walking through the wall was like nothing
she had ever experienced before. When she came to describe
it later to herself (for the only person she ever told about the
whole business was her daughter Jane, a few years later, but
Jane was too young to understand her words), she could only
describe it as "walking through a wall of icy flaming swords",
words that made no sense when she repeated them to herself,
but were the only way that she could even vaguely describe
her sensations at that time.

It should have been pitch-black inside the windowless

shed, but her companion's head and body seemed to glow with an unearthly, eerie, blue-green light. She could hardly see his face on account of the glow that surrounded it. Even so, she was almost painfully conscious of his eyes looking her up and down.

"Yes, you are the one. You will be mine," he said. Once again, the sound of his words had an almost physical effect on her, and she staggered slightly.

"Me? Why me?" She was half-flattered by his attentions, but at the same time deathly scared of where all this might be leading.

"You are one of us," he said. "There are not many of us now living in the land on the other side of the sky. We are an old race, much older than mankind. So old that we are dying. There are no young women, and there will be no children."

"I am one of you?" she asked incredulously. "How can that be?"

"Your mother's father was one of us. Your grandmother never knew, and she died believing that the man you knew as your grandfather was your mother's father, so you would never have known. Surely you must know that even as a child you were different to others?"

Abbie thought back to the occasions when she had refused to join in her friends' play – play which had somehow resulted in an accident causing injury, or even death in two instances, to those taking part. Her insistence that there was something "horrid" in the corner of the room where she slept, until they prised up the floorboards and discovered a human skull, which Parson said showed clear evidence of its owner having been foully done to death. Her knowledge of things that happened on the other side of the village, almost as soon as they had happened. Yes, she was different.

"If you had not been your grandmother's granddaughter, you could never have walked through that wall with me."

She was forced, against all reason, to acknowledge that she had walked through the solid wall of the shed, and nodded in agreement.

"Now, will you help me?"

Dumbly, she nodded once more. Having grown up on a farm, she knew how bulls and cows, rams and ewes, cocks and hens, behaved, and she had heard enough sniggered innuendo from her friends to know that men and women did much the same. Was this what was going to happen to her? She felt inside her an unholy mix of terror and excited anticipation. Was this what growing up was all about?

"No," he said, and she knew – how? – that he had read her thoughts. "That is not the way that these things work." He held out the dish that had held the bread and milk. In place of the food there was a small dark sphere. "Take it."

She took the dish from his hand, and instantly felt the weight of the ball as it rolled around the dish.

"You will marry," he told her. It was not a prediction, but a command. "It does not matter whom you marry, but you will marry, and that right soon. When you do, and when you do what husbands and wives do to make a child, you must do it holding this," pointing to the ball, "in your mouth."

Abbie, despite herself, blushed.

"If it is still in your mouth when your husband is finished with you, you must take it out and keep it ready for the next time. But if it is gone from your mouth as he draws himself away from your body, then prepare yourself to bear my child in nine months' time. Do not fear. Although it will outwardly resemble your husband so that he never suspects anything, it will be my child, not his. Guard my gift to you well, and on no account lose it. There will be consequences if you do not do as I say. Do you understand all that I am telling you?"

There was nothing she could do except nod once more. Even though she appeared to be in an outlandish dream, all made sense to her.

"Good. Now I must take you back." Once more she traversed the wall of icy flaming swords, and found herself outside the shed – and instantly realised that she was alone. She removed the ball from the dish and placed it carefully in the placket of her skirt before laying the dish on the ground.

Now she could hear Mrs Jowett's voice. "Abbie! Abbie! Where are you, girl?" There was no anger in the voice, though, only what sounded like concern. The back door of the farmhouse opened, spilling golden light onto the gloom. "There you are! What have you been up to?"

"Sorry, ma'am, I was looking at the stars," she pointed vaguely upward to where Orion hung in the sky, "and I must have forgotten the time."

"You daft 'ap'orth, Abbie." Despite the words, Mrs Jowett's voice was kindly. "The sooner you find a good man to look after you, the better it will be for you."

Abbie sighed. She hadn't seriously considered marriage before that night, other than as a remote event that might or might not happen in the future, and now two people were pushing her, admittedly not entirely against her will, into finding a husband.

It was Harry Machin, some five years older than her, on whom her eye finally settled. If truth be told, she had had her eye on him for some months, even if she hadn't fully realised it at the time. Harry was not the wealthiest, or the best-looking boy in the village. Nor did he appear at first sight to be the cleverest, though this was more due to his disguising his intelligence to avoid envious comments, than it was to a lack of ability. He had also about him an air of dependability which ensured that the farmers trusted him with those tasks usually given to older men with considerably more experience. Abbie had noticed his quiet competence, and the way in which he was often able to find a solution to a problem that defeated those around him, as well as his kind and friendly manner, and despite the censoriousness that the young often display towards their elders, she found herself approving of him.

If she was to marry, and more and more she felt herself drawn to the idea, almost despite herself, Harry Machin was the one she would choose.

He quite often found work on the Jowetts' farm, giving Abbie a chance to talk to him as she took his midday snap to him from the farmhouse (for the Jowetts treated their workers well, almost as members of the family).

Harry had never been anything but polite and kind to Abbie, but without her encouragement, it is unlikely that he would ever have made any move towards her. As bold and confident as he was when facing an angry bull, or the problem of a field of hay to be gathered in with black storm clouds rapidly approaching, he was almost painfully shy when it came to dealings with the opposite sex.

But as Abbie let her fingers dawdle touching his for ever longer periods as she handed him the basket of bread and cheese, to which she sometimes added a scrape of honey or even a prized strawberry filched from the Jowetts' garden, and smiled up at him, he began to give more than red-faced monosyllabic replies when she asked him how he did. For her part, these questions regarding his health and well-being, which she had originally seen as being routine politenesses, became enquiries to which she genuinely wished to know the answer.

Soon Harry also found himself actively anticipating the hour when he could spy her form, silhouetted against the dark oaks at the edge of the field, making her way towards him. Eventually he found himself asking, albeit haltingly and stammering, "Abbie, is there ever a time when you are not working for the Jowetts?"

"Oh yes," she said, smiling. "Every Sunday afternoon is a holiday, and on two Tuesday afternoons each month when the market is held in the town, although I must buy things for them in the market, Mrs Jowett has no objection to me taking my own time to do it."

"Then would you…" He flushed red. "Would you consider walking out with me next Sunday afternoon?"

Her smile would have disarmed a much more confident man than Harry. "With the greatest of pleasure, sir," she replied, sweeping a low curtsey to him.

"You are mocking me?" he enquired, taken aback.

"By no means, I assure you, Harry. I will be waiting for you to call for me on Sunday afternoon."

This put poor Harry in something of a quandary. He had envisaged that Abbie and he would meet quietly, hopefully unobserved by anyone else. By calling on her, he would be proclaiming his interest in Abbie, if not to all and sundry, at least to the Jowetts, who were the largest farmers in the area. But if that was the price to pay for an afternoon's pleasant companionship, then so be it.

"I look forward to it."

"Ta ra."

"Ta ra a bit."

It is a matter of record that Harry and Abbie were married in the parish church of Saint Chad some six months after this conversation. The Jowetts, sorry was they were to lose such a maid as Abbie had been, and whom they had treated almost as a daughter, were delighted that she had awakened the interest of Harry Machin.

A few weeks before the wedding, old man Jowett spoke to Harry.

"Can I have a word with you, lad?"

"Of course," Harry said, nervously.

"No, it's nowt you've done wrong." He went on to explain that he had been impressed by Harry's skill at repairing and maintaining some of the newfangled farm machinery that was then coming into use. "You've got brains, Harry, as well as a strong back, and don't let anyone tell you different. You can read and write with the best of them, as well. And I've seen you do reckoning up in your head that most men couldn't do with a pen and paper. Now," he went on, warming to his theme, "there's a man down in Birmingham called Matthew Boulton. One of those toy makers – buttons and bits and pieces for swords, and ladies' bits and bobs, that sort of thing. But he needs people like you, Harry, to work in his manufactory. He's got plans, I heard. Plans that need you if they're going to come to something,"

"In Birmingham? I'd have to move away from here? *We'd* have to move away," he corrected himself, remembering that he was to be married.

"Aye. But you'd be close enough to come back and see your folks from time to time."

"Do you know this Matthew Boulton?"

"I know of him, and I've met him once or twice. He's a bit full of his own importance, but he means well, and by all accounts, he takes care of his people. If you felt you wanted to do better for yourself and Abbie, I dare say I could put in a word or two for you with him."

"I'd have to talk to Abbie about it."

"Of course you must do that. It would be a great thing for you, lad, and we'd all like to see you get on, though we'd miss you."

When Harry talked to Abbie, she appeared to be thrilled by the idea of moving to Birmingham.

"It's not going to be like here," he warned her. "They talk strange down there."

"You get yourself down there and talk to this Matthew Boulton," she told him firmly. Harry had no choice but to obey, and he made his way to Birmingham a week before the wedding, a letter from old Mr Jowett in his pocket.

He came back exultant. "It's something you wouldn't believe," he told Abbie. "It's a new manufactory, with all the trades under one roof, hundreds and hundreds of people. Soho, near Handsworth, just a bit north of Birmingham, so we'll still be in Staffordshire. And I met Mr Boulton. He's offered me a job working on a new kind of steam pump which he and Mr Watt, who's a Scotchman, are making. I told him I'd start in two weeks, when we're married and all."

"And where will we live?"

"There's hundreds and hundreds of little cottages, just for them that works for Mr Boulton. It's like a new world, Abbie. You'll love it there, you see."

II

The Manufactory

AND HARRY WAS RIGHT. She did love it at Soho, where it
really did seem that Harry was valued for his abilities.
The house that they were given to live in was smaller than the
Jowetts' farmhouse, and she missed the clucking of chickens
and the mooing of cows in the early morning when she lay
in bed, but there really wasn't a lot to complain about, except
the smoke and dirt.

"It may be all modern and up-to-date, Harry," she said to
him, "but them coal smuts get everywhere. Can't you talk to
Mr Boulton or Mr Watt about them?"

But Harry just laughed, and told her it was impossible for
the work to be made cleaner.

The best thing about life for Abbie, though, was Harry. She
hadn't expected to be so happy with him. Yes, she'd liked him
well enough before they were married, but now she felt really
fond of him. She had always reserved the word "love" to describe the girlish crushes of her and her friends, not that she

11

had had so many of those, but it now seemed to her that the word might have a rather deeper meaning.

Harry, who had become one of Boulton's most trusted employees very soon after moving to Soho, once obtained permission to take her into the factory to see the great engine that he and Mr Watt were developing. A monstrous great thing, all rods and levers and hissing steam – almost like a dragon out of a child's tale. She watched the great beam swinging up and down, up and down, and marvelled at its incessant power. Mr Watt himself, who was visiting Soho from Cornwall, she found a little difficult to understand thanks to his Scottish accent and what seemed to be shyness on his part, though Harry told her that he could be fierce enough when he came to defending his ideas against those whom he considered were stealing them. Harry had tried to explain the ideas of Mr Watt's engine, telling her that there had been steam engines in Cornwall for some time, pumping water out of the tin mines there, but that Mr Watt's inventions made for a far superior engine, using less coal and pumping more water.

With all the business of setting up her home with Harry, and the excitement of Mr Boulton's enterprises, Abbie had forgotten the dark stranger and the ball that he had given her. On their wedding night, and for several nights after that, she had remembered to slip the ball into her mouth when Harry's attention was elsewhere, though she felt somehow that this was a betrayal of Harry's trust in her, but it had obstinately refused to disappear.

Then came the move to Soho, and the ball was temporarily out of mind until the time when Abbie awoke screaming in the middle of the night.

"What is it?" Harry asked, putting his arms around her.

But she couldn't tell him that the dark stranger whom she

had met in the shed all that time ago had just returned to her in what she hoped was merely a dream, had shown her terrible things – things beyond her most nightmarish imaginings, and had told her that these would happen to her if she failed to obey his commands.

As his figure had faded away, she had been left with his words ringing in her ears. "Your husband seems like a good man. It would be a pity if something were to happen to him."

As she lay in Harry's arms, she started to sob. "Don't leave me, Harry. Don't leave me."

"I'm not thinking of leaving you, Abbie," he reassured her.

"No, I know you're not. I'm just thinking of your work. All those big machines and that steam hissing away. What if you had an accident?"

"I won't," said Harry. And somehow that simple statement seemed to make everything better. The butterflies left her stomach, and her breathing slowed. Harry noticed.

"Good girl, Abbie. Now sleep, and no more silly dreams, all right?"

And that's just what she did.

AND AS IT HAPPENED, the next night that Abbie and Harry joined together, the ball was in her mouth as they started, and to her surprise, as they lay together afterwards she found it had disappeared. A feeling of great peace together with a contradictory anticipatory excitement came over her as she lay awake with Harry breathing noisily on the other side of the bed, with the certain knowledge that a new life was starting inside her.

Within a few weeks, she was able to tell Harry that she was

expecting a child, news that he greeted with a cry of surprised joy – a sound that she had never heard before from his lips.

Her pregnancy was smooth and uncomplicated. Matthew Boulton arranged for the most highly regarded midwife in the region to attend her, and old Mother Palfrey, as she was known, gleefully prepared Abbie for the unspeakable torments that lay in wait for her as she gave birth for the first time.

Much to Abbie's relief, and seemingly to Mother Palfrey's disappointment, the birth was an easy one. Abbie spent only a short time in labour before giving birth to a healthy baby girl.

"She's got all the right bits attached to her," Mother Palfrey sniffed, "but that much hair on her head, it ain't normal, it ain't."

"Don't all babies have hair when they're born?" said Abbie, holding the newborn and looking down at her.

"They do, but not that much," said the midwife. "Now I've seen your husband, and your little scrap does look like him, I must say. And I've seen her come out of you. But I tell you something, and that's that if I hadn't seen your Harry, and seen you, I'd have said that was a changeling – one of Them – with that hair and all. And look at her little nails. Never seen nails that long on a new baby. But she's no changeling."

Abbie said nothing. If the change had taken place, it wasn't as simple as Them snatching a child out of the cradle and replacing it with one of Their own. But something *had* taken place, she knew that, and she didn't want to know the details of it. It was enough that the baby, *her* baby, whoever else's it might be, was alive and well, and she herself seemed to have suffered no ill effects.

Harry chose this moment to arrive. Mother Palfrey had dispatched a boy to fetch him from the manufactory as soon as the baby had arrived and the cord had been cut, but he had only just been able to get away. Even if he had arrived earlier, it was almost certain that Mother Palfrey would have barred the door to him until all was over.

He beamed at his wife and his daughter as he stood in the doorway.

"She's beautiful," he said. "And so are you, my dear."

"As beautiful as Mr Watt's new steam-engine?" she teased him. "Old Bess?"

He laughed. "What's her name?"

Abbie hadn't even thought about a name. Or rather, she'd thought of too many names, and was now unable to make up her mind.

Harry seemed to have decided, though. "Jane," he said. "After my mother."

So Jane it was, and the baby was baptised Jane Machin a week later.

DESPITE THE UNUSUAL AMOUNT OF HAIR on her head when she was born, Jane Machin seemed to be perfectly normal, at least in her appearance. Harry was devoted to his little daughter, and as soon as he returned from the manufactory and washed the dirt and grime from his face and body, made straight for little Jane, picking her up and murmuring sweet nothings into her ear. Only then would he proceed to Abbie and salute her with a kiss.

But for Abbie, who spent more time with her daughter, there seemed to be some cause for concern. Jane would sometimes lie motionless on her back, hardly breathing, and with her eyes wide open. At first Abbie thought she might be asleep with her eyes wide open – she had heard of such things – but when she passed her hand in front of Jane's face,

15

the infant blinked, and started to squall, as if she had been interrupted in some sort of pleasurable activity. And it was then that Abbie noticed that at these times Jane's eyes were not still, but were darting from side to side, as if the child was engaged in watching something which was invisible to others.

Jane began to speak at a very early age. It was only a few days after her first birthday that she pointed a chubby little finger at Harry and said, "Da da", and less than a week after that when she pointed the same finger at Abbie and mumbled "Ma ma". A few other words followed, but strangely, Jane seemed to have little inclination to sit up, let alone crawl or start walking. Her uncanny habit of wide-eyed daydreaming (for that was the only way that Abbie could interpret it) for extended periods of time continued, but it seemed that it did no harm to her. Abbie was content to let it continue, though she was convinced that it was connected in some way with the dark stranger who had claimed to be Jane's true father, even before her birth.

However, when Harry first encountered Jane's strange habit, he was concerned. "Should we call a doctor?" he asked. "I've never heard of a child behaving like this."

Abbie was not keen on the idea of a doctor examining Jane. Who knew what he might find? "No, I'm sure there's nothing wrong with her. Look at her." She pointed to little Jane, who was clearly observing them from her crib. Abbie fluttered her fingers at the girl, and was rewarded by a "mama" and what was clearly an attempt to wave back. "It's not like she's always mardy or anything like that."

"I still don't think it's right," Harry complained. "But you see more of her than I do, it's true, and I'll take your word for it that there's nothing wrong with her. It does seem that she's a bit different, all the same."

Abbie had no intention of telling Harry exactly what it was

that was different about Jane. She'd come to rely on him, and she was terrified that if she told him about the dark stranger, he would desert her – and then there was the question of what the dark stranger might do if she made his existence known.

It came as some relief to her when she discovered herself to be pregnant again some two years after Jane was born. This would be the child of Harry and her, she told herself, not of some dark stranger.

For Harry's part, he was delighted. "Maybe it will be a boy," he said, and taking Abbie's wedding ring from her finger, tied it to a hair taken from her head, and swung it over her pregnant belly as she lay on their bed.

"It's not going round in a circle – just in a straight line. That means it really will be a boy."

Already, a few months before the baby was due, he had named it "James".

"Jane and James Machin. It sounds good, doesn't it?"

And Abbie agreed. "James" was on his way.

She was about seven months gone when the great frost came. The canals froze, ice covered the ground, and even the birds seemed to stop singing, except for one tiny robin, which perched outside the Machins' front door and greeted Harry as he set out for work in the morning.

He was concerned about the now heavily gravid Abbie and always offered her a welcome supporting arm whenever the two of them went out together onto the slippery roads.

ONE DAY, Abbie was busy preparing the evening meal, awaiting Harry's return from the manufactory. The night was drawing in, and a solitary candle added to the fire's light as she carefully cut two rashers of bacon, one thick and one thinner, from the hock that hung from its hook in the corner. Little Jane appeared to be watching the operation with interest from the crib.

She was about to lay the bacon in the pan when there was a knock at the door.

"Mrs Machin," came a voice through the door which she did not recognise, but nonetheless tugged at the strings of her memory. "Mrs Machin, your Harry's had an accident. They want you up there now."

"Who are you?"

But there was no answer.

She took the pan off the fire, placing the bacon beside it. Should she take Jane with her? She hesitated, but her daughter seemed perfectly content, and she had been left in the house on her own before with no visible ill effects.

Abbie snatched up her shawl and wrapped it around her shoulders before opening the back door and hurrying out into the freezing night air. The manufactory was not far from her house, but there was a dark track sloping down to the tow-path of the canal, now covered with ice. She hesitated. To avoid that icy path would mean taking a much longer route, and she was already cold. She decided to make her way carefully down the track.

Not carefully enough. Her feet gave way from under her, and she landed on her backside with a jarring thump before sliding down to the tow-path, only avoiding sliding into the canal itself by a matter of some inches. She picked herself up painfully, and started slowly along the unlit tow-path towards the manufactory.

The pain inside grew worse with every step. She would have cried out if there had been anyone to hear, but the path was deserted. As she walked, she was horrified to feel a

Sticky wetness between her legs. Fear gave her strength, and she managed to reach the manufactory door where light and warmth beckoned.

"It's Mrs Machin, Harry's missus, Ned," said the porter on duty, Jabez, whose job it was to take all deliveries and greet visitors.

"You look all in, me duck," said Ned. "Sit you down here," indicating the chair on which he had been sitting.

"What's that?" asked Jabez, pointing to a red smear, leading from the door to where Abbie was now sitting. "That's blood, that is. Where do you hurt, me dear?"

"Inside," Abbie said briefly. It hurt too much to say more.

The two men exchanged looks. This was strange business. Women's business. And they wanted as little to do with it as possible. "I'll fetch tha Harry, duck," said Ned. "You stay there."

Abbie didn't have the strength to tell him that Harry had had an accident and might be in an even worse state than she was herself. She steeled herself to sit and wait patiently, but even sitting quietly was agony, and with it was the fear that she would lose her baby, James. Tears started to roll down her cheeks as Jabez watched in helpless embarrassment.

And just as she was convinced she was going to die of pain and loss of blood, Ned returned with Harry. Even though her half-closed tear-filled eyes she could see that he had never been in any accident. He seemed to be as strong and as whole as ever. And at that moment, she suddenly remembered where she had previously heard the voice that had told her of Harry's accident. It was the voice of the dark stranger in the shed, one of Them.

Harry appeared to take in the scene at a glance, and rushed over to Abbie.

"My God!" he gasped as he took in the sight of the blood-stained floor. "How are you?"

"I... hurt..." is all she could manage to gasp out before pitching forward, semi-conscious.

"Jabez, give me a hand," said Harry, helping her to sit up straight. "Ned, you find the gaffer."

"Mr Boulton?" said Ned, clearly a little nervous at this request.

"Yes." Harry seemed about to let loose a torrent of oaths, something he only did when he was seriously angry or upset, but thought better of it. "There's a doctor with him. Visiting him from Lichfield. He's meant to be one of the best in the country. Get them both to come down here as quickly as they can."

IT WAS A MATTER OF ONLY A FEW MINUTES before Matthew Boulton entered, followed by a large stout man with a face marred by smallpox scars. Despite his ugliness and generally uncouth appearance, there was a warmth and humanity in his face that gave Harry confidence that something good was going to come of all this.

"This is my good friend, Doctor Erasmus Darwin. Doctor, this is Harry Machin, one of my best workers, working with Mr Watt, and this here," indicating Abbie's almost unconscious form, "is Harry's wife, Abbie."

Dr Darwin did not seem a man to stand on ceremony, but looked at Abbie, looked down at the floor, and shook his head sadly.

"How far along is she?" he asked Harry.

"About seven months, sir."

Darwin shook his head. "She should be lying down. Is there anywhere she can be taken?" he asked Boulton.

"There's a sofa in my office. She can lie on that."

"But, sir," said Harry. "The blood…"

"Damn the blood, man!" said Boulton, almost angrily. "Your wife is more important than a sofa. Find a plank or something she can be carried on, you two," to Ned and Jabez, "and a couple of men to help carry her."

"What do you think, sir?" Harry asked the doctor.

"Too early to say, lad. Let's wait until she's comfortable before I make any pronouncements, shall we. And less of the 'sir'."

"Yes, s— doctor."

"That's better." Harry wasn't sure whether Dr Darwin was referring to Harry's mode of address, or the return of Ned and Jabez with two men and what seemed to be a door.

Darwin supervised the careful placing of the now unconscious and unmoving Abbie onto the door, and its removal into Bolton's office. As they reached the door, Harry stopped and hesitated, obviously unsure as to whether he should enter.

"In you go, lad, and don't be so daft," Boulton said. "Where's your little one?"

Up to now, Harry hadn't considered Jane. "I don't know," he said, helplessly. "I suppose Abbie must have left her at home."

"I'll get one of the girls from my house to go over to your place and check on her. Don't you worry, lad. Dr Darwin here's a fine doctor. They say the King himself asked him to be his doctor, and the Doctor refused, saying he was happier where he was. Can you believe that? Your Abbie's in the best of hands, so don't take on so. In you go now."

Abbie was lying on the sofa, her skirts pulled up to above her knee. Harry noticed the bloodstains marking the damask covering, and immediately felt guilty, but he remembered what Boulton had said, and felt a little better, though it was clear that Abbie was far from well. Darwin was bending over her, and as Harry entered, he straightened up and turned to Harry, a concerned expression on his face.

"It's not going to be good news, I'm afraid," he said. "I don't believe in building up false hopes, only to dash them to the ground. I am reasonably certain that the child, if it is born, will be born dead. I am sorry," he added simply.

All of Harry's hopes for his future son vanished at these words; his head hung, and his shoulders slumped.

Darwin's hand rested heavily on Harry's shoulder. "I am sorry," he repeated.

"What about Abbie – my wife?" Harry asked.

A deep sigh from Darwin. "I cannot tell. I hope that she will recover, but who can say?"

All life seemed to ebb visibly from Harry as he heard these words.

"You and Abbie and your little one will want for nothing." These words came from Boulton, who had been standing behind them. "You're too important, Harry. You mean a lot to us all. Whatever it takes, rest assured that I personally will take care of things."

"Thank you, sir," said Harry.

"You're a good man, Matthew Boulton," said Darwin. "You're lucky to have him as your master," he said to Harry. "Now, if you have no objection, I would like to perform a rather intimate examination of your wife. You may stay if you wish, Mr Machin, though I warn you that you may find it a trifle upsetting. Mr Boulton, I must ask you to leave the room."

"I will leave with him," Harry said. He was feeling sick and weak.

Outside the room, with the door closed, Boulton looked

at Harry critically. "You're not well, lad. If Darwin wasn't in there with your wife," he jerked his head towards the door, "I'd go in there, fetch the bottle of brandy in my desk and give you as much as you wanted. Don't you worry about your little one, though. She'll be looked after by the same girl as looks after my children."

"Thank you, sir," Harry said weakly. The two men stood in silence by the closed door, studiously avoiding each other's gaze. At length there was the sound of footsteps, the door handle rattled, and Dr Darwin stood there, a look of anxiety painted on his face.

"Once again, it gives me no pleasure to be the bearer of bad tidings. Your wife, Mr Machin, is seriously injured. Her fall and the resulting complication appear to have seriously damaged her womanly parts, and it seems impossible for me to stop her bleeding. I am sorry to have to tell you that I have my doubts as to whether she will last the night. You should go in and say farewell to her."

Darwin and Boulton exchanged a look. "I'm going to get that brandy," said Boulton, and followed Harry into the room.

Harry, distraught, was standing over Abbie, holding her hand, and speaking softly to her, so softly that the other men were unable to catch the words. He wordlessly shook his head as Boulton offered a glass of brandy to him.

Unoffended, Boulton placed the glass on the desk beside the sofa. "It's here if you feel you want it, lad," he said. "You stay here as long as you want to. I'll make sure your little one's being cared for, and before I go home for the night, I'm going to get someone to wait outside this door who will call me or Doctor Darwin if you want us, and I'll arrange for some food to be sent to you. You can't keep a vigil on an empty stomach."

He turned to leave as Harry thanked him. Darwin placed his hand on Harry's shoulder once more. "I'm stopping the night with Mr Boulton," he said to Harry. "Don't worry about calling me. It doesn't matter about the time – we doctors are used to this."

"Thank you, Doctor Darwin," said Harry. "It's a great comfort to me."

For hours Harry sat by Abbie, holding her hand. He was interrupted by a servant from the Boulton household, who brought him a dish of warm soup and some bread, and informed him that little Jane was now in the Boulton house, where she was being well cared for, if not actually spoiled, by the cook and the housekeeper. Despite himself, Harry managed to smile a little at this news.

At one point, Abbie's eyes, which had been shut, fluttered open, and she seemed to recognise his face.

"Harry?" she whispered faintly. He nodded. Her next words were difficult to make out, but he seemed to hear, "Keep... Jane... away..." There was a long pause. "From... the... other... side... of... the... sky..." Her eyes closed, and all his words and desperate holding of her hand and caressing of her face would not open them again. He had no idea what was meant by these words, or even if he had heard them correctly, as Abbie lay there, silent and unmoving.

There was no way of knowing the time, as it had grown too dark to see the clock on the mantelpiece, but he guessed it was past midnight when the pattern of Abbie's breathing changed, to slow irregular gasping. He released her hand and made for the door where, as promised, a man was waiting outside.

"Please go to Mr Boulton's house, and ask for Doctor Darwin to come here."

The man scuttled off, and Harry returned to Abbie. To his horror, she had ceased breathing, and involuntarily, tears came to his eyes, as he realised he had lost the woman who had become the centre of his life.

The silence was suddenly and shockingly broken by Abbie's rasping breath, followed by another and another, and then, after a few minutes, silence once again. Harry jumped as the door behind him opened, and the doctor entered. As he approached, Abbie started to breathe again in shallow rasping breaths.

"This, I fear, is the end," Darwin told Harry. "I have seen it too many times, alas, for there to be any doubt. There is nothing I or anyone can do for her."

Harry wept openly as Abbie's breath stopped once more time. This time she did not start breathing again.

III

The Farewell

FOLLOWING ABBIE'S DEATH, little Jane often seemed distraught.

"Where mama?" she would ask Boulton's servants on waking in the morning, and at regular intervals throughout the day. The only answers they could give her were vague non-committal statements that "she's gone away" or similar. This seemed to content her, at least for a few hours, after which the question would be repeated.

The episodes of staring at nothing for minutes on end continued, as they had done when she had lived with her mother and father.

But more worrying and unsettling were the episodes where she appeared to be listening to an invisible friend while asleep. Though she was not old enough to form full sentences, she seemed able to understand and react to what was said to her. It frightened the servants when they peeped into the room where she was sleeping to see her head cocked on one side in an attitude of attention, eyes closed, and nodding in a startlingly adult fashion as if in agreement with some conversation, audible only to her.

This was bad enough, but added to this was the sense of *something* there, a *something* that was at the same time visible and invisible, which could only be described, and that with difficulty, as a black light. What its shape was, no one could describe precisely, but all were agreed that there was something almost human about the something, of a quality that frightened them "to their very bones" as Mrs Baddeley, the housekeeper, described it.

Although the housekeeper reported these fears to Matthew Boulton, saying that it was only the kitchen-maid who had expressed her concern, the truth was that all the servants in Soho House were frightened of these episodes. At other times, however, little Jane was well-behaved, smiling and gurgling like any other child of a similar age, and if it had not been for these strange disturbing episodes, she would have been loved and spoiled beyond redemption by the whole of the servants' hall, from Lucas the butler downwards.

Abbie's funeral was attended by almost the whole of the Soho manufactory workforce, as well as Matthew Boulton and his family. Having lost his own wife several years previously, Boulton was more than sympathetic.

"Your little one is doing fine with us," he told Harry. "I think that she's a grand little thing, and it's a joy to see her face when you come to visit her each evening."

Harry knew there was something else. "But?" he asked.

"Aye, I'm afraid there is a 'but'. It's probably nothing, but

Annie, our kitchen-maid, says there's something queer about little Jane, and she won't even go near her after dark."

"That's rubbish," said Harry. "Abbie and I lived in the same house as her for nearly two years, and there was nothing strange about her, except…" His voice trailed off.

"Except what?" Boulton's voice was sharp.

"She had this trick of looking off into nothing for minutes on end. We thought she was asleep with her eyes open, but then we thought differently."

"According to our housekeeper, Annie says she's seen that a couple of times. But she'll grow out of that. What I've been told Annie says is that she's looked into the room where Jane's sleeping, and seen some sort of light by the side of the bed. She said it was some sort of black light, which makes no sense at all, does it?"

"Sounds like a load of old rubbish to me, sir. And if you don't mind me saying so, your Annie sounds a bit daft in the head."

Boulton chuckled. "She's not the sharpest chisel in the tool-box, that's for sure. But she's not as daft as all that. Anyway, I'm afraid that's upset the other servants, and the long and the short of it is that they don't want your Jane in the house any more."

Harry's face fell. "I don't know what to say. It's been very good of you to look after her this past month or so—"

"It's the least I could do for you, Harry. Couldn't she live with your parents?"

"Both dead, I'm afraid. Abbie's as well. They died several years ago.""

"Sorry to hear that, lad. No brothers or sisters?" Harry shook his head. "Well, we will have to put our thinking caps on, then won't we? What would you say if little Jane were to live in Lichfield?"

Harry looked surprised. "Why there, sir?"

"Because Dr Darwin lives there, and whoever he doesn't know there isn't worth the knowing. I'd wager that he could find the perfect home for Jane in an hour if we asked him."

"But I can't afford to pay someone to look after her," Harry objected.

"I can, so don't you worry."

"But…"

"Listen to me, lad, and I'll tell you a few home truths. One, you're my right hand when it comes to working with Mr Watt. I've said it before and I'll say it again. And Mr Watt will tell you the same. All those things that make our steam pumping engines the best in the world – you've had a hand in all of them. And that means I want you to keep working for me. And if I can make your life easier, then that's what I'll do. And the second thing is that I can afford to do it with no problem. If you prefer, I'll give you the money for Jane's keep in your wages, so you pay them, and I don't. How does that sound?"

"More than I deserve, sir."

"Rubbish. Nonsense. Less than you deserve. Tell you what, you get Saturday afternoons and Sundays off, don't you?"

"Yes."

"Now you get all Saturday and all Sunday off. Same pay as before – you're not going to lose out on it, and you can take yourself off to Lichfield for two days to see your daughter. I can even help pay your way there if you need it. Now, what do you say to that?"

"Thank you, sir. I don't deserve all that."

"I said it before, and I'll say it again," he repeated. "That's nonsense. If I was to tell you what I really thought of you, do you know what?" Harry shook his head. "Your head would swell up so much you'd never get out through that door."

Boulton's shoulders shook in merriment at his own joke, and Harry, despite his anxiety, found himself joining in.

"So what I'll do," Boulton said, "is to write a little billet-doux to your friend and mine, Dr Darwin, and we'll get an answer back very soon if I know my friend."

MATTHEW BOULTON WAS PROVED CORRECT in his forecast of Dr Darwin's extensive range of contacts in Lichfield. It was only three days before an answer arrived from that city. Erasmus Darwin wrote in his letter that he knew of a Mrs Kate Perkins who "lives in Dam Street, not five minutes' walk from my house (provided one walks a little faster than do I), and is a most worthy and respectable woman, sadly now widowed, who has in the past acted as nurse to one of the Canons of the Cathedral here when his child fell sick". He added that she had two children of her own, both a little older than Jane, but both were said to be of "amiable character" and she would be happy to welcome Jane Machin and treat her as one of her own. As to the money she would expect, it came to ten shillings a week.

"It sounds good," said Harry. "But I am not sure that I can afford it."

"I will make sure you see that extra ten shillings in your pay packet each week," Boulton told him.

There was one singular matter concerning Mrs Perkins that Erasmus Darwin had failed to mention to Matthew Boulton. Boulton had informed his friend about the mysterious fear that little Jane had inspired in his servants. Curious about all matters that were connected in some way to science, especially those that dealt with the mind and the body, Darwin was initially tempted to dismiss these fears as simply the product of the over-active imaginations of those in Boulton's household at Soho House. Even so, it was not in his nature to come across a strange and possibly complex phenomenon without investigating it further.

Mrs Perkins had a reputation in Lichfield as a "wise woman", who combined her work as a children's nurse – a duty which she performed admirably, according to all those who had used her services – with healing, using herbs and potions, sometimes of her own devising, accompanied, some said, by certain practices which verged upon the magical. Indeed, Dr Darwin had often consulted with her on the uses of various herbs and other medicines, and it must be said that both gained from the exchange of information. On the one hand Darwin learned about a wide variety of folk cures that often proved more efficacious than the approved medical nostrums. On the other hand, Mrs Perkins' patients were spared the application of newts' bladders and the like to their injuries, since Darwin had been able to demonstrate to Kate Perkins that such "remedies" were only of use in that they excited hope in the patient and had no other therapeutic value.

Regarding her reported magical skills, Darwin restrained his curiosity, and was simply aware of the whisperings about her that went around Lichfield. For the most part, it was agreed that if she did indeed possess any powers denied to the mass of mortals, such knowledge was always used discreetly and benevolently. The cathedral canon to whose children she had acted as nurse was almost certainly aware of these stories, and had clearly dismissed them as irrelevant. Even so, if there proved to be something of the uncanny and weird about the Machin girl, Darwin was convinced that Mrs Perkins was more likely to discover and understand it than he himself.

THE FIRST MEETING between the Machins and Mrs Perkins appeared to be a success. Boulton had generously allowed Harry Machin the use of his carriage on the Saturday when he made the first trip from Handsworth to Lichfield, carrying Jane and a quantity of clothes and other necessaries for her use.

As he knocked on the Dam Street door, and waited for it to be opened, Harry Machin felt an ice-like stab at his heart. What if, he asked himself, this Mrs Perkins was not all that had been promised? Would she neglect little Jane, and take the ten shillings and use it only for herself and her own children? And would Jane be able to manage without seeing him every day, as she did at present?

He had half a mind to turn around and take the carriage back to Handsworth, when the door opened, and a middle-aged woman who could only have been Mrs Perkins opened the door.

"You'll be Jane," she said, addressing the girl first. "And you're her father, I take it? Doctor Darwin told me all about it. Shocking business, that. But if Doctor Darwin couldn't save your poor dear wife, then I'm sure that there's no one as could have saved her."

Her manner was brisk and efficient, but there was a warmth to it which came through, and provided Harry with a sense of hope and some calm. For her part, Jane solemnly regarded Mrs Perkins' face for about twenty seconds, before breaking into a beaming smile, and stretching out her arms towards her new friend.

"Oh, the little darling," exclaimed Mrs Perkins, mirroring the child's smile. "I can see we're going to be friends."

Harry was relieved. He'd had visions of squalls and temper tantrums. He was even a little jealous of the bond that seemed to have been instantly created between his daughter and her new foster-mother. As he watched, two children came up and stood peering at him from behind their mother's skirts. As Darwin's letter had said, they appeared to be a little older than Jane.

"This is Will," patting the older child's head. "He's four."

"Nearly five, Ma," said the boy.

"Nearly five," she smiled. "And Mary here, who's three."

Mary dipped a little curtsey to Harry, who smiled at her and was rewarded with a smile in return.

"Would you like to see where she'll be sleeping?" Mary's mother asked Harry. He nodded, and she led the way up the narrow stairs to a small room at the back of the house where a window looked out onto the fields and what seemed to be a small lake. The room was clean, and airy – better than any room in his house, Harry thought to himself.

"She'll be sharing with Mary," said Mrs Perkins, pointing to two small beds. "Mary's a good girl, and she doesn't quarrel with other children. Nor does Will, come to that. And your little Jane, she'll get the same food as my own. I can see," she added, looking at Jane, who was still beaming at her, "that we're going to be great friends."

"I'm sure you will," said Harry, leaving the bag of clothes and toys on the bed marked as Jane's. He was glad that Jane was going to be with someone who clearly was a good mother to her own children, and still had enough kindness left over for others' offspring. Even so, he was sad to be leaving his daughter behind, and his feelings must have shown in his voice, because Mrs Perkins said to him, "I understand that you'll be coming up every Saturday and Sunday to see her. You're always welcome to come and see her – I'm just taking care of her until you're in a better position to look after her yourself. So don't you mither yourself about this. Jane's your daughter, and I'll never forget that, even if I look after her as if she was one of mine."

They went downstairs, and Harry bent to kiss Jane farewell. "Until next week, duck," he said to her. He turned to Mrs Perkins. "I think I should go and thank Doctor Darwin for all this."

"You'll be lucky to find him in," she told him. "He's a busy man. But his house is just up that way. Go up the street to the cathedral, turn left, and then past the cathedral there's a little snicket to the right of the road that takes you to the Stafford road and that'll bring you through his garden to his back door."

Harry thanked her, and set off for Darwin's, a sense of emptiness in his heart.

The Doctor

JANE SEEMED TO THRIVE under the care of Mrs Perkins. She cheerfully seemed, with the apparent callousness of the very young, to have accepted her new "mother" and forgotten the old one, though Kate Perkins discouraged Jane from calling her "Mama", and reminded her as often as possible that "Dada" was coming to see her.

Little Mary took instantly to her new foster-sister, and the feeling seemed to be mutual. The two of them were often to be seen toddling around hand in hand and speaking to each other in a language of their own which only they could understand.

Kate Perkins had been called to see Erasmus Darwin a couple of weeks after Jane's arrival. She presented herself at the back door of his house at the requested hour, and was shown into the room that served as his study.

"Come in, come in, my dear Mrs Perkins," he greeted her, heaving himself to his feet. "Thank you so much for coming

35

to see me here. Please sit down." He indicated a comfortable chair facing the one on which he was sitting.

"It's nothing, sir."

Darwin acknowledged this with a nod of his large head. "And the little one, Jane Machin? How is she settling in? All well, I trust?"

"She is indeed, sir. She and my little ones are getting along fine."

"And she's no trouble?" There seemed to be more than casual interest in the enquiry.

"No more than any other little one of that age, sir." She paused, studying the doctor's pock-marked face. "May I ask why you are asking me that, sir?" Her tone was a little sharp. "Is there something you haven't told me? She's not sick or anything, is she?"

Darwin sighed. "No, she's not sick. But there is something that I haven't told you." He leaned forward and his voice dropped as he proceeded to tell her of what Matthew Boulton had written to him about little Jane's condition and the strange sights that had been seen in her bedroom when she was supposedly asleep.

Kate sat back in her chair, thinking for a while. When she finally spoke, her voice was tinged with anger. "I don't think it was fair of you to ask me to look after such a one without telling me first," she said.

"I apologise, Mrs Perkins," Darwin told her. "You're being paid ten shillings each week to look after her, aren't you?" She nodded. "Then let me add another five shillings of my own each week to that as some sort of compensation."

"That's very generous of you, sir, but it's not the money as worries me. Why did you put such a one as that with me in the first place?"

It was some time before Darwin spoke, choosing his words

carefully. "Because I respect your judgement on many matters, Mrs Perkins."

"Sir? You're a great man, a doctor. You're famous, the King himself has asked you to be his doctor, and you say you respect me? I'm sorry sir, but that's got to be some sort of a joke."

"Not at all. I have learned from you. Cobwebs to stop bleeding. Mouldy bread to stop a wound from going foul. The art of the foxglove. How can I not respect someone who has taught me these things?"

She smiled faintly. "And I suppose I can say that the same is true for me. You have taught me many things. But what has all this to do with Jane Machin?"

"Mrs Perkins, you have a reputation in this city." He paused.

"You mean like some say as I'm a witch, sir?"

Darwin waved a large flipper-like hand in front of his face. "That is what some say, yes. I would rather say that you are capable of perceiving things hidden from others. I have seen this in you, when you have told me of matters concerning patients of mine which only the patients themselves would have known, and were completely unknown to me." He paused. "And what has all this to do with Jane Machin? Surely that is obvious."

"So you chose me to look after your friend's man's daughter because I am called a witch?"

"I would not put it is as crude terms as that, but yes."

Kate Perkins' face displayed her anger as she rose. "Then it is time that my arrangement with you and Mr Boulton, and Harry Machin, pleasant enough as he may be, came to an end. You will have the kindness, Doctor Darwin, to write to your friend in Handsworth, and arrange for Jane Machin to leave my house. I admit that I shall be sorry to lose her and the ten shillings a week, but I cannot accept having such a one thrust upon me with no warning. You didn't play me fair on that, sir, and I'll not be having it."

"Please, please, my dear Mrs Perkins." Darwin struggled to his feet and interposed his bulk between her and the door. "Do not leave, but sit and hear what I have to say, if you would be so kind. You are an intelligent woman, and I know that you listen to reason when you hear it. May I offer you a glass of something while we talk? I tend to prescribe a glass of Madeira at this time of day."

She relaxed her posture a little. "You're a right charmer, you are, Doctor," she half-smiled. "Yes, I'll take that glass of Madeira, thank you kindly. I warn you, though, I am still more than a little mithered by what you have done."

Darwin rang the bell, and he and his visitor sat in silence until the decanter and glasses were ordered and brought in. He poured a glassful for Kate Perkins with his own hands, and handed it to her before pouring a glass of water for himself. The two raised their glasses to each other and sipped. It was Darwin who finally broke the long silence.

"Mrs Perkins, at several points in our conversation today, you used the phrase 'such a one as that'. Enlighten me, if you would, as to the meaning of that phrase."

"This is going to sound daft, sir, but…" Her voice tailed off.

Darwin waited for her to go on, and his patience was rewarded.

"Well, there's Them as comes from the other side of the sky."

Darwin was startled. "I've never heard those words before. What do you mean? There is no other side to the sky. I mean, the sky is…" He found himself lost for words. How could he explain the principles of the refraction of light to her?

"Them's the words, sir. The words They use." There was a

subtle inflection on that penultimate word, and Darwin seized on it.

"'They'?"

"I'm saying too much, sir, but They are there. On the other side of the sky, waiting to come to visit us and use us."

"Demons?" he asked.

"Not like you'd hear talk of in church, no, sir. They're more than likely the Good Folk you'll hear them up in the moors in the north of the county talking about."

"Fairies?" Darwin did not laugh.

"If that's what you want to call Them, yes."

"And you think that Jane Machin is one of Them?" Darwin copied Kate in emphasising the pronoun.

"From what you've told me just now, yes, sir. But I haven't seen anything with my own eyes yet. She's clearly not all of her one of Them. A sort of half-breed or mongrel, if you like."

"But Matthew Boulton wrote to me that she looks like her father."

"They are cunning, sir. They can disguise themselves to look like anything They choose."

"You're not saying that her father is one of Them?"

"I'm saying that the man who believes himself to be her father is not her real father. Don't ask me to explain how it works, sir, because I don't know, and that's the truth. I'm not saying anything against her mother, mind. She was probably a good honest woman, and a good mother to her daughter. But my guess is that They tricked her and her husband."

"Do you consider there to be any danger?"

Doctor Darwin, to her amazement, wasn't laughing at her. She considered how absurd it was – 'daft' is the word she used to herself – that one of the great men of England should be sitting opposite her, asking for advice. "This is all what I was told by an old woman when I was a young girl. She told me that They can walk through walls, and appear and disappear," she informed him. "They make milk go sour, and the bread will never rise properly in a house where They are." She stopped. The milk *had* turned sour quite a lot recently in the house on Dam Street since Jane arrived. "What she also told me is that other than that, these mongrels are relatively harmless on their own, but they are like that metal spike that you had put on the Cathedral some time ago for the thunder."

"The lightning conductor, yes." Darwin had been instrumental in the installation of a lightning conductor on Lichfield Cathedral some years previously.

"What I mean is that They can come from the other side of the sky to our side through these mongrels. And when They are here, there's no end to the mischief."

Darwin seemed sunk in thought as he considered her words. "Would you know, Mrs Perkins, if They had decided to come here from – what did you say, 'the other side of the sky'?"

She nodded emphatically. "I would, sir. Trust me on that."

"And would you let me know?"

"I would that, sir. If there's one person in Lichfield who could take Them on and beat them at their own game, I reckon you're that man."

Darwin smiled. "Thank you for the confidence you place in me. Now, I mentioned another five shillings each week in addition to the ten that Mr Machin is paying. After our little conversation, will you take those five shillings? On condition, that is, that you look after little Jane Machin and alert me regarding anything that pertains to what we have just talked about."

"I can do that, and thank you, sir. I am sorry for what I said to you just now."

"No apologies needed, Mrs Perkins. Another glass of Madeira before you leave?"

KATE PERKINS SIGHED as she let herself back into her house. There was one thing that she hadn't told Dr Darwin – the fact that as far as she was aware, she herself was one-eighth one of Them. Not that she owed any allegiance to Them – but it was that one-eighth that had made her so successful in her healing, and which had brought the title of 'witch' down upon her head.

It was strange, though, that They had not been attempting to make contact with little Jane, though, if she really was a child of one of Them. Were They biding their time, and waiting for a chance to come out and strike?

This was not her first encounter with Them – or even her second or third. As one with Their blood in her veins, she knew from childhood what it was like to be accosted by strange dark figures who appeared out of the wall to molest her tranquillity with their frightening unblinking gaze.

And that blood also allowed her to see Their presence in others. Several times she had been called to a child-bed where she had been unmistakably aware of Their presence in the newborn baby. Her instincts had almost always been to take the child's life speedily and secretly, telling the mother that it had been stillborn, and on two occasions she had actually done so, mourning the humanity that had been destroyed, but rejoicing in the fact that one more of Them was no longer free to walk the earth.

Her conscience had nagged at her, though, and she now regretted what she had done. She did, however, keep a list of those children she recognised as being partly Them, and from a distance, observed their progress.

It was noteworthy that these children, for the most part, lived in areas which were distant from the Cathedral, and usually far from the other churches of the city, St Mary's in the marketplace, St Chad's at the other end of Stowe Pool, and St Michael's on the top of Greenhill.

Her own house on Dam Street was between the Cathedral and St Mary's. Perhaps, she thought to herself sometimes, that proximity was the reason for the lack of visits by Them, either to her or to Jane. Maybe she could ask Dr Darwin about this, she thought. He hadn't laughed at her description of Them, any more than he'd laughed at her remedies of spiders' webs and mouldy bread. And from what she understood, he was no friend of the established Church, though there were always rumours flying around about him and Canon Seward's daughter, Anna.

She was still angry that Darwin had not consulted her first about Jane Machin, but at the same time she was relieved that should anything in the future transpire that showed that They were coming into our world, she would be listened to and believed by a man who was generally considered to be one of the wisest in the kingdom.

As MATTERS TURNED OUT, it was not long before Kate came into contact with Them once more. Her sister, Anne, lived in the village of Streethay, a little way outside the city of Lichfield, and Kate went there one day to collect some eggs from her sister's chickens, taking her two children and little Jane with her.

It was a slow journey. Jane was unable to walk far, and had

to be carried much of the way, and little Mary and Will struggled to walk the one and a half miles to their aunt's.

Once there, the three children were entranced by the sight of Aunt Anne's chickens and the pig. Will especially spent a long time talking to Wickens, the pig, and translating the snuffles and snorts that formed the pig's contributions to the 'conversation' for the benefit of the other two children who were soon giggling uncontrollably.

As Kate watched her two children and Jane from the kitchen window, she suddenly noticed that though Will and Mary were still engaged in their 'talk' with the pig, Jane had stopped participating, and was sitting with her head cocked on one side, listening, but clearly not to Will.

At the same time Kate herself became aware of another, malign, presence. She could see nothing, but she knew that it was one of Them, and it was standing just beside Jane. From long experience, she knew that her sister did not share her powers, such as they were, relating to Them, so it would be useless to ask her for confirmation.

Without a word to her sister, then, she raced outside, and immediately the presence made itself even more apparent to her, even though she was still unable to see any sign of it. The feeling was like how she imagined that being enveloped in an uncomfortably warm thick sticky black cloud would be – unpleasant and stifling.

"Ah, so it's *you*," said the deep thrilling voice in her head; a voice she had heard several times before, but never as loudly and as clearly as this. "It is you taking care of my little one."

"Yours?" she asked, wordlessly.

"My daughter, yes. I have been talking to her, telling her what she can expect in her life. What else should a father do for his child?" There was an unpleasant chuckle.

"And what is she to expect?" she asked silently.

"Oh, she will suffer the usual lot of humanity. Pain, grief, unhappiness, misery. That is inevitable, given her mother. But from the other side of the sky she will also have strength and power and might. Now," the voice continued, "will you leave her and me together?"

"No!" This time the word came out in an audible shriek. Instantly her head was filled with a searing pain that refused to abate. She could only describe it to herself as being stung by a swarm of wasps – inside her head. "I'll go, I'll go!" she screamed aloud.

Her children and Jane, startled by her cries, turned and stared at her wordlessly. Mary and Jane both started to cry as Kate fled back to the house. Will was clearly upset, but moved to comfort Mary and Jane by throwing his arms around the pair and holding them tightly.

Once inside the house, Kate's head cleared a little. "Anne," she said to her sister. "Get the children inside as soon as possible, and help us back to Lichfield. There is something out there which will not harm you, I am sure, but it is intent on hurting me and little Jane. I am not even sure that Will and Mary are safe. Please, for the love of God."

Anne knew enough of her sister to realise that such a request was to be taken with all seriousness. She called to her husband that Kate had suffered "a queer turn" and that he was to look after their child, who was crying at the thought of his cousin's departure, while she escorted her sister and her children back home.

The walk back to Dam Street proceeded in near silence. Will and Mary were seemingly too stunned by recent events to speak or to ask questions, and Jane appeared exhausted as she dozed on Anne's shoulder. Kate's headache seemed to recede as they walked closer to Lichfield, and as they reached the bottom of the slope up Church Street that led to St Michael's on Greenhill, it had disappeared entirely.

All the children seemed to be almost dead on their feet when they arrived at Dam Street, and despite the early hour, Kate put them all to bed.

THE NEXT DAY, Kate decided to see Doctor Darwin to inform him of the previous day's events. She made the short trip through the Close, taking Jane with her, only to be informed that the doctor was presently seeing a patient in Rugeley, some miles away, but was expected back soon.

Darwin's housekeeper, whom Kate had often seen in the market and around the city, invited Kate and Jane to sit in the kitchen with her if they wanted to wait.

Kate gratefully accepted, and soon it was clear that Jane, who seemed to have completely recovered from the previous day's events, charmed Mrs Griggs, who presented her with a cup of milk, and a slice of bread and dripping.

The sound of a carriage drawing up, followed by the sound of the front door opening and closing, with footsteps on the flagged hall floor, came down to the kitchen.

"Sounds as though the Doctor's home," Mrs Griggs said to Kate. "I'll go and see if he's ready to see you." She returned a few minutes later. "He says if you don't mind waiting another five minutes or so, he'll be happy to see you then. Them carriage rides don't half take it out of him some days, I must say."

"Thank you," Kate told her. They waited, and Kate and Jane were led upstairs by Mrs Griggs, who showed them into Darwin's study.

"I am always delighted to see you, of course, Mrs, Perkins, but I take it that this is not merely a social call," he greeted her. "And do I see Jane here? Good day to you, my dear." His heavy face broke into a charming smile as he extended a hand towards her to pat her on the head.

"Not a social call, no sir," Kate told him. "Last time, I said that you hadn't played fair with me, and you hadn't told me everything about Jane here."

"That's all over and done with as far as I am concerned, Mrs Perkins. I don't hold it against you, and I hope you don't hold anything against me."

"Well, I have to confess that I haven't been fair with you, either, sir."

"How so?" Darwin leaned forward in his chair.

"Well, sir, it's not something that I like to shout about, but… I am in the same position as Jane here, but not to quite the same degree, if you take my meaning."

"You mean that you are one of Them?" Darwin frowned. "The ones about whom we talked last time, and you used the phrase 'the other side of the sky' to describe where they come from?"

"Yes, sir. Them. Now Jane here, I now know for sure that her father is one of Them. I'll tell you how I know in a minute. Me, so far as I can tell, I'm just one part in eight. My great-grandfather was one of Them. My great-grandmother told my grandmother, who told me when I was a scrap not that much older than her here."

"And that is what makes you…" Darwin groped for the word, "…special?"

"Well, I can't say as I can be certain about it, but yes, sir."

"And you say you are certain that little Jane here – and what a darling little creature she is, to be sure – has a parent who is not human?"

"I am, sir." Kate told Darwin about the events at Streethay the previous day.

"And yet nothing like this has happened in the city here?"

"I have noticed, sir, that being near the Cathedral, and churches generally, seems to keep Them away."

"The power of religion, eh? Who knows? It may be so, or it may not. It would seem dangerous to attempt to prove or disprove this through experiment, though. It would hardly seem just to subject you to the tortures that you described to me just now."

Kate smiled faintly. "I am glad you say that, sir. I would not want to go through that again for any amount of money."

"Remind me again. What did her father, for I suppose that we may suppose him to be truthful in this description of himself, say was to be young Jane's lot as regards her other side?"

"Strength and power and might. And that is what I believe They all want, sir. It is their goal. Kindness and love mean little or nothing to them, but power over others is what They seek."

"Hmm…" Darwin sat in thought. "Could you bring Jane here more often? Several times each week? I am interested to see how she may grow."

"My Will and Mary will be sorry to lose her company, sir."

"No matter. Bring them as well. My own children will welcome new playmates. And as for me, I wish to see how little Jane will take to my company as I attempt to educate her."

"Sir? You'd let my little ones mix with your own?"

"Of course I would. It would be good for everyone, including you, my dear woman. You could have some moments in the day that you could call your own, instead of attending to the wants and needs of your little tyrants." He smiled. "A glass of Madeira?"

DARWIN KEPT HIS WORD. Over the next few years, Will and Mary, together with Jane, were regular visitors to the Darwin house, where they endeared themselves to the staff with their good manners, and to the Darwin children with their good nature.

As might be expected, Darwin was particularly interested in Jane, in whom he discovered a keen intelligence. At the time of her third birthday, she was able to recognise her letters, and a few months after that she was reading simple words, clearly understanding their meaning.

It seemed to Darwin that she was possessed of singular abilities, and he took care to meet and converse with her father, Harry Machin, who continued to visit Lichfield every Saturday and Sunday. It became obvious to Darwin in their conversations that Harry Machin was a man who had been handicapped by the circumstance of low birth, for in the doctor's eyes, his powers of understanding were equal to those of any of the members of the Lunar Society, a group to which he and Matthew Boulton belonged, together with Josiah Wedgwood and several other like-minded 'natural philosophers'. Indeed, he was seriously tempted to ask Harry to accompany him to a meeting of the Society, but on reflection determined that it would be a cause of embarrassment, not only to the members of the Society, one of whom was, after all, Harry's employer, but also to Harry himself.

Nonetheless, he took great pleasure in the conversations he held with Harry, and lent him several books which he felt might be of some interest to the younger man.

He continued to be aware, though, of what Kate Perkins had told him about Jane's true paternity, and bore in mind that though both Harry and Jane Machin displayed unmistakable signs of high intelligence and natural ability, this might well be little more than coincidence.

For his part, Harry was sensible of Darwin's interest in Jane, and his kindness to her and the Perkins children, though he was a little worried that being overly exposed to the comfortable and prosperous aspects of Darwin's household would cause her to be discontented when these ceased, and she was forced to adopt what he would regard as being her proper station in life.

ONE SUNDAY IN SUMMER, Harry, in company with Jane, came to visit Darwin at his house, following his attendance at the morning service held at the Cathedral, to which he had also taken his daughter (Darwin had not attended, taking a more sceptical view of organised religion).

Darwin greeted them, and as soon as Jane had been sent to play with the other children, examined the younger man's face closely.

"There is something wrong, Mr Machin? You appear to be somewhat disturbed."

Harry was often, as now, amazed by Darwin's perspicacity, but reminded himself that these powers of observation formed a large part of his skill as a doctor.

"Yes, indeed. Well…" He hesitated. "There is something that is troubling me. My wife, Abigail, died some time ago, as you know."

"I am sorry that I was unable to save her life."

"No, sir, that is not what I am trying to say. I know that you did everything in your power to save her, and since I have come to know you a little better, I recognise that there is no doctor in England who could have done more. No, the problem lies elsewhere."

"Another woman, perhaps?"

Harry sat up straight, and looked at Darwin, astounded. "How in the world could you know that?"

"A bow drawn at a venture, but a venture with some reasoning behind it. I will not delve into the specifics, but there are various elements of your appearance and your manner that led me to make the pronouncement that I did."

Harry sighed. "Very well, then. I wish your advice, sir. I am torn in two. A few months ago, I met a woman, a fine woman. I swear to you that I had not looked at another woman in that way since Abigail's death, but Martha somehow seemed to attract me in some strange fashion."

"Her name is Martha, then?"

"Martha Claybourne, yes. She is a widow, a little older than I, with five children from her late husband. She lives in Cornwall, near the town of Redruth. I met her when I was down there helping to set up an engine, and we have seen each other several times since then when I have been there." Harry seemed to be awaiting some response from Darwin, but none seemed to be forthcoming. "I am sorry to say that she does not wish to become Jane's step-mother, nor does she want to move from Cornwall. Should we marry, she would want Jane to remain here, in her present position with Kate Perkins."

"And you yourself?"

"I love little Jane, though I see her so infrequently. She is my daughter, and flesh of my flesh, as they say. However…"

"…You feel you cannot live without this Martha Claybourne? Am I correct?" Darwin's words were uttered in a tone that was far from sympathetic, and Harry winced under their impact.

"Yes, that is so. Even though it may seem strange to you, doctor and philosopher that you are, a man may find himself in need of female company."

Darwin smiled inwardly at this. His beloved wife had died some years previously, and Darwin had soon turned for comfort to his children's governess, who had then proceeded to bear him two daughters. "I make no judgement," he told Harry. "But surely, you are not intending to shut Jane out of your life for ever?"

"I have no wish to do so. But…" Here Harry paused. "It is a question of money."

"Aha! It will be more expensive to keep five children and one wife than to keep you alone?"

"Of course, even though Martha has some money left to her by her late husband. I have already talked to Mr Boulton and Mr Watt about the situation, and they will find me a well-paying position in Cornwall – we do a lot of work down there with the steam-engines, as I am sure you are aware."

"Enough to keep your proposed wife and her brood?"

"Yes, and enough to keep up sending my ten shillings each week to Mrs Perkins. But, I am sad to say, not enough money for me to keep visiting Jane here in Lichfield."

"And what exactly do you propose that I should do? I am, of course, friends with your employer, but I happen to know that he has a very high opinion of you already – as do I, I may add – and I am sure that no words from me would have any further effect on your wages, even though he will certainly increase them if you marry and he learns of your situation."

"So it seems that I must either abandon my daughter, or live alone for the rest of my life."

"Come, man, you make it sound like one of Mr Garrick's tragedies. You are not abandoning her. If you were a seafaring man you might be away from her for months, years, on end. You can write epistles to her, can you not? And I for my part, will ensure that she answers them, with my assistance if necessary, though I can tell you that she is coming on admirably in her reading, and is starting to write her letters. You will be closer to your daughter than thousands of those at sea. And I am sure that you will be able to come to visit her sometimes, maybe not as often as you would like, however.

"Come, man, cheer yourself a little. Your daughter is a fine little thing, and I know that Mrs Perkins is almost as fond of her as she is of her own. And for myself, I find her to be a perfect delight. She will be as well cared for and even loved as any child in the country. Now, what do you say to that?"

To which, Harry could only mumble his agreement.

The Philosopher

A FEW YEARS PASSED. Jane Machin lived happily with the Perkins family, and Kate Perkins seemed almost to have forgotten that Jane was not one of her own children. All the children continued to visit Erasmus Darwin regularly, and he soon became "Uncle 'Rasmus" to them, much to Kate's initial horror, but she was reassured by the doctor that there was little he enjoyed so much as the affection of children.

Kate was very reluctant to let Jane out of the immediate vicinity of the city and the cathedral and churches which she was convinced formed a protection against Them, so when Darwin suggested that he take the children some way away to a friend's house near Derby to witness a number of philosophical experiments, she was less than enthusiastic.

"I know you mean well by my little ones and by Jane, but I do consider it to be putting them in some danger by taking them out of the city."

"I assure you, Mrs Perkins, that I will take every effort to protect them, and I shall be alert regarding the possibility of anything untoward happening. I will take full responsibility for any consequences."

"Even so," she answered him, "I cannot say I shall be quiet in my mind until they return safely with you."

"Have no fear," he answered her. "Some of the most eminent minds in the country will be present, and between us, I believe that we will be a match for anything that dares to set itself against us."

And with that, Kate had to be content. She went away from Darwin's house, more than a little apprehensive about what the future might hold in this regard, and cursing men, especially clever men, for their arrogance in believing in their superiority over things that they did not understand.

ON THE APPOINTED DAY, Darwin and the three children set off in his carriage to the house where the philosophical demonstrations were to take place, to be given by a member of the Royal Society, James Ferguson. Darwin's carriage was designed by him, and typically there was only room for him in it. However, since he typically travelled with a pile of books to read in one corner of the carriage, and a heap of food and drink to refresh himself between visits to patients in the other, these necessities could be removed, and the spaces taken up by the three children.

It was the first time that they had travelled in a carriage, and the motion made Mary feel queasy. When she complained about feeling unwell, Darwin merely smiled, and gave all of them leaves of peppermint to chew, which he correctly predicted would remove any feelings of nausea.

On arrival at the house, the children were welcomed by the

housekeeper, who gave them some supper (the adults were taking refreshment in another room) and helped them get ready for the demonstration by combing the girls' hair and brushing the horse hairs from their clothes.

At the appropriate time, they joined the adults, and to her delight Jane recognised one of the guests, a Mr Joseph Wright, who at one time had been a resident patient at Darwin's house. He was a skilled artist, and Jane had spent several happy days sitting quietly by his side when she visited Darwin as he drew pictures of animals for her amusement. She was particularly fond of his drawings of cats, but he also drew pictures of large baggy-skinned animals she had never seen in Lichfield, and told her their names – elephants and hippopotamuses.

She ran up to him, holding out her arms to him, and he smilingly returned her embrace. Darwin chuckled at the sight, as Wright drew out a notebook and pencil and rapidly made a sketch of the three children.

The demonstrations began, with the Scottish philosopher first showing how sparks could be made to fly between two of the audience, with one holding a metal cord attached to an electrical machine.

"This," he pronounced, "is the lightning from the skies, as shown by Mr Franklin of America some years ago, but brought to you in this very room."

Towards the end of his demonstrations, electrical, alchemical, and other, including the demonstration of a model of the sun surrounded by planets, which revolved in their proper motions as he turned a crank on the side, he produced an astonishing piece of apparatus.

"This," he declared, "is an air-pump. In the same way that a pump may be used to draw water from a well, so this pump draws the invisible fluid which we term 'air' from a container."

He took a candle, and placed it on a surface which he covered with a glass jar, connected to the pump by a hose. After a while, the candle went out.

"Now, observe," he said, turning the jar so that its mouth was uppermost, and plunging a lighted taper into it, which was immediately extinguished. "The candle has replaced the phlogiston with what we call 'fixed air' by its combustion. This can also be proved by my removing all the phlogiston with the aid of the air-pump here." He relit the candle and placed the jar over it once more before cranking the pump rapidly. This time the candle guttered and went out in a much shorter time than before.

"And now, here I have a sealed pig's bladder, which I place in this glass jar, so." The flaccid wrinkled object was placed in the jar, which was then attached to the pump. "Now, young man," Ferguson said to Will. "When the air is removed from the jar, what do you think will happen to this bladder?"

"I cannot tell," said Will, scratching his head.

"Then watch!" He worked the pump, and to the surprise of the children, the bladder expanded until it became the size and shape of a foot-ball. He let the air back into the jar, and the bladder deflated.

"And now, we will substitute this bird for the bladder in the jar," taking a small song-bird from a cage that had been hanging from the ceiling above him.

As he placed the bird, which struggled and fluttered in his hand, into the jar, Jane's face took on an expression of anxiety. Mary noticed this, and put an arm around her foster-sister's shoulders.

"And now," the philosopher addressed himself to Will once more. "What will happen to the bird as the invisible fluid is withdrawn?"

"It will blow up like the bladder?" offered Will.

"Let us see." He worked the pump once more, and as he did so, the bird fluttered wildly, its wings beating against the glass. Mary covered her eyes from the sight of the little creature, which was now clearly in some distress. Jane appeared ready to burst into tears, and as Ferguson continued to turn the crank, the bird's frantic struggles became ever more feeble.

"Let him go!" Jane protested, but her voice was so feeble and so distorted by what appeared to be grief that no one took any heed of her words.

One of the gentlemen attending the demonstration attempted to explain to the two girls how this experiment proved that air was necessary for life in the same way that air was necessary for combustion, and that there was therefore some connection between burning and breathing, but his words fell on deaf ears, as Mary continued to look away from the bird, while still holding Jane in her arms.

Jane, too, seemed unable to look at the struggling bird. "My head hurts!" she complained, and her voice showed she was on the verge of tears. "Stop it!" she shrieked, and without warning, there was a splintering crash as the glass jar shattered, and the newly freed bird weakly flapped its wings, seemingly gathering strength with each movement.

The philosopher appeared astounded. "I have used that jar in over two hundred demonstrations such as this. I confess that I have no conception of how it could have broken in that way."

While he was talking, Will had carefully captured the bird in his cupped hands and returned it to the cage, where it appeared to be recovering.

Darwin, who had been standing in a darkened corner of the room, came over to the two girls. "I am sorry that this distressed you so much," he said, in a kindly voice as he bent over them. He stood and addressed the philosopher. "I consider it a grave error of judgement on your part to subject a poor harm-less creature," indicating the caged bird, "to these tortures as part of a public demonstration. As you can see, the children here are sorely affected by this, and even I, who am a doctor and thereby accustomed to witnessing the suffering of others, felt more than a little uncomfortable just now witnessing the plight of that poor bird. If there were not ladies and children present, sir, I would address you in stronger terms. I trust that you will not repeat this as a part of your demonstrations in the future."

Erasmus Darwin was as angry as the children had ever seen him. He was far from being the 'Uncle 'Rasmus' who would explain to them about his plants, and birds and animals, and always had time to chat with them, even when he was meant to be going to visit one of his patients.

"Come," he said abruptly to the children, and they left the room. "Wait here," he told them, settling them by the fire in the hall, and returning to the room. He rejoined them with Mr Joseph Wright in tow.

"Jane," said Mr Wright to her, "did you ever see my picture of an experiment like the one we've just seen?"

"No, sir. I've only seen your drawings of animals and things like that when you stayed in Lichfield."

Wright scratched his head. "I really don't know how to ex-plain this, Darwin. I painted that picture of the air-pump ex-periment ten years ago – more – and what happened tonight before the jar burst was exactly what I painted. The people, the faces, the poses – everything."

"But you created that painting from life, did you not?" Darwin asked.

Wright shook his head. "It is true that I attended an exper-iment of this kind, but the audience there was very different from the one I painted. Usually I paint from a model in front of me, but in that case, it was different. Many of the details and some of the faces just appeared in front of me, and I drew them, as if in a dream."

It was Darwin's turn to shake his head. He called for his carriage and settled the children in it before hoisting himself inside.

After a few miles, it seemed that Will and Mary were asleep, but Jane was wide awake, but in some kind of reverie, eyes open but seemingly unfocused.

"Jane," Darwin spoke softly. "How did you break that jar?"

"I'm sorry. I didn't mean to," she said, almost tearfully. "It was an accident. I didn't like to feel the birdie in there, so I wanted to let him out. I didn't mean to break it. Are you very angry with me?"

Darwin smiled to himself. "No, not at all angry. Perhaps you can tell me how you managed it?"

"I just wanted the bird to be free, and then…" She stopped. "He didn't want me to do it."

"Who was that? Mr Ferguson?"

"No, Him from the other side. I don't know his name."

"Do you often see him or speak with him?" Darwin's voice was light, but there was an undercurrent of wariness.

"No. Not hardly ever. But he seems to know me when he speaks."

THE NEXT DAY, Darwin recounted the whole of the previous night's proceedings to Kate Perkins, taking himself to her house in Dam Street to do so.

"I did warn you, sir," she said, after listening stony-faced to his explanation.

"You did indeed, Mrs Perkins. I should have listened to you.

Now, are you sure that nothing like what I have just described has happened in this house?"

"I'm sure enough of that. Plates get broken and chipped here, like they do in any house, but it's usually because someone's dropped them on the floor. My Will, for the most part. He's a butterfingers, that one."

"And you've never seen or heard anything unusual about her?"

Kate Perkins shook her head. "Nowt. And I still say that's because we're so close to the Cathedral."

"You may well be right, Mrs Perkins," Darwin told her.

"Now, sir. Something I have to ask you. Did you see or feel anything unusual in that 'philosophical demonstration'?" There was an element of scorn in the way she pronounced those last words.

"I will be honest with you. Yes, I did. I cannot describe exactly what I felt, but I was aware of another person— no, it was not a person, but another being of some kind, who was in the room with us, though he or it was invisible." He reflected for a few seconds. "No, I cannot describe it. It seemed to be near Jane. As to what I felt? I cannot tell you with any clarity, I am afraid."

"Jane said you knew that it was her who broke that bottle or whatever it was. How did you know that, sir?"

Darwin smiled. "You are asking all the right questions, Mrs Perkins. You are a natural philosopher."

"After what happened last night, I'm not sure as I should be taking that as a compliment."

"Hmph. Yes, well… As to your question… I was convinced that she had broken it. How she achieved that end, I am unsure. I am also unsure as to how I know that fact. I was simply certain that she was responsible." He scratched his head, seemingly forgetting that he was wearing his wig. "But you are perfectly correct, Mrs Perkins. There is something very strange about little Jane. I am starting to believe in Them on the other side of the sky. And there's another thing," he added. He told her about Joseph Wright's painting of the air-pump, which was of a scene and subjects who had not existed until ten years after the painting had been finished. "So what do you make of that, eh?"

"You're asking me, sir? You with all your learning have no answer to this?"

"My learning does not encompass the impossible, Mrs Perkins. It is clearly impossible for a man to paint a scene that does not exist at the time he paints it, but exists ten years later."

"But you say it has happened?"

"Yes, and that is the devil of it— pardon me for saying that."

"Do you or any of your philosophers think it is possible to travel in time, like we travel from here to Rugeley, say?"

Darwin laughed. "How would you even begin to think about doing such a thing?"

"I don't know, sir. That's why I asked you."

Darwin could see that Kate Perkins was wishing to say more, and encouraged her to continue.

"Well, it's not quite the same," she said, "and it probably sounds a bit daft to you, but you know the stories about the people who say they've been to see Them on the other side of the sky?"

"I've heard of some of these tales."

"Well, they think they've been there for years and years, but when they come back to us, they find they've only been gone for a day or so at the most. Sometimes it's the other way round. They think they've been gone for a day and a night and they come back and it's been twenty years, and all the folks they knew are now dead. I think all these stories mean that They can control time – make it slow down and speed up.

Maybe They can even send memories backwards, if you see what I mean."

"So little Jane somehow managed to send that scene back to Joseph— Mr Wright, to a time when she wasn't even born? Is that what you are saying?

No, sir, not her what's doing it. Him. The one you thought was there last night, and the one I saw at Streethay who says he's her father. He's there, and He's doing things."

"Doing things with time? That would be very disturbing. Why, it would mean…" Darwin paused, and this time remembered to take off his wig before scratching his head and replacing the wig. "I don't even like to think what that would mean. I wish you hadn't told me that, Mrs Perkins. I will get no sleep tonight thinking about it."

"Sorry about that, sir."

"No, no, not at all. Someone's got to ask these questions, and I'd sooner it was a woman of good sense like you than some of those opinionated fools down in London." He smiled, but it was obvious that Kate's words had given him pause for thought.

VI

The Concert

SOME YEARS LATER, Jane Machin was firmly established as a member of the Perkins household at ten years old. Kate Perkins had almost forgotten that Jane was not her own daughter, other than the ten shillings each week she received from Jane's father, and the five shillings from Erasmus Darwin. Harry Machin, though he clearly had not forgotten his daughter completely, visited once each year at most, and Jane's birthday remained unremembered by him.

Jane was now able to read and write fluently, taking her lessons with the Darwin children, and had long since eclipsed Mary in these matters. Since Kate was careful not to let her stray too far from Lichfield, there had been no recurrence of the incident at the philosophical demonstration.

As well as English, Jane was starting to learn a little Latin, and Kate worried that she was going to have "too much learning for what she is", as she put it, but Darwin assured her that if Jane continued to develop in the way he expected, there would be no problem in her taking up a position as a schoolmistress or governess in a good family.

But it was Jane's musical talents that astounded everyone. From a very early age she had been able to sing, in tune and time, and with a memory for the simple songs and rhymes that amazed all who heard her.

She had to hear a song only once before it lodged in her memory. Even one week after hearing it, she could reproduce it, words and music, near perfectly. Nor was this talent confined to songs, but she could also memorise instrumental music.

She was especially taken with the spinet at Darwin's house, and once she had grasped the principle that musical sounds could be put onto paper in the same way as words, immediately demanded to be taught how to interpret these strange symbols. At seven years old, she was considered too young to learn by the Darwins' governess, but following orders from Erasmus Darwin himself to attempt to teach her the basic skills of musical notation, Jane surprised them all by her almost instantaneous grasp of the subject and her ability to read at sight, handicapped only by the size of her hands, which prevented her from playing some of the chords and arpeggios.

ERASMUS DARWIN WAS ENTRANCED by Jane Machin's musical talents, possessing little skill himself in this area. When she practised her music, he would often be discovered sitting quietly in a corner, reading and writing, listening to the music coming from the spinet with a smile of pleasure spread across his broad face.

He mentioned his young protégée's skills in a letter to his friend Matthew Boulton, and received in return an invitation for Jane to visit Soho House and give a musical recital to the Boulton family and some guests, including a few members of the Lunar Society.

"Alas, it will not be possible for Jane's father to attend, much as I, and I know you also, would wish that to be the case," he wrote. "He is engaged with Mr Watt in business of an extraordinary delicacy which requires his constant attendance in Cornwall. I trust that young Jane will not be too sorely disappointed."

Since it was now the best part of a year since Harry Machin had visited Lichfield, Darwin felt that Jane would not be unduly upset by this. He asked Kate Perkins' permission for Jane to visit Boulton at Handsworth, and she agreed, but only on condition that she was able to accompany her. As she explained, Darwin, for all his good nature, and his skill at dealing with children, was not the girl's mother, and it was important that Jane felt herself supported.

"And," she went on, "who knows what might happen when she's away from here?" meaning Lichfield. "I'm sure we both remember what happened at that philosophical demonstration. I think it's important that I'm with her."

To which Darwin could only agree, not that he had any strong objection to Kate Perkins' company – if truth be told, he enjoyed his conversations on medical matters with her. Even so, he was a little unsure how she would manage at the gathering in Soho House.

As it transpired, Darwin was more than happy that Mrs Perkins had been included as a member of the party at Soho House that evening.

Jane, dressed in a new gown (for which Darwin had secretly

65

provided a large part of the purchase price) was introduced to Matthew Boulton's family. She had met Boulton himself on a number of occasions previously when he had visited Darwin's house for meetings of the Lunar Society, but she had no memory of the other members of the family, even though she had lived in the house for some time when much younger.

She did, however, seem to recognise the layout of the house, and was able, under gentle questioning from Darwin, to describe rooms of the house which she had not entered during this visit. At one point, she described a room as having walls painted with a light green.

"No, they are hung with maroon-coloured hangings," said Mrs Boulton.

"But, my dear," her husband replied, "at the time when Jane was with us here, the walls were indeed a light green."

Darwin, who had been making notes as this mild interrogation proceeded, wrote furiously in his notebook at this point. "Remarkable," he could be heard muttering under his breath. "I must revisit my whole theory of memory." He shook his head.

Jane was led to the spinet, and seated at the keyboard. She touched a key and shook her head.

"Why, what's wrong?" Kate Perkins asked her, recognising Jane's characteristic pout.

"It's the wrong sound." Jane said. "It's too sharp."

"She says that about the cathedral organ, too," Darwin commented.

"Well, it is too sharp," Jane told him. "Compared to your spinet, anyway."

"I don't understand," said Mrs Boulton. "Surely that's a middle C, and that's that. It's like saying that a yard of cloth in your house, Doctor, is longer than a yard of cloth here, and that's just ridiculous. This is a very fine instrument, I'd have you know, young lady."

"Yes, I know it is," Jane said humbly. "It has a beautiful sound. It's just that when I play on Uncle— I mean, the Doctor's spinet, when I play this note," and she pressed a key, "it sounds like this." Here she sang a tone which was almost, but not quite, the same as the note that she had produced from the keyboard.

Darwin turned to Mrs Boulton. "Actually, it is not quite the same as a yard of cloth differing in length in two different places. Here is something that was recommended to me by a friend in London." He reached into his waistcoat pocket and produced a small, forked piece of metal. He struck it gently against the palm of his hand, and placed the handle of the fork on the table, leaving the two tines standing vertically. The room was filled with the pure tones produced by the fork, and amplified by the table. "That, Mrs Boulton, is the sound of the A to which my spinet is tuned. Jane, my dear, if you would be good enough to play the A on the keyboard in front of you. Thank you. You see," he triumphantly concluded, "the tone is different, and young Jane is perfectly correct. The spinet here is tuned higher than mine back in Lichfield."

"Well, I never!" exclaimed Mrs Boulton. "But who is to say that yours is the correct sound, and ours is not?"

Darwin smiled. "That is a very different question, and I refuse to give an answer to it. All I can say is that Jane Machin here has a wonderful talent for fine discrimination when it comes to sound. And not only of sound, but of music, too. Come, Jane, may we hear that courante by Handel that you have been practising?"

Without further ado, Jane launched into the piece, confidently and precisely, but with a feeling for the music, and at the end launched into a faster gigue from the same suite.

At the end there was silence, other than a low "Bravo" from Matthew Boulton, followed by a burst of applause from all in the room.

"May I play something of my own? Something I made up?" Jane asked them.

"By all means," Boulton answered enthusiastically.

Jane plunged into a complex piece which sounded to the listeners to be almost the equal of the Handel they had just enjoyed. Again, at the end, there was silence, followed by loud enthusiastic applause.

"That is your own music?" said Mrs Boulton. Her tone was incredulous.

"If it is not, I have no idea from where it came," Darwin told her.

For her part, Kate Perkins sat quietly in a corner, thunder-struck. There was, of course, no instrument at the Dam Street house, and all of Jane's practising had been carried out at Darwin's house. This was the first time that she had heard her ward performing, rather than merely carrying out mechanical practising of scales and exercises.

As the party sat in wonder at what they had just experienced, the young virtuoso spoke. "Are we going to eat soon? I'm hungry."

BOULTON LED THE WAY into the dining-room, where the table was set. Jane was seated next to Kate Perkins, and it was hard to tell which of them appeared more intimidated by the array of knives, forks, spoons, and glasses set before them.

Kate watched Darwin carefully, and copied his movements, and Jane copied Kate as best she could.

There was a lull in the conversation, and near-silence reigned for a few seconds before Darwin spoke.

"Hark! Listen carefully."

"What do you hear?" asked Josiah Wedgwood, who as a friend of both Darwin and Boulton and a lover of music, had been invited to enjoy Jane's performance.

"I would sooner that you told me what it is that you hear," said Darwin. "I fear that my ears are playing tricks on me."

"I hear music," replied his friend. "The spinet. And if I am not mistaken, I hear the same piece that was composed and played to us just now by our little friend."

"Impossible!" said Boulton. "Who could possibly be playing? I am certain that none of my servants has hidden musical talents. And are you sure that the piece is the same that we have just heard?"

"Thank you for confirming my suspicions, Josiah," said Darwin. "I had feared my wits had deserted me. With your permission, madam," with a nod to his hostess, "I would like to interrupt this delicious feast and see for myself who is playing this music."

"Have a care, Doctor," Kate Perkins warned him with a meaningful glance.

"I will indeed, my dear Mrs Perkins. I see that I will not be alone." Boulton too had tossed his napkin onto the table in front of him, and Wedgwood was heaving himself out of his chair. "Please excuse us, madam," he said, opening the door and letting himself out, followed by his two friends, who closed the door behind them.

The two women sat in silence for a few minutes, ears pricked to listen for any untoward sounds.

"These men," said Mrs Boulton to Kate Perkins with a nervous giggle. They were almost the first words that she had spoken directly to her guest since she had arrived. "Always wanting to find out things which should be left well alone, in my opinion."

"I could hardly agree with you more," Kate replied. Since she was a guest at the table, she hesitated before finally deciding to omit a 'madam' at the end of her speech. "There are things better left unexplored."

"Is that what you meant when you warned Doctor Darwin to have a care?"

"Indeed so." She stopped and looked around her. "Jane! Jane, where are you?"

Jane's chair was empty, and there was no sign of her.

"Hiding under the table, I'll be bound, the little imp," said Mrs Boulton, but on examination there was no one to be seen under the table. "Well, she can't have gone out of the door, because I'm facing it, and I would know if it had been opened."

"This is the only door to this room?" asked Kate.

"It is. And my husband designed this house himself, and I know that there are no secret passages hidden in the walls, as there might be in an older building." She shook her head.

"I am responsible for Jane," Kate told her. "I must find her." She rose, but as she reached out her hand for the door handle, the door opened, and Darwin entered, leading Jane by the hand.

"There you are!" exclaimed Kate. She seemed about to ask Jane where she had been, and what she thought she had been doing, but Darwin gave her a glance and she held her peace.

"So here we all are, safe and sound," Matthew Boulton remarked in a manner which Kate felt was falsely jovial. "And now let us continue our meal."

"But who was playing the music?" Mrs Boulton asked. "Did you not discover that?"

"Imagination, my dear Mrs Boulton," Josiah Wedgwood informed her. "It seems that Doctor Darwin here was using us as materials for an experiment in suggestion. He pretended to hear something, asked us all what it was that we heard, and convinced us all, including myself, that we could hear a spinet being played."

"Well!" said Mrs Boulton. "I find it hard to doubt the evidence of my own ears, but if you say that is the case, Doctor, I suppose I have no choice but to agree with you."

"The mind is a powerful thing, madam," Darwin solemnly informed her. "Our imagination can play strange tricks. I do apologise unreservedly for any inconvenience my little enquiry may have caused."

"But Jane?" Mrs Boulton persisted. "One moment she was with us, and the next she was nowhere to be seen in this room."

"She slipped out with Mr Wedgwood here," Darwin told her. "Did you not observe her?"

Kate was certain that this was not the case, but held her peace. The meal proceeded, and talk of experiments and the mind was studiously avoided by all.

"It is time to go," said Darwin to Kate and Jane after the meal was over. "Jane can sleep in the carriage, and there are plenty of rugs for her to wrap herself in and keep warm. And some left over for you, Mrs Perkins, so you will not feel the cold, either."

Once settled in the carriage with Jane wrapped in blankets, and seemingly asleep, and they were firmly on the road to Lichfield, Kate turned to Darwin. "What really happened, Doctor? I am not as easily deceived as that Mrs Boulton. That was no experiment of yours."

"You are far from being easily deceived, my dear, and indeed you may well know more about this business than do

I. I can only tell you what it is that we experienced, but I am unable to tell you how it occurred.

"There was no one playing the spinet – no one that was visible, that is. The spinet was definitely being played, though. I was first into the room, and I could see the keys being depressed. As soon as whatever it was realised that it was being observed, the playing stopped."

It was one of Them, wasn't it?" asked Kate.

"I lack your experience in these matters," Darwin admitted, "but from what you have told me, yes, you are correct."

"And what did you feel?" Kate asked.

"There was a most uncomfortable feeling. Somewhat similar to the feeling one has when coming inside on a rainy day in wet clothes, and standing in front of a fire. And also a most distressing feeling of being trapped in some sort of viscous liquid, such as honey, but with the impression of a foul odour. The other two, by the way, described that feeling of warmth and wet and the feeling of the sticky liquid, but neither was conscious of an odour."

"It was one of Them," Kate told him. "Without a doubt. Jane's playing brought one of Them to the place. And what of Jane? She did not leave with that Mr Wedgwood, I'd take my oath on that. Nor did she go through that door."

Darwin sighed. "I cannot believe what I saw. Mrs Perkins, would you say that I was drunk this evening?"

"No, sir, I would not. You never drink wine, as I well know. And for myself, I know that I drank very little."

Darwin smiled faintly. "Thank you. As I stood looking at that abandoned spinet, which so recently had been played by someone or something unseen, I saw, with these two eyes, Jane Machin step through the wall of the room, and stand in front of me."

"It's one of Their tricks, sir. I have seen it myself once. The child of one of the Vicars Choral here, long since moved away. What did the other two men say?"

"Their backs were turned, and I was able to persuade them that Jane had come from the dining-room with us, unnoticed by anyone until now, since our attention had been fixed on the spinet. Frankly, I doubt if they truly believed me, but it was more convenient to accept this explanation than to believe the impossible – that a young child is able to walk through walls at will."

"You and I must talk tomorrow, Doctor," Kate told him. "If her music is a gift from Them, we must not encourage it. And we must ask Jane tomorrow what she remembers of tonight's adventures."

"As always, Mrs Perkins, you are correct. I would all my friends and colleagues had a fraction of your good sense."

THE NEXT MORNING, Jane seemed terrified by the idea of going to see 'Uncle 'Rasmus'.

"Will he be very cross with me?" she asked.

"I don't think so, dear," Kate told her, though she was worried that Darwin might well be less well disposed towards her following the events at Soho House.

As it turned out, Darwin had been called out to a patient in a nearby village, but his housekeeper informed Kate that he was not expected to return for some time, and suggested that she called later that afternoon, or the next day.

Kate was careful to keep her eye on Jane for the rest of the day, as far as she was able. Something in the air didn't seem right. As she looked out of the back of the house over Stowe Fields, black clouds hung in the air over towards Curborough.

"Looking a bit black over Bill's mother's," she said to herself, wondering yet again who the Bill was who was mentioned in the local saying, and why his mother's house should be the focus for storm clouds. She went out into the back yard to fetch in the washing before the threatened rain appeared, and just managed to fetch in the last of the clean clothes before the first large warm drops of rain spattered on the dry ground.

She shut the kitchen windows against the rain, though the air seemed warm and damp and stifling, almost making it difficult to breathe. She could hear Will's and Mary's voices from the other downstairs room, but listened in vain for that of Jane.

She wiped her hands on her apron and went into the front room. Mary and Will were watching the rainstorm splashing in Dam Street, and pointing out their neighbours who were battling their way home through the deluge. Jane was nowhere to be seen.

"Where is she?" asked Kate, but neither Will nor Mary could give her an answer. In fact, Mary seemed surprised that Jane was not in the room with them.

"She was here," she protested. "I never saw her go out."

Kate knew better than to ask how long ago it was that Jane had been in the room. There was no clock, and even if there had been, Mary was unable to tell the time.

Kate stood, hands on her hips, wondering how to make her next move, when there was a crashing sound from upstairs, followed by a tinkling sound. Kate snatched up her skirts and rushed up the stairs to the back room where Mary and Jane slept.

The wind was howling through the smashed window, driving rain onto the bed, with a sound so loud that it made it difficult for Kate to think rationally. There was no sign of Jane. Thinking that Jane might have made her way to one of the other upstairs rooms, Kate went in search of her, but her efforts were fruitless – Jane was nowhere to be seen – and she returned to the back room again with the intention of covering the broken window with the blanket she had snatched from her own bed.

The wind continued to roar and howl, but Kate could hear another noise through the storm – the sound of Jane's voice. She was unable to make out the words, but it was definitely Jane's voice, and quite impossibly, it appeared to be coming from outside the window.

She struggled to the window against the gale and rain pouring in, and was immediately enveloped by the sticky black feeling that she had experienced at her sister's in Streethay. There was a presence near her. One of Them, she knew. The one who had been playing the spinet at Soho House the evening before.

WHEN DARWIN HAD MENTIONED some time ago that she had been called a witch by the other inhabitants of the city, she had deflected the conversation away from the subject. The truth was that by most people's standards she was indeed a witch. To be sure, some of the healing that she performed was based on old folk remedies, with the addition of some of Dr Darwin's recipes. It was the other healing that was "special". On these occasions the medicine that she gave to cure her patients was little more than water with a little vinegar and pepper mixed in. The poultices that she placed on wounds were simply composed of flour, water and salt. There was no reason why they should work, but they worked many times more often than Erasmus Darwin or any of the other doctors in the city might expect. In fact, the number of patients who failed to respond to these treatments was so small as to be almost unworthy of mention.

Not that Kate was attempting to cheat or bamboozle her patients. When she gave these nostrums to her patients, she did so with the absolute certainty that she was doing the right thing. The healing power was not in the materials, but derived from the mind of something outside Kate – she took no credit for these cures. And, to be sure, these were not given out on every occasion, only when she had the inner knowledge that the cure was certain, and in those cases, she refused to take money for them – though she did accept presents and gifts given in gratitude by those she had cured.

Over the past few months she had taken little Jane with her to see some of her patients, and somehow knew that Jane was able to summon more of the healing power from Them than she, Kate, would ever achieve.

But there was a price to be paid on Kate's side, which she had been told about when she was seven years old. She and her grandmother had been left alone in the house for some reason.

"Come here, little Kitty," her grandmother had told her. "I want to tell you something important. Roll up your sleeve. No, the left sleeve." And Nana had drawn a strange mark on her left arm with a piece of burnt rowan wood.

"This," she had told the young Kate, who looked in wonder at her small pale arm, now covered with intricate tracery, "is a mark that will never leave you. Oh yes," she had addressed Kate, who was rubbing a wet finger over her skin. "You can rub off the ash, but the mark will always be with you, and They can see it, and know you are one of Them."

"Who are They, Nana?" Kate had asked.

"They have no names, but They come from the other side of the sky. And They can help you. While you live, you will never want. You will be able to tell who lives and who dies, with Their help. Look at your arm by the light of the moon, just as you are looking at it now, and They will know you are calling for Their help. Ask, and They will give it. And folk will bless you for it." She had paused. "But there is a price to be paid. Every life you save with Their help is half a year of your life gone. So use that gift carefully."

The young Kate had not understood most of what had been said to her, but the words her grandmother had used stayed in her mind and she gained a fuller understanding of their meaning as she grew older.

She first, slightly reluctantly, bared her arm by moonlight before she was married, at the age of seventeen, but already with a reputation as a gifted healer, using her grandmother's herbal remedies, if not actually as a witch. To her amazement, the pattern that her grandmother had painted with rowan ash all those years before appeared again, as a glowing tracery of light on her skin. Somehow, she knew that They were present, watching, waiting to be called – and greedy for their six months of her life. She was young, she was careless and un-married – and six months didn't seem to matter. She asked for Their help. Again and again. The first few times seemed like a coincidence. Her patients recovered, but she put it down at least partly to the herbal infusions that she had prescribed. But now she knew Their power, and no longer bothered with the infusions, but simply prescribed the vinegar and pepper for her patients' ills when she performed these special healings.

She had kept note of the number of times she had used this power. Now thirteen and a half years of her allotted lifespan were gone, and she was increasingly reluctant, with Will and Mary still young, to throw away many more years of life.

But when Jane was with her, even though she knew They

would help, she would pay no price. But she feared for Jane – what sort of price were They asking her to pay?

IN THE BACK ROOM, Kate looked out of the broken window into the swirling storm outside, and to her amazement saw Jane, seemingly floating in mid-air, motionless despite the tempest swirling around her.

"What are you doing? Come back!?" she shrieked into the wind battering her face.

"I can't come back. He won't let me," came the reply. Jane's face was contorted in an expression of terror.

As Kate watched, Jane suddenly moved further away, as if being pulled by some invisible force, and let out a wail of fear. "He's taking me away!" she screamed, but her words were only just discernible over the howling of the wind.

Kate knew who He was. She rolled up her left sleeve and exposed the symbol, glowing faintly in the moonlight, in a desperate attempt to talk to Them, to beg them to let Jane go and return her, but she was enveloped by the dark sticky mass that had assailed her at her sister's house, and by the excruciating pain in her head that had accompanied it. She sank to the floor, senseless, and as her vision faded, so did the sight of Jane, riding the storm to the other side of the sky.

KATE HAD NO IDEA how long she had been lying on the floor when she awoke. Night had fallen, and the storm had abated somewhat, but wind and rain were still coming through the open window. She struggled to rig a blanket over the smashed pane, and to mop up the water on the floor. Thank goodness, her headache was gone.

Her next thoughts were of Will and Mary. What were they doing while she'd been unconscious? She raced downstairs, to find them sitting, seemingly asleep, in the kitchen. As she entered the room, Will awoke and complained he was hungry. She prepared some sort of meal for him, and woke Mary, who shared Will's bread and bacon. For her own part, Kate found it impossible to eat.

"She's gone all mardy like," Will whispered to his sister in a voice that wasn't meant to be overheard. Kate said nothing. She was well aware that the children had been in danger, and she felt guilty and protective towards them.

Later that night, Kate found it impossible to sleep. She was uncomfortably aware of the presence of Them near her, and the realisation that Jane had gone – where? She supposed that she had been taken to the other side of the sky.

As she lay awake, she tried to imagine what that place would look like, if it really was a place at all. But They had to come from somewhere, didn't they? So there must be a place on the other side of the sky, whatever Doctor Darwin had to say on the matter.

When morning came she wasted no time in going to see Darwin.

He seemed none too pleased about being disturbed, but invited her to sit. "My dear Mrs Perkins," he said. "I can spare you a few minutes of my time. I have a patient at Rugeley who is expecting me."

"In that case, sir, I'd better go, hadn't I? I just came to tell you that Jane is gone."

Darwin looked at her in shock. "She has run away?"

"No, sir." Kate proceeded to tell Darwin about what had happened the previous night, Darwin's face turning to a shocked ashen grey colour as she proceeded. "And now, sir,

I think I'd best be going and leave you to your patient in Rugeley."

Darwin waved a hand. "She's not so sick that an hour's delay will kill her," he said. "What you are saying seems incredible."

"I can assure you, sir, that I was not dreaming or drunk."

"I believe you," Darwin told her. "So much that is unexplained happened at Boulton's the other night, that I have no choice but to believe that They, whatever They turn out to be, have taken one of Their own. Have you ever heard of anything like this happening before?"

"No, I have not. There are tales of babies being snatched from cradles, and one of Their children being put in their place, but never of a grown child being taken away like this." Kate began to weep, and Darwin offered her a large linen hand-kerchief with which to wipe away her tears. "I was very fond of little Jane, you know, sir. Almost loved her as much as one of my own. Such a clever little thing, and good-natured with it."

"I know," Darwin said. "I am so happy to be 'Uncle 'Rasmus' to her, and also to your own children, I hasten to add. But come, let us be practical. Do you feel you and your children are now in danger from Them?"

Kate took her time before answering. "No sir, I do not. Though I feel that They attacked me, and I was worried sick about my own children after Jane had been snatched away, now I believe it was only as a distraction to allow Them to steal Jane."

"Do you think Jane was happy to go with Them?"

"Not at all. The poor little mite was scared out of her wits."

"Do you expect Jane to be returned to us?"

Another long pause. "I cannot say."

Darwin smiled thinly. "Excellent. You refuse to commit yourself to a particular view on a subject of which you possess

insufficient knowledge. I wish that some of my medical colleagues displayed the same amount of good sense."

"I suppose all we can do is wait," she said at length.

Darwin shrugged. "I really cannot think of anything that
we might do that would bring Jane back to us. So, if you will
excuse me, I should be making my way to Rugeley." He looked
at Kate a little more closely. "And do take care of yourself, Mrs
Perkins. Distressing as this whole business may be, you must
not let it affect your health."

"Thank you, sir." She smiled faintly. "It's been some time
since someone worried about me like that."

Two days later, Jane returned to the house on Dam Street.

Kate was just washing the plates after the midday meal
when there was a knock on the door. She opened it to see a
middle-aged man, dressed in what she called "village clothes",
that you might see on the folk who came into Lichfield on
market days from the villages round about. He was not alone
– a small child was visible behind him, but it was impossible
even to tell whether the child was male or female.

"Now don't you go mithering me," she said, assuming that
he was some sort of beggar looking for charity. "I've hardly
got enough to spare for me and the little ones as it is."

"That's not it, if you don't mind," he answered her stiffly. "If
your name's Kate Perkins, this one here says she's with you."
He stepped to one side, and to her delight, Kate beheld Jane.
Bedraggled, still wearing the nightshirt in which Kate had
last seen her, and more than a little dirty, but her face had lit
up with the joy of seeing her foster-mother.

"Oh my Lord, so she is. Thank you, thank you, thank you,"
she repeated as if it were a charm. "Where…? How…?"

"My name's Jim Degg. I live just outside Yoxall, and as I was going along to the Crown yesterday evening, I comes across this one," pointing to Jane, "in the lane, just as you see her now. Except she hadn't no shoes or stockings or nothing. Those as she's got on now is my little one's."

He paused for breath, and Kate invited him into the house. He entered, and Kate scooped up Jane in her arms and held her tight.

"Thank goodness you're back, you little terror," she said kindly to Jane as she placed her on a stool in the corner. "We'll get you cleaned up in a minute. Sit down," she invited the man who had brought Jane here. "She told you where she lived?"

"She said that she lived near the Cathedral, like, with Kate Perkins. So I took her back home with me, and the missus asked what I was doing with her, and said I should being her here this morning. So I told the gaffer what was up, and I've got the morning off to bring her here."

It seemed clear to Kate that he was expecting some kind of reward for his trouble, so she went to the jar on the mantelpiece and found five shillings, which she gave to him.

"Why, thank you," he said, "but I really couldn't take all of this. I see you've got two other little ones," (Mary and Will had quietly come into the room, and were staring openmouthed at the spectacle of a muddy Jane in her night clothes sitting on the stool, and a strange man talking to their mother) "and they're going to need feeding. I'm not saying that a little money wouldn't be welcome, but that's too much." He handed three shillings back to Kate, who took the money silently.

"You're a good man, Jim," she said at length.

"I try. And that's all any of us can do, ain't it?" He rose and went out of the door, only to return half a minute later. "Sorry to be a trouble. But she's got my little one's shoes on."

Kate hurriedly removed them, and handed them back to him, apologising.

"No, my fault," he said. "Forget my head if it was loose, my mother always used to say to me."

He left for the second time, and Kate turned to Jane.

"Now we'll get you all cleaned up, you mucky little pup, you."

Jane began to cry. "I couldn't help it," she sobbed. "His house was all muddy and dirty."

Kate felt a shiver run down her back. She didn't need to ask who "He" was. "I'm not cross with you," she assured Jane. "Are you all right? Are you hurt?"

"No, but I'm a bit tired and hungry."

"There's some bread and a bit of cheese, and I dare say I can find some milk for you. That's better," as Jane started to smile. "But first things first," and she cleaned the child's face and hands. "Where did He take you?"

"He said it was his palace, but it wasn't anything like the Bishop's Palace where Miss Anna lives. It was nasty and dirty and muddy and very cold. And He would keep talking."

"What did he say to you? Mary, Will, you go into the other room now. Jane can tell you all about things later if she wants to. Off you go. Shoo! Now, what did He say to you?"

"He told me all about what he called his palace when we got there. Golden walls, and jewels in the lights, and all the rich cloths covering things. But I never saw any of those. Just mud on the walls, like a hole in the ground, and a smelly old lamp which didn't have any jewels on it, and there were no cloths except for an old sack in one corner. And it was cold. I'm not nesh, but I really was cold. I told him this, and he kept saying, 'Can't you see? Can you really not see what I'm telling you?' I don't know what He was thinking." She shook her head. "Then He said he was my father, but that's not true, is it? Father lives down in Cornwall, doesn't he?" Kate nodded. "I thought so."

"Did He tell you his name?" Kate was aware that possessing the name of one of Them was a powerful weapon that could be used against Them.

Jane shook her head. "I did ask him, but He told me it wasn't important. He just wanted me to call him 'Father'. But I wouldn't, and he sort of sulked, rather like Will does when you don't allow him to put honey on his second slice of bread. And then He kept saying that I could have anything I wanted from him if I just told him what I wanted. I couldn't think of anything except I wanted to go back home, so I kept telling him that." She shook her head. "He kept saying I could be queen of the world, and silly things like that. I couldn't be queen, could I?" she asked Kate. "I'd have to live in London, I suppose, and I don't think I'd like that. I like it here with you and Mary and Will. And Uncle 'Rasmus." She shook her head again. "No, that's not what I wanted. I kept on telling him that I wanted to go home to you. In the end He agreed, but He told me that He couldn't go too near the Cathedral. But I did tell him that a little money would be nice, though, and He gave me ten gold pieces. Here they are." She pulled out a knotted hand-kerchief from the sleeve of her night-gown, and carefully untied it. Look."

Kate gazed at the golden coins that shone at the bottom of the hand-kerchief, but as she gazed, they faded and changed their shape. After about half a minute, there was nothing in the cloth except a pile of bright orange nasturtium petals. Jane started to cry. "I was so pleased with finding this money for you," she sobbed, "and it's just dead flowers."

"Faerie gold," Kate said. "You're not the first to be deceived by Them, and I'm sure you won't be the last. You did well not to trust him and ask him for anything more than this. Don't cry, poppet, we're no worse off than before you went. And what happened next?"

"He seemed angry but told me that if all I wanted was to go back, then that's what would happen. And the next thing I knew, I was walking along the lane, and then that man found me and took me back to his house where they gave me some bread and some gruel, and let me get warm by the fire." She shivered. "The place He called his palace was muddy, *and* it was cold. Not like here."

"Well you're back now, and that's all right," Kate told her.

DARWIN WAS SOMEWHAT LESS than his usual cheerful self when he greeted them the next morning, but he appeared to be worried and anxious rather than angry.

Seating Jane on a chair with a glass of milk and a slice of cake, he asked her gently what had happened after she had gone to bed on the night when she had been abducted by Them.

Jane clearly found it difficult to express in words what she had experienced, but from what she said, it appeared that she had dropped off to sleep in her bed, and had suddenly been awakened by the feeling of someone lifting her up.

"I couldn't see anything," she said, "but it felt as though someone had picked me up in his arms."

Darwin seized on the word. "His?" he asked. "You are sure that it was a he who picked you up, and not a she?"

Jane nodded emphatically. "Oh yes. Definitely." She paused. "Though if you ask me how I can be so sure, I couldn't tell you."

"And has that happened before?" Kate asked.

"No. But somehow it didn't really feel all that strange, even though it was the first time that it has ever happened."

"And then what happened?" Darwin asked.

"I was carried towards the window, and then we – that is, me and whoever was carrying me – went through the window without opening it." She shrugged. "I don't know how that happened, but it did. And then I could see him. Not all of him, but just his hand. He pointed it towards the window that we had just come through, and the window broke. And then after a minute or so, you came into the room," looking at Kate, and you saw me. "And I wanted to go back, because I was frightened and I was cold." She started to cry.

"Don't take on so," Darwin told her. "You're back here with friends and people who care for you, and you're warm and safe." He passed her his large pocket hand-kerchief and she wiped her eyes before handing it back to him. "What happened next?"

"We flew like a bird. At least, He flew, and He was carrying me," Jane said with a tone of wonder in her voice. "It was quite frightening, but quite wonderful at the same time. "But don't ask me where we flew to, because I don't know. It was dark and I really don't know the places near here very well. I know that we flew over some hills, and I think we flew over some water, but I really don't know."

"And then?"

"We were in that muddy hole that He called his palace, just as I told you yesterday," she said to Kate. Darwin looked at Kate, who proceeded to repeat what she had been told by Jane.

"I heard of such things from the village folk when I was a lad growing up in Derbyshire," Darwin said, "but I had always thought of them as merely tales to be told around a fireside of an evening. But who is this person and what sort of person is he?" asked Darwin.

"I don't know what He looks like," Jane told her. "I have never seen him clearly. His palace, if that's what it really was, was too dark for me to see him clearly. I think He's tall and dark, but I really don't know. But sometimes in the past I have heard him, only at night when it's too dark to see. He spoke to me when I was lying in bed. He says He's my father, but you know this isn't true, don't you?" She started to cry. "I was too frightened to tell you about him talking to me, though, because I knew that you wouldn't believe me, or you would say I was daft or something like that."

"Now, now," said Darwin, holding out his hand-kerchief once more to Jane, who accepted it gratefully and mopped her eyes. "Can you tell us his name?" Jane simply shook her head. "Does that mean you don't know his name?" She nodded. "I see. Well, can you tell me what sort of things He has been saying to you?"

She sniffed. "I know that it sounds like nonsense, but He's been saying the same sort of things that He told me when he carried me away to his hole in the ground. He said to me that I would be one of the most important people in England. And He told me all about the nice things that I would have to wear and to eat and everything." She stopped. "But I guess that if the nice things He was talking about are like his palace, then they wouldn't be worth anything, would they? They'd just be like those gold coins that turned to flowers." Darwin lifted his eyebrows at that, and Kate explained what had happened.

"I see," said Darwin, shaking his head. "Please go on, Jane, dear."

"And anyway, if I was to be queen, or whatever it was that He was suggesting to me, He said that I would have to do what He told me to do. And I wouldn't like that at all. It's different from when you," looking at Kate, "or you," looking at Darwin, "tell me what to do, because you're both sensible and I like you both. He seemed to be silly, and I didn't like him or his smelly old 'palace'."

There was silence in the room.

"Did He say why He had taken you away? And why He brought you back again?" asked Darwin.

Jane frowned. "I think He took me away so that He could have more time to talk to me. He likes the dark, I think, and it's difficult for him to do things in the daytime."

Not impossible, though, Kate thought to herself, remembering the way in which she had been attacked at her sister's house in Streethay. But it was worth remembering that light was possibly a way of weakening his powers.

"So in his nasty dark hole He could talk to me all the time," Jane went on. "And I think it was because I kept telling him that I wanted to go home that He let me go."

"I'm sure you are right, my dear," said Darwin. He settled himself more comfortably in his chair as he changed the subject. "Who was it who wrote the music that you played at Soho House the other evening?"

"Well, no one actually wrote it, I suppose. Not on paper, I mean," Jane told him. "But I heard it all by myself."

Darwin exchanged a look with Kate. "Where did you hear it?" he asked, gently.

"Well, it was sort of in my head and sort of outside my head," Jane told him.

"Was there someone else in the room with you when you heard it?"

"Oh yes, He was singing it to himself. That's how I heard it."

"But who has taught you music?" Darwin asked. "That piece you played us was not just a tune, but a full piece of music with harmonies and developments and..." Darwin, although he enjoyed listening to music, had never made a study of it, and was unsure of the technical terms that might be used.

"That was easy," Jane told him with all the confidence of a young child prodigy. "The difficult part is the tune, but He sang it to me."

"Does He often give you tunes to play?"

"Sometimes, but not often."

"He teaches you about music?"

Jane shook her head. "No, all that, the harmony and the development of the tune. That's all from me."

""I have heard you playing here on my spinet, but I have always assumed that you were playing works by other people." Darwin shook his head. "I never heard that Mozart child when he came to this country and gave all those concerts, but by all accounts, you are as talented as he was."

He seemed about to go on, but Kate was obviously anxious to ask a question. "How did you leave Mrs Boulton and me that night and meet Dr Darwin and his friends in the other room?" she asked Jane. "I could see the door the whole time, and I'll take my oath on it that you didn't go through it."

"It's difficult to explain," Jane told her gravely. "I think I walked through the walls, but I couldn't have done, could I? I mean, people can't walk through walls. But I'm sure that's what I did, and I know it sounds daft, but I'm sure that's what I did."

"You're right it sounds daft," Kate told her. "Are you telling me the truth now?"

Jane started to sniffle. "Honest. He did give me some help, though."

"He? The same one who tells you you're going to be important? The same one that teaches you all that music? He talked to you at Mr Boulton's house?"

"Yes, him. I knew it was him. I could feel him near me. He told me to be brave and just go to the other room the quickest way that I could. So that's what I did."

"Didn't it seem strange to you?" Darwin enquired.

"It seems strange now, sort of like a dream. It doesn't seem real. But that evening I just knew that I had to walk through the wall, and it didn't seem strange or anything like that just then. Did it really happen?"

"I think that it did, but I don't know how it happened. I was really hoping that you could tell us."

She shook her head. "I can't explain it. Perhaps He can explain it better."

"I'm not really sure that we want that," said Darwin. "But you don't think He's a nice person, do you?"

Jane took a little time before she answered, frowning. "I'm not sure. Probably He isn't a nice person. Because He said in his nasty dirty hole that He might have to hurt Will and Mary if I was going to have all the things that He talked about. I don't want all those things, like I said. And I don't want Will and Kate to be hurt." She turned to Kate, who had drawn in her breath sharply. "Please don't be cross with me because I didn't tell you that before."

Kate seemed about to speak, but it was Darwin, overcoming his stammer, who replied promptly. "I am sure she won't be cross with you, but now she and I need to talk together for a while. Why don't you run along and play with my Mary and Susanna?"

JANE LEFT, and Kate addressed Darwin. "This girl, innocent as she herself may be, is a danger to my family, and almost certainly to me if she remains with me."

"I agree." Darwin sat, his great head bowed in thought.

"She is too young to leave the protection of a home. How old is she now?"

"Ten years old."

"A musical prodigy such as we can only dream of. And a charming little thing. And a poisoned dart in the flesh of whoever has charge of her." Darwin paused. "I have been reading... Not books of science, but books of alchemy and books about the Rosicrucians – have you heard of them? No? No matter. Specifically, I have been reading about characters that these people called 'Elementals', creatures only visible to certain individuals."

Kate drew in her breath. "Such as Jane?"

"And possibly you at times. These Elementals are reported to be bound to the four classical elements of fire, water, earth and air, and they have names and very distinctive properties. For example, the Elemental associated with fire is called a 'Salamander' and can survive flames and fire. The Italian artist Cellini wrote that he had seen one in the kitchen fire at his home when he was a child. A water Elemental is named an 'Undine' and, as you might expect, can live in springs and fountains. They have beautiful singing voices, according to those who have described them."

"Jane sings very prettily."

"That she does. I have heard her many a time. Now we come to the earthen Elementals – the 'gnomes'. These have the power to walk through walls and earth, and other solid materials— Ah, that surprised you, did it? It did me, when I realised what Jane must have done the other evening at Soho House. And lastly we have the aerial spirits who are known as 'Sylphs' who, as you might suppose, are able to move through the air. So..." He placed his hands on his knees and leaned forward. "How do you think?"

"The same sort of stories have been told for years in the

villages. Maybe more confused than the way you have just described, but similar. Faeries who live underground, can fly, or live in lakes and rivers. The fire faeries are not ones I have heard of elsewhere."

"So what of the one who calls himself her father? It seems He can move through walls and earth, and also fly? What is He? Is He one of those earthen Gnomes? Or an airy Sylph? Or both? Or perhaps a fiery Salamander as well? Or even a watery Undine?"

Kate shook her head. "I really cannot say, sir."

"Nor I. Of course, the descriptions by these Rosicrucians may be fanciful. Perhaps all of Them are seen as one kind of Elemental at one time or by one person, or something like that. We simply do not know, do we?" He sighed. "Or is this 'father' in fact a king or some sort of lord over these things? And, of course, it could all be imagination."

"You know very well for yourself that is not the case, sir. Even if I was lying to you—"

"I assure you, my dear Mrs Perkins, that I do not believe for one moment that you have been telling me anything that is not the simple truth."

"Thank you, sir. But even if I had not been telling you the truth, you have just told me that you saw for yourself that little Jane must have walked through the wall at Mr Boulton's."

"I know. But these Rosicrucians spoke in riddles. They believed themselves to be in possession of knowledge that was hidden from others."

"Then why did they write about these things?"

Darwin shrugged. "Who knows? It is the way of all those in possession of a supposed secret, I suppose – that they must let the world know that they are in possession of the secret, but yet not to reveal the full nature of that secret."

"Pardon me, sir, but is not your Lunar Society somewhat similar?"

"By no means – we make it very clear to all what we have discovered. In any case, we do not claim to have a monopoly on truth. We are merely climbing the first steps of a long ladder that may or may not lead us to understanding." Darwin sounded indignant.

"I am sorry, sir. I appear to have misunderstood."

"No matter. Perhaps you are correct. Maybe we should make our Lunar Society discoveries more readily available to those who wish to learn. But that is a matter for the future, rather than now." He paused for a while, clearly deep in thought, and continued. "And these Elementals are supposed by the Rosicrucians to conjoin themselves with human beings— that is to say, to have children with them…"

"I understand you, sir. You and I have seen enough over the years to know what is what."

"Yes, well." Darwin coughed. "And this is apparently to gain immortality for these beings, but here the rules governing such relationships appear to be rather complicated."

"You mean that Jane is immortal?"

"I really do not know. And I know no way of proving whether this is so other than by attempting to…"

"To kill her?"

"Yes. Needless to say, that is not an experiment that I wish to undertake or to see undertaken."

"I am glad to hear you say so."

"I confess that I am fond of her. I would be sorry to lose her. However…"

"I agree. She cannot stay with you any longer, but we must not condemn her to the poorhouse."

"Then let me propose an alternative to the poorhouse. I have friends in Switzerland. I will make enquiries."

PART TWO

THE ALCHEMIST

(1790)

VII

The Lecture

THE SUN BURST FORTH from behind a cloud and shone through the windows of the inn's bedroom onto the unlovely face of Otto Esquibel-Schultz, who stirred in his sleep. His lank grey hair, within which lice could be seen if one cared to look close enough, straggled across the pillow.

He opened his eyes, and not for the first time asked himself what the hell he was doing in Zürich. The answer was a long and rather complex one, involving as it did the disappearance of a Geneva widow's life savings following a visit to her house by Otto one evening, and a subsequent warrant for the arrest of one Philomentor, other names unknown. Well, Philomentor was now gone, along with his long straggly beard. For some time, Otto had considered losing his grey mane, but in the end decided that he should keep it as an essential part of his performance, but tie it back, rather than leave it loose as he had in Geneva. The clean-shaven Hermecritus, as he now styled himself, would bear little

95

resemblance in his smart new mystical robes to the bearded and theatrically ragged Philomentor.

The act would have to change as well, he told himself. Batteries of Leyden jars were all very well, and created an impressive effect, but for obvious reasons, he had been forced to leave them behind in Geneva, and he had no wish to create a stir by attempting to procure half a dozen here in Zürich. At least his glass armonica had survived the flight from Geneva with only minimal damage, which had been repaired in a morning. When the instrument was played softly during a healing session, the electric shock, when it came, was made more effective by contrast.

Animal magnetism, though less dramatic, would provide a suitable alternative effect and would help to refill his pockets, requiring only a suitably modest outlay. But for this afternoon… Otto tried to remember the title he had proposed for his lecture at the Kessel Institute. "The Rosy Cross and Animal Magnetism", if he remembered correctly. It would be easy enough for him to stitch enough together to hold their attention for the best part of an hour, especially if he gave a demonstration of his mesmeric talents, making a smartly dressed young fop bark like a dog, or persuading a pretty little bit of stuff to leap screaming onto a chair at the presumed sight of a horde of imaginary mice. These had always made them laugh and admire the skill of the magnetiser.

It was a far cry from Franz Mesmer's mystical "healing" sessions, at which Mesmer's handsome young assistants (Otto was never one of these) held fashionable ladies from behind between their knees, resulting in "interesting" reactions from these ladies.

It was a shame that Otto had to give his lecture in German, though. French or Italian were far more suitable languages for that kind of nonsense. For though Otto was fluent in all three, and English and Basque (his cradle tongue) in addition, together with considerable competence in Latin, Greek, and some in Hebrew, he had definite views on which language was suitable for different occasions.

In fact, given a completely free choice, he would have preferred to deliver the whole address in Latin, partly because of the effect of learning that it induced, and partly because it enabled him to invent new words with which no one could argue in order to describe the ideas he expounded.

And once this lecture had been given, he would have enough money to purchase an old wash-tub which could be appropriately decorated and re-named as his *baquet* or receptacle for "magnetised" water, along with a visit to a blacksmith to procure some curiously wrought iron rods to transmit the benefits of the water to his mesmeric clients.

And then, thought Otto, as he at last arose, and prepared himself for the day ahead, he, or rather Hermecritus, would be ready to make the move to other countries. He wasn't sure how far the long arm of Geneva's law could reach within Switzerland, but he was willing to believe that it did not extend into any of the Italian or German states, or into Austria. Sadly, the current political climate in his greatest potential market, France, made it impossible for him to ply his trade there. So for the moment, it was the Kessel Institute this afternoon.

THE ROOM AT THE KESSEL INSTITUTE was large enough to seat two hundred people, Otto, in his full persona of Hermecritus, calculated, and it was almost half-full. Better than he had hoped, but it still pained him to see the empty seats.

For now, he sat impassive in the most throne-like chair that the Institute could provide, wearing his imposing robes of purple fringed with gold, his hair neatly brushed and tied back, and the glass armonica by his side. He gazed steadily at the audience as it assembled, only his eyes flickering to and fro as he took in the details of the crowd, sizing up potential candidates for his demonstration of animal magnetism later on in the afternoon.

A small clock chimed the hour, and the President of the Institute made a short oration introducing the speaker. It was a speech that Otto had written himself several years before in order to assist the conveners of such events, and contained references to several years of meditative contemplation in a secluded mountain retreat in Sicily, a year lecturing at the English university of Oxford, and the great love borne for him by his former mentor, Franz Mesmer. Some of these references had a grain of truth to them – for example, he had indeed visited Oxford for one night, at which time he had given a lecture to a dozen drunken students who had pelted him with rotten fruit until he was forced to stop talking. It was not an incident he cared to recall. Nor, if truth be told, was his relationship with Mesmer as he had described it. Indeed, he doubted if Mesmer would remember the name of the younger vagabond who, together with half a dozen others, had helped set the stage for his healing sessions. But Otto had learned from Mesmer, oh yes, indeed he had. He had watched as the great man held men and women in the palm of his hand as he talked to them, cajoled them, laid his hands upon them, and emptied their pockets.

As the introduction closed, and the audience applauded politely, Hermecritus rose to his feet, and started to address the audience in his correct, but accented, High German. He was able to speak fluently and accurately on the appearance and subsequent history of the Brotherhood of the Rosy Cross, throwing in names and dates with evident ease, and through mental sleight of hand was able to produce a link between the Rosicrucian movement and animal magnetism.

"But first," he announced, "I will play for you some music which is surely the earthly equivalent of the music of the spheres. Music which will ravish your hearts, and will soothe your spirits to the point where animal magnetism will have the greatest benefit. While I play, please join hands with your neighbours, close your eyes as I play, and we will create together a space of living peace and spiritual harmony." There was a rustling and a shuffling as men and women delicately extended their hands towards strangers, and the weird, slightly unearthly sounds of Benjamin Franklin's glass armonica issued forth as Hermecritus ran his fingers, somewhat less than expertly, over the glass bowls. As he played, he cast his eye over the audience, and noted with satisfaction that all eyes appeared to be closed. All, that was, except those of one younger girl, sitting near the back next to an elderly couple who appeared to be worthy burghers of Zürich. There was something about her that marked her in some indefinable way as being different from the rest of the audience. It was not her dress, which appeared to in a similar style to that of the others, though of slightly poorer quality (Otto had an eye for such things) than that of most of the audience. It was more to do with the quality of her expression and her attitude, which, even while she was seated, seemed to indicate a keen interest in Hermecritus, or even, he sensed, the person behind the mask of Hermecritus. There was an uncomfortable feeling that he was being stripped of his disguise and laid open, as if on an anatomist's table. His fingers, rubbing the glass bowls, became sweaty, and the tone of the instrument became noticeably harsher.

At length he brought the piece to an end, and the audience, almost as one, sighed and opened its eyes. He picked a doltish-looking young man from the audience, and with a few passes easily magnetised him. He was unsure of the manners of this audience. Had it been a German audience, he would have convinced the young man that his shoe was covered in the leavings of a dog, but after Geneva, he knew that the sober Swiss were less likely to find this amusing, so he contented himself with giving his subject a raw potato to eat, telling him that it was a delicious apple.

The poor man bit into the vegetable and devoured it with obvious relish, to titters of embarrassed laughter. It was noticeable that his fair young companion moved a noticeable distance from him when he returned to his seat.

Next, an elderly matron danced an arthritic jig to a tune only she could hear, to the amusement of the crowd. All this time, Otto was uncomfortably aware of the girl's eyes upon him, analysing him, and seemingly wordlessly mocking him.

As the old lady returned to his seat, Otto fixed his silent interrogator with a gaze that had never failed to have an effect on clients who had been reluctant to pay for his services, and invited her to join him on the stage. No, 'invited' was too weak a term. He wordlessly commanded her to join him as he spoke the polite words of invitation.

"With pleasure, sir," she answered in German as accented as Otto's own, accompanied by a winning smile. He had expected resistance, but there was none, and she walked to the stage, along the aisle between the seats, smilingly confident.

He asked her name.

"Jane, sir."

"Very well, Jane. Please stand just so," he demonstrated, "and relax." He began the magnetic passes that he had learned from Mesmer years before, but he could tell that they were having little or no effect on her. Indeed, it almost felt as though he were the one who was being magnetised. It was becoming more difficult for him to speak, and he found it hard to move his arms.

He watched, powerless to stop her, as the girl made her way to the armonica and started operating the pedal that turned the glass bowls. Then she put her fingers to the glass, and produced sounds sweeter than anything he had ever been able to produce, with a tune and harmonies that almost stopped his heart. As he watched, he could see the audience also reacting to the spell of the music. As he listened, the sound grew fainter, and his eyes started to close.

The next thing that he heard was the sound of raucous laughter from a crowd, and when he opened his eyes, he found himself crouched on the floor, his arms dangling by his side like those of a monkey, and a turnip clutched in one hand, out of which, he realised with disgust, a bite had been taken. The taste of raw turnip was still in his mouth.

He stood up with as much dignity as he could summon, dropping the vegetable as he did so, and looked around the stage for the girl. She was nowhere to be seen.

Then he looked out into the audience, and saw her, sitting demurely in the seat she had previously occupied, a faint smile on her lips, as she watched him slowly recover his composure.

Never, he told himself, had he been so humiliated, but he forced a smile and addressed the audience. "*Gnädige Herren, gnädige Damen,*" he began, and then stopped, unsure of what to say next. He decided to throw caution to the winds. "Today you have witnessed my assistant, Jane's, performance on the glass armonica, and I am sure you will agree with me that her playing puts my poor attempts to shame." There were murmurs, followed by a round of applause. "And furthermore, as you have seen, she is able to impart animal magnetism even to myself, to an almost incredible degree." Another round of applause, during which he and Jane locked their gaze on each other. She has the power to destroy me, he thought to himself, and instantly wondered from where that thought had come. He knew that he must be her ally, rather than her enemy. "Come here, Jane," he smiled at her. "Join me and take the applause that is your rightful due."

She rose, and with that faint, half-mocking smile on her face, once more mounted the platform, and faced the audience.

"We must talk, you and I, when all this is over," he hissed almost inaudibly to her as the audience clapped with occasional shouts of "*Brava!*" from some of the young blades.

"Very well," she answered him.

OTTO SAT FACING JANE, each occupying a hard-backed chair in the small room that led off the hall in which the lecture had been given. He still felt ill at ease, for reasons that remained unclear to him.

"Jane," he said. It was not quite a question. "You are not from these parts, I take it?"

"I am English," she answered.

Otto spoke in English. "Indeed? Would you prefer that we speak in your own language?"

She shrugged. "It is the same to me. I have lived here in Switzerland for nearly ten years now."

He changed back to German "How old are you?"

"Does that matter? Nineteen, if you must know."

"And you live here with your parents? The couple sitting in the seats next to you just now?"

She smiled. "They are perfect strangers to me. I never saw them before today. And no, I do not live with my parents.

I lodge with a family who are friends of friends of mine in England."

Otto raised his eyebrows. "You yourself come from a wealthy and well-connected family, I take it?"

This time the smile was accompanied by a laugh. "My dear Hermecritus, or whatever your true name may be, you could not be further from the truth," she answered in English. "It is true that one of my friends is indeed well-connected – indeed, his name is known throughout Europe, and I suppose by some he might be considered wealthy, but I can assure you that I myself spring from the humblest of beginnings." This was spoken with an air of self-assurance that belied her age.

"I was surprised by your skill with the armonica. Where did you learn to play?"

"I saw one only once before, when Mr Franklin brought his instrument to my friend's house. I was four years old at the time."

Despite himself, Otto was impressed by the way in which she casually referred to the inventor of the instrument that had played such a prominent role in his presentations. "But you played with such skill," he pointed out. "As if you had been playing all your life."

"I have been described as a musical genius," she stated simply. There was no hint of boasting or superiority in her tone, simply a statement of fact. "I play the forte-piano and the spinet in addition to the flute. I also compose music, as you heard just now. That was one of my pieces, composed on the spot, and heard for the first time by your audience."

Otto desperately wanted to know what had happened earlier with regard to the magnetism, but felt impelled to sidestep the question for the moment. "Why did you come here this afternoon?" was the question he ended up asking.

Again that faint half-mocking smile. "One hears such a

lot of nonsense," she used the German word *Quatsch* in the English sentence, "about the Rosicrucians. I was hoping to hear something new on the subject."

"And did you?"

She considered for a moment. "Not really. I thought that you placed too much emphasis on the influence of John Dee and Robert Fludd on *The Chymical Wedding*."

Otto laughed. "You are how old? Nineteen, I believe you said, and you dare to criticise one who has spent his life in the pursuit of wisdom?"

"Should we not term it as the pursuit of others' wealth? Or perhaps I am mistaken?" Once again she looked at him in the way that had so disconcerted him when she had been in the audience before the lecture had started.

"That, too," he grudgingly admitted. There was a silence of a few seconds as he considered how to proceed. The question had to be asked, and the words tumbled from his mouth in a rush. "How did you do it? Magnetise me, I mean?"

"I just made it happen. I wanted it to happen, and it did. I didn't like what you did to that old lady. It wasn't fair to have people laugh at her like that. The boy, that wasn't so bad, but you shouldn't make fun of people like her. You know who she is, don't you?"

He shook his head.

"She's a cousin of the Burgomaster. You may have made an enemy in this town. A rather powerful enemy. When word gets round…"

He swallowed, and his throat seemed to have gone dry. "Are you trying to get me to leave here? Are you threatening me in some way? Because if you are…"

"I, threaten you?" She smiled and shrugged. "How could a young girl like me threaten the great Hermecritus? I'm just saying what I think would be best for you. If you want my advice—"

"I'll listen, anyway. I don't promise I'll take your advice, though."

"—you should leave here immediately and cross into Bavaria." He nodded. "And you take me with you."

Otto sat up straight. "What?" he exploded. "Why on earth would I want to take you with me?" He paused. "And why on earth would you want to come with me?"

"I can play the armonica better than you can. And I'm not sure that I can't magnetise better than you can, but I'd let you do that anyway. I don't think people would like a girl doing it."

"Generous of you," he muttered sarcastically.

"And why do I want to go with you? Because you're not really a magnetist, I could tell. You're an alchemist, really, aren't you?"

He started. "Yes. What of it?"

"I need answers. Answers that alchemy might provide. And I think you're the person who can help provide those answers for me."

"What about your guardians?"

"They're not my guardians. They are only a family in whose house I am staying. I am free to come and go as I please. With whom I please."

He looked at her. He saw a slim figure, slightly taller than himself, with a face that, while not pretty in the usual sense of the word, still managed to attract and hold attention. Her hair, arranged in a rather simpler style than was the current fashion, was a deep lustrous black, which contrasted with her pale green eyes.

"It's a tough life," he said. "Do you think you can manage?"

"If not, then I'll leave you, won't I? Where are you staying?"

"The Black Boar, Seidengasse. Do you know it?"

"I'll find it. I'll be there at eight o'clock tomorrow morning. Be ready to set off for Bavaria with me then."

"Wait! What about money? Are you expecting me to pay for your coach and everything?"

"I'll pay my own way to start with. And then, you see, we'll start making enough money that neither of us will have to worry about these things." She rose. "Eight o'clock tomorrow. Be ready." He rose and moved towards the door to open it for her. "Don't bother," she told him, and walked out of the room, through the wall.

OTTO STOOD, STUPEFIED. He could hardly believe what he had just seen. A girl, to all intents without anything special about her, if a little more mature for her age than others he had encountered, had stood up, and with no obvious preparation simply walked through a solid wall as if it was the most natural thing in the world. It *was* solid, he told himself, after feeling around the place where she had vanished, searching for a secret spring or panel which might have opened and closed silently, giving him the impression that his visitor had actually walked through the wall.

But, as he had known all along, there was nothing there. Had he been magnetised or mesmerised into believing something that had never actually happened? That seemed unlikely, but it was preferable to believe that he had been mesmerised into believing the impossible than that he had witnessed something that was completely contrary to the laws of nature.

But were not the angels that John Dee had summoned able to pass through solid barriers? Was not the transmigration of matter one of those secrets known to the Masters of the Rosy

Cross? And were not the earth Elementals supposedly able to pass through solid barriers, according to the Rosicrucians?

Otto shivered. Either he was going mad, or he had agreed to ally himself to one of the greatest adepts of all time, greater than the Masters of the Invisible College, or he was dealing with something that had been to him so far only words in a book. Either way, the future promised to be a change from his past experience.

THE NEXT MORNING SAW OTTO, with all his belongings, including the glass armonica, neatly packed in bales, waiting outside the door of the Black Boar inn. After reflection, he believed what Jane had said to him that the Burgomaster would almost certainly seek some sort of revenge for what he had done to his cousin. The Swiss, he reflected bitterly, were somewhat lacking in the robust sense of humour of their German neighbours.

As the church clocks struck the hour, he saw a figure that could only be Jane at the end of the street.

"I am glad to see you ready," she said with a smile as she approached him.

He looked at the small travelling-bag in her hand. "Your luggage?" he asked.

"Yes. I will buy what I need when we arrive at our destination. For now, what I have with me will meet my requirements."

"And what will you use for money?"

"What we earn together. It may be that I have to use my savings at first."

"So you do have some money with you?"

"I do. And it is hidden in a place where I strongly advise

107

you not to go looking." She extended her arm, revealing the hilt of a dagger hidden under one sleeve. "It is small, but it is lethal. A scratch might kill you, if you are lucky." A sudden movement of her arms, and the dagger was in her left hand, the point directed towards him.

He laughed nervously. "If I am lucky, you say? What would bad luck be, if death is lucky?"

"The salve on the tip of this weapon has varying effects. For the lucky ones, as I say, death in a matter of a few minutes is the result. For those less fortunate, a future as an incurable drooling idiot is all that they can look forward to."

He felt a cold sweat breaking out on his brow. "Are you not afraid that you might yourself fall victim to this venom?"

She laughed. "I have a potion that negates the effects."

"Where do you learn such things?"

"That is something that I may tell you, in time. Come, let us make our way to the stage where we may take the coach out of Switzerland."

ALAS, THERE WAS NO COACH leaving that day, or indeed for the next three days.

"Then we will hire a carriage – or maybe a cart," she added, looking at Otto's impedimenta.

It was left to Otto to negotiate the deal. He had a sneaking suspicion that Jane was capable of driving a harder bargain than was he, but eventually he was able to settle a price with a farmer who lived some fifteen miles in the direction of Waldshut over the border, allowing them to ride in the cart which had brought turnips to Zürich the previous day.

He heaved his luggage into the cart with some difficulty, and made himself as comfortable as he could in a nest of possessions, envying Jane, who hopped lightly onto the front of the cart beside the driver, and immediately struck up a conversation with him.

As they slowly clopped their way down the street leading out of the city, Otto wondered whether he would be able to leave Switzerland safely. He had visions of the Zürich watch riding after him and haling him back to the city where… He preferred not to dwell on the subject.

The houses became fewer, and they were in the countryside. If it were not for the circumstances, he might almost find this ride in the cart a pleasant experience.

He called to Jane in English, "Won't your guardians be missing you? What did they say when you told them you were leaving them?"

"I told you, they're not my guardians. And I didn't bother speaking to them. I just left a note that I was leaving, but I wrote to them I was going to Basel. I am not bound to them, and they knew that I would leave some day."

"So I am in no danger of being accused of abducting you?"

She laughed. "I rather think that it is I who have abducted you, don't you? No, I see no danger on that front."

Well, that was one less thing to worry about, Otto told himself. He stretched out and tried, unsuccessfully, to ignore the potholes as the cart slowly bumped its way towards its destination.

VIII

The Performance

EVENTUALLY, THE JOLTING STOPPED, and the driver announced that they had arrived in Windisch.

"Can't take you any further," he told them. "There might be someone going up the river to Koblenz or even to Waldshut in Germany tomorrow. It would be more comfortable for you," he grinned to Otto, "than the road there. You think the road to here from Zürich is bad?" He laughed. "Go to the wharf over that way tonight, and find yourself a boat going downriver."

Otto removed his possessions from the cart and turned to Jane. "And now where?"

"I suggest that we find a place to stay the night before we find a boat. Preferably an inn where we can entertain the locals and make a little money for ourselves. Though," she added, looking round, "I wonder if there is anywhere here where they would let us do that."

"Entertainment?" he snorted. "Listen, my girl, I'm a serious student of the Art, and I would never lower myself to mere shows."

"It's lucky for us that I don't share your scruples, then, isn't it?" she said to him. "And also lucky that I have the talent to entertain the good people of this town. Look." She reached out and displayed her open palm, and then turned her hand over to show the back.

"So?"

"You are interested? You know how we refer to curious people in English. We say that they are nosy. They poke their long noses into things. I wonder what you have been poking your nose into?" Without warning, she grabbed his nose and twisted, then pulled her hand away, displaying a silver thaler in her hand. Otto rubbed his eyes, astounded.

"Pick it up. Feel it. Bite it, and then put it back in my hand," she ordered him.

He did so, and satisfied himself that it was a genuine coin, but whence it had come, he had no idea.

He dropped the coin into her palm, and she closed her hand, trapping the coin in her fist.

"Now tap three times on my hand with the little finger of your left hand," she commanded him.

Feeling more than a little foolish, he did so, and she opened her hand to reveal a soft white downy feather. The coin was nowhere to be seen.

"That is a truly remarkable piece of prestidigitation," he said. "I have never seen such." It should be noted that Otto was himself a conjurer of no mean ability, though it was not a skill that he advertised too widely, but even so, he had not the faintest idea of how the trick had been performed.

"It is not prestidigitation," she said, simply.

Otto remembered her seemingly walking through the wall of the Keller Institute in Zürich, and said no more. Did she possess the power to conjure silver (and possibly even gold) from the air – and then to return it to the air?

OTTO COLLECTED HIS BAGGAGE, paying a boy to carry the heavier pieces, and asked him for a recommendation of a place to spend the night. The boy's suggestion of the Three Pine Trees appeared promising enough when they reached it, and the innkeeper was happy to let them have a room.

"May I make a suggestion?" Jane asked him, smiling sweetly. "My colleague and I are entertainers. We can perform tricks that will delight your customers, and keep them in the taproom all night, buying your food and drink. My proposition is this – we will happily pay what you ask for the room – on the condition that your takings tonight do not exceed anything you have ever taken in one evening before. If they do come to be higher than your previous record, then we owe you nothing."

"Conjurers, eh? I've had them in here before and they couldn't draw flies."

"Maybe they were not as skilled as are we," Jane told him. "See." She plucked a large pewter tankard from behind the bar and placed it upside-down on the table. "Hermecritus here will now use his magical art and we will see what we will see."

Otto rose to the occasion. In a deep sonorous voice, he intoned a Latin formula, which had a duly impressive effect, and made mystic passes with his hands over the tankard without touching it.

"Let us see what he has wrought," said Jane. With a flourish she lifted the tankard to reveal a beautiful red rose in full bloom.

"Now how did you even find a rose like that at this time of year, let alone did it get under there? Again?"

Jane replaced the tankard over the rose, and Otto went through his magician's flourishes once more.

"And now," Jane said, lifting the tankard with a dramatic flourish to reveal a small ginger kitten curled up underneath it. The kitten mewed faintly and stretched its tiny paws toward them.

The innkeeper rubbed his eyes. "I have to admit that I have no idea how you did that. Where is the rose, and where did that kitten come from? Again."

Jane replaced the tankard over the kitten, and Otto intoned his mystic words once more while waving his hands over the tankard.

This time when Jane lifted the tankard, a fat toad sat in the place previously occupied by the kitten.

"Get rid of it at once! Foul thing!" exclaimed the innkeeper. "Toads have no place in my tavern."

"Certainly," she answered him, replacing the tankard over the offending amphibian and instantly lifting it again to reveal the surface of the table, with no sign of either toad, kitten or rose.

"I'm impressed," said the innkeeper. "Hans," he called to a young man who was standing by. "Get yourself into the town and spread the word that there's going to be something worth seeing here tonight." To Jane he said, "You've got yourself a deal, miss. Now let me show you and your father up to your room."

Despite himself, Otto grinned and winked at Jane as they followed the innkeeper up the stairs. To his surprise, she winked back.

The room was small, with room for one double bed and little else once Otto's belongings had been brought in.

"Just because we're sharing a room, doesn't mean…" Jane told Otto sternly.

"Of course not," Otto answered her indignantly. He was uncomfortably aware of the dagger that he had seen earlier. Not that he had much interest in that direction, to be honest. It wasn't that he found Jane to be especially unattractive – it was simply that he had left this sort of thing behind him some years ago.

"I'll take one of the quilts and sleep on the floor," he told her. "You have the bed."

"Thank you," she said, and smiled at him. "You're not as much of a rogue as you like to think you are, are you?"

There was no sensible answer that Otto could make to that, and he remained silent, unsure of whether or not he had been paid a compliment.

"We should go to the wharf and find a boat for tomorrow while there are still people around," Jane told him. "It will be getting dark soon."

As they made their way from the inn, Jane turned to Otto. "You did well with the Latin just now. It was inspired."

Otto smiled. "Thank you. And you did well with the kitten and rose and the toad. I confess that I have no idea how you did that. I have never seen conjuring like it."

"It's not a conjuring trick," she said simply, but again refused to explain any further. "And what was the Latin, anyway? I don't speak it like that, though I can read a little, and I seemed to recognise a few words."

He laughed. "It was a description of the symptoms of dropsy from an old book on medicine. Somehow it must have become lodged in my memory, and there it was, ready to recite."

Jane laughed with him. "It was certainly impressive."

They arrived at the wharf, and somewhat to their surprise, discovered a boat that would be setting off for Waldshut in the morning which was willing to take them for what seemed to be a very reasonable sum of money.

They arranged a time to meet the next morning, and started their return to the inn.

"Do you trust that boatman?" Jane asked Otto.

"Why? Don't you?"

"I have a bad feeling about him. There is nothing definite that I can say that makes me distrust him, but there is something about him that makes me uneasy."

"You're imagining things. You're tired and hungry and it's been a long day. Let's get back to the inn, get some food in our bellies, and things will seem better. And then we'll give the show of our lives. Glass armonica and all." He chuckled.

THE EVENING was a great success.

Jane and Otto worked together as if they had been doing it all their lives. Jane's performance on the glass armonica produced genuine tears of emotion from the listeners, who then roared with laughter as Otto mesmerised volunteers from the audience, and requested them to perform ridiculous tricks, most of a somewhat coarser nature in this rustic setting than the ones he had shown in Zürich. The man who was told that he had stepped in the leavings of a dog screwed up his face in disgust as he continued to scrape the imaginary offending mess from the soles of his shoes.

Then, in the same way they had demonstrated to the innkeeper, Jane and Otto produced fresh flowers from hats they had borrowed from members of the audience.

Otto performed an illusion which he described as "The Miser's Dream", where he appeared to pluck golden coins from the air, and dropped them one by one into an empty pewter tankard, where they made a satisfying clink as they fell. When the last coin had been snatched from the ear of a small child sitting in the front row, Otto asked the landlord to fill the tankard with beer, before handing it to one of the farmers who had been watching the performance open-mouthed with a look of the purest avarice on his face.

The poor man's surprise when he drained the beer and looked greedily into the depths of the tankard to discover nothing there was the cue for the whole company to laugh at him.

All the time, the audience was eating and drinking with gusto, with Otto and Jane exhorting them to enjoy themselves, and the innkeeper smiled at the small fortune he saw accumulating from that evening.

At length the evening came to an end. The final performance involved a large chest, borrowed from the inn, which was examined by three members of the audience who pronounced it sound and empty. These three then sat on the lid of the locked chest, with the keys held by one of their number, while Jane played the armonica and Otto uttered impressive-sounding sentences in his sonorous voice. At the end of his recitation, the three unlocked and opened the chest, to discover a live goat inside. Whence it had come, and how it had appeared within the chest was the subject of conversation in the town for long after Jane and Otto had departed.

At the end of the evening after the customers had departed, the landlord thanked Jane and Otto for their performances.

"When can you next visit?" he asked them, and appeared to be deeply disappointed when they informed him that they were leaving the next day, and had no definite plans to return.

"Your lodging, and anything you care to ask for tonight and tomorrow, is yours," he told them, setting a plate of veal stew before them. "Just ask if you need any more."

After their meal, Jane and Otto retired to their room.

"We make a good team," said Otto, smiling.

"I told you that we would," Jane answered him. "Now, I am tired and wish to sleep. Might I trouble you to turn away while I make myself ready?"

The delicate task of preparing herself for bed was soon over, and Otto in his turn made himself ready to sleep on the floor.

Both soon fell fast asleep, and the next sound that either heard was that of the cocks crowing in the yards outside the inn, and the sun shining through the windows.

They broke their fast on ale and bread, and made their way to the wharf, followed by the thanks of the landlord.

The boatman with whom they had arranged their travel the previous day was waiting for them, and helped Otto stow his baggage safely.

"Are you going to sit with him?" Otto asked Jane, "like you did on the cart coming here?"

"No," she smiled. "I think today is a day for talking, don't you?" So saying, she perched herself on a sack of vegetables beside Otto, and watched the boatman casting off from the quay as the boat started its journey downstream, a gentle breeze aiding it as the countryside glided by.

THE TWO TRAVELLERS SAT side by side in silence, enjoying the fresh breeze and the sunshine.

At length, Otto spoke. "Today is a day for talking, you said. But I know very little about you. I take it that you are from what might be termed a good family?"

"Not at all." Jane shook her head. "I come from the opposite – a very humble background. My mother died when I was very young, and my father worked in a manufactory. He found that he could not support me without my mother, and

I was placed in the care of a widow with two children. I have nothing to complain of with regard to her. She took care of me, and I dare say that she loved me as much as she loved her own children. I was happy there." She paused, sighed, and continued. "And, perhaps more important of all, she introduced me to the cleverest man I have ever known, and perhaps one of the cleverest of all time. His name is Doctor Erasmus Darwin."

"I have heard of him!" exclaimed Otto. "The poet?"

"Poetry is but just one facet of his talents," Jane told him. "He is a doctor, a scientist, an inventor. A truly remarkable man, but there are some things beyond even his understanding." She paused. "But Kate, the widow with whom I was placed, understood some of them and explained them to me."

"What sort of things?" asked Otto.

"This is not the time to tell of them," she said. "I will simply say that they were things that made it impossible for me to live with her any longer. In fact, she thought that it would be best if I left England."

"How old were you when this happened?"

"I was nine years old."

"And yet you say that she loved you? What sort of person sends a young girl into another country all alone? That does not sound like love to me."

"She did – does – love me. It was for my own safety that she sent me to Zürich."

Otto looked at her, but it was clear that she was not going to say more on the subject of why she had been sent away – at least at that time. "Why Zürich?" he asked.

"That was thanks to Erasmus Darwin, Uncle 'Rasmus we used to call him. He had a friend who is an artist who came from Zürich. His name is Henry Fuseli, and he creates paintings of subjects that many regard as being imaginary or fanciful."

Otto caught the note in her voice. "And you do not? Regard them as being imaginary?"

She shook her head. "I do not." And then, as if afraid of revealing too much, sat, gazing at the cows in the fields by the banks as the boat glided down the river.

Suddenly she spoke again. "Mr Fuseli has friends still in Zürich, and it was through him that I came to live there."

Otto was curious. "Were you not lonely? No friends, in a strange country?"

"Yes, I was lonely. The Müllers were a very kind family, though. Mr Fuseli knew that they could speak English and High German as well as the *Schwyzertüütsch* they speak in Zürich. So they could talk to me and I could make myself understood enough to tell them of my needs. Believe me, I lacked for nothing in the material line. I did not ask from where the money came to keep me there. Perhaps Uncle 'Rasmus. I felt it would be impolite to enquire too deeply." She sighed. "But the Müllers, kind as they may be, are an elderly childless couple, and their ideas of what a girl such as myself might enjoy were not always mine." She laughed. "I was thrown very much onto myself and the contents of Herr Müller's library, which contained many interesting books. Books on subjects in which I have a particular interest."

"I take it that is how you became familiar with *The Chymical Wedding*?" Otto asked.

"That and many more similar books," she confirmed. "Books in German and English, and of course Latin, all dealing with these subjects. And no," she held up a warning hand, "I have no intention at the moment of revealing to you the full nature of my interest in them. I will simply state that these books confirmed for me what I had been told by my English foster-mother, Kate Perkins, before I left England. Indeed, they used longer words and finer language to describe what I had been told by her, but the principles were the same."

Again she fell silent, as if deliberating within herself whether to reveal more. At length she spoke again. "But now you must return the favour. Tell me more about yourself, if you would."

Otto sighed. "Like you, I am a traveller far from his native land, which is the Basque country, lying between France and Spain, with its own tongue, near impenetrable to outsiders. I can teach you the rudiments of the language, if you like, and you can then write your secrets, secure in the knowledge that no one will be able to read them. Other than myself, of course." He smiled, displaying a set of decaying teeth. "However, my father, a glover, decided his trade would be better carried on in Paris, and the whole family moved there when I was just under five years old.

"My father wished me to continue in his trade, but as you can imagine, I could see little future for myself fitting five fingers into gloves. However, my own fingers proved cunning enough for me to learn a few tricks." Here, Otto reached into his purse and proceeded to demonstrate the appearance and disappearance of a coin. Jane shook her head and smiled deprecatingly. "Yes, trivial, I know, but this passed as true magic to the companions of my youth. And then I heard of Franz Mesmer, who by all accounts was working something that seemed closer to true magic than anything I had ever heard of.

"I apprenticed myself to him, but in such a way that he could not suspect that I was attempting to learn from him. No, no, I simply helped prepare the stage for his magnetic salons. But I watched and I learned, and what I discovered was that there was no magic, but a simple trick of the mind, by which the mesmerist persuades the mesmerised to do something that perhaps they secretly wish. Maybe they do not absolutely wish it, but in any event, I have discovered that it is impossible to make someone do an action that they absolutely do not wish to do. Even the old crone who danced in Zürich – maybe she felt ridiculous afterwards, but there was a look of enjoyment on her face while she danced."

"And the young man with the potato in Zürich and the man with the dog dirt on his shoes last night?"

"Did you not see afterwards when they returned to their friends? Both of them were the hero of the hour. Neither young man would have had to pay for any food or drink for the rest of the evening, if I know that sort. But…" He paused, and seemed about to stroke his beard, then remembered that he was no longer wearing one, and dropped his hand abruptly. "I have no wish, even in the deepest corners of my mind, to act like a monkey and eat raw turnip. And yet…"

Jane said nothing, but simply smiled faintly.

Otto realised that he was not going to obtain much more information on the subject, and continued. "And through what I learned from Mesmer, though he had no knowledge that he was my professor in the subject, I was enabled to earn a living. An honest living?" He shrugged as he answered his own question. "Maybe it is not entirely honest, but I flatter myself that I do more good than harm. People walk out of my séances feeling better than when they walk in. I have cured the lame – or rather, with my assistance, they have cured themselves."

"You sound like Doctor Erasmus Darwin," Jane told him. "He too is a great believer in the sufferer's powers to end his own suffering."

"But," Otto held up a dirty finger in warning, "what I wish for myself are the true secrets, the true magic. So I have delved into the secrets of the alchemists, into the mysteries that have entranced great minds for centuries. I am convinced that the truth lies somewhere there." He looked at Jane. "And it appears that you have a path to that truth."

THERE WAS A PERIOD OF SILENCE following this remark, which lasted for some thirty minutes, during which the boat continued to drift downstream.

Otto closed his eyes, and dozed in the sunshine, but was awakened by a tug at his sleeve.

"Wake up," Jane whispered to him. "Look."

Otto noticed that the boat was making its way from the centre of the stream to a part of the riverbank which appeared to be uninhabited. Not only was that stretch of the bank devoid of people, but there were no houses or other obvious signs of human habitation to be seen.

The boatman was watching his passengers with what appeared to be a predatory gleam in his eye. Otto became uncomfortably aware of the long knife (or was it a dagger?) that hung from the boatman's belt.

"Ah, you're awake, then? That's good to see," the boatman remarked.

"Does it matter to you or the boat whether I'm awake or asleep?" Otto replied.

"Oh, it doesn't matter one bit to the boat. But it matters to me." The bow of the boat gently bumped against the shore of the river, and the boatman deftly tied a rope around the overhanging branch of a tree growing on the bank.

"Why have you stopped the boat?" asked Otto.

"Well, you see, it's like this," answered the other, seating himself on one of the thwarts of the boat, and almost absent-mindedly withdrawing his dagger from its sheath, and starting to clean his nails with the point. "I happened to hear what went on at the Three Pines last night. Seems like you two are pretty good at what you do. My mate Fritz, though, he was a bit put out by what you did to him. You gave him a pot full of beer and gold coins and when he'd drunk the beer, there was no gold coins left. And that really made old Fritzy mad, it did. So he came to me early like, before you two come along, and he asked me to put things right for him."

"How do you mean?" Jane asked.

"I'd have thought it was pretty simple. You make some more gold coins for me, and some for Fritz, let's say fifty each, but this time they don't just disappear."

"And if we don't?" Otto asked.

"Well, it's a nice quiet bit of water, this. Not many folks come this way. Mind you, it's a tricky stretch. Lot of people fall in and drown around this way. Be a shame if two more were to join the rest, wouldn't it? Of course, I'd be very sorry to lose my important passengers, but then I'd have all their belongings as a sort of compensation, wouldn't I? They're probably worth a bit."

Otto held up his hands. "Let me explain. We're not magicians. We're *prestidigitateurs*, using the skill of our hands to create illusions."

"So you're not real magicians?"

"No," said Otto, but Jane simultaneously chimed in with an emphatic "Yes".

The boatman looked from one to the other. "One of you isn't telling the truth. Well, I was told by my dear mother, God rest her soul, never to doubt a lady's word. So, my dear, will you make some gold coins for me and Fritz?"

"Yes," Jane answered him. Otto looked at her. She seemed calm and composed enough. Of course, she had that nasty little dagger to take care of any opposition. And she somehow seemed able to perform impossible feats.

"And do you swear that once you've made them they won't just vanish?"

"Yes."

"Go on, then. I want to hear you say it."

"I swear by all that I hold precious and sacred that I will produce one hundred golden coins for the use of our friend here and his friend Fritz and that furthermore these coins will not vanish."

"Excellent. Will you use this to hold them?" He held out a leather bag.

"That will do excellently. Please give it to me."

Otto watched as Jane performed a version of The Miser's Dream, plucking coins from mid-air, and dropping them with a satisfying chink into the bag. He grudgingly admitted that she was performing it with a much better skill and grace than he had ever achieved.

"Ninety-eight... ninety-nine... one hundred," counted the boatman. Jane handed the bag to him, and he plunged his hand into the bag and brought out a shining gold piece. "They're there, right enough." He bit into one. "Seems good to me. And you give me your word that they're not going to vanish?"

"I give you my word on that," Jane said.

"Then let's be off, shall we? I hope you don't mind if I leave you a little outside Waldshut. You see, I don't want you to go around telling people about what's just happened. I'd like to be a little way away from here if you're going to do something like that."

"Now why would you ever think we'd do that?" Jane asked him, smiling sweetly.

"Just this funny old mind of mine," he said, casting off, and poling the boat into the current once more.

True to his word, he brought the boat to shore a little way outside Waldshut.

"He even helped you unload your belongings," Jane said to Otto.

"And he didn't take anything that wasn't his," Otto replied. "Mind you, why would he with a hundred gold coins in that bag of his?"

Jane started to laugh.

"What's so funny? You promised him that they wouldn't disappear. So he has a hundred gold coins. Where they came from, I really have no idea. You know something, though? I wager that his friend Fritz won't see any of them."

"You're almost certainly right," Jane said. She was still laughing.

"How do you know?"

"Because I only promised that the coins wouldn't vanish, right?"

"Yes."

"I never promised that they wouldn't turn into something else, did I?"

Light dawned. "Oh, like what?"

"Venomous spiders and scorpions. When he next puts his hand in the bag, he'll feel more than the prickings of conscience."

"Oh, that's clever, that is. And then the spiders and what-not will run away, nowhere to be found, and he'll be found dead with his hand in a bag – his bag – nothing to link him and us together, except whatever Fritz might have to say."

"If there really is a friend called Fritz who wants his gold pieces. And if there is a Fritz, is he really going to say that he asked to have us killed for a few pieces of fairy gold?"

"Fairy gold? Is that what it is?"

"It's as good a name for it as any."

IX

The Castle

WALDSHUT TURNED OUT to be somewhat smaller than they had expected, and it turned out to be in Further Austria, under the control of Vienna.

"Let's go on to the next town where they have a German Landgrave in charge," Otto told Jane. "I'm not that keen on the Austrians."

"Or they on you?" suggested Jane, not without a hint of malice.

"That, too," Otto agreed, but there was a smile on his face as he said it.

Tiengen turned out to be close enough for them to walk, though by the time they reached the town's only inn, Otto was beginning to feel the strain from his luggage, even though they had paid a boy to carry some of the heavier boxes, and Jane had taken some of his other bags and carried them for him.

The inn had two rooms available, and they had no need to

share, a fact for which Otto was thankful. He was becoming increasingly wary of Jane, and had little doubt in his mind that she was capable of destroying him utterly if she chose to do so.

"What are we going to do here?" she asked him as they sat down to their evening meal.

"We must go to the castle. I will present myself as Philomentor."

"Who?"

"It was the name I had before Hermecritus. It will, perhaps, be a little more familiar to them than Hermecritus. And any misunderstandings associated with my previous name that might possibly have reached these can easily be explained away here, a safe distance from Geneva."

"And what will Philomentor offer the prince or duke or whoever it might be who lives in the castle?"

"Gold."

Jane laughed. "You can make gold from lead?"

"I can persuade the Landgrave that I can do so."

"And will you require my assistance?"

"I have seen your fairy gold, have I not? I have no wish for that to turn into scorpions and spiders."

"It will not do that unless I make it so."

"But will it remain as gold, even if you do not make it vanish or transmute into something else?"

"No. It will either vanish or change to something with no value – dead leaves or petals of a flower, for example – at the break of the next day." She shrugged. "I do not know why this is, but it is so. Believe me, I have attempted to change this state of affairs often enough, but without success. But the gold that you will produce for this Landgrave?"

"It will be real enough, believe me. And it will survive a sunrise. But it will not be of a sufficient quantity to prove useful, other than to inspire the confidence that more will be forthcoming from the same source."

"And what do you hope to gain from this?"

"A roof over my head. A table against which I can tuck my belly three times a day. And time and quiet to study."

"You are serious? About the study?"

"More than ever, since I met you. You have shown me things that I did not dare to believe before now. They appeared too fantastical. But I know what I have seen with my own eyes. Now I want to understand more."

"Why, you are a natural philosopher at heart."

"Rather, I am an unnatural philosopher. I study those things which are beyond the sky."

Jane started. "What did you just say?"

"I study those things that are beyond the sky."

"You mean on the other side of the sky?"

"If you want to put it that way, yes. Why? Do you know what is there?"

Jane shook her head. "I cannot tell you, as I do not know. I simply fear."

THE NEXT DAY saw Otto and Jane make their way to the castle, where Otto introduced himself, and presented Jane as his niece.

They were shown into a chamber, somewhat sparsely furnished, and told to wait for a chamberlain.

After about thirty minutes, the court official entered.

"So you are Philomentor?" he asked Otto.

"That is my name," said Otto.

"Lately of Geneva?"

"That is so."

"And why, may I ask, have you left there to come here? This is, after all, a rather smaller town than Geneva." He smiled.

"But I believe that the Landgrave has an interest in matters which are, shall we say, not for the common man. I do not know whether Your Excellency has ever had the misfortune to visit Geneva."

A smile. "Alas, no."

"There is no regret necessary. You have missed little. The people of Geneva are without imagination, without the ability to be inspired with a sense of wonder. Now here, I believe things are somewhat different."

"If you are referring to the Landgrave's interest in alchemy…"

"I am indeed. I myself possess some little skill in the art, and I would be happy to present His Highness with the last of my Philosopher's Stone." He withdrew from an inner pocket a small leathern pouch. "No, sir, I beg you, do not laugh. After many years, I was able to produce a small quantity of the Stone, following the most exacting procedures as laid down in various texts, however, none of which had the procedure correctly described. It was left to me to extract from Albertus Magnus, from Robert Fludd, from Elias Ashmole, and from Paracelsus himself, among others, those aspects of the procedure which were true, and to combine them into a method which resulted in my possession of a small quantity of the Stone."

"And what is this Stone supposed to do?"

"Why, it will transmute base metals into gold, as I will show His Highness, should he desire the proof of my words."

"And if you are successful in this transmutation, what would you then expect from His Highness?"

"A place where I may create more of the Stone, though I should warn you that it is a lengthy process requiring many months of intensive work. Also lodgings for my niece and myself, and a small sum of money on which we may live. Our needs are simple. A small sum would be sufficient. And," as he held up a finger, "I would be indebted if I were able to make use of the library of His Highness from time to time. Naturally, should I discover anything which I consider would be of interest to His Highness, he will be the first to be informed of my discovery."

"I will put the matter to His Highness and bring you word within the hour. Wait here."

He left, and Jane turned to Otto. "And what happens when you cannot make the gold?"

"The gold will be made, never fear. I may not have your gifts, but believe me, I have a few little talents of my own which have helped me to survive for the past twenty years or more."

"And what am I supposed to be doing while you peddle your nonsense here?"

"Did you not hear? I am giving you the chance to explore one of the finest libraries in Europe on subjects where those such as you and I have an interest. What languages have you besides German and English?"

"Some Latin. Tolerable French."

"No Italian? Spanish? Greek? Arabic? Hebrew?"

"No."

"No matter. There will be enough here to entertain and inform you. I am very hopeful that I have set my demands low enough that after my demonstration, we will be made welcome here for as long as it takes me to produce the Stone."

"And when you cannot produce it?"

Otto winked. "The production of the Philosopher's Stone is a lengthy and tedious process. Furthermore, it is very complicated and one small mistake can mean that the whole business must start again from the beginning."

"I see."

They sat in silence for a while until the chamberlain re-entered.

"His Highness will see you both now."

They were ushered into a room furnished as a study. The Landgrave, an elderly man, bald-headed with a fringe of white hair, and wearing spectacles, was seated at a table, peering at a book. A stack of leather-bound volumes, apparently of great age, stood on the table beside him. He removed his spectacles and peered short-sightedly at Otto. He appeared not to have noticed Jane.

"Franz here tells me that you have some of the Philosopher's Stone. Is that true?" he asked, with no preliminaries.

"It is true, Your Highness. I must warn you that it is only a small amount."

"Not worth my while to have you killed for?" The Landgrave chuckled unpleasantly. "Very wise of you. Pardon my humour. Some find it amusing. Others, not so much. Franz here," gesturing towards the flunky, "is one of those others."

"Highness," Franz protested.

"But you have some of the Stone, and you are willing to make a demonstration?"

"I am, Your Highness."

"And if the demonstration should fail, or you are found to have used sleight of hand or trickery to achieve a result, you are aware of the consequences?"

"No, Your Highness."

"You will be broken on the wheel in the town square. It is, as a man of your education is aware, a slow and painful death. I have had too many fraudulent tricksters posing as alchemists attempting to buy my favour with promises of gold.

However, I am not a cruel man at heart, so I have given you fair warning of what will happen to you should you fail or attempt to deceive me. I now ask you again if you are prepared to make the demonstration, before and during which there will be strict controls applied to guard against trickery. If you now change your mind and tell me that you do not wish to make the demonstration, then you will be free to leave. There will be no punishment, and naturally no reward, other than the satisfaction of being an honest man. So, are you prepared to make the demonstration?"

Otto's voice was steady. "I am."

"When? What will you need?"

"A half pound of saltpetre. Two quarts of human urine passed by young females – they need not be virgins, but they must be under thirty years of age. A half-pint of *aqua fortis*. The tail of a young male lamb without blemish. Two ounces of sulphur. An ounce of quicksilver. And an ounce of lead which will be transmuted to gold."

"That seems to be remarkably simple compared to what these," he gestured towards the books on shelves around the room, "seem to prescribe."

"Highness, the complexity of the operation lies in the preparation of the Stone, not the transmutation of the lead to gold. However, I will also require a small cauldron and a furnace, as well as a crucible."

"Franz, you will record all these needs. And how long will all this take?"

"Highness, the best part of a day as I reduce the liquids and combine them with the saltpetre. Then a few hours with the crucible. It should all be completed within the space of one day and one night."

"I will have these prepared for you in due course. You are staying at the inn? I will send word for you when these are ready in a few days. You are dismissed." Reseating his spectacles on his nose, he returned to his book.

The chamberlain, Franz, ushered Otto and Jane out of the room.

"You are sure you wish to continue?" he asked Otto. "It is not too late for you to change your mind."

"I am sure," said Otto.

"In that case, tell me again what you will require, and I will arrange for it to be brought here."

As they walked down the stone passage, Otto repeated his list of ingredients, adding at the end, "If possible, I would like to see the laboratory where His Highness would have me perform this feat."

"Certainly," Franz answered, and led the way to a small chamber in the corner of the building.

"Excellent," said Otto, surveying the furnace and the alchemical apparatus neatly stored in the corner. He bent to examine the furnace and the stack of fuel beside it. "You use charcoal?"

"I believe that is what most have used in the past. Unless you have any other requirements?"

"No, no, charcoal is the best and this certainly seems to be of the highest quality. It gives the most constant heat, and burns well. Have there been many others trying to make gold for His Highness?"

"In the past ten years, there have been four others."

"And…?"

For answer, Franz drew the edge of his hand across his throat.

"I see," said Otto.

"One seemed sincere, but failed to produce his gold. The other three attempted to use simple trickery to achieve their ends, but were easily detected. However, I ensured that they were strangled before the torture of the wheel. It is not right to make a man suffer so."

"Amen to that," Otto agreed.

As THEY WALKED OUT of the castle down towards the inn, Jane turned to Otto.

"Can you do it?"

"What?"

"Produce the gold."

"Of course. There is going to be no problem."

"No problem, you say? Well, it's your body on the wheel, not mine."

"If they execute me they'll probably burn you, too."

"Why would they do that?"

"Because you're a witch helping me with the aid of the Devil."

She shrank back away from him. "Do you mean that?"

He laughed. "Of course not. But how do you prove you're not? If they say you're a witch, you're a witch, and they burn witches in these parts. So you'd better trust that I can do what I say I can do."

"Are you sure you don't need my help?"

He laughed. "Your fairy gold? As soon as they saw a pile of dead leaves the next morning, that would be the end of both of us. Leave it to me."

"You've done this before?" she asked curiously.

"Enough times that I'm confident."

"Are you going to use magnetism to make them believe that they will see gold?"

"I am not."

135

"Then what are you going to do? I really don't believe that it is possible to turn lead into gold."

"Maybe it's not. Maybe you're right. But believe me, they will have gold, and none of your fairy gold, either. Now stop talking about it, or you'll make me nervous."

IT WAS THE AFTERNOON OF THE NEXT DAY when a messenger came from the castle to the inn, to inform Otto that his presence, and that of his niece, were required by His Highness the Landgrave on the following morning.

"Me, too?" asked Jane.

"Who knows why? Maybe they intend you as a hostage for my good behaviour." He shrugged. "Who can tell with the people living in these parts? Neither Swiss nor German nor Austrian. They are a race unto themselves, and they have their own ways of doing things."

"What should I wear?"

Otto laughed. "I have hardly seen you carrying chests of garments with you. Do you even possess any clothes other than the ones you stand up in?"

"No, but…" Her voice tailed off.

"I suppose you can produce a new outfit of clothes as easily as you produce gold coins and scorpions?" She nodded in reply. "I can tell you now, that would be the worst possible thing you could do. Were you to turn up in new clothes, and should anything go wrong with the transmutation – which I can assure you it will not – but if it should, then they will search your effects here at the inn. Indeed, I expect them to do just that while we are in the castle. And if they find no trace of any other new clothes, then you are for the stake."

"What do you want me to do?"

"We will take the armonica with us to the castle, and you may play it when I direct you to do so."

"The music will help to produce sympathetic vibrations to assist the transmutation?" Her tone was mocking

"It might just do that. It will certainly distract the attention of those attending, and help to soothe their suspicions."

THE NEXT MORNING, they set off for the castle. Otto was carrying, though not wearing, the robes that he wore when securing or giving his magnetic demonstrations. Jane, naturally, was wearing her everyday clothes.

One of the men from the inn followed them, wheeling a small handcart on which was perched the glass armonica.

Franz, the chamberlain, met them at the gate. "You are sure that you wish to continue?" he asked anxiously. "Believe me, I hate to see anyone suffer unnecessarily under the weight of their pride."

"And for my part, I hate to see anyone suffer unnecessarily under the weight of their kind-heartedness. Cheer up, man, it will never happen." He clapped Franz on the shoulder as they made their way to the laboratory where the transmutation was to take place.

Once they had entered, Jane instantly became aware of the two guards on either side of the Landgrave, who was seated on a carved wooden chair.

"Good day to you, Philomentor. I trust you will not mind if we take a few precautions."

"By no means."

"Very well, then." He turned to the guards. "Search everything that he and the girl have brought with them, and when you have done that, strip and search him. You know what sort of things you should be looking for – you have seen them often enough over the years. And as for you, my dear," looking at Jane, "I am sure you will not object of two of my ladies take you into the next room and examine your person."

"I was not expecting this, Your Highness," Jane told him. "But yes, I am ready."

"Excellent. Martha! Elizabeth!" he called, and two middle-aged matrons entered. "Take her," he ordered, nodding towards Jane. "And be gentle. There is no need for roughness in her case."

The two led Jane to another room, where she was stripped naked and examined by one of the searchers for anything that might have been secreted about her person, while the other meticulously examined her clothes. Though she shrank from the touch of the other's hands on her naked flesh, the search, as had been ordered by the Landgrave, was as gentle as such an operation ever can be.

At what seemed like the end of an eternity, she was ordered to dress herself again, and to go into the next room.

To her relief, Otto was there, dressed and smiling.

"Excellent, my dear niece," said Otto. "I do wish His Highness was a little more trusting, though." He smiled at the Landgrave, who did not return the expression. "Shall we set up the armonica together?"

"I am puzzled," said the Landgrave. "Are we to have music while the transmutation is proceeding?"

"I have found, Your Highness," Otto said, "that the celestial vibrations produced by the armonica during the distillation of the elixir in which the transmutation takes place impart a smoothness and a subtlety to the final liquid which greatly enhances the process of transmutation. Your Highness is surely aware of the thoughts of Pythagoras on this and related matters."

"Oh, quite so, quite so. Even so, this is a novelty to me, I admit. Are you the first to have employed this technique?"

Otto bowed slightly. "I believe I may claim that honour."

"Very well. Proceed."

The armonica was duly set up, and Otto donned his robe.

"Is this, too, part of the procedure?" asked the Landgrave, clearly amused.

"It is for my own satisfaction, I admit. Clothes maketh the man, as you are aware, Your Highness, and by presenting myself to the Universal Spirit in this garb, I feel myself to be on a higher plane, and more able to perform this delicate operation."

Otto busied himself with scrupulously weighing and measuring the various substances which had been provided, and placing them in a brass beaker which he had previously wiped clean. He picked up a small red silk bag from the table where it had been left following the searching of his possessions.

"And that is?" asked the Landgrave as Otto threw two pinches of a white powder from the bag into the beaker.

"Unicorn horn from Africa, many leagues to the south of the Pyramids, as I earlier explained to these gentlemen here," replied Otto, indicating the guards. "I was unsure of whether Your Highness would have any such readily available, and so I took the liberty of bringing my own."

"And this?" as Otto added a small amount of a brown powder from a yellow bag.

"The powdered bark of the sacred holy thorn of Glastonbury in England. I was privileged to visit there some years ago, and was graciously allowed to take a small amount of this most potent vegetable for my own use. I have discovered that the addition of even a few grains has a beneficial effect on any alchemical operation. And now, my dear niece," as he placed the beaker above the fire, "if you will play for us."

Jane played, and the sounds of the armonica soon cast their spell over the assembled company, including the two serving women, who had been watching with interest.

"Sweet music," the Landgrave proclaimed.

"Thank you, Your Highness," Jane answered him, managing to bob a curtsey while continuing to play.

The liquid boiled as Otto diligently stirred, and a foul smell began to make its presence felt.

"This is to be expected?" asked the Landgrave, coughing.

"Unfortunately so, Your Highness. If the window may be opened, the stench will be dispersed, and in a few minutes, the elixir will cease to produce the smell."

"By all means, let us have the windows open," exclaimed the Landgrave.

Soon the air was clear, and Otto announced that the windows might be closed once more.

"Your Highness, could I make a request for some beer?"

"Is this part of the transmutation elixir?" laughed the Landgrave.

"No, but it is thirsty work sitting over this furnace. And something for my niece, if possible. You may stop playing for now," he told Jane. "The vibrations have killed off the noxious fumes."

Beer was ordered for all and brought, and Otto drained his tankard at one draught. "I congratulate Your Highness on the quality of your beer," he told the Landgrave, who acknowledged the compliment with a nod.

A few hours passed, during which the Landgrave left the room, and the guards changed. Despite the chimney, the heat of the furnace and the fumes made Jane feel drowsy.

She seemed to be on the point of dropping off to sleep when the Landgrave re-entered, presumably having eaten his meal, and all except Otto, who was busy stirring the elixir, rose.

"Sit, sit," commanded the Landgrave. He was clearly in a good mood. "How have matters progressed, Sir Alchemist?"

"Very well, Your Highness. A matter of less than an hour should see the elixir ready to be used in the transmutation."

The room's occupants settled themselves, and silence reigned. At length, Otto used a pair of tongs and removed the beaker from the heat of the furnace. He placed the beaker carefully to one side, and then carefully fed sticks of charcoal from the pile beside him into the furnace.

"I am making the fire hotter for the final transmutation," he announced. "Niece, you may start playing once more."

The flames grew, and the charcoal became a bright glowing orange as the fire was expertly built up, Otto feeding it stick by stick.

Jane, her eyes fixed on the furnace as she played the armonica, gave a sudden cry, stopped playing in mid-note and pointed at the mouth of the furnace. "Look!"

Obediently, all followed her pointing finger.

"What is it?" asked one of the guards, clearly thunderstruck. "It looks like a small snake or lizard, dancing in the flames. How can it be?"

"But it has a human face. It is what the adepts term a Salamander," said the Landgrave in an awestruck voice. "A fire Elemental. I have never seen one before. I have read of them, but I confess that I have not truly believed in their existence until now. My congratulations, Sir Alchemist, if this is your doing."

Otto sketched a slight bow, and continued his preparations, seemingly unimpressed by the appearance of the Salamander. He took a crucible, and brought it to the Landgrave.

"Your Highness, I wish you to drop this leaden pellet that you have provided into the crucible. This is what will become gold." Obediently, still entranced by the sight of the

Salamander, which continued to dance in the flames, the Landgrave did so.

Otto returned to the furnace, poured a quantity of elixir into the crucible, and with great ceremony, opened a small wooden box that had been taken from him and was now standing on the table with the other powders and items. He added the contents – a black powder, and stirred the contents.

"The Stone?" enquired the Landgrave. There was no mockery in his voice.

"Indeed so, Your Highness." Otto placed a lid on the crucible and set it on the fire. "The quality of your charcoal is excellent, and I do not expect we will have to wait long."

"How will we know?"

"You must trust me when I tell you that this is something I will know in my innermost being, Your Highness. Maybe the Universal Spirit will tell me, or maybe she," pointing at the Salamander will give me a sign."

All fell silent and observed the creature writhing and dancing in the flames. As the guard had said, it appeared to be lizard-like, but from what could be observed of its head, it had a human face, female, and of an almost unearthly beauty. Its eyes were of the deepest black, and a forked tongue seemed to slide between its bloodless lips from time to time. The Landgrave was clearly entranced and kept his eyes fixed on it.

Suddenly the silence was broken by a loud popping sound, a flash of light from the furnace, and sparks and live coals leaping onto the floor. The guards rushed to extinguish these last before the wooden floor caught fire.

"The Salamander has gone!" exclaimed the Landgrave. "Is that your sign, Sir Alchemist?"

"Aye, that it is," said Otto. He removed the crucible from the heat. "May I request Your Highness to join me here?"

"With pleasure," said the old man, rising.

"As you can see, Your Highness, the elixir has calcified," Otto pointed to the contents of the crucible, from which he had removed the lid. "I shall now remove it."

An amorphous blackened lump tumbled from the crucible onto a metal plate that Otto had placed on a stool beside the furnace.

"And now, if Your Highness would be good enough to smite this calcification so that it shatters…" Otto suggested, offering a metal rod to the Landgrave, who accepted it, and brought it down smartly on the black mass.

The lump dissolved into powder, and in the middle of the heap was a golden mass of approximately the size and shape of the lead that had previously been placed in the crucible. The Landgrave reached out his hand to touch it.

"Your Highness, it will still be hot," Otto warned him. "Use these tongs, and place it in this water to cool it."

The Landgrave did so, and after about a minute retrieved the gold.

"Spirits of nitre," he commanded. Otto located the bottle on the well-stocked shelves of alchemical materials and carefully poured a little into a glass beaker.

The Landgrave dropped the golden sample into the acid, and watched carefully. The lump of gold, for so it was, having passed the acid test, remained unchanged.

The Landgrave turned to Otto, and embraced him. "Sir Alchemist, even if the transmutation had failed, I would have spared your life, in gratitude for allowing me to see the Salamander. But as it is, you have indeed produced gold from lead. All that you have asked for and more shall be yours. This laboratory shall be yours in which to labour, and anything you require in the production of the stone – whether it be from

India, Cathay, Zipangu, or the Americas – you merely have to ask me, and it shall be yours."

JANE AND OTTO SAT in the chamber that had been allotted to them, following the Landgrave's enthusiastic acceptance of the gold that had so miraculously appeared in the crucible.

For the first time since they had entered the castle, they were alone. Otto had just opened the door of the chamber, and left it ajar, ensuring that no one could overhear their conversation without being detected.

"How did you do it?" he asked Jane.

"I think I should be the one asking that question," she answered him. "And what exactly do you mean by 'it'?"

"Why, the Salamander, of course. Like the Landgrave, I have read of these things, but I never fully believed in them. I assume that it was you who summoned it."

"Not deliberately, I assure you. I was playing the armonica and gazing at the fire. I had no intention of summoning the thing."

"Have you ever seen one before?"

"Never. I was as astonished as the Landgrave. How were you able to regard it so calmly?"

"Practice, my dear, practice. In my life, many unexpected things have happened to me, and I have found out that the best thing to do is invariably to make an accident look deliberate. And as you can see, the Landgrave fully accepted that it was my art that had summoned it. What did you make of it, by the way?"

"I do not think it wished us any harm," Jane said. "Nor, I think, was it there to assist us. It was simply present, for its own reasons, we must assume, which are unknown to us. But there are Those who dwell beyond the sky, as you say, or on the other side of the sky as my English friends would say, who are not well-disposed towards humanity."

"That does not accord with many of the writings. The Elementals are to be sought out and given all due respect."

"With all due respect to the gentlemen who wrote these books, I doubt if they ever had contact with any of these beings. They were simply repeating legends and stories that had been passed down through the ages. In the city in England where I come from, they are to be feared and flattered so that they do not cause harm." She paused for a moment and sipped at her wine. "My turn. How did that gold get into the crucible?"

"I carried it in the pocket of my breeches," he explained, smiling.

"But... but..."

"I was stripped, and my garments were examined, as was my body? Yes."

"And they failed to find it. How did they miss it?"

"They did not miss it. Because it was not there." By now, Otto's smile had changed to a broad grin.

"Oh, you are infuriating. You carried it in, and yet it was not there. And yet it was there, clearly. I do not believe all that hocus-pocus about virgins' urine."

"They did not have to be virgins," he corrected her.

"Does it matter? They might have been ninety-year-old great-grandmothers for all the difference it would make. Admit it, all that business with the elixir and the unicorn's horn and the Glastonbury thorn bark was nonsense, wasn't it?"

"Yes. Nonsense. Come on, you're an intelligent person. Think."

"We were stopped and searched, and our persons and garments and possessions were searched most thoroughly. At least, mine were. I do not believe that the search conducted on you was any less thorough. There is no time at which you could have brought that gold into that room without anyone being aware of it."

"Wrong. Think." He sat back, goblet in hand, watching her.

Obediently, she cast her mind back to the events of the day, and of all that had occurred since they had arrived in Tiengen. A slow smile spread over her face. "You crafty devil," she said.

"Go on."

"The day when we came here first and talked to the Landgrave…"

"Yes…"

"After we had talked, you asked to see the laboratory." She closed her eyes. "I see it now. You examined the furnace and the charcoal, and slipped the gold from your pocket among the sticks of charcoal. Then after the Landgrave dropped the lead into the crucible, you used your skill in sleight of hand to remove it, and replace it with the gold as you put it over the fire." She stopped and looked at Otto, who was still grinning. "Am I right?"

"Bravo, my dear, you are completely correct."

"But if I can guess it, surely the Landgrave can also work this out?"

"I doubt it. The most effective blinkers to blind a man to the truth are those made of gold." He took a pull at the goblet of wine that stood before him. "Even if he ever suspects the truth, your miracle of the Salamander, even if it was unintentional, will convince him that what he saw was genuine." He rubbed his hands together. "And what we have before us now, Jane, is a veritable feast of learning spread out for us. The library here is famous, going back for several generations.

Much to learn for both of us. Perhaps we may discover what you truly are." The grin returned to his face.

Medicine has a fortune of us. Philosophers may di.. over whi.. out move. The gun and us. To the race

The Salamander

ABOUT NINE MONTHS after Otto had "produced" gold for the Landgrave, he and Jane were still living in Tiengen. To all eyes, Otto appeared to be diligently attempting to re-create the Philosopher's Stone, but at each attempt, the process of which might occupy many weeks, there appeared to be some fault in the apparatus, in the ingredients used, or even in Otto's own implementation of the method that he claimed had originally produced the Stone that he had used to produce the gold.

Even so, the Landgrave, even if he might have been inwardly impatient, was tolerant of the repeated failures. The memory of the Salamander was very much with him, and he often found himself drawn to the laboratory where Otto was working, and engaged him in conversations on esoteric matters.

For her part, Jane was bored. She had attempted to discover more about Them by reading some of the books in the

Landgrave's library, but she found most of the books, as she had said once to Otto, to be either commonplace, stating obvious truths, or to be works of the author's invention, with what might seemed to be imaginings with no basis in reality. It was a rather depressing exercise. As Otto had warned her, some of the books were in Greek, and though she had tried to teach herself the language, it defeated her. Arabic was completely beyond her reach, but her Latin improved considerably.

Sometimes she asked herself why she was still here, and the answer was that she found herself enjoying Otto's company. She had persuaded him – or perhaps it was the rather affluent surroundings in which he found himself that had persuaded him – that he should keep himself cleaner and tidier, and she found it easier to be with him. Occasionally he would call her to the laboratory where he and the Landgrave would be discussing some point of natural philosophy.

"Why, Sir Alchemist," the Landgrave had remarked on one of these occasions, "you are more than a mere distiller, as I have heard them called."

"Your Highness is too kind. I have dabbled in the study of the mysteries."

"More than dabbled, my friend. Tell me," he leaned close to Otto, and spoke low so that Jane had to strain to catch his words, "I wish to have for a wife a Salamander, as described in the book of the *Comte de Gabalis* by the Abbé de Villars. Not as the reptile guise in which she appeared when you transmuted the gold, but in her human form. This is something I desire more than gold, to be the father of heroes. Can you achieve this for me? If you say you are unable to do so, I shall take no offence. I know of no one, no, not even Paracelsus himself, who has achieved this in our age, though de Villars claims that a Salamander became enamoured of Noah's wife, Vesta."

"Ah, Your Highness wishes me to invoke the Salamander through the concentration of the Fire of the World in a crystal globe."

"You have it exactly, Sir Alchemist," the Landgrave exclaimed. "And when that is done, and the Solar Powder is removed from the globe and prepared according to the receipts laid out in the works of the philosophers, then, a Salamander may become my lover."

"Is this your full desire, Your Highness, that I should labour on this, rather than the transmutation of the gold?"

"It is."

"Very well, then. I shall need to have made a perfect crystal globe, to be ready for the summer, when the Sun's rays will have their full efficacy. Much of the work I can do myself, but it will be necessary to employ one or two workmen to assist me."

"As many as you require. If anyone questions you on this matter, refer them to me." And with that, the Landgrave left the room.

"IT IS PROVING DIFFICULT to produce a crystal sphere of sufficient quality to create the Solar Powder, Your Highness," Otto told the Landgrave a week after the conversation just described.

The Landgrave's face fell. "So, there will be no Salamander?" he asked sadly.

"I did not say that, Your Highness. I am exploring different avenues which will, I trust, bring us to the Salamander. The method as described by the Abbé de Villars may well work, but if, and only if, the crystal employed to create the sphere is of a sufficiently high quality, and the sphere itself is manufactured to a standard of near-perfection, a process which I estimate would occupy the best part of ten years."

"By which time I will be too old and decrepit to enjoy the embraces of even a Salamander," complained the Landgrave.

"Your Highness is doing himself no favours by saying this," said Otto. "However, I have been searching through ancient texts in Your Highness' library, and I have found a connection between the *Rosarius Philosophorum* of Arnaldus de Villa Nova and the *Viridarium Chymicum* of Daniel Stolcius where he mentions the work of Michael Sendivogius on the central nitre and the so-called 'food of life' which he extracted from common air. To my knowledge, no man before me has been fortunate enough to have made this discovery, which will enable a Salamander to be summoned, and will persuade her that the summoner is worthy of respect. Your Highness, naturally, will perform the summoning ceremony once all has been prepared by me, and the Salamander will come to you as her master."

"You put my mind at rest," said the Landgrave. "How long before you can achieve this?"

"A matter of weeks at most," Otto told him.

The Landgrave's nephew, Ludwig, who had been standing behind his uncle, suddenly burst out with, "And when is my Salamander to be expected?"

"I was not aware that I was to make preparation for two Salamanders to be summoned, Your Highness."

"Nor I," said the Landgrave. "Ludwig, you are not of an age and you do not possess sufficient knowledge to be initiated into these mysteries."

"Even so, Uncle, if this alchemist will not give me his niece, he may give me a Salamander."

"What is this about your niece?" asked the Landgrave incredulously.

"A misunderstanding, Your Highness, no more. I believe that your nephew has somehow formed the opinion that my niece was available as a partner for him."

"In marriage? Ludwig, that could never be."

"I never mentioned marriage," the boy answered sulkily. "Just because this old fraud here is tupping her, and does not wish to share her with his betters, does not mean that he may contradict my wishes."

"Ludwig, your thoughts and words are dishonourable, and unworthy of the name you bear. You may leave us." The boy did not move. "I said," he repeated in a louder voice, "that you may leave us." There was no reaction from Ludwig. "Will you leave, or must I have the guards carry you out?" he shouted at his nephew.

The boy turned wordlessly, and walked out of the door.

"I apologise, Sir Alchemist," said the Landgrave. "He is the only child of my poor sister, who died giving birth to him. His father, the Graf von Kettelburg, was killed by a boar while hunting some years later, and I took young Ludwig under my wing. I confess that he has been a disappointment to me in many ways."

"Your Highness?"

"He has been responsible for the disgrace of at least two maidservants in the last two years. And goodness knows what sort of other things he has been doing that have not reached my ears. He is, however, my heir. When I pass away, he will inherit this title and my lands, and it would not do for me to be seen to enquire too closely into the affairs of my heir."

"I too have heard things about him, Your Highness, but I prefer to judge them merely as idle gossip."

"I wish that were the case. I cannot say that I actively wish any harm to come to him. Should, however, a serious accident befall him, I would neither be surprised nor overly sorry."

"I believe I understand Your Highness."

"But what is he talking about with regard to your niece. She *is* your niece, is she not?" he asked curiously.

"She is, but the matter between her and your nephew is not worthy of discussion. Nor, for that matter, is the relationship between myself and her, which I swear to you, Your Highness, is nothing but honourable. Now, Your Highness, this is the way in which I will summon your Salamander.

"I will require some vulgar quicksilver out of which I will separate the sulphur using that artificial fire called the Burning Star, and then recombine this celestial mercury and sulphur, that is to say, I will produce a quantity of the First Matter, or the Physical Chaos as it is sometimes referred to, and from there I may produce the Elementary Gold from common or vulgar gold, and this Elementary Gold differs from the Vulgar Gold as being the most pure of all the metals. You follow me?"

"I have heard these terms, yes."

"Now, the next step is to proceed to transmute the Astral Gold from the Elementary Gold, and from there, we may be allowed to bring forth the Salamander and bend her to our wishes."

"And how is this final transmutation to be achieved?"

"Through the power of thunderbolts."

"And if there is no thunder? Must we wait until the thunder falls upon us?"

"By no means – I can create thunder and lightning for our purposes."

"Heaven preserve us, Sir Alchemist! If you can achieve all this, you are a master above all the sages of antiquity and of the present day? Quicksilver, you say? I shall have brought to you as much as you require. Vulgar gold? How much?"

"An ounce or two only. Perhaps I will not need that much."

"I am relieved. I have heard of some who claim to require pounds of the metal for their work."

"I am not one of those, Your Highness."

"Excellent. Then, to work, Sir Alchemist, and keep me informed of your progress."

"WELL, THAT LOOKS LIKE A JOB for you, Jane," said Otto.

"What, helping you to make a crystal sphere to produce sunpowder?"

"No, that's complete nonsense, like so many of the books here. Do you know, I think I shall write a book like these, put in the most ridiculous ideas I can think of, and watch everyone try them out."

"But you do believe in Salamanders and Elementals?"

"Yes. Don't you?"

"Me? I suppose I have to, don't I? I've seen them, after all." She thought about the times she had walked through walls, and flown with the one who called himself her father. "Yes, you're right. They exist, don't they?"

"If you don't know that, no one does," Otto told her sharply. "It will be your job to summon a Salamander."

Jane put her head in her hands. "If I could do such a thing, I'd sooner the Salamander burned him to ashes," she half-whispered.

"Who? The Landgrave?" Otto was shocked. "He's been good to us both, hasn't he? Why do you want to see him burned up?"

"No, not him, that nephew of his, Ludwig. He's after me. Always trying to catch hold of me when we pass in the corridor or meet. He tried to put his arms round me and put his hand down the front of my dress the other day, but I managed to break away in time. Ugh!"

"You know," Otto reminded her, "you have many powers. Like turning gold into scorpions, like you did with that boatman. You could get rid of Ludwig quite easily, I would have thought. And you still have your poisoned dagger, don't you?"

She laughed. "It's not really poisoned. Do you think I'm so stupid as to wander around the place with a deadly blade next to my skin?"

Otto sat back, stunned, and then began to laugh. "Well, of all the… I really don't know what to say. Here am I, having lived in fear of being pricked by your little pig-sticker, and all the time…"

"I can use it, even if it's not poisoned."

"I'm sure you can, and I know now that you can do much worse, anyway. I'll remind you again that you do have some rather frightening powers, and I'm sure neither you or I have seen all of them."

"Of course I could do worse. Do you think I haven't thought of that? But if I do something obvious, then the Landgrave's going to suspect something, isn't he? And then we're both thrown out of here. Or worse. They seem to execute a lot of people round here. It's almost as if the Landgrave enjoys hearing them scream for mercy."

"Then you have to think of something that isn't obvious, don't you? Make it look like an accident."

She sat, elbows on the table, head in her hands. "Otto," she said, without looking at him. "How long are we going to stay in this place? You seem to be finding lots of interesting things in the library here, and getting on well with the Landgrave. But what about me? I can't read half the books here, the other half is either rubbish or things that I know already, and I'm tired of dodging the attentions of a spoiled young brat of a princeling who thinks it's his God-given right to molest whatever woman takes his fancy at the moment."

"Get that Salamander for the Landgrave. Maybe it will burn up young Ludwig – and I agree with you, he's a pain in the arse. Then we can leave, with a happy Landgrave, and probably more gold in our pockets than he ever expected to get from my alchemy."

"Promise?"

"Promise. Where do you want to go after this, anyway?"

"France. Paris."

Otto sighed. "I don't think I'm very popular there. I made quite a lot of gold vanish out of people's pockets there some years ago."

"Those people have probably had their heads cut off by now. Haven't you seen the reports? The people you took the gold from are the enemies of the people."

"Perhaps," Otto admitted. "But are you really sure you want us to go to Paris?"

"Well, I suppose I could go on my own if you don't want to come with me."

He laughed. "My dear, there is no doubt in my mind that you are an exceptional person. But you should realise that you need your Uncle Otto near you to protect you if you're going to make it to Paris alive and unharmed." He smiled. "I've actually got quite fond of you, you know. As a niece," he added hurriedly.

She laughed out loud. "Thank you, Uncle Otto. It's nice to hear that." She extended a hand towards him, and he grasped it. They sat there for a few minutes, content in each other's company, before he released her hand, they caught each other's eye, and simultaneously burst into peals of loud unquenchable and inexplicable laughter.

OTTO ENTERED THE CHAMBER where Jane was sitting reading, flushed, and breathing heavily.

"What's the matter?" she asked him when she had taken in his condition.

"It's your bloody boyfriend," he said. "Ludwig. He can't have you – the Landgrave practically said as much to him in so many words – so he wants a Salamander – which the Landgrave has also forbidden him."

"And?"

"And I ran into him in the corridor just now and he threatened to have me broken on the wheel if there was no Salamander coming his way."

"Well, I'd better get him a Salamander, hadn't I? That's what you're saying, isn't it?"

"Yes. Because you and I both know that I can't do it. I spun a wonderful tale to the Landgrave just now – so wonderful I almost ended up believing it myself – but it's complete rubbish." He sighed. "Sounded great, though. I must remember it when I start giving lectures again."

"So we are going to leave here, after all."

"When we have the Salamander, yes."

"Suppose I say that I don't know how to bring them here?"

"Suppose I say you'd be lying if you said that."

"I don't know. Really I don't."

"I do know. But I can't do it myself. Only you are capable of doing it. You have to play the armonica and gaze into the fire."

"What?"

"You're playing the music of the Elementals, whether you know it or not. The used to call it 'the music of the spheres'. You know why?" Jane shook her head. "You know about the spheres?"

"Yes, of course I do. They imagined in those days that there were crystal spheres with the planets and stars attached, and that they turned round to make the planets and stars move."

"Exactly. But that music that you play was and is the music of the ones you call Them – those who live on the other side of the sky, that is to say, the spheres, and of the Elementals. You can call the Elementals, and they will come and they will respect you. You know their music."

"If…" Jane stammered a little. "If I were to use the music to summon a fire Elemental – a Salamander, would she do what I commanded her?"

"I do not believe that you should command these beings. You make courteous requests of them."

"Very well, then. If I were to make a courteous request that she embrace Ludwig and…"

"…and that she consume him with her fire?"

"Yes. That. What would she do?"

"They bear no goodwill or malice toward human beings generally. She would almost certainly do what you ask. And that would be a relief to the Landgrave."

"How do you mean?"

"He has as good as told me just now that he would like me to arrange a serious accident to befall young Ludwig. Apparently you are not the only one on whom he has cast a lustful eye. He has a certain reputation."

"Then that is a problem solved for us and the Landgrave," Jane said.

"Hardly. We will not be alone with him in the laboratory. Almost certainly there will be at least one servant, probably Franz, with us. We cannot afford to appear to be the direct cause of his death."

"Oh, very well, then. It seemed like a good idea. Who will make the request of the Landgrave's Salamander when it appears?"

"The Landgrave himself is the one who must make the request when the Salamander appears and the Salamander will then obey his request."

"You're sure of this?"

"As sure as that you will see lightning and hear thunder tomorrow."

Jane looked out of the window at the clear blue sky and sighed.

THE FOLLOWING DAY saw Otto hard at work, unpacking some of the boxes with which he had travelled, the contents of which Jane had never seen. He dispatched a servant to the kitchens to request four large identical glass jars.

"I see," said Jane, as he filled the jars and stoppered them with wax before driving a long nail through the wax to have its tip resting in the water, "that you are creating a 'battery' of Leyden jars."

Otto looked up, a look of surprise on his face. "How the—how on earth do you come to know about Leyden jars? And a 'battery'?"

"Uncle 'Rasmus – Doctor Erasmus Darwin, remember? He used electricity a lot to treat his patients, and he sometimes allowed me to see his electrical experiments. And his American friend, Mr Franklin, sometimes visited. Wasn't he the one who got the idea of tying them all together with wire and calling them a 'battery'?" She sighed. "That does all seem a very long time ago now."

"I had forgotten that you had told me," Otto said. "Of course."

"And where is the electricity to come from?" asked Jane.

"Look," said Otto, pointing to the armonica.

"Oh yes, of course. The treadle you use to spin the bowls could spin a glass sphere instead, and you could create the electricity from there."

"Actually, the bowls themselves will suffice."

"And there's your thunder and lightning."

"That's right."

"So now all you have to do, if I understand you correctly, is to create this Elementary Gold from the Vulgar Gold using the Burning Star."

Otto smiled. "Exactly."

"And what is this Burning Star?"

For answer, Otto extracted a small cloth bundle from the bottom of one of his boxes. He unwrapped it carefully, to disclose a small bottle three-quarters full of liquid, with a small lump of some solid inside.

"This is dangerous," he warned. "Stand a little apart from me."

Jane did so, and watched as he used a slim blade to detach a part of the lump from the main body, while it was still under the liquid in the bottle, and then a pair of long forceps, such as she had seen at Erasmus Darwin's, to remove the small piece from the liquid and place it on the top of the unlit stove that stood in the corner of the room.

As she looked at the small grey lump, it started to smoulder, and then burst into a fierce flame.

"And that is what, exactly?" asked Jane.

"Piss. Distilled piss."

"Come on, what is it?"

"It's what it is. It's called phosphorus."

"Oh. I'd heard of it from Uncle 'Rasmus, I think, but never seen it."

"Horrible stuff. As you can see, it burns with no flame applied to it. It is also, apparently, poisonous. Not that I have ever eaten it or even handled it."

"Why do you keep it with you? It sounds as though it's terribly dangerous to have around."

"It is, but then you never know when you might need to produce a Burning Star." He laughed. "So now, let us assemble our electrical generator."

He and Jane worked to assemble the armonica, and Otto connected two copper chains leading from attachments at the bottom of the instrument to the Leyden jars.

"Now," he told Jane, "this will not be the music of the spheres. Do not concentrate on making music, but use this leather pad to rub the bowls."

Obediently Jane operated the pedals, and pressed the pad against the bowls until Otto indicated that she might stop.

"And now," he said, taking on the air of a stage conjurer, and taking a wooden handle which was attached to a chain, which in turn was attached to the Leyden jar. "Thunder and lightning!" he exclaimed triumphantly, as he touched a metal spike attached to the wooden handle to a metal window frame, and a large spark and a near-deafening crack split the air.

"Most impressive," said Jane. "When can we get Ludwig his Salamander?"

"His Highness comes first. Clearly. What hope do we have of presenting a Salamander to him if his nephew is consumed by fire first, eh?"

"I see what you mean."

"Very well, then."

WITHIN A WEEK, Otto pronounced that the transmutation of the vulgar quicksilver into the Physical Chaos was now complete. The Landgrave, who had been invited to witness the operation of the Burning Star, accompanied by the music of the spheres produced by Jane on the armonica, was suitably impressed.

"Now," declared Otto, "I am able to produce the Elementary Gold from the Vulgar Gold, but this is an operation that requires complete concentration, and I am afraid that I must undertake it alone."

"Is it dangerous?" the Landgrave enquired anxiously.

Otto shrugged. "To the neophyte in these matters, yes, it must be admitted that there exists an element of danger. Even to one such as myself, the merest lapse in concentration may render me senseless at best, and dead at worst."

"Heaven preserve us, Sir Alchemist," exclaimed the Landgrave, crossing himself. "I would not have asked you to proceed with this operation had I known these hazards to exist."

"It is no matter. Believe me, if I was not confident of success, I would not have offered to undertake the operation."

"Very well, then," said the Landgrave, but he appeared to be unconvinced.

Two DAYS LATER, Otto presented the Landgrave with a lump of gold that he claimed as now being the Elementary Gold.

"It may look and behave similarly to Vulgar Gold, Your Highness," he explained, "but though the accidents remain the same, the substance has changed, as explained by Aristotle."

The Landgrave nodded wisely in agreement.

"So tomorrow, if your Highness is agreeable, we will proceed to the summoning of the Salamander, and you may then ask of her what you will."

"Excellent. At what hour?"

"Sunrise is generally reckoned to be the time at which such a summoning is considered to be most effective."

"I shall give orders to be awakened well before that time. Until sunrise, then, Sir Alchemist."

"I HAVE NEVER," Otto said to Jane as he stoked the furnace in the laboratory to a near white heat, "been less confident of the result of such an operation."

"You have never attempted to summon a Salamander before," Jane pointed out.

"Exactly. And the operation is under your control, not mine. But it is I who will suffer should this whole business come to naught. Remember that."

"I will, Sir Alchemist," Jane said, dropping a curtsey in mock humility.

"What we must do," Otto reminded her, "is for you to start playing the music of the spheres, and concentrating on the fire as you did before. I think you will be able to bring the Salamander in her lizard form quite easily. There are three of us longing to behold her. Then, when I give the signal, the armonica becomes the electrical machine, and you use the leather pad until I give the signal to cease. I will then produce the thunder and lightning, after which you start playing again, and we will ask the Landgrave to summon the Salamander in her human form. Meanwhile you will concentrate silently, as will I, on bringing her out of the fire into the room."

"And then?"

"We will see if the tales of Salamander lovers are true."

At that moment, the Landgrave entered, accompanied by Franz, the chamberlain, and splendidly dressed in embroidered silks and furs.

"Good morrow to Your Highness," Otto and Jane said together. The Landgrave acknowledged the greeting, and took his seat on the chair that had been prepared for him, at a safe distance from the furnace, but from which he had an excellent view of the proceedings.

Otto explained to him the order in which he expected events to proceed. "Do not be alarmed, Your Highness," he advised, "when we create the thunder and lightning in this room. Once that is done, and we have thereby contacted the inner spirit of the Salamander, you may ask her to step forth in her human form. Now," turning to Jane, "it is time to begin. Let us hear the music of the spheres, and summon the Salamander to the furnace."

Jane began to play the armonica. Without any conscious effort on her part, she found herself playing music that was unearthly, in the best possible sense of the word. The Landgrave sat, seemingly entranced by the sound, as he gazed into the fire.

As Jane continued playing, gazing into the fire, she became aware of the Salamander once more, playing in the flames, writhing and darting in apparent pleasure. The beautiful human face was set in an expression of near-ecstasy, and the body wove its way sinuously through the flames.

"She is dancing!" exclaimed the Landgrave.

"Indeed she is," said Otto. "Now we will use our thunder and lightning to reach her inner spirit."

Jane recognised the signal to stop playing, and used the leather pads to produce the charge which was carried to the Leyden jars by the chains. After only a few minutes, Otto signalled that she should stop.

With ceremony, he grasped the wooden handles of the metal spike, and held it close to the metal window frame.

There was a crashing sound, as loud as a genuine

thunderstorm, and a brilliant flash that left them all blinking, unable to see anything clearly for a minute or two.

"Summon the Salamander," Otto commanded the Landgrave, who slowly rose to his feet.

"My Salamander," declaimed the Landgrave. "My love, the desire of my heart. Please be kind enough to grace us with your presence in human form."

A loud crash and a blinding flash of light once more, and all were forced to close their eyes. When they reopened them, they realised they were not alone in the room. A tall slender female figure, swathed in red silky material, stood before the Landgrave, seemingly awaiting his words.

"My dear," he stammered. "How good of you to join us."

"How could I do otherwise?" Her voice was smooth and somehow serpentine, with a hissing quality to it. "I am powerless to resist when I hear such music."

"Play," Otto ordered Jane. "Softly."

Jane started the music again, and the Salamander writhed in apparent ecstasy once more. Her face was the most beautiful that Jane had ever seen, and her figure was of the kind that men find irresistibly attractive. The Landgrave was clearly entranced.

"What is your name?" he asked.

"My name is Ignia," said the Salamander. "And yours?" Again that hissing quality of the voice.

"I am Landgrave – that is to say, lord – of the lands around here. My name is Philip." He reached out a hand towards Ignia.

"I am to take your hand, Philip?" she said. "Be warned, my lord. Should I take your hand, I will be yours, since I sense you wish this to be so. But should you play me false, I will be gone from you for ever, and you will regret it. Now, do you wish me to take your hand? There is no going back on this covenant."

The Landgrave rose, and with a certain ceremony took the hand of the Salamander. The couple left the laboratory, the Landgrave casting a look of triumph mixed with gratitude in Otto's direction.

When they had gone, Franz, who had been wordlessly ordered by the Landgrave not to follow him and his new partner, turned to Otto. He bowed.

"I had believed all alchemists were frauds and cheats up to now. But you, sir, you are the wonder of this age."

"AND NOW," SAID OTTO, "it is time for Ludwig's Salamander."

He and Jane were waiting in the laboratory, about a week after the appearance of Ignia. Since that time, the Landgrave had always made his appearance with Ignia by his side, and all who beheld her had declared her, not without some sincerity, to be the most beautiful creature they had ever beheld. For she was beautiful, no doubt about it, but her beauty was of an unearthly kind, only slightly marred by the reptilian tongue which occasionally protruded from between her lips.

As for the Landgrave, all remarked that they had never seen him so invigorated, or with such a spring in his step. However, having been informed by Franz of the processes by which Ignia had been called forth, only one person had decided – nay, had insisted – on a Salamander of his very own. That person, needless to say, was Ludwig.

His lust, for such it was, for a Salamander as a partner, had brought one possible benefit. He no longer bothered Jane with his intentions, possibly as a result of being told by Otto that her talents were necessary for the Salamander's appearance, and if she were seriously annoyed, she would not be well-disposed to demonstrate those talents. Ludwig took the hint, and for the past week he had been oleaginously polite to Jane whenever he encountered her. She was unsure whether she preferred this or his previous rapacious manner.

"I can't believe you ever consented to this," Jane whispered furiously to Otto.

"I have my reasons," he said. "It will be highly educational."

"For whom?" she asked, but before he could answer, Franz entered, announcing the arrival of Ludwig.

He was dressed in the height of fashion, and like all who follow the look of fashion slavishly without thought as to its deeper meaning (for, strange as it may seem, all fashion has some hidden meaning to it), he looked more than a little ridiculous.

Otto explained the procedure to him.

"First, we must produce the Salamander in the furnace, which as you can see, I have prepared ready for her arrival."

"And then?"

"We create thunder and lightning by means of this apparatus here. This summons the Salamander from the fire into her human form, where she will join us. You are then free to ask of her what you will, since we have declared ourselves her equal in power. But until that time, I must charge you to remain silent."

"If you say so," Ludwig answered. His tone was scoffing, and it was not clear what, if anything, he had understood of this, even though Otto had explained the principles to him several times over the previous few days.

Jane began to play the armonica, but the sound was somewhat removed from the music of the spheres that had summoned the Landgrave's Salamander. There were weird discordant notes that set Otto's teeth on edge, and caused icy shivers to run along his spine. He looked at Jane's face, and saw that she appeared to be concentrating on the flames in the furnace to the exclusion of all else. He turned his own gaze to the furnace. Could it be? Yes it was, the flicker of a tail in the fire.

"She's here! She's here!" shouted Ludwig, springing to his feet. "Come forth! Show your full power and love me as long as I shall live!"

Otto shook his head in disgust, and signed to Jane to stop playing, and to start operating the armonica as an electrical generator. She applied the leathern pads, and the bowls revolved under their pressure, transmitting their charge to the Leyden jars.

After a couple of minutes, Otto signalled that she should stop, and he grasped the wooden handle of the metal rod, touching it to the window-frame.

A flash and a crack of thunder, at least equal to that which had accompanied the appearance of the Landgrave's Salamander, deafened and blinded them all.

Otto became aware of a foul smell, and the weak voice of Ludwig.

"I think... I think I've messed myself."

Otto said nothing, but he could hear a faint sniggering sound coming from Franz's direction.

As their eyes regained their ability to see, once again, a beautiful tall woman dressed in a red silken shift was standing before them. Her face was stern.

"Was it you who summoned me?" she asked, pointing at Ludwig.

"Yes... Yes it was."

"And you wish me to show you my full power?"

"Yes."

"And to love you as long as you shall live?"

"Yes! Yes!"

"Then so be it."

She stepped forward facing Ludwig and placed her hands

on his shoulders. Instantly there was a small of scorching, then burned flesh, as Ludwig began to scream in wordless agony.

The Salamander bent her face towards that of Ludwig. Her forked tongue slithered in and out of her mouth as her lips approached his. His scream was choked off as she pressed her mouth over his mouth, but his limbs were writhing in what Otto could only imagine to be excruciating pain. To the watchers' horror, smoke started to issue from Ludwig's nose and his ears as his arms and legs stopped their insane dance, to be replaced by spasmodic twitching, and then stillness.

The Salamander stood up, releasing her grip on Ludwig, who sagged to the floor, apparently lifeless. She turned and addressed Jane. "Mistress, I bear you no ill-will for summoning me, but I would fain return."

"What did you do?" Jane asked. "Or rather, why did you do it?"

"I gave him his heart's desire as he expressed it to me. I showed him my power, and I loved him for the whole of his life. He never specified how long that life should be. Now let me return, Mistress."

"You are free to go," Jane told her.

With a pop and a small shower of sparks, the Salamander vanished, leaving Otto, Jane, and the dumbfounded chamberlain gazing at the motionless body of Ludwig.

"How am I to explain this to the Landgrave?" wailed Franz.

"I think you will find he will not be quite as heartbroken as you imagine," Otto told him. "His Highness is well acquainted with the dangers of such operations as we have just witnessed. You will bear witness that Ludwig was strictly enjoined against speaking until such time as the Salamander had left the furnace."

"Indeed, I remember you saying that most clearly."

"And that contrary to these instructions, he summoned the Salamander, giving orders which could be – indeed were – interpreted in a fashion that was not altogether to his benefit."

"Yes."

"As I say, His Highness is no fool. He understands that with great power comes great responsibility. There is danger also, and those who disregard the wisdom of others who inform them of that danger must necessarily pay the price."

"Nonetheless," Franz stammered. "I do not want to be the one who brings him this news."

"Then I will do it myself," Otto told him. "But on one condition."

"What is that condition? How much money do you need?"

Otto laughed. "No money. I simply wish you to confirm the truth of what I shall say to His Highness. I assure you that it will be a truthful account of what has just happened. If he wishes to see the body for himself, the truth of my words will be confirmed, of course, but your words will add authority to my account."

"And that is all you ask of me?" Franz said, with a sigh of relief.

"Yes. I would, however, suggest that you find a sheet with which to cover that poor wretch, and then summon a couple of servants to take him to his room and lay him on his bed."

"It shall be done," said Franz, and left the room.

Otto carefully closed the door before turning to Jane. "Well, that didn't go too well, did it?"

"Oh, I think the Salamander enjoyed herself," said Jane. "Ugh. Can we open a window? It smells like overdone pork in here."

"One thing," Otto said to her as he obediently opened the

window. "The Salamander talked to you, not me, and addressed you as 'Mistress'."

"I know," said Jane. "But it was I who summoned her through my music, was it not?"

"I suppose so. And that's another thing, now I come to mind it. Why was the music so different today?"

"I cannot say precisely," said Jane. "It was not me playing, or rather, it was someone or something else playing through me."

"The one who calls himself your father?" Otto asked.

Jane nodded. "Yes, I am certain of it. He was angry at Ludwig for having dared to approach me. I am sure of that."

"But Ludwig brought that on himself," said Otto. "That was not the doing of anyone or anything else, was it?"

"I do not know. Maybe the Salamander who came today was sent by Him especially to destroy Ludwig."

At that point, Franz re-entered with a sheet. Jane re-arranged the corpse into a posture which was a little more seemly, and Otto and Franz arranged the sheet around it.

"I realise this is a terrible imposition on you, sir," said Franz, "but there is no one among the servants I can trust not to look under this sheet and see the terrible sight that is there. And once they see it…"

"Very well," sighed Otto. "I will help you."

Between them, the two men lifted the body. Jane went ahead of them, ensuring that the passages were empty and that they would meet no one on their way to Ludwig's room.

Once the cadaver had been disposed on the bed, Otto sighed. "Come with me, Franz, while I tell His Highness of what has happened. And Jane, you come too. Perhaps your presence will help calm him."

MUCH TO OTTO'S SURPRISE, and his great relief, the Landgrave, with Ignia seated beside him, took the news of his nephew's death with equanimity. When Otto explained that Ludwig had disobeyed the instructions given to him, and thereby brought about his own fate, the Landgrave stirred in his chair.

"This is true, Franz?" he asked his chamberlain.

"All that occurred took place exactly as the alchemist has described it," Franz confirmed.

"Then I cannot feel that any blame attaches to any of you," said the Landgrave.

"Nor to my sister, whoever she might turn out to be," said Ignia, speaking for the first time. "She was summoned, and she was commanded. She obeyed the command, as we are bound to do when one in power issues it."

"Quite right, my dear," said the Landgrave, looking at her with the eyes of a lovestruck youngster.

Franz coughed. "If I may remind Your Highness…"

"Yes?"

"Ludwig was your heir. There is no other relative of yours who can take your place. You must declare a successor."

"'Must', Franz? 'Must'? This is not a word to be used to me."

"Your pardon, Your Highness. May I say that it would be highly advisable for you to name an heir in Ludwig's absence."

"Oh, very well. Sir Alchemist, how would you like to sit here as ruler of this part of the world, eh?"

"Your Highness," stammered Otto, obviously flustered. "I am not worthy—"

"Nonsense, Franz. Sir Philomentor is now the official heir to my lands and titles."

"But…" Otto recovered himself. "Your Highness does me

too much honour. May it be many years, many decades, before you... before I..."

"Quite so," smiled the Landgrave. "I completely concur with you in these sentiments."

As it turned out, it was less than a week before Franz burst into Otto's bedchamber early one morning with the news.

"His Highness is dead, Your Highness."

"What?" said Otto, sitting up in bed and rubbing his eyes.

"The Landgrave died in the night. You are now the Landgrave, Your Highness."

The news slowly penetrated Otto's sleep-addled brain. "How?"

"His heart appears to have given out."

"And the Salamander? Ignia?"

"Gone. No sign of her anywhere in the castle."

"Probably gone back to where she came. No sign of burning or scorching, as there was with Ludwig?"

Franz shuddered. "No. He was... naked."

"Probably died in the act of love," Otto said simply and without emotion. "Happens quite a lot you know. Though not so often with a Salamander," he added reflectively.

"Quite so, Your Highness."

"Oh, for God's sake, cut that out. Forget that I am the Landgrave for a bit. Wait until I feel like a Landgrave and start executing people in the town square." He looked at Franz's horrified expression. "I'm joking, you fool. I have no intention of executing anyone."

"I'm glad to hear it, Your..."

"Oh, call me Otto for God's sake," Otto said. "You'll never

know if it might or might not be my real name, but I'll answer to it. I suppose I'd better go and tell my niece."

JANE SEEMED UNSURPRISED by the news. She had not yet arisen, and sat up straight in bed as Otto told her the news.

"I thought so," she said calmly. "I had a dream last night."

"About Him?"

"Yes. It was more of a nightmare than a dream, I suppose." She frowned. "It's not clear to me now, but I remember feeling that there was death and violence."

"Did the Salamander, Ignia, appear in the dream?"

"I don't recall that." She began to beat on the coverlet of the bed with her fists. "Damn! Damn! Damn!"

"What?"

"I thought I was safe from Him here, out of England. Has He got stronger, or have I got weaker and less able to defend myself against him?"

"I cannot say, but I have my suspicions, which I will tell you later. For now I have other worries."

"Such as whether you are to be the Landgrave of Tiengen?"

"That, yes. Indeed. Am I to be called "Your Highness" for the rest of my life? It would be a comfortable existence, to be sure." He waved his arm in a gesture that presumably took in the whole castle and the lands surrounding it. "All this, mine to do with as I please." He sighed. "I don't know the first thing about being a ruler. I know something about being ruled, though."

"That's a start," Jane said, encouragingly.

"No, that's not really what I mean. All the little details that I would have to deal with. The nuisance of it all. Papers to sign, land leases to take care of, and ceremonies on saints' days. All that sort of thing. I'd have no time for reading or experimenting."

"Then give it all to Franz. He seems to enjoy that sort of thing."

"What, give him the work?"

"And the title. Appoint him your heir and then abdicate after a month or so. Don't tell him that you're going to do that, of course."

Otto scratched his head. "It might work."

"It would work very well, Your Highness."

Otto stooped, picked up one of Jane's slippers lying on the floor and flung it in her general direction. It missed, as he had intended. "Don't call me that, please."

"Or you could name me as your heir and then abdicate," Jane mused.

"You? A woman ruler? Here in this part of the world. Sorry, my dear, but they're never going to accept that as an idea. You'd have to marry a stupid wooden puppet and rule through him. There are lots of blockheads around here – just throw a stone out of the window and marry the one it hits."

"Sorry. I have no intention of marrying anyone – just yet, anyway, so that's really not an option."

"Then Franz it is."

"And then?"

"Move on somewhere else. I need to keep moving, even if I'm not running away from something."

"And could I come with you?"

Otto looked at her in surprise. "I was assuming that you would be joining me."

"Never assume anything about me," Jane told him.

"I never do," Otto laughed.

PART THREE

THE REVOLUTIONARY

(1793)

XI

The Road to Liberty

"**A**ND WHERE ARE WE GOING?**" Jane asked Otto. They were riding north, each mounted on a fine horse from the castle stables and leading another, laden with their baggage. Jane was wearing a pair of men's breeches which she had obviously acquired from somewhere, and rode astride her horse, rather than side-saddle, somewhat to Otto's discomfiture.

"It may be safer for me if I'm not immediately recognised as a girl," she had said in answer to his unspoken admonishment.

Otto had abdicated his position and title as Landgrave the previous week, leaving a surprised Franz as the new Landgrave.

"You'll make a better job of it than I ever would," Otto had told him. "You know everyone around here for a start. I'm a stranger here. And it seems that people like you. You'll make a success of it, I know."

"But I'm not born to the position."

"Neither am I. And if anyone asks, I'd say you were in a much better place than me to take on the job. So here's your chain of office, Your Highness."

"And what are you going to do, Your— I mean, Otto?"

"Go away. Travel here, travel there, until I can find somewhere that pleases me and I feel I can stay."

"Not here?" Franz had asked, almost wistfully.

"Not here. I've read all the books in the library that I need to. And you don't need me round here any more."

"And your niece?"

"She's travelling with me. One favour, if I may, Your Highness?"

"Yes… within reason."

"Actually, two. First, lock up the alchemical laboratory and lose the key. Forget that room ever existed. Believe me, I have reasons for telling you this."

"I shall be glad to. I never felt comfortable with the old Landgrave's interest in those things. For someone like you, I suppose it's all right, but it was unbecoming in one of his rank. And then of course, there's what happened to Ludwig, and of course the old Landgrave himself, though it may be said that at least he died happy." At this point, Franz had sighed deeply. "And the other favour?"

"There are a few books in the library which should not fall into the wrong hands, for the same reason that I entreat you to lock up the laboratory. If I may, I will take them with me."

"Feel free to take as many as you can carry. And you may have a riding horse each and another one each for your baggage, and sufficient gold to pay your way to Cathay, if that is where you wish to go."

Otto had smiled. "Cathay was not where I had set my heart

on going, but it is a kind thought, and I accept with deep pleasure and gratitude."

"WHERE ARE WE GOING?" repeated Otto. "You're off to Paris, aren't you?"

"I want to go there, yes. Aren't you coming with me?"

"I think not. I fancy a nice easy life in one place with no responsibilities."

"And where will you find that?"

"I thought Heidelberg would be a good place to start looking. Failing that, Utrecht, perhaps, or if I could stand the climate, Uppsala."

"A university? Why not Oxford or Cambridge in England?"

Otto shuddered. "The food, my dear. Even Swedish herrings or Dutch cheese are better than that eternal roast beef. And the weather. No, not England. No offence meant to you."

"None taken. But I shall miss you."

"And I you. But I think before we part, we should talk very seriously, and this seems like a very good time to do it."

"About us?"

"About you. What do you know about your father?"

"You mean my human father, or the one from the other side of the sky who calls himself my father?"

"Aha! There we are. Who is your father?"

"I was always told that I looked like my father. My human father, that is."

"All children take after their fathers, even the ones who don't. Could your human father fly? Walk through walls?"

"Don't be silly. Of course not."

"Can the Other who calls himself your father do these

179

things? You know very well that he can, and so can you. You've told me this."

"I can't fly. I've never even tried."

Otto stopped his horse and looked around. There was no one in sight. "Try now."

"What?" She was incredulous.

"Take your feet out of the stirrups and let yourself rise up in the air."

"How?"

"How should I know? I can't fly. Just do it."

Jane shook her head. "You're insane." Nonetheless, she took her feet out of the stirrups and closed her eyes.

After a few minutes, "Open your eyes," Otto commanded her.

She did and, to her obvious astonishment, discovered that she was floating in the air about a yard above her horse, though still in the same posture as if she was still sitting in the saddle.

"Now come to me," Otto told her.

A frown of concentration, and then a smile as she glided over towards him. "This is ridiculous," she said, but her smile was now an open grin. "And back again," she said, moved over to her horse, and settled herself on its back.

"See?" Otto said, with more than a little air of triumph.

"So what?"

"Are you a Gnome? You can walk through walls. Are you a Sylph? You can fly."

"Next you'll want me to live underwater to prove I'm an Undine. Or walk through fire or something to prove I'm a Salamander."

Yes," Otto said simply. "When we come to the next stream, I want you to put your face in the water for as long as you can manage. Can you swim?"

"Yes, I used to swim in Stowe Pool in Lichfield when I was a child."

"I'll wager you can keep your face in the water for five minutes at a time, by my watch."

"All right."

Within an hour, Otto had won his wager. Jane seemed perfectly happy to keep her face under the surface of the stream as long as she cared to do so.

"I don't even feel uncomfortable," she said. "And it's quite pleasant. So," after a pause. "How will we tell if I'm a Salamander? I don't have the looks of Ignia or the other one, do I?"

"Not as you are, that's true. But as a Salamander..."

"Can we take it for granted now that I'm a Salamander, then?"

"For now, let's assume that. Now I've only heard of one who has the powers of more than one Elemental. That's the one who calls himself your father."

"Now, your mother was mostly human, so he has probably obtained some sort of immortality by somehow begetting you through her. And you do have this tough streak in you."

"Really?"

"Quite probably. I won't try testing it. But it seems to fit the facts. And that means that whatever you may think of yourself here, you are quite an important person to Them on the other side of the sky."

"What sort of important?"

"I would say that you are quite a threat to your father. You can command Elementals. If you wanted, I am sure you could summon a couple of Sylphs out of the air right now."

"Do you want me to try?"

"No!" Otto almost shrieked the word. "You will draw unwelcome attention to yourself if you do."

"My father?"

Otto nodded. "Sooner or later, my girl, you are going to have to go up against him if you want to stay alive, despite your immortal streak. Right now, my guess is that you have more ability than he does, but he has more experience and skill."

"You frighten me."

"Good. Because I want you to be frightened. I want you to be aware of what's happening around you in the places you can't see."

THE PAIR TOOK THE ROAD for Heidelberg.

"What if they won't take you on as a professor?" Jane asked Otto as they approached the city.

"I think they will. Some of the books that I took from the old Landgrave's library – with Franz's full permission, mark you – will almost guarantee that any university in Europe will welcome me with open arms."

"Isn't that bribery?"

"I'm increasing their store of knowledge. And what could be more honest and straightforward than that?" he chuckled. "But what about you. What are you hoping to do in Paris?"

"Find out more about myself and about Them."

"Why Paris? Why not with me at the University?"

"Evil things are happening there. And I believe that He is there, making them happen."

"You want to meet him? You of all people should know better than that. You know how dangerous He is. You may well have greater powers than him, but they have yet to be tested."

"All the more reason why it should be I who defeats him."

Otto was visibly taken aback. "Are you certain He can be defeated? And why?"

"Why? He killed my mother. I have seen it all too often in dreams to know otherwise. And yes, I can defeat him. But to do so, I must learn more about evil, and Paris is that place."

"You do not consider me evil?"

Jane laughed. "My dear Otto, I said once that you are not the rogue you believe yourself to be. I stand by that judgement. You will make a superb professor. The university here, or any university lucky enough to have you will admire you and shower you with honours. But I will not be with you to share them. Farewell," she said, turning her horses away from him. "I will try to let you know how things fare with me."

"Farewell," Otto replied simply. To his surprise, his sight blurred as his eyes filled with tears. If he had but known it, Jane's eyes were in the same condition.

MOST PEOPLE would have considered it unsafe, if not downright dangerous, for a young woman of Jane's age to make her way through Europe alone, given the times and the suspicion that almost every community had of outsiders.

There was, however, a certain presence that hung about Jane that made others decide that this was one person with whom it would be foolish to interfere. Though no beauty in the classical sense, she was attractive enough, despite her male attire, to draw attention to herself from the young men in the villages through which she passed or the inns in which she stayed, but only occasionally would a foolishly brave would-be suitor attempt to approach her, and then was instantly repelled for reasons he was later unable to explain to his friends.

Though she did not obviously rebuff any who attempted

to ride with her and share her journey, these fellow-travellers seemed to tire of her company and soon found a reason to take another road.

She was obviously well-off – her clothes were of good quality, the horses she rode and led were no nags, and plans were laid by dirty men in dark corners of the inns where she spent her nights. They spoke of the riches that would be theirs if they were to take her horses and money. Strangely enough, none of these men ever returned from the lonely forest trails where they waited in ambush.

Through the mysterious dispersal of news that exists in country districts, Jane found she had acquired some sort of status, though not of the kind that is generally welcomed. As she passed through the towns and villages, and when she met another lonely traveller on the road, she often noticed, especially in Catholic districts, the locals crossing themselves. When she asked for lodging at a village inn, the innkeeper (if a man) was obviously reluctant to grant her request, but clearly fearful about refusing her. If the innkeeper was a woman, there was perhaps slightly less fear in the equation, but the fear was still there.

She learned to take her meals in her room, and to sleep with her dagger under her pillow. Sometimes she heard whispering outside the door of her room, and she would slip stealthily out of bed, grasping the dagger in one hand, with a blanket wrapped around her other arm to act as a shield, should that become necessary. However silently she made her moves, though, the noises outside always stopped as she stood barefoot, waiting, shivering with cold, but unafraid to face whatever might come through the door.

In this fashion she made her way to the Low Countries, whence she would pass into France.

XII

The Fellow-traveller

JANE ENTERED THE TOWN OF HASSELT, which at first glance seemed to be almost devoid of interest. There were some handsome buildings in the Flemish style, but Jane had seen quite enough of those recently. However, for some reason she felt that she would be safe here, and she searched for a suitable inn in which to stay the night. She still had most of the money with which she had left Tiengen, and she accordingly decided on the inn with the most prosperous appearance.

She received the usual stares and suspicious looks that a young woman travelling alone always seemed to attract, but to her relief, there seemed very little in the way of hostility.

"You're not from these parts?" asked the innkeeper as she handed over her money for the night's lodging.

"I've come from Switzerland," she told him.

"Ah, I could tell," he said. "Not often we have two folk from out of country staying here at the same time."

"Oh?"

"He usually sits in the parlour of an evening, reading and writing. I'm sure you'll have a lot in common, being from abroad and all that."

Jane doubted the truth of that. Why would she have anything in common with a random traveller from goodness knows where? She gave directions for her horses to be cared for, and made her way upstairs to her room, which was clean and pleasantly furnished. She opened the window to listen to the noises of the town, and was somehow reminded of Lichfield. The sound of the market closing, and the tolling of a bell some way off brought back memories of Dam Street and the cathedral.

The evening meal, like the room, was of a somewhat better quality than most of the others she had encountered on her travels, and having dined, she decided to at least see the mysterious foreigner who occupied it in the evenings.

HE WAS SEATED BESIDE THE FIRE, and as the landlord had predicted, was reading, and making notes as he read. As Jane entered, he noticed her out of the corner of his eye, put down his pen and his notebook, and stood to greet her. She noticed he was elegantly dressed, though not in the local fashion, and his middle-aged face, though handsome enough, appeared more than a little lined by weather and care.

"Good evening," he said in French — clearly not his native language, it seemed to Jane, followed by the same greeting in Flemish. Though she had only a few words of the language, Jane felt this was not his native language either.

She replied in German, and he smiled.

"I am sorry," he replied in his accented French, "I don't

speak German." He paused, and cocked his head on one side, looking at her curiously.

She frowned, embarrassed by his looking at her. He appeared to realise her discomfort as he seemed to pull himself together, and stopped his stare. "I am sorry," he said in French. "It seemed to me that maybe we had met somewhere before."

"Perhaps it would help refresh your memory if we told each other our origins," she suggested.

"Very well. I am English," he answered in French. "From the middle of the country."

"Oh!" she replied. "I would not have taken you as English." She realised she had spoken in French, and with an embarrassed cough changed to English. She was glad that she had had a chance to practise the use of her native language with Otto at times. "Although I have just come from Zürich, with a protracted stay in Germany, I too am originally from England. Also in the middle," she added.

He smiled. "And you are travelling alone?" he asked. "No companions? No servants?"

She shook her head. "None. I did have a companion until Heidelberg, however. He is now, I assume, a professor at the University there."

He raised his eyebrows. "Most interesting. Pardon my curiosity, but are you travelling back to England?"

She shook her head. "Not for some time yet, if ever. My aim is to go to France, and to discover what is happening there."

It was his turn to shake his head. "Some very bad things are happening there. It is no place for you to visit at this time. You might be able to persuade me otherwise, however." He stopped and looked at her once again. "Pardon me, but where did you live in England?"

"In Lichfield," she said.

"Really? I used to have friends there at one time. Then I am sure that is where I must have seen you."

She in her turn looked at him more closely. "I have to say, sir, that you seem wholly unknown to me, as I am sure I am to you. I left England when I was a mere child – nine years old, in fact. I trust that I have changed sufficiently in the time since then to be somewhat less recognisable?"

"Possibly. I do remember seeing at Doctor Darwin's house one time a small child who – forgive me – might well have been you. This little girl had an air of seriousness, and called the good doctor 'Uncle 'Rasmus', which amused me, as it obviously gave him great pleasure to be so addressed. I made enquiries, and discovered that this little girl was lodging with a widow close by, having lost her mother, and that her father had remarried and now lived in another part of the country."

"Then, sir, you are describing me. And what a memory you must have, to be sure, not just to remember my face, but all those details that you just recited."

"It is my job to remember things," he said, enigmatically, but did not expand on his words. "Will you take a glass of wine with me? It is a lonely business, being the only Englishman in the neighbourhood, and it will do me good to speak English again. You, too, I do not doubt." Seeing her hesitation, he laughed. "My dear young lady, believe me, I have no designs on you, other than to sit here by the fire and listen to you tell me a little about how you come to be here from Switzerland, in company with a man who is to be a professor in Germany."

"And will you tell me something of yourself? How a friend of Uncle 'Rasmus comes to be sitting here in an inn here in Flanders, in a town which seems on first inspection to be totally devoid of interest?"

"Maybe, maybe. But first, some wine? Or have you

developed a taste for beer since your move to Switzerland—how many years ago did you say?"

"I did not say. I said I left England when I was nine years old. You may guess how many years ago that was. And thank you. Wine, if you please."

He poured from a bottle that stood beside him on a table, and handed her the glass. "Your health," he said, raising his own glass.

"And yours," she answered him.

They drank, and he motioned to a chair facing his on the opposite side of the fire. They settled themselves, and Jane started to speak.

"I lived in Zürich with a family from the age of nine, as I said. I need not at this time go into the reasons that caused me to leave England, and I would beg you not to press me on that matter. You must believe me when I say that it was nothing that I had done that caused this move."

She paused, and he spoke, with a question that she had not expected. "Why Switzerland? It seems like a strange choice for one who was forced to leave England at such an age?"

"It was the choice of Doctor Darwin, who asked a friend of his, an artist called Henry Fuseli, to find a place for me."

"Fuseli, eh? The 'Nightmare' man. Interesting."

"Yes, I have seen engravings of his work. They are... disturbing."

"Indeed so. May I know your name?"

"I am called Jane."

"A good, solid English name. Not Jeanne or Juanita or any of those. Pray, continue."

"I grew up in Zürich, learned German and French, the first of which I now speak as fluently – perhaps more fluently now – than English. I received some formal education, and also spent many hours in the library of my foster-father,

Herr Müller, who had some books with subjects that are, shall we say, interesting." She looked to see his reaction, but his face had not changed, and his expression of intense interest did not change. "About a year ago, I attended a lecture by a mesmerist who was to speak on the Rosicrucians. The lecture itself told me nothing that I had not already discovered for myself in my foster-father's library, but the man himself was interesting. At first sight he appeared to be nothing but a common cheat and mesmerist, whose chief conjuring skill would appear to be making coins disappear from the pockets of his victims to reappear in his own."

"He has a name?"

"He has been forced by circumstances to take several names at various times. When I attended his lecture, he went by the name of Hermecritus. Before that, I later discovered, he had performed under the name of Philomentor."

Her interlocutor gave a nod as if he recognised the name. "And his real name?"

"Forgive me if I do not wish to reveal it at this time."

"You intrigue me. More wine?"

"Thank you, but no. In any event, I persuaded this man to leave Zürich, and travel north with me. We finished in Tiengen, where the Landgrave there wished my new friend to create gold for him."

"An alchemist, eh?" He laughed. "And did he create gold? These German princelings must be even more gullible than I had imagined."

"He did much more than that. And I would ask you, sir, not to laugh at things of which I suspect you of knowing nothing."

"I beg your pardon."

"No doubt you think me deranged, or deluded at best, perhaps blinded to the truth of the matter by the feelings I have or had for this man. Let me assure you, sir, that the relations between us were no more than that of a niece for her uncle or an uncle for his niece. Indeed we were friends, but no more than that. As to what my friend achieved there, I am now less than willing to tell you."

His laughing tone vanished from his voice. "Once more, I beg your pardon. I have the impression that you are about to tell me something of importance."

"Very well. I will tell you what occurred in Tiengen." Jane then proceeded to recount a version of the events that had led up to the demise of Ludwig and the Landgrave, to which her companion listened spellbound. She omitted her role in the summoning of the Salamanders, and her subsequent dismissal of Ludwig's killer, but gave all the credit for these to Otto, without, however, giving his true name. She finished her recital with the parting from Otto at Heidelberg.

There was silence for the space of a few minutes when she had finished. At length, he spoke to her. "These 'Elementals', as you call them. From where did he learn about them? And where did you learn, for that matter?"

"They are well-described in books of alchemy and by the Rosicrucians," she answered.

"Clearly you believe in them," he said. "And I can assume that from what you say, if I were to make enquiries of this place – Tiengen, you said – that your story would be confirmed?"

"I believe that the Landgrave Franz whom we left in charge of the town of Tiengen would be happy to confirm the events that I have just described to you."

"More wine? No? Very well. I must tell you that I can draw one of two conclusions. One, that you are completely insane, and that I should waste no time in talking to you further, and that you should be committed to an asylum forthwith. Two, that you are telling the truth, and that any previous beliefs of mine regarding natural philosophy that you have assumed me to hold are no longer to be regarded as valid."

"There is no middle ground?" she enquired, somewhat mischievously. "That I may in fact be deranged, and also that your assumptions about the world may be mistaken?"

"If you were in fact deranged, I do not believe that you would offer this as a possibility, other than if you were extremely cunning and devious. Are you, in fact, extremely cunning and devious?" He smiled, showing that he was not to be taken altogether seriously, and robbing the words of any malice.

She smiled back, but it was not an altogether pleasant smile. "Some would say so."

"I would ask you to prove your assertion that there are Elementals near us, but I imagine that you would find some reason not to do so."

"My main reason would be one of self-interest. Why should I do so? What advantage is there for me if I show you an Elemental, or demonstrate some of their powers myself?" Her eyes widened as she realised that she had just admitted to possessing qualities over the normal.

He pounced. "Aha! So you also have some of these powers? No, do not bother to answer. You do, it is clear from your reaction. Stop shivering girl, I am not about to denounce you as a witch or have you burned or worse for heresy. That is not what I do. You have told me something about yourself – perhaps more than you intended, but no matter. Let me now tell you about myself, and what I may offer you.

"My name is Thomas FitzAlan. I come from a minor titled family, though as a younger son I have no title myself, and unless my elder brother perishes, I will have none. I am currently employed by His Majesty's Government in a somewhat confidential business. Of that, more later, perhaps, if I see fit to do so. However, that business requires me to travel to France, possibly to Paris. It seems that you would like your path to lead that way also. My work would be infinitely easier if I were to travel as a married man."

He paused, and she blushed. "Sir, your proposal, if I am to understand you correctly, is unwelcome and grossly insulting."

"Why? What is it that you assume that I am proposing to you?"

"Why, you are either proposing marriage to a young woman with whom you have been acquainted for less than a single hour. Some to whom such a proposal is made might find this flattering. For my part, I do not. Alternatively, you are proposing the semblance of such a marriage with no obligations on your side, which is a proposal I find even more odious and less to my taste. I therefore," rising, "bid you goodnight, and wish never to speak to you again." She turned towards the door as if to leave, but FitzAlan rose in his turn and held out his hand.

"Miss Machin, wait. Hear me out before you decide whether to leave or not. I should have said that my work will be much easier if I appear as a married man, with my wife beside me. I am not asking you to be my wife. What I would ask is that in public, and in public only, you play the part of my wife. In private, we are two individuals, linked together for mutual protection and that alone. I give you my word on that."

She turned back from the door to face him. "It appears that I may have misunderstood you. Very well. But I will need to know more before I agree to any proposal you may make to me. Perhaps I might have another glass of wine while you inform me."

"Very well." He refilled her glass and handed it to her. "A little more about me. As you know, France is in turmoil. Every day new rumours from Paris reach this place. The King is dead. The King has escaped to England. The King is chained in a dungeon in the Tuileries. Which report is correct? Where in truth is the King? We do not know. We – that is to say, the English – need to know what is happening there. Else, how can the ministers of our King, poor man, train and equip our navy? Will this new France wish to invade England? If so, how can we prepare?"

"And your task is to discover these things?"

He nodded. "As you have no doubt noticed, though my knowledge of the language is good, I cannot pass as a Frenchman. I therefore have to remain as an Englishman, though with sympathies towards the revolutionaries. There are indeed many such in England, our mutual friend Erasmus Darwin and other members of the Lunar Society among them."

"I see."

"Thomas Paine is a well-known sympathiser – you have heard of him? No? William Wordsworth?"

"You forget, sir, that I have been immured in the castle of a minute German state for the past year. Such news as arrived there chiefly concerned the hunting exploits of the other princelings of the area."

"William Wordsworth is a poet of some facility who has written several pieces in praise of the chaos that now obtains in Paris." He half-closed his eyes and declaimed,

"Bliss was it in that dawn to be alive,
But to be young was very heaven!—Oh! times,
In which the meagre, stale, forbidding ways
Of custom, law, and statute, took at once
The attraction of a country in romance!
When Reason seemed the most to assert her rights,
When most intent on making of herself
A prime Enchantress—to assist the work
Which then was going forward in her name!" He opened

his eyes. "Well, what do you make of that? There you have William Wordsworth extolling riots and bloodshed in the name of Reason and freedom. And soon I expect the French to make the acquaintance of Thomas FitzAlan, an enthusiast for the glorious principles of Liberty, and, if you are agreeable, also of his wife, Jane, a fellow enthusiast for their cause. What can I offer you in return? you ask me. In one word, protection. France is not an easy place in which strangers can make their way at any time. In these days, it verges on the foolhardy to make one's home there. However, you should know that I am not without some skills in survival – I will not bore you against your will with my exploits in the war against the American rebels – and it may be that you will welcome my protection at some future date."

"It is possible," she said, guardedly.

"I am not as sceptical of the matters to which you alluded earlier as you might think," he added. "I witnessed some strange events in America when I spent some time among the natives there. Things which could not easily be explained by Darwin and his philosophers. It may well be that you and your Elementals might prove to be my protection on occasion."

"Then you believe me?"

"Of course."

"You are not just humouring me?"

"By no means. I am known to dissemble on occasion, but this is not one of those times."

She looked at him closely. "So you have knowledge of Them?" she said.

"Them? Oh, you mean your Elementals?"

"Yes. Them and their masters. They live on the other side of the sky."

"The other side of the sky." He seemed to be rolling the phrase around in his mouth, savouring its taste. "I've never heard that phrase before. It makes no sense at all, and yet I know exactly what you mean by it. I think that my American Indian friends would understand that immediately." He smiled. "I think we will make good fellow-travellers."

FITZALAN (Jane had yet to think of him as Thomas, let alone Tom) indeed proved to be an enjoyable companion with whom to share the road to Paris. He was possessed of a fine tenor voice, and treated Jane and the surrounding country-side to a selection of airs from the popular operas of the day. He was still singing as they passed through a village on one occasion, and a few small coins were pressed upon him as the villagers thronged about his horse to listen.

He smilingly accepted them, but Jane was pleased to see that they went into the outstretched hand of a vagabond beggar a few miles down the road.

When he was not singing, he was clearly relishing the company of someone to whom he could relate his stories of America and the rebels there. At one point, Jane asked him if he had ever met Benjamin Franklin.

"Indeed I did, on more than one occasion, and I have to say that there are few men who have impressed me as much as he. Perhaps Erasmus Darwin, if he had been a statesman, might have matched him in scientific, philosophical and lit-erary ability, but other than that, I would venture that Ben Franklin is perhaps the greatest man ever to have walked this earth. Did you ever meet him when he visited Lichfield?"

"I was little more than a babe when I was introduced to him. I have faint memories of him – mainly of his smell, which was not unpleasant, but was somewhat strange to me."

FitzAlan laughed. "It is strange what children remember of the past, is it not?"

When they stopped at an inn for the night, FitzAlan invariably requested one room with but one bed in it for both of them, as befitted the fiction that he and Jane were a married couple. The first time he did that, Jane looked at him in horror.

"You said that we were not going to share a bed, and all that implies," she said. "You give me no choice but to leave you, since I now see that you are not a man of your word."

He held up his hand, palm facing her. "Wait," he told her. "You will occupy this room alone. No one else will enter unless you specifically wish them to do so."

"You?"

"I will stay downstairs in the taproom, drinking, or at least making a pretence of drinking, until I fall insensible in the corner. Or maybe I will sleep in the stable with the horses to guard them. In any event, our landlord will not think it strange that I am not sleeping in the same room as you."

Her face cleared. "I beg your pardon," she said. "It seems that I misjudged you."

"No offence taken," he smiled. "I do trust, however, that I will have the pleasure of your company at dinner tonight."

"Of course, Milord FitzAlan," she smiled.

"Oh, if only I was a Milord," he sighed as they ate roast pork with turnips. "Sometimes I think it would be a pleasant life to sit in Shawborough Hall, with servants around me to fulfil my every wish, and have nothing to worry about other than the vintage of the claret to accompany my dinners. And then again, if I were my elder brother, Sir George FitzAlan, who inherited the baronetcy, I would never have gone to America, met the Indians there, and seen sights which would take your breath away. I have seen the great waterfalls at Niagara when

I accompanied Colonel Davies on his expedition there, and he made paintings of them. They are—" he paused, clearly lost for words. "They are beyond description – vast, powerful, and fill one with a delicious sense of terror and awe."

She perceived another side to this man – a man who was more than a mere soldier. "You sound as though you might be an admirer of M. Rousseau," she said.

"Ah, that dreamer," he laughed. "I met him when he was staying with Sir Brooke Boothby at Ashbourne. Pleasant enough, but hopelessly self-indulgent in his emotions, like Sir Brooke himself. But one does not need to be an admirer of his to appreciate what is wonderful in nature. I quoted William Wordsworth to you once, did I not? Well, he and his fellow poets are finding 'tongues in trees, books in the running brooks, sermons in stones, and good in everything'. It is the fashion now, you see."

"And you are a follower of that fashion?"

"Hardly. One does not need to follow any fashion to be impressed beyond the power of speech by Niagara, or indeed, by the immense unspoiled beauty of the American continent."

"Tell me more," Jane begged him.

"With pleasure." And for that evening, and for the remaining evenings on the road to Paris, FitzAlan regaled her with tales and descriptions of America and its natives, for whom he held a particular regard.

"For the most part, they are not Christians, as you probably know," he told her. "But when they are not at war with themselves or the invading Europeans – war which they conduct with a brutal savagery – they comport themselves with an almost Christian set of virtues towards each other. More so," he sighed, "than many of the European Americans there. The ideas of these last with regard to 'liberty' sometimes seem to me to be a freedom to do whatever they wish, with few regards to the comfort, or even the safety of their fellow human beings, among whom I naturally include the poor African wretches brought over as slaves to increase the wealth of a few. Another of their supposed freedoms from government naturally includes the idea that taxation should be almost abolished. Now," wagging a finger at her, "no sensible man likes to pay more tax than he deems necessary. But taken to extremes," and here he shrugged, "a government starved of money has no power to defend itself, or to increase the happiness and welfare of its citizens. Should another war with England ever come about, it is my opinion that the Americans would suffer a crushing defeat, despite their innate belligerence, and in any event, the poor in America will find themselves neglected even more than is the case in England, which God knows is bad enough."

"You sound like a Revolutionary yourself."

"In my heart, perhaps I am," he admitted. "But I do not feel it right to use the violence that some advocate and, that I fear, is being committed in France at the moment."

"If you were indeed installed as master of Shawborough Hall, I am sure your tenants would have little to complain of," she told him.

"You flatter me, Mrs FitzAlan," he told her. Over the past few days he had taken to addressing her in this way, partly, as he explained, to accustom her to respond to that name, and partly, it appeared, as some sort of antic humour on his part. At first Jane had resented this, but it appeared that this was not meant with any hidden or sinister intent, and she had learned to accept it with a smile.

As THEY LODGED IN THE INN before the next day's journey

which would take them into Paris, FitzAlan did not tell his usual stories of wild forest landscapes and Indians, but turned to Jane with a serious look on his face.

"Miss Machin," he said to her, and she knew that his usual half-jesting attitude had disappeared. "I asked you to pose as my wife as we travel to Paris and stay there. This is still something that I would ask of you, but there is one more thing I would ask. Not for me, you understand, but for England." Jane nodded in response, but uncomprehendingly. "There is an English lady staying in Paris at the moment. Her name is Mary Wollstonecraft – have you heard of her? No? She is a rather remarkable person in her way. If she were a man, she would probably be regarded as one of those philosophers in the forefront of the fight for liberty, along with your friend Darwin and his circle. As it is, she seems to think that women are the equal of men."

"And you believe that they are not?" Jane responded hotly.

"I do not," he answered, smiling broadly.

"This is no laughing matter," Jane responded. "How can you say such a thing and smile?"

"Wait," he said. The smile had not yet disappeared from his face. "I did not say that women are inferior. I said that they were not the equal of men. I believe them to be superior in many respects – the fact that most lack the physical strength of men is but a trifle."

"And in what respects, pray, do you believe women to be superior?"

His expression and tone of voice changed to seriousness. "Why, in their power of feeling and sympathy, in their ability to love, in their ability to withstand pain – have you ever witnessed childbirth? I have, in an Indian village, and what that poor woman suffered I would not have believed it possible for any human being to endure. There are so many aspects in which women are superior to men, and many others in which they are at least equal to them. There have been talented woman mathematicians, for example, who give the lie to the ridiculous notion that women are incapable of rational thought. Some women, true, lack this capacity, but then so do many men. There are excellently talented female artists, for example, Élisabeth Vigée Le Brun, who painted at the court of the French king. Her portraits, particularly of women and children, lack the sickly sentimentality of a Greuze, and reveal the true character of the sitter." He paused for breath. "Am I forgiven?" The smile returned.

"You are forgiven, Milord." Jane returned his smile.

"Very well, then. It is believed by some that this Miss Wollstonecraft has to Paris in search of true love."

"Oh?"

"With your friend, or rather, Doctor Darwin's friend, Henry Fuseli."

"Oh? I had heard he was married. Has his wife died?"

"No, he is still married, but according to the gossip, this is not the sort of thing that worries Miss Mary Wollstonecraft unduly. I mentioned that I considered her a leading exponent of the idea of liberty. She is some sort of philosopher, to whom the constraints of society have little appeal. She has written several books, well-written, I might add, such as 'A Vindication of the Rights of Women'."

"I think I might find myself somewhat in agreement with Miss Wollstonecraft," Jane said thoughtfully. "Though not, I feel, in the matter of Mr Fuseli."

"I thought you might enjoy her company and her ideas," FitzAlan replied. "Which is why I want you to make friends with her, as one English expatriate to another."

"Why do you wish me to do this?"

"Because it is not so much I who wish it as the government

of the day. You and I may be in sympathy with many of her views. However, she appears to hold the Girondins in high regard. Though they are not the most extreme faction of the Revolution – we may reserve that honour for the Mountain – their ideas, if imported and promoted within England, could cause chaos."

"And the loss of Shawborough Hall?" she teased.

"Almost certainly that would occur, though if I am honest, it would be no great loss. But the lack of order is a state that would set a country back to a level of near barbarism. And if Miss Wollstonecraft is thinking of writing something that will extol the virtues of the revolution here, there are those in England who will ignore it, but a significant number who will see it as a call to action, a call to arms. And that must not happen." There was no hint of humour now.

"And if I do find out that she is planning to publicise her ideas? What then?"

"That, happily, is not my decision. I must get word to London, and then they will decide."

"Will harm come to her?"

"I can give you my word of honour that I do not know the answer to that. However, in the event that I am forced to make some sort of report, I will endeavour to frame it such a way that the least possible harm comes to Miss Wollstonecraft. I would not like to think that she will be expunged from history."

THEY ENTERED PARIS, and were able to rent rooms in a house in the Faubourg Sainte-Antoine, close to the site of the Bastille, which had been attacked for the gunpowder stored there, and its seven prisoners freed, on the fourteenth day of July in 1789, and had subsequently been demolished.

FitzAlan quickly established that the better of the two rooms designated as bedrooms should be Jane's, and hers alone, and that he was not to enter it unless given her explicit permission. She found herself to be more and more attracted to him as a trusted friend as time went on. From time to time his occasionally perverse sense of humour grated on her, but on the whole, she preferred being with him to being alone.

As FitzAlan had promised, Jane was taken to meet Mary Wollstonecraft. She felt handicapped by not having been able to finish Miss Wollstonecraft's writings, but Thomas had been able to provide her with a summary of the lady's thought, and she was able to at least understand the gist of the discourse. She was thankful, however, that her paramour, the American Gilbert Imlay, was not present.

"They are not married," FitzAlan had explained to her, "but he claims to the Revolutionary government that she is his wife, and is therefore an American citizen, and is therefore no threat to them. I trust that this arrangement does not disturb you too much?"

"Hardly," Jane replied. "I am anxious to discover what sort of person she is." Nonetheless, Jane would have found it difficult to know how to behave towards a man who was neither husband, nor the true love (if FitzAlan's reports regarding Fuseli were to be believed) of her hostess.

Even so, she was intrigued by her conversation with the female philosopher, and she reported back to FitzAlan that she stood in a fair way to becoming her friend. However, as events turned out, she was never to see Mary Wollstonecraft again, a circumstance that was to be a lifelong cause for regret.

A little over a week since their arrival in Paris, and two days after her meeting with Miss Wollstonecraft, she was thankful for FitzAlan's presence in her life. Without quite understanding how she had reached that state, having taken herself to bed early, she found herself standing in her nightgown, barefoot on the cold uncarpeted floor, screaming loudly. She had no idea of the hour, but guessed that it

Her screaming was stopped by a knocking at the door of her room, and FitzAlan's voice.

"Miss Machin, what is wrong?"

"A... a dream," she sobbed, for by this time she was starting to weep uncontrollably.

"May I bring you something? Some brandy and water, perhaps?" he asked.

"If you would be so kind," she said. She suddenly realised that she was cold, and took herself to her bed. As she got under the sheets once more, she felt a shiver of revulsion, and the horror of the dream came back to her in all its hideousness.

There was another knock on the door. "Miss Machin, I have your brandy and water."

No, she could not get out of bed to meet him. She had serious doubts as to whether her legs would support her again. "Please come in," she called, a tremor in her voice.

"You are sure?" he asked.

"Please." There was a note of pleading in her voice.

He entered, bearing a glass in one hand, and a candlestick with a lighted candle in the other. He placed the candle on the small table beside the bed, and handed the glass to her. "Shall I go now?" he asked.

"No, please stay a while, if you would be so kind."

He sat on a chair on the other side of the room.

"No, please sit on the side of the bed. I have the need to see a human face."

He crossed the room and sat down. He was wearing a wrapper of some kind over a nightgown, out of the bottom of which his bare legs poked. His face seemed to display some concern, but he appeared to be in no hurry to speak.

She sipped at the brandy and water and coughed.

"Too strong?" he asked. "I can add more water if you require."

"No, no, this is fine," she answered him, and sipped again.

He sat still, seemingly waiting for her to speak.

"I'm sorry to disturb you," she said at length. He remained silent. "I had a dream," she told him. "A nightmare, like one of Fuseli's paintings. I thought I had escaped the visits from Them – the ones on the other side of the sky. He was there – the one who calls himself my father." She was aware that her breathing was becoming fast and shallow, and she sipped again.

"Go on," he said, and was silent, waiting like one of the American Indians he had told her about who seemed able to freeze motionless for hours, waiting for their quarry. Only in this case his quarry was her words.

"He is— king, perhaps, of Them."

"The Elementals that you have mentioned?"

"Yes, and more than them. These are—" she stopped, not sure of how to describe what she felt.

"Demons?"

"No." Her voice was definite. "They are not evil, in the sense that the Church would describe demons. They do not automatically wish harm to come to human beings and they do not automatically seek evil over good. But they are totally selfish, totally without regard for humanity, and for each other as individuals. Insofar as they recognise the one – my 'father' – as king or leader, it is out of fear of him, not love or respect as we would understand it."

"Faeries?" he asked.

"As good a term as any," she said. "The Good Folk, yes." She paused. "You are not laughing."

"I do not laugh at these things. I believe you, but even if I did not, I would not laugh at you. That would be an act of considerable discourtesy."

"Thank you. They are here, in Paris. The chaos here suits them. They sense human beings like themselves – amoral, ambitious, without scruples. They can use these people for their own purposes. He wants me to join Them. To act for Them against human beings who would foil their plans. You are one of those He wishes me to act against."

"Thank you for the warning."

There was no answer. Her eyelids drooped, and she was having to concentrate to keep them open. "Thank you," she repeated, holding out the glass.

He rose, and took it from her. Their fingers touched, and on an impulse she reached out and put her hand around his. He simply stood there for a few minutes, silently watching as her eyelids closed, and her hand fell away from his. He carefully picked up the candlestick and took it and the glass to the door. As he opened it, a faint voice came from the bed. "Thank you – Thomas," she said.

AFTER HE HAD GONE, she lay half-awake despite her fatigue, reflecting on the events that had just taken place. She was very conscious of the fact that she had not told FitzAlan the whole truth. While on the previous nights since they had moved to Paris, she had suffered from frightening dreams, which were almost hypnotic in their intensity, the visit she had just experienced was no dream.

She had known, with absolute certainty, that her visitor that night was no phantom illusion or a dream, but the being who called himself her father. The tone of his words as He had spoken to her was hideously unmistakeable, even after all the years that He had been absent from her life.

"You must help us here," He had hissed at her. "The city is in ferment – we may rule this place through some of those who seek power here. But there are those who would be against us. The one with whom you travel is one of those, and we wish you to ensure that he does not hinder our plans."

"How should I accomplish that? What should I do?" she had asked.

"That, daughter of mine, is something that you must decide for yourself."

The only thing she could think of was that she should kill FitzAlan, and as soon as the thought had formed itself in her brain, his words had come hissing back at her.

"Of course, you do not have to do it yourself, if you are so delicately minded. You might denounce him to the authorities as an English spy. You would only be telling the truth, after all. Or, if you prefer, you might wish to accuse him of an assault on your person, and let the courts here, such as they are, decide on his punishment."

"And if I do?" she had asked. "What do I gain from this?"

"You will take your place by my side," He said. "Indeed, you will rule over this city in my place. And when your time comes, you will take my place on the other side of the sky. Power beyond what you can imagine will be yours."

She had found herself unable to speak as her mind wrestled with what had just been put to her. At length she had stuttered, "And if I do not?"

"Expect visits from me every night until you do." And with that, a sudden pain had exploded within her head, a pain that went beyond anything she had ever experienced in her life, surpassing even the pain of her monthly cramps which had at times left her almost unable to move for hours at a stretch.

"Leave me!" she had shrieked, and instantly the pain had left her, with a sound of hollow mocking laughter ringing in her ears. It was at that point that she had discovered herself standing in the middle of the floor, shivering and screaming, at which point FitzAlan had knocked on the door to ascertain what had befallen her.

How was she to defend herself against His attacks? The easiest way would be to accede to His commands. It was tempting, if only to avoid the agonising pain. But to do so would deliver thousands of men and women into the hands of Them. And as she had said to FitzAlan, though They were not evil in the traditional sense, Their egotism and selfishness meant that the inhabitants of Paris, and by extension, those of France, would suffer.

It was possible, she considered, that her power over some of the Elementals would save her from the worst that He could do. She remembered the fact that the Salamander which had killed Ludwig had addressed her as "Mistress", and requested her permission to leave. Could she, perhaps, guard against attacks by Him by enlisting a bodyguard of Elementals?

When she had summoned the Salamander, she had been playing music on the armonica, an instrument which was now with Otto in Heidelberg. She doubted if there was another such in the whole of France. Would her flute, which she had kept carefully packed in her baggage, although unplayed for months, serve as a substitute, she wondered?

She rummaged in her bag, and withdrew the instrument. Concentrating on the thought of a Sylph, or air Elemental, she started to play, softly, for fear of drawing FitzAlan's attention.

As she played, the air in front of her seemed to solidify in the shape of a man, taller by at least a head than her, and naked, other than for a wisp of what might have been cloth strategically placed over his midriff. His skin was a shade of blue, slightly lighter than a summer sky, and his teeth gleamed disturbingly white as he drew back his lips and spoke to her.

"You summoned me, Mistress," he said, and bowed. "What would you have of me?"

"Protection," she answered simply.

"From what or from whom?" he asked.

"From my father," she answered, trusting that he knew who she was, and her relationship to Him.

"Ah," he said. "I cannot do that."

"Why? Has he been a good master to you?"

He shook his head sadly. "No, not that. I did not say that I would not do it. I said that I cannot do it. He is too strong. I cannot protect you. In any case, what would I gain if I were to protect you?"

"Your freedom."

"Ah." He appeared to think. "For me and my friends, if they agree to work to protect you as well?"

"Yes," she said without further reflection.

"I will go and ask them," he said. "May I have your permission to leave?"

She nodded, and he was gone.

THE NEXT MORNING when she awoke, FitzAlan was nowhere to be seen. The French girl who had been engaged as their maid and general servant informed Jane that "Citizen Fitz", as she called him, had gone out early without saying where he was going or when he would return.

Jane ate her breakfast of dry bread soaked in her bitter coffee thoughtfully. It seemed clear that she had some influence and power over the Sylphs, and possibly over the Salamanders, if her experiences in Tiengen were anything to go by. She knew that FitzAlan had not laughed at her when she had mentioned her fears, and it was quite likely that he would attempt to be of some assistance to her should he feel it to be necessary.

But at the same time, despite his obvious good will and what he claimed to have experienced in his time in America, she could not, with the best will in the world, believe that he was able to hold his own against the masters of the Elementals. She needed more reinforcements.

She finished her breakfast, and retired to her room. The maid, Annette, had told her that the *sans-culottes*, the popular group supporting the radical Jacobin faction in the Assembly, were out on the streets. "It is no place for a young lady to be there," she had said to Jane. "As for me," she shrugged, "I can easily pass for one of them". Time dragged slowly as Jane read through one of the books that she had taken from the castle at Tiengen, seeking inspiration in its accounts of interactions with Undines, Sylphs, Gnomes, and Salamanders. From outside in the street there came the sound of shouting and what sounded like scuffling and the breaking of glass, but Jane felt no need to go to the window and observe what might be happening.

At a time she guessed was about midday, she heard the sound of the front door opening, and heavy footsteps, possibly a man's, making their way upstairs. She had no idea who was there. Maybe FitzAlan, maybe not. The little dagger which she always kept up her sleeve slipped into her hand as she faced the door of her room, ready for whatever might come through it. To her relief, the footsteps did not go to her door, but she heard the sound of the door to FitzAlan's room opening and closing, and then a heavy thump as if something had fallen to the floor. There was silence as she waited for further sounds, but there was nothing.

She cautiously opened her door, and went over to FitzAlan's door, where she knocked loudly.

"Are you there – Thomas?" she asked. "What is happening?"

There was no answer, and she tried the door handle. The door was locked, clearly from the inside.

Now she was worried. Whether it was FitzAlan in trouble, or whether it was some enemy who might be going through FitzAlan's papers – perhaps one of the agents of the Committee of Public Safety, seeking evidence of his spying, Jane knew that she had to enter the room.

Gripping her dagger firmly in her right hand, Jane pushed her way through the locked door, experiencing a strangely familiar feeling of icy swords as she walked through the wood.

On the floor in front of her, she saw FitzAlan lying face-down on the floor, with a small pool of blood forming near his head. She replaced her dagger to its hiding-place, bent down to turn him over, and was relieved to see that he was still breathing. A nasty gash near his eye seemed to be the source of the blood, and she stopped it with her hand-kerchief. There was still some water in the jug on the washstand, and she brought the jug and slop-basin over to him, and gently cleaned his wound. As she was wondering how to move him onto the bed, he stirred a little and half-opened his eyes.

"Miss Machin, how—?" His hand fluttered and gestured weakly towards the locked door.

She did not answer, but simply allowed her face to fall into a faint smile. "What happened?" she asked.

"I was taken for an aristo – one of the aristocracy. They threw stones at me and then chased me through the alleyways and the back streets. Luckily, none of them seemed able to throw with any skill – or rather, only one of them managed to actually hit me, here." He pointed to his forehead. "And I found it easy to outrun them. Because I don't speak with the accents of a Parisian, they assume I am from the provinces, and they then assume that because I am from the provinces, I must be one of the federalists or Girondins. I suppose I was lucky not to be recognised as an Englishman," he said. "Those damned Hébertist *sans-culottes*. Ignorant peasants. Throwing stones at their betters. They have no idea of what is going on or where they are driving themselves. Gadarene swine, rushing towards the cliff of anarchy. And then they will suffer. We will all suffer. Why do Robespierre and Saint-Just and the rest of them tolerate this rule by the mob?"

This was all on the outskirts of comprehensibility to Jane, as he ranted on about the various factions of the Revolution, most of which was completely unknown to her.

"It is not even as if this crowd of illiterate fools were being led by true representatives of the people," he complained as he attempted to rise, Jane supporting him as he did so. "Failed lawyers, Grub Street hacks, would-be philosophers, for the most part. Too idle or incompetent to be true representatives of the people. More ambition than brains," he groaned, sinking onto the bed.

"Don't think about it," Jane advised him. "It's only upsetting you and will make your headache worse. Now, what can I get you?"

"There's some brandy over there," he said. "Don't bother with a glass. Just pass me the bottle."

He drank a few sips from the bottle, and coughed. "That hurts," he complained, wincing, but there was a grim smile on his face. "Just put a little of the brandy on that cloth of yours and clean out any dirt that's still there from the wound, would you?"

"It will sting," she warned him.

"I know that, damn you, woman!" he almost shouted impatiently, and then appeared to think better of what he had just said. "I do beg your pardon, my dear Miss Machin," he said in a much quieter tone. "I promise to behave myself."

Indeed, when his wound came in contact with the spirit he started, but did not cry out as she gently dabbed the wound, which was bloody but shallow.

"There you are," she said at length, dabbing at the lesion with a clean cloth. "Do you want me to bandage it?"

"No, thank you. I shall wear my bloody wound as a badge of honour. Maybe it will be a testament to my true *sans-culottisme*." He laughed. "Ouch, that hurts." He paused a while, looking curiously at the door, the key of which still stood in the keyhole. "How did you…? I mean, I don't understand."

She waited a little before replying, deciding to see how he would react to the truth. "I walked through it," she said, simply.

To her surprise, her words seemed to have little or no effect on him. "I see," he said at length. "From the little you have told me, I assume that you have other powers? No, do not bother to tell me now. I must sleep now. Perhaps they will prove their value later on." He closed his eyes, and his breathing slowed and became regular. Jane perched herself on a chair where she could watch him.

After a few minutes, she rose, and without removing the key from the lock or opening the door, walked through it in the same way that she had entered.

As the cold sharp tingling left her body, she heard a laugh from the room on the other side of the door.

"I saw you, Miss Machin," came FitzAlan's slightly

213

mocking voice. "I confess to being mightily impressed. Now I really will try to sleep. Please wake me at about five this evening. Don't bother to knock. Just walk straight in." There was a chuckle, and then silence.

IN THE EVENING, FitzAlan seemed to be almost recovered from the incident earlier in the day. He joined Jane at dinner that evening and joked with her as if nothing had occurred.

After the plates had been cleared, and Annette had retired, his mood seemed to change. He leaned forward across the table and spoke in a low, urgent voice.

"Tell me more about your father. Who He is, what you feel when He is near. Everything." It was not a request, it was an order.

"Why should I do that?" she asked.

"Because I wish it," he said, with a smile that owed nothing to humour.

"And if I decide not to grant your wish?"

He spread his hands out, palms upward, in a gesture of helplessness. "I feel that it is best for you if I do not tell you." There was a chill in his voice as he said these words, which communicated itself to her spine. Suddenly Jane felt that she was in the presence of authority. From where that authority derived, she was unsure, but Jane now felt that she had no choice but to obey him.

"I hardly feel that I know Him," she confessed, "but my experiences with Him have never been happy ones." She told FitzAlan of the time at Streethay where Kate Perkins had met Him, of the time that she had first discovered her ability to pass through walls at Matthew Bolton's house at Soho, and when she had been abducted as a child and taken to his "palace" which was no more than a muddy hole in the ground. She then proceeded to inform FitzAlan of the details of the previous night that she had omitted to tell him earlier.

"You are telling me that this being, demon or Faerie or whatever He may be, is seeking to use the Revolution here for his own purposes, or rather those of his species. Hmm." He sat, cupping his chin in his hands, and appeared to be lost in thought. "It would seem to be of a piece with what we know."

"We?" she asked, pouncing on the pronoun.

"Yes, there are several of us working together with— no, I will not name him, but he stands high in the opinion of the government under Mr Pitt as well as leading a group devoted to the study of matters which might otherwise be overlooked by those such as our mutual friend Doctor Darwin."

"You are Freemasons? Rosicrucians?" she asked.

"We do not use those names, but yes, it is true to say that many of our beliefs and practices have their roots in those organisations. We had come to the belief was that there were intelligences other than those of mankind, which can and do influence us. The tales of Faeries and their like can be found all over the world, it seems. Certainly, though there are differences, my Indian friends in America described many such instances. We found it hard to believe that such a people as the French, who, despite their several faults, are creatures of reason and logic, could descend into the madness that now envelops them without some encouragement from outside. Since we were unable to discover any human influence…" His voice tailed off.

"…you concluded that there was someone or something from outside." Jane finished the sentence for him.

"Those from the other side of the sky, to use your phrase, yes. I suppose the churches might call them demons, but they hardly fit the classical description of those beings, from what you say."

"So what does that make me?" Jane asked. "Half-Other as I seem to be."

FitzAlan put his head on one side and smiled. "You appear to be on our side, at present, at least."

"You believe I might change sides, and betray humanity?" Jane flashed. "You do not trust me?"

"My dear Miss Machin, I trust you as much as I trust anyone, including myself." He paused and flashed a mirthless smile. "Which is, in the business I now find myself, not at all."

"Earlier you talked about this Mary Wollstonecraft," Jane reminded him. "Is that all now to be forgotten?"

"By no means," he answered. "There are wheels within wheels, or covers covering covers would be a better analogy. To our French friends, we are a man and his wife in sympathy with the principles of this damnable Revolution. To the vast majority of the British government, I, and by extension you, are working to discover the true sympathies of British subjects, including Miss Mary Wollstonecraft, who are currently resident in France. To a select few, whom I shall not name, we are looking for something much deeper and more fundamental than political squabbles between human beings."

Jane sat digesting this for a few minutes. "I take it that it was no accident that we happened to be staying at the same inn in Hasselt?"

"Ah, well done. No, of course it was no accident. Your exploits, and those of your friend at Tiengen were more widely reported than you might imagine. It was clear to us that a Salamander had been summoned. A few enquiries about your friend Philomentor or Hermecritus, or Otto—" Jane started. "Yes, of course we know his name – as I was saying, a few enquiries into his past told us that although he had some skills in the arcane arts, we did not believe it was he who had summoned the Elemental. It must therefore have been his mysterious assistant, and it was, you may be surprised to know, relatively simple for us to determine your whereabouts as you made your way from Tiengen."

"I was not attempting to keep my movements secret," Jane told him.

"Thank you for that. It made our task much easier. The question now is how I can protect you best."

"Why do you want to protect me? Do you not trust me to take care of myself?"

"To answer your last question first, no, I do not. You have powers, I am sure, but you are unused to using them. The Others living on the other side of the sky set against us will have practice and competence in their use, even if their raw power is less."

"I see. And the answer to the first question?"

"Properly trained and experienced, you are our best weapon against Them." He paused, and smiled at her. "And there is another reason."

"Yes?"

"I have become very fond of your company – please do not take this amiss – I mean no harm by these words. I would indeed be sorry to be deprived of it."

"Thank you. It is most kind of you to say this. For myself, I find myself to be hardly averse to your company, and I am most grateful to you for your offer of protection. But since we are speaking freely to one another…"

"Yes?"

"Please do not doubt my loyalty in the matter of this conflict. Pray remember that it is not by my choice that I am— whatever it is that I am, and that I possess powers outside the ordinary. My experiences with Them have not been pleasant, and give me no reason to have more to do with Them than is absolutely necessary. Indeed, I find that more and more I am motivated by a reason which some might consider to be wrong. That is to say, revenge."

"Revenge?"

"Yes. Revenge on Them for making me what I am. For killing my mother. For sending me away from a family I loved to a strange land. And for forcing me, almost against my will, to lead the life of a friendless wanderer." Despite her strivings, Jane's tears began to flow, and she sat, sobbing silently to herself.

After a minute or so, she felt the pressure of an arm around her shoulders. She knew it to be FitzAlan's, and still sobbing, she moved her hand to meet his and closed her fingers around it. So they remained for several minutes more, until she ceased her silent weeping and withdrew her hand from his.

"Thank you, Thomas," she half-whispered. "You are kinder to me than I deserve."

DESPITE THE THREATS that had been made earlier, her sleep that night was not disturbed. She was puzzled about this until she awoke in the morning, and noticed several heads of garlic in various parts of the room, each with a silver cross embedded in it. Around her bed, chalked on the bare floorboards, were several strange characters which she recognised as Hebrew letters, though she had no idea of their meaning or significance. It was clear that on the previous night when she had made herself ready for bed, the faint candlelight had been insufficient to illuminate these marks or the garlic.

She had a memory of FitzAlan slipping out of the room for

a few minutes the previous evening following their conversation, and noises coming from upstairs, but she had assumed that he had temporarily left the room for the usual reason following a few glasses of wine. Clearly this was the sort of thing he had in mind when he had talked about protection. And when she came to consider it, she had thought she had smelled garlic as she undressed for bed. At the time she had put it down to imagination, or perhaps even to an after-taste of the chicken that they had eaten that evening. Clearly the source of the smell was immediate, and real.

It was obvious that FitzAlan was much more than he seemed – his true self was not the soldier from the American wars or the dilettante aristocrat that he occasionally seemed to be, but here was proof before her very eyes that he had a deep knowledge of the esoteric arts, or at least had contacts with those who did.

Thoughtfully she dressed, and made her way downstairs, where FitzAlan was already sitting over bread and coffee.

"Did you sleep well?" he asked with a slight smile, his eyebrows raised.

She smiled in return. "Yes, thanks to you, I wasn't disturbed."

"Thanks to me?" he asked with an air of incredulity, his eyebrows raised impossibly even higher.

"I am sure it was not Annette who placed the garlic in my room."

"Why not?"

"Have you any suspicion that she can read and write Hebrew? And has knowledge of the Sephirod that comprise the Tree of Life?"

"No," he admitted. "And what do you know of the Sephirod? Was this one of your travelling mesmerist's little tricks?"

"No, this was something that I discovered for myself in the library in Tiengen."

"And what do you make of it all?"

"Very little, I'm afraid. Robertus de Fluctibus' Latin is…"

"I think the word you are looking for is 'eccentric'. And yes, Robert Fludd's thoughts are muddled. Many have been led astray by persuading themselves that they have understood his work."

"So it is all nonsense?" Jane poured herself a bowl of coffee, and dipped a crust of bread into it.

FitzAlan shook his head. "That is a very harsh judgement, my dear Miss Machin. It does seem that he had some sort of idea of how certain of the Sephirod might be applied to the Elementals."

"How is all this connected?" Jane shook her head. "I can understand the garlic, since there were many peasants and even educated men and women in Germany who believed in it as a charm."

"None in Lichfield?" smiled FitzAlan.

"We knew very little of garlic when I was there, and I doubt very much if anything has changed in that regard. The silver and the cross, yes, in Zürich there were some who believed that. But this Hebrew…? How come you to know of it?"

"There are those who are more versed in these esoteric arts than I," FitzAlan explained. "For myself, I am unable to read or understand these things, but I am at least able to copy them."

"And these others? Are they philosophers?"

FitzAlan laughed. "Not in the sense that the world terms our friend Erasmus Darwin or his friend Joseph Priestley as philosophers, no. But yes, they are lovers of wisdom, which is what the Greek term denotes by the word."

"And they are in London?"

"In England, yes. And they have links with others in London, Zürich—" Jane started. "Oh yes, indeed. Geneva,

Florence, Rome, Leipzig, Uppsala, Edinburgh…" He paused. "Even some in Paris."

"Can I meet them? I wish to know more about the other side of the sky, and these are the first people I have met who may be able to tell me?"

"This is not the best time, but yes, I can manage this. You must meet Mary Wollstonecraft once more and I can arrange for one of these men to be there too. Allow me a few days to make the preparations."

ONLY TWO DAYS LATER FitzAlan invited Jane to accompany him once more to the house where Mary Wollstonecraft was staying.

She was anxious to see more of Paris. Since their arrival, she had hardly been outside, other than for her previous visit. She had no real idea what to expect in the city, other than what Annette had told her, and what she had observed of FitzAlan the other day. She made sure her little dagger was safely tucked into her sleeve as they set out.

FitzAlan watched approvingly. He had tucked a brace of pistols into his pockets. "Never hurts to assume the worst," he said curtly.

As they stepped out of the door, Jane became aware of a change in FitzAlan's manner. No longer the almost languid urbane gentleman, his whole attitude and manner changed to that of a man in a forest, anticipating an attack by wild beasts that could come at any minute. She wondered from where this sudden wariness had been learned, remembered his stories of American wars, and wondered no more.

"Stay close," he warned her, but his advice was unnecessary. Jane was following him, a step or two behind him, and a little to one side, to allow his right arm free play to draw a pistol or a knife should it become necessary.

As they turned the corner at the end of the street, Jane saw a group of men, meanly dressed, wearing the cap of liberty, adorned with the tricolour rosette. Although FitzAlan had told her to dress in an unostentatious fashion, even so it was clear that she was of a different class to the *sans-culottes*, who started moving menacingly towards her and FitzAlan.

A few paces away from them, one who seemed to be the leader of the group, carrying a pike, stopped, spat on the cobbles, and uttered a foul oath as he demanded to know who they were, where they had come from, and where they were going. "On the orders of the Committee of Public Safety," he added.

"From there," FitzAlan told him, jerking his head backwards, "and we're going there," drawing his hand, now holding a pistol, from under his coat, and pointing it at the man. "As to who we are, that is none of your business, Citizen," he said in his accented French.

"We know who you are and where you're going, anyway. So you're a foreigner, then, and no true patriot? Come on, lads, this looks like two for the republican razor."

The gang moved forward. Jane could see that two of them had drawn wicked-looking knives, and she let her own dagger fall into her hand, while keeping it out of sight.

"I advise you to keep your distance, Citizens." FitzAlan spoke with a hardness in his voice that was new to Jane.

"'Advise', you say?" The leader levelled his pike so that the point was pointing directly at FitzAlan's throat. "Let me advise you, Monsieur Rosbif, that this little toothpick can go through you faster than you can blink." The pike moved menacingly forward, and the point stopped a matter of inches from FitzAlan's Adam's apple.

There was an explosion and a puff of smoke as FitzAlan fired his pistol. The ball hit the pike-bearer in the shoulder, and he dropped his weapon with an anguished cry.

"Oh, you've done it now, monsieur," he growled. "I will stand by the guillotine and drink your blood when your aristo head is taken off those shoulders of yours. Seize them both!" he ordered his companions.

FitzAlan was unable to prevail against the simultaneous onslaught by four ruffians, though he laid one out unconscious on the ground with a mighty punch to the jaw, and Jane managed to nick the wrist of one with her small dagger, forcing him to drop his knife and howl in agony.

At the end of the struggle, FitzAlan was writhing in the grip of the two uninjured ruffians, and Jane stood, glaring at the leader, who was advancing towards her, one hand covering the bleeding wound in his shoulder.

"You will come with us, madame," he ordered her, making a mocking parody of a courtly bow. "You may choose to come of your own accord, or we can force you to accompany us. The choice is yours."

Jane was deathly afraid. FitzAlan, still struggling against his captors, looked her full in the face, and seemed wordlessly to urge her to flee. But how could she flee? Dressed as she was in a long skirt, and unfamiliar with the layout of the Parisian streets, she stood no chance of escaping.

"I will—" she started, but stopped abruptly as she suddenly realised that her feet were no longer touching the ground, and she was hovering in the air. In addition, she realised that this was of her own doing, and that no Elemental was helping her do this.

The leader of the *sans-culottes* stared open-mouthed at her, as did his companions. One of those restraining FitzAlan relaxed his hold, crossed himself, and dropped to his knees.

Seizing his opportunity, FitzAlan twisted free of the grasp of his other astounded captor.

Without any conscious effort, Jane flew to him, seized hold of his hand, and bore him effortlessly with her as they sped down the street at a height of only a few feet in the direction of the Seine, leaving their would-be captors confused and confounded.

"Turn left here," said FitzAlan as they came to a street junction. His voice was as calm and untroubled as if he were in a fashionable salon. "And now right," he added after a short interval. He continued to give directions until he finally announced that they were at their destination.

Again without any conscious thought on her part, Jane gently dropped to the ground, FitzAlan following. Only now did she start to comprehend the enormity of what had just happened. Her knees started to give way, and if FitzAlan had not swiftly moved to put his arm around her shoulders, she would have collapsed.

He looked at her with what appeared to be awe. "My dear Miss Machin. I cannot believe what has just happened."

"Nor I," she answered, and started to giggle almost hysterically, unable to control herself. "Did you see," and the words struggled to escape between her giggles, "their faces?"

"I was otherwise engaged," he replied gravely, but he found himself unable to maintain his gravity, and smiled broadly. "Let us go inside. We are marked fugitives now – or perhaps worse – and we should not remain on the streets for longer than is necessary." He knocked on the door.

XIII

The Underground

AFTER A BRIEF INTERVAL, the door was opened. A wizened old man, clad in a dark robe of what appeared to be velvet, peered cautiously at them. A smile spread over his face as he recognised FitzAlan.

"My dear Thomas," he exclaimed in accented English. "And this must be the famous Jane Machin."

She wondered at the adjective. How could she, who had spent her adult life in near-seclusion, ever be considered as 'famous'? "I am Jane Machin," she replied.

They were ushered into a meanly-furnished room, and invited to sit.

"I am Montalba," said the old man to Jane. "At least, that is the name you may use to address me. Thomas and I are old friends, and I trust that you and I will very soon become friends." He smiled. "Did you have much trouble coming to this place?" He sat back, hands folded in his lap, and a faint half-smile on his lips.

Jane looked at FitzAlan, who returned her look, and they both started to laugh.

"We were stopped by a group of *sans-culottes* who wanted to drag us to the guillotine," FitzAlan told Montalba.

"I see," said the old man. "But you escaped their clutches, obviously."

It was Jane's turn to speak. "I... I... managed to escape them and brought FitzAlan – Thomas, I mean, with me."

Montalba's eyebrows shot up.

"She flew," said FitzAlan simply. "Flew like a bird, snatched me in her talons, and we soared through the streets of Paris, leaving the *sans-culottes* far behind in our wake."

"Is that all?"

"I laid one out with a good punch." He paused. "Shot another of them. Leader. Shot, not killed." His words were almost staccato.

"Oh, that was a very unwise thing to have done," Montalba said. There was sadness and regret in his voice, but no perceptible anger. "You have stirred up a hornets' nest, my dear Thomas. They will find where you have been living, have no doubt about that. They may even find where you were going. We are none of us safe. We must move from here as quickly as possible." He sighed. "These old bones will not stand such excitement."

FitzAlan laughed. "Your old bones will seem young when compared to the others down there."

"It is no joke, young Thomas. My dear," he turned to Jane. "I do not believe you will have the pleasure – and believe me it is a pleasure – to meet our Mary."

"Ilmay?" asked FitzAlan.

"He is out of the house at the moment, arranging some shipment of tobacco or molasses or some such. He is importing these things from America," he explained to Jane, "supplying the French with luxuries which otherwise would be supplied by English ships, but cannot now be obtained in that way, thanks to the English blockade."

"You will leave him and Mary above?"

"Of course. To do otherwise would attract suspicion, would it not? Now, young man, my bones, as I said before, are older than yours. Prepare the entrance." He stepped off the rug on which they had been standing, and motioned to Jane to do the same.

FitzAlan took one edge of the rug and pushed, so that the rug, curiously rigid, crumpled into a set of folds along its width to reveal a trapdoor, which FitzAlan opened. Jane could just make out a flight of stone steps leading down into... what?

Montalba took a candle from the table and lit it with a flint and steel. "I shall go first," he announced, "and you," turning to Jane, "will follow. Our young friend here will make all safe when we are safely down there and then depart to finish his business."

So saying, he cautiously started to descend. Jane watched as his head sank below floor level, and then prepared to follow him. She abruptly turned to FitzAlan. "We will be safe down there? It reminds me of the nasty dirty cold brugh that my father once took me to."

"You are safer with Montalba than with me, believe me when I tell you this. He is so old that he remembers the birth of the stars – at least that is what he says, and you would do well to at least pretend to believe him when he tells you these things. And with that great age have come great learning and great wisdom – not the same thing at all, as I need hardly remind you. And like you, he is no friend of Them."

"You *are* joining us?"

"In time. I have matters to attend to first. Have no fear.

Farewell for the present." And before Jane fully realised what was happening, he had taken hold of her hand and kissed it.

"Thank you, Thomas," she smiled. "Farewell for the present," turning and making her way down the stairs, where Montalba was waiting at the bottom. He had exchanged the candle for a resinous pinewood torch which smoked and spluttered, though it provided better light than the candle.

Above them, the trapdoor closed, and Jane heard what she assumed was the sound of the carpet being dragged over it.

"He will join us?" she asked Montalba, seeking reassurance.

"He will. In a few hours. We cannot afford to leave alive those who attacked you. Fear not, Thomas will take care of them. They are not expecting him."

"Come," he told her, and led the way down a narrow passageway, on each side of which were cavities, filled with sticks. Though Montalba was able to stand upright, Jane had to bend her neck a little in order to avoid bumping her head on the roof of the gallery. "Take care, the floor is uneven," he warned her, but Jane had already discovered that fact for herself.

As she recovered from her stumble, she found herself looking into the empty eye sockets of a skull in the niche next to her. She gave a start and a little cry.

"What... what is that doing there?" she asked.

"What?"

"That skull."

"Oh, we are in the old stone quarries under the city. Some years ago they decided to move some of the bodies from the cemeteries down here. As you can see, they were just bones and fragments of dried flesh by the time they came here.

"But they smell," she objected.

"So you say, but I cannot smell it myself. Several hundred bodies which were not mummified have been brought here at various times in the Revolution. They are a long way away, though. For obvious reasons, we do not go there."

With a start, Jane realised that the sticks in the niches in the wall were actually the long bones of arms and legs.

"How many are down here?"

He shrugged. "Why knows? Who has counted? Perhaps one million, perhaps two. Maybe even more. Does it matter? They are only bodies. Those who inhabited them still live on." They walked on a few paces. "Or maybe they do not," he added. "In any event, they do not bother us down here."

It seemed like hours that they walked through the bone-lined galleries, turning into side-galleries now and again, following a path that seemed clear to Montalba. Jane began to feel a sense of panic. If she needed to get out of this place, there was no way that she could find the exit on her own. Her breathing became rapid and shallow, and her steps faltered. Montalba sensed the change in her, and stopped.

"I sense you are worried," he said. His tone was kindly. "Naturally, there is more than one entrance to these catacombs. In fact, there are many, scattered around the whole city. You are never far from being able to reach the surface. In any case, to one as close to the Elementals as are you, the presence of walls of rock should pose no obstacle. You do possess that power, do you not?"

She nodded. His words provided some relief, but the feeling of being shut in failed to disappear as they continued their journey. However, in a relatively short space of time, they found themselves in a larger cavern, lit by more flickering bluish flames. By the light provided by these flames, Jane could discern two more hooded robed figures of indeterminate sex, seated on what appeared to be dining chairs at a table, playing cards.

One of them looked up, and the hood turned towards Jane.

"So this is she?" the figure said. The voice was old and dry and dusty. If the bones that lined the gallery had a voice, it would have been this. Jane peered through the gloom and tried to make out the face, but all that she could see was a white oval, with two black holes where eyes might be. "Where is FitzAlan?"

"He has unfinished business. He will join us soon."

"Excellent." The hood swivelled in Jane's direction. "Jane — that is your name, is it not?" She nodded. "Come closer, if you please. My eyes are not what they were—"

The other hooded figure spoke for the first time. "They were never much even then, great-grandfather," it said. The voice was that of a young woman.

"True, but one must make do with what one is given," said the first.

Jane approached, and was conscious of being scrutinised closely, though there was no movement from the other.

"Good," came the voice at last. "You are not beautiful. That is good."

Jane could not help asking, "Why is it good that I am not beautiful?" She was not offended by the judgement. She considered herself to be moderately attractive, but no one had ever referred to her as 'beautiful'.

"Beauty is a distraction. A curse. A way of taking away men's reason."

There was a muffled laugh from the other figure, and a shrug from Montalba.

"I have told you my name," Jane said. "May I know yours, sir?"

"You may call me— let me see, what shall we have? How does Ortolanus sound to you?"

"Very poetic, sir. The same as the author of *Liber super textum Hermetis*?"

A chuckle. "Oh, excellent. You know your ancient adepts. And my great-granddaughter, Florella."

"Delighted to make your acquaintance," Florella said, speaking to Jane for the first time. "Pray, come and join us at the table." She indicated a chair.

JANE EXAMINED THE CARDS spread out on the table. They seemed to be the usual suits: cups, coins, wands, and swords that she knew from her time in Zürich, but there were other picture cards which did not seem to correspond to anything that she had seen before.

"What are these?" she asked, pointing to a card with a picture of a man hanging upside-down from a tree branch with a rope tied around his ankle.

"That's the Hanged Man. He connects Gevurah and Hod." Florella's words meant little to Jane.

"And this?" she asked, pointing to another.

"Fortune, connecting Chesed and Netzach. Do you really not know the Major Arcana and its relation to the Tree of Life?" Florella's voice indicated astonishment. "I had heard that you were an adept, and that you could summon the Elementals."

"Yes... yes, I suppose that last is true. But none of this was in any of the books I have read."

"And your master never told you about the Tarot? And its links with Kabbala?"

Jane shook her head. "My master? Do you mean Otto?"

Montalba spoke. "Florella, my dear. Jane here has talents of which you and I only dream. But they are talents gained, not from knowledge, but from nature itself. These cards there," and his hand indicated the squares on the table, " have deep meanings. By studying them, it is possible to learn a little of one's place in the grand scheme of things. This pattern in which they are arranged mimics the Tree of Life, as I am sure you have deduced already, and it represents the universe and our place in it."

"Or if you prefer, God, and our relationship to Him," added Ortolanus. "And by studying this, and learning the inner secrets of the universe, we hope to be able to defeat Them."

"But it seems," Montalba went on, addressing Jane, "that with your innate powers you have no need of these toys."

"They are not toys!" Ortolanus replied with more than a touch of anger in his voice. "They are guides to a better life and greater powers, as I have told you many times before."

"Have it your own way," Montalba answered him peaceably. "If you discover how to summon an Elemental before I am able to do so, I will cease to regard these scraps of pasteboard as toys."

"Can you really summon Elementals, as we have been told?" Florella asked in wonder.

"I have summoned Salamanders, yes."

"I would love to see a Salamander. Please, I wish to see one."

"The last person to say that to me was burned to death by the Salamander," Jane told her. "Salamanders are not pets to be cooed over and stroked."

"You are wise," Montalba told her. "Wise not to abuse your powers."

Jane felt the absence of FitzAlan. Those she was with might well be learned and experienced in things of which she knew little or nothing, but there was something about them that told her they were not to be trusted with practical matters. How could scraps of pasteboard and Hebrew letters possibly be of any use? While FitzAlan... She sighed.

"Where is he? Thomas FitzAlan, I mean."

"You are right," said Montalba. "He should have returned by now."

"What was the business that you talked of that he must finish?"

"Why, to kill those rogues who attempted to kill you," he remarked in a matter-of-fact voice.

"What if he does not return to us soon?"

"Then we must leave here. It is he who has brought us our food and water, and supplies of the materials to produce the inflammable air, or 'hydrogen' as M. de Lavoisier would have us call it, that we burn for light down here."

Jane looked, and noticed that the blue flames she had seen earlier emanated from the end of pipes connected to flasks in which liquid quietly bubbled.

"Where will you go? Back to Mary Wollstonecraft?"

"No, we must find another place, where our presence will not be suspected. If he does arrive here and finds us gone, he will know where to find us, never fear."

"How long do we have to wait?"

Montalba pulled a large watch from his pocket. "We will give him three hours more. Then we must leave. Agreed?"

The next three hours seemed interminable to Jane. She sat on the chair, watching Florella and Ortolanus discussing things which were largely beyond her understanding. Occasionally when she could make out the sense of what they were saying, they seemed to be giving overly complex answers to what seemed to be very simple questions.

Her legs grew stiff, and parts of her body started to grow numb as she sat silently on the chair. Even if she had felt that she was allowed to talk, it was doubtful if she could have found anything meaningful to say.

Her eyes closed, and she drifted into a half-slumber. At the back of her mind, she was conscious of the presence of him who called himself her father, and she recognised his voice, but it was as if a fog overlaid his words, and she was unable to make out anything of what he was saying.

Without warning, a sudden pain shot through her head, and she sat up, fully awake, and let out a cry.

"What is it?" asked Montalba. "Is it him?"

Jane nodded wordlessly. The pain had gone as swiftly as it had arrived, and she was no longer conscious of his presence.

"It is nearly time," Montalba said. "We may leave."

Ortolanus swept together the cards on the table, tucking them into a pocket of his robe, and Florella assisted him to his feet.

"We will leave the lamps burning," Montalba said. "They may serve to confuse any who attempt to follow us. Come."

He led them through a narrow opening on the opposite side of the cavern to that which Jane and he had used to enter. Again Jane had to stoop, in places nearly bent double, as they made their slow and difficult way along a gallery which seemed to slope slightly upward. In this part of the catacombs, there were fewer bones to be seen.

The journey underground was a relatively short one. Montalba stopped, and pointed upwards. "Can you reach that?" he asked Jane, indicating a small ring set in a slab over their heads. "It should slide sideways."

Jane was easily able to do this, and Montalba retrieved a rude ladder from where it had been lying on the floor of the gallery.

"Florella, you first. Look carefully and make sure that the place has remained unvisited since the last time we were here."

Florella carefully ascended the ladder. Her feet disappeared from view, and the sounds of her moving around were carried down to them. After a few minutes, she appeared to return, and she said, "All is as we left it. Either no one has visited…"

"…or we are up against enemies more cunning than usual. Thank you. Ortolanus." He indicated the ladder, and Ortolanus made his slow ascent, assisted by Jane from below and Florella from above.

Jane followed, and Montalba ascended, with surprising ease for one apparently so old. The chamber in which they now found themselves was clearly in a meaner area of Paris than the one from which Jane and Montalba had started their journey. There was a metallic smell in the air, which caught at Jane's nostrils. She sniffed.

"It is blood, my dear."

"Are we near a slaughterhouse?"

Florella laughed bitterly. "You might well say that. The guillotine is but a hundred yards away in the next street but one."

"There is method in this madness," said Montalba. "Believe me, if the Committee of Public Safety were to discover us, we would…" He drew his hand across his throat. "And who but a madman would hide himself next door to the guillotine, on the very street where the tumbrils bring the sheep to the slaughter? We are safe here – as safe, that is, as anyone in Paris can be in these times of insanity."

As he finished speaking, the sound of excited shouts and cries came to Jane's ears, along with the sound of a horse's hooves, and the rumbling of wheels.

"Down, down," hissed Florella, shrinking to the floor below the level of the windowsill. Jane followed her example, but not before she had caught a glimpse of three men, clad in their breeches and white shirts, standing in the cart, tied together.

"Poor souls," said Florella with what sounded like genuine sympathy in her voice. Jane took the opportunity to examine her companion in full light for the first time. She was, by most standards, beautiful, almost as beautiful as a Salamander, thought Jane. It was no wonder that she had laughed when Montalba had made his little diatribe against female beauty. It had clearly been directed at her.

Her hair was, however, unkempt, and her face was dirty, but neither did much to diminish the astonishing effect of her appearance. Jane turned her attention to her great-grandfather, who seemed even more shrunken and wizened in daylight than he had in the light of the inflammable air lamps.

He noticed her studying his face, and slowly and deliberately winked at her. She had no idea what this might mean, and turned away from him.

The sound of another tumbril approaching, accompanied by shouts and jeers, grew louder, and Jane could not resist a cautious peep.

What she saw horrified her. Alone in the cart, clad in white shirt and breeches, and standing tall and defiant, was Thomas FitzAlan. "No!" she shrieked. "We must save him!" as she leaped to her feet.

Immediately Florella pulled her down to the floor, but not before she, too, had looked and seen FitzAlan. "It's Thomas! He's taken!" she hissed to Montalba and her great-grandfather.

"He is lost," Montalba answered. "There is nothing we can do for him."

Jane groaned as if in physical pain.

"It will soon be over," Florella told her. Jane had closed her eyes, but felt an arm which could only be Florella's around her shoulders, and the sensation of a warm soft body pressed against hers. "There, there," said Florella. "It is hard, I know. I am older than I may appear. I too have known pain and loss and the suffering that goes with them." She held Jane a little closer, and Jane's anguished cries faded to a stifled sobbing.

Other than the sounds of Jane's distress, there was near silence in the room, broken by a sequence of sounds from outside. A hissing swishing sound, a thump, and the sound of cheers.

"Madame claims another victim," observed Montalba. "Be comforted, my dear. It is a quick and painless death."

"I have heard it said that the head lives on for minutes after it has been severed from the body," said Florella.

"Nonsense. Old wives' tales," countered her great-grand-father, but his words went unheard by Jane who had fainted away.

She came to her senses, and it took her some time to re-member where she was, who her companions were, and then, most terribly, what had caused her to faint.

Florella regarded her with a face of some concern. "How are you?" he asked.

"Terrible," she answered simply. "Is he…?"

"Almost certainly by now, I fear."

"And what will happen to his body?" She paused "And his head?"

"They will be thrown in a cart, together with those of the others killed today, and taken to a pit outside the city."

Jane turned to Montalba. "Florella said that the head lives without the body. Would it be possible to… to bring back the head and the body and make them live?"

"Old wives' tales, as I said. But if there is one person who could do that thing, it would be you," Montalba said. "But there is the small problem of obtaining the head and the body. We cannot simply leave this place and ask for them, you know."

"But we can steal them away," Jane answered him. She turned away from the others and faced the corner of the room away from the window. She put her hands to her temples, and with the sound of a mighty wind, two shapes stood before her, silvery and half-transparent. It was impossible to tell whether they were male or female, though they stood considerably higher than Jane or Florella.

"Sylphs," Montalba breathed. "Air Elementals. That I should live to see this day."

"What would you have of us, Mistress?" asked one of the forms.

For answer, Jane closed her eyes, and recalled the image of FitzAlan as she had known him, and also as she had last beheld him in the tumbril.

"I see him, Mistress. What would you have of us?" the Sylph repeated.

"His head is no longer joined to his body. Find the head and the body and bring them both here, I command you!" Her finger shot out and pointed at each Sylph in turn. The Elementals quivered visibly as she ordered them, and as suddenly as they had come, vanished with the same sound of wind as they had made on their arrival.

THE FOUR WAITED IN SILENCE, which was broken only by the rumble of tumbrils passing, and, all too frequently, by a swishing sound followed by a dull thud, which in turn was succeeded by cheers. Jane felt that the wait for "her" Elementals to appear was one of the longest in her life, but at length, the same sound of wind announced their arrival.

One of them bore a human head, which Jane recognised with horror as being that of FitzAlan. The eyes were still open, staring at her, and the face seemed to bear an expression of amused contempt – an expression that she recalled seeing on him several times while he had been alive. The arms of the other Elemental bore a lifeless body, which she also recognised by means of a distinctive mole on the back of the left hand as being that of her companion. Both the head and the body appeared to her to be waxen images, and it was almost impossible for her to associate them with the lively and vibrant personality with whom she had passed the last few days.

Her eyes filled with tears, and she had to turn away for a few minutes. At length she turned round. FitzAlan's body was now placed on the ground, arms folded over its breast, and the head was placed on the neck. "You may go," she said to the Sylphs, and as before, they departed.

"It was a clean death," Florella reminded her, not unkindly. "He would not have suffered."

"And now…" Montalba said.

"And now? What?" Jane asked. "Can you, with all your wisdom, restore him to life? Please, I beg you, do not delay, but do it now."

Montalba shook his head. "I cannot. Ortolanus cannot, for all his purported knowledge of Kabbala and Tarot. And I am certain that Florella cannot."

The three of the others looked at Jane expectantly. "I?" she asked.

"You assured us that you could," Montalba told her gently.

"I did no such thing!" she retorted. "Where would I start?" Completely overcome by grief and frustration, she started to sob helplessly, unable to stop the flow of tears. Florella, seemingly moved by some sisterly impulse, moved to her and embraced her. After a brief resistance, Jane accepted the embrace and continued to weep on her new friend's shoulder.

Ortolanus shrugged. "It seems our quest has ended, unless Miss Machin here can be persuaded to do what is necessary to bring about what is needed."

"Your quest?" Jane asked, pausing in her grief for long enough to ask the question.

"Perhaps my friend spoke in a way that you misunderstood," said Montalba. "Our quest for knowledge."

"Knowledge?"

"Yes, the knowledge of the Humour of Life, the Ignis Primus, that can create life from inanimate matter."

"If your experiment—"

"*Our* experiment, my dear," Montalba replied in silky tones.

Jane went on as if he had not spoken. "—fails, then he is no more. He is bereft of life, and you are no better off than before. And if he is somehow to be restored to life, then you are the gainers—"

"And so are you, for your friend will be with you again."

"And why do you think that I am the one to do this?"

"You have the power to summon Elementals. I have seen this," said Ortolanus. "All you have to do is summon the one who calls Himself your father, and I am certain that He has the power to restore Thomas FitzAlan to life."

"And what will He ask in return?" asked Jane. The others all shook their heads. "I will tell you. He will want my consent to allow those from the other side of the sky to rule Paris, and from Paris, all France, and from France, all Europe. And we humans will be no more than dust in their path to be swept away. Or perhaps pawns to be moved and sacrificed at will. Believe me," she said desperately, her voice rising to a shriek. "I know this. Do not ask me how I know, but I know it as certainly as I know that I can make fire like this."

She held up her hand, palm facing outward away from her, and as the others watched open-mouthed, flames grew from the tips of her fingers as if they were candles.

"Enough," she said, and the flames vanished.

"Jane," Florella said, "I feel I must ask you something. What did Thomas FitzAlan tell you about himself, and about us?"

"He said that he was an agent for the English government

working against the revolutionaries here…" Montalba nodded, and Jane added, "…and that there was another group, also connected with the English government working against the designs of Those from the other side of the sky."

"The first is correct," Montalba confirmed. "Thomas was indeed working for the English government as a political agent. As to the second—"

"It is untrue," Florella broke in.

"He lied to me?" Jane asked.

"No, he was lied to," Florella explained. Ortolanus looked at her with fire in his eyes as she continued to speak. "My wicked great-grandfather, or so he likes to style himself, and a more selfish and self-obsessed man you would have to go a long way to find, and this man who calls himself Montalba – the white mountain, would you believe – wish to discover the secret of eternal life. And for that reason, if only to protect their feeble selves, they pretended to Thomas that they were still in the employ of the English government. Though it is true that they had at first been employed as such, their own wishes to discover the hidden secrets of the ages led them to give false reports to London, and to deceive their supposed masters there of the progress they were making in their fight against the Others. When Thomas was sent to join them, they knew somehow of his American experiences, and the time he had spent with the Indians, which in their eyes would make him more receptive to their fables when they spun their lies of treachery and deceit. I was likewise sent to join them, in the belief that they were working for the benefit of humanity. I was soon undeceived, but was prevented by force from telling Thomas, let alone London, of the treachery of these two."

"It would behove you to keep quiet, wench," hissed Ortolanus.

"Or else?" Florella replied mockingly. "What more can you do to me? Look," she exclaimed to Jane, and pulled up her sleeve. Jane saw with horror that her arm was covered in scars and the marks of burns, some of which were hardly healed. "And they did worse to me, but we will not speak of these things. What could I do, one woman against two men, strong despite their age?" She rolled down her sleeve again and faced Montalba with a fierce expression on her face. "You cowardly mountebanks. There will be a special place reserved in Hell for you two." She turned to Jane. "You can have no conception how good it is for me to be able to say these things to you. It was they who discovered your association with Hermecritus—"

"Is Otto part of this affair?" Jane asked.

"No. These two invited him to join them, while you were staying in Tiengen, but he refused. It seems that he had somehow heard things about them – there seems to be some connection in the past between him and this precious pair. They then set Thomas FitzAlan to track you and to bring you safely to Paris. Thomas believed he was doing you, and the English, a good turn, while in actual fact he was only serving their purposes."

"I have warned you," Ortolanus said. "Be quiet now, or face the consequences." There was a look of pure savagery on his face.

"I will not be quiet," she spat back and turned her back on him. "The *sans-culottes* who attacked you…"

"Yes?"

"They knew who you and Thomas were, and when and where you would appear. They had been told by these two."

Jane thought back to the incident, and remembered the words of the leader. "I see."

"Either he would be killed at the first meeting, or he would be victorious, and then sent out to eliminate the attackers as witnesses, in which case he would certainly die, one way or another. Then you are to perform the task of restoring him to life. Then they will know the secret of life – the secret for which they have killed and tormented not just Thomas and myself, but many others throughout the years."

"So you are treating poor Thomas there as no more than a bird in an air-pump. He was simply an animal for you to torment?" Jane flashed at Montalba, who merely shrugged. "And you, Florella? Why are you still with these two men?"

"I told you, I had no choice," she replied, "I—" and her words were cut short by a horrid gurgling sound as blood spilled from her mouth. Behind her, Ortolanus still brandished his dripping dagger. Ignoring him, Jane rushed over to the dying girl, and cradled her in her arms. The two men stood by, watching impassively as Florella's ragged breathing slowed, became shallower, and then stopped. Jane laid her head gently on the floor and closed her eyes. She stood and faced Montalba and Ortolanus defiantly.

"Now you have two corpses for me to exercise my skill. Very well. You will see marvels."

"You will do this for us?"

"I will show you the power of life and death," she said. "That is what you want, is it not?"

"You can do this? You will do this? You swear it?" The face of Ortolanus bore an expression of almost obscene lust as he licked his lips.

"I can and I will do this, and I swear it by all that I hold precious."

Time, she told herself, to use some of the tricks she had

learned from Otto. "We must wait until after dark." Montalba made as if to protest, but she held up her hand. "No arguments. You will do exactly as I say, or else I cannot and will not perform this. Do you understand?"

Both men nodded dumbly.

"We will need a fire in the stove there." She pointed. "Do you have fuel? No? One of you must obtain fuel. Wood, charcoal, whatever you can obtain. Are there any musical instruments here?" she asked, expecting it to be a forlorn hope, but was surprised when Montalba produced a recorder from the folds of his robe. She held out her hand and he gave the pipe to her. She ostentatiously wiped the mouthpiece, and played a short melody. "Very good. You have incense?" This time it was Ortolanus who produced a small lacquer box. She took the box, careful to avoid touching his hand, opened it and sniffed. "Excellent. And now, before you find the fuel for the stove, let us see what your cards have to say to us. One card for you, Ortolanus."

He pulled the pack from his robe, shuffled, and placed one card face down on the small table that stood in a corner of the room.

She turned it over to reveal the Judgement, upside-down. Ortolanus' face went white. "I have been judged and found wanting," he said.

"Your words, not mine," Jane said. "Now you," turning to Montalba.

His card was the Wheel of Fortune, reversed. His face showed shock and surprise at the sight.

"As bad a fortune as mine," Ortolanus cackled.

"It's all foolery, anyway." Montalba retorted. "Now you," he commanded Jane. She drew the High Priestess, and the other two drew back.

"Perhaps we need not see your powers tonight," Montalba muttered.

"Or at all," Ortolanus added, making some sort of sign with his hands which Jane took to be a charm against harm.

"But I swore that I would, did I not?" Jane reminded them, smiling sweetly. "Let be draw for Thomas," she drew a card from the pack, "and for Florella."

The card she had selected for Thomas was the Tower. Florella's was Temperance. The two men looked aghast. "You say you do not understand these cards, and yet…" stammered Ortolanus.

"Correct. You may please yourselves as to the meanings of these cards." She raised her voice. Now go, and bring the wood or the charcoal for the stove."

"You won't run away?" Montalba asked.

Jane continued smiling innocently. "Where would I run?" she asked. "In any case, I gave you my word. Maybe you are not used to people keeping their word. In any case, this is something that I want to do for myself. Now go."

Without a word, the two men left her. Jane noticed with some amusement that Ortolanus made a half-bow to her seemingly unconsciously as he left the room. She heard the door to the street open and close before she collapsed on the floor, and allowed herself to weep for the friend – the friends – whose corpses lay stretched out beside her.

THE TWO MEN RETURNED less than an hour later, bearing a small sack of charcoal and a bundle of firewood.

"Will this be enough?" Montalba asked.

Jane pretended to consider. For a moment she thought

of sending these two evil old men out into the Paris ftreets again, but decided againft it. "It is sufficient," she said simply.

She took the fticks and charcoal and ftarted to lay a fire in the ftove. As the sun set, she sat in one of the chairs in the place, and ftarted to play the recorder, trying hard to ignore the two bodies lying side by side in front of her.

The two men ftood liftening, seemingly mesmerised by her playing. As she finished one of her pieces, she ordered Montalba to light the fire, but to leave the doors of the ftove open.

As the flames danced and crackled, she played on sweetly, thoughts of revenge burning in her brain.

"Look!" exclaimed Montalba, pointing. "There is something living in the fire!"

"A Salamander!" whispered Ortolanus in awe. "Two Salamanders!"

Jane played on, and with two loud pops, the Salamanders burft from the ftove, and ftood in front of her.

"Miftress?" queried the taller and more beautiful of the two.

"These two," she indicated Montalba and Ortolanus, who were ftanding open-mouthed, "admire you immensely. Is that not so?" she addressed Montalba directly.

"Oh, yes… yes…" he ftammered.

She turned back to the Salamanders. "I wish you to express my feelings for them. Look into my heart for my feelings and take them." There was a faint tingling sensation as the Salamanders took Jane's hate from her, leaving her ftrangely dispassionate.

"We may ftart, Miftress?"

"Yes."

The taller Salamander made her way to Montalba, and the other to Ortolanus. Almoft simultaneously, they grasped their prey by the shoulders, and faftened their lips to those of the old men. A smell of scorching arose, with smoke arising from the mouths, noses, and even the ears of the Salamanders' victims, and their screams of agony erupted, stifled by the kiss of death. Soon, the Elementals released their grip, and the two bodies slumped to the floor.

"They now know the power of life and death," Jane said. "As I promised. Thank you," she said to the Salamanders.

"What now, Mistress?" asked the taller.

"You may feed," Jane told them. "I will leave this place. Wait a short while, and then consume the house, and all that is in it." She indicated the four bodies on the floor, and despite herself, tears came to her eyes as she gazed on FitzAlan's face for the last time. "Then you may return whence you came."

The two Elementals bowed. "Your command is our pleasure, Mistress."

"Farewell," Jane said, and stepped out of the house to the dark Paris street. As she turned the corner, she looked back. Flames were already shooting out of the windows of the house she had just left, and the smell of smoke, overlaying the stink of burning flesh, came to her nostrils. She hurried on.

As she raced through the streets, nearly deserted at this time of night, she became aware of the sticky suffocating presence of the one who called himself her father.

"Where are you going to, daughter?' the words inside her head enquired. The sound of the voice could only be compared to the sensation of an aching tooth. It was painful, and there seemed to be no escape from it.

She did not answer and the question was repeated. In hopes that she could silence the pain she answered, "As far from this cursed city as I can."

"Where do you wish to go? Let me take you."

For a moment she considered this. Perhaps to America, to see the wonders of which Thomas FitzAlan had spoken so enthusiastically. Perhaps to… She cut off this train of thought, conscious that all her thoughts were open to Him.

Suddenly two things burst upon her consciousness. First, He was asking her permission to take her where she wanted. If He truly had power over her, He could stop her in her tracks, or scoop her up and carry her as He had done when she was a child. And then she remembered escaping from the *sans-culottes*, flying effortlessly and tirelessly down the streets of Paris at a speed that could not be matched, even by the fastest runner.

Without any further thought, she found her feet now some inches above the filthy cobbles, and the houses sped by her in a blur.

"Very good, daughter," came the toothache voice. "For the last time, will you join us?"

"No!" she shrieked with all the force at her command. "Never!"

"Then I will leave you for now. Next time, remember that our meeting will not be so friendly. And make no mistake, there will be a next time."

Jane felt as though she had been set free from an abominable trap as He left her, and she continued speeding through the air, now outside the city,, automatically following the course of the river, knowing that it would eventually bring her to the sea, and passing through the villages dotting the banks of the Seine as it wound its way towards the sea.

It was time, she knew, to go home – back to England and the place where she had been born and the places where she had spent her childhood. She felt a sense of loss. Somehow she had come to believe that Thomas FitzAlan would be her protector for the foreseeable future. He had seemed so confident, so completely in control of the situation. And now, betrayed by a group of… whatever they had been. She could only think of them as traitors to their own race. Tears pricked her eyes, making it more difficult to see. Angry with herself for what she saw as weakness, she wiped away the tears and continued to fly ever westwards.

How fast was she flying? She really had no idea. A few owls and bats were in the night air around her, but she swept past them as if they were motionless. It seemed to her that she had spent her whole life flying, but she remained unfatigued. As her journey continued, the sky behind her in the east started to lighten as dawn broke. Now she could make out some of the fields and hedges of the French countryside, and a collection of houses some way ahead which could only be Rouen, if her memory of the geography of France was correct.

She had seen no one as she had flown past the small villages, but it was perfectly possible, she considered, that a larger city like Rouen would have at least a few citizens awake and moving about the streets. She changed direction, and steered across the loop of the river on which Rouen was situated, rejoining the Seine a little further on. The sun had now risen sufficiently for her to now see that the river looped and twisted, and she could cut across these loops on her way towards Le Havre.

The coast was now in clear sight as daylight dawned, and she could hear a clock in a village church striking the hour.

She decided to come down to earth just outside the port. She was not tired, amazingly, but she was hungry. It seemed as though she had not eaten for days, but she was unsure how she might find something to fill her stomach. She had no money of any kind with her, and despite her skill in conjuring gold coins from thin air, she felt that the sort of person who might be persuaded to part with a crust of bread might be more than a little suspicious at the offer to pay for it with a piece of gold. Theft would seem to be the only option available to her.

As she approached the next farm, rather than swerving to avoid it, as she had been doing up to that time, she slowed, and dropped to the ground. Her feet and legs responded to the unaccustomed strain of supporting her weight, and she staggered slightly as she moved cautiously towards the farmhouse, whose back door stood invitingly open.

There was no one inside the kitchen that she could see, but half a loaf of coarse brown bread stood on the table. As fast as she could, she dashed into the kitchen, scooped up the bread in her hands, and rushed out again, leaping into the air just in time to see a man, presumably the farmer, appear from around the corner of the barn, and stand, open-mouthed at the apparition before him.

Too late, she realised that what she had first seen as a stick under his arm was a shotgun. He shouted something in his almost unintelligible Norman French, and then there was the sound of a loud explosion behind her, immediately followed by a whistling sound as most of the pellets flew past her, and a sharp stinging pain in one leg where she had been hit.

She faltered a little in her flight, shocked by the pain, but soon recovered, and rapidly sped out of sight of the farmer, and hopefully out of range of the gun. Her leg was still hurting, so she landed, and gingerly examined the sore spot. To her relief, the pellet did not seem to have broken the skin, but the place where it had struck was bruised and discoloured.

She was now near the coast, and as she chewed on the bread she had stolen, she realised that she must make a decision on how she would cross into England.

Though it was clear that flight was possible, the idea of a long trip over water without any land in sight frightened her. It was true that she might well have Undine powers of survival in water, but she was certain that the sea would be cold, and she might very well die from the cold, if not actually drowning. In any event, she had no wish to put this to the test.

A boatman might well be more willing to accept gold for a passage across the Channel than would a farmer for a loaf of bread, but there were dangers in sailing from Revolutionary France to England over and beyond the dangers involved in a sea voyage.

The French Revolutionary government was far from enthusiastic about the idea of their mariners making their way to England, and the English were naturally hostile to the idea of French boats arriving in England.

Jane remembered that FitzAlan had told her that there was a regular smuggling trade between France and England. French fishing boats would start out with a cargo of brandy, tobacco and silks, and meet English boats in mid-Channel. There the contraband cargoes would be transferred, and English gold received in exchange – both sides considering that they had profited by the deal.

Very well, her task was now to go to a small fishing village, and keep her ears open for news of smuggling. It would take some time, she believed, but in the meantime, she hoped that she might be able to earn a living through her music or maybe telling fortunes or the like.

IT HAD TAKEN SOME TWO WEEKS before Jane had been able to find a boat that would be willing to take her to England. She was lucky, she was continually told by the inhabitants of Villers-sur-Mer, the small village where she had ended her journey, that they were not supporters of the Revolution. At first they had treated her story of being English with suspicion, but eventually she had managed to convince them that she was not an agent of the Committee of Public Safety.

She'd overheard one of them talking to his friend.

"If those buggers in Paris had wanted to send a spy to seduce us, they'd have picked one a bit prettier than that one."

"Nah, she's not that bad-looking. Better than my old woman, anyway."

"That bloody cow in the field over there is better looking than your old woman, Pierre."

"Oh, give over. Look at yours."

"I know, I have to, don't I?"

It was hardly the witty talk of the Paris salons which she had been anticipating, but it made her smile. She knew she was no beauty, but it didn't worry her. She smiled to herself as she wondered what Pierre's reaction would be if faced with a Salamander.

The men of the village told her that the villagers would be starving, were it not for the generosity of the English fishermen, who were kind enough appear in mid-Channel to buy from them their brandy and calvados, and the silks that mysteriously appeared in the village from time to time, with no one admitting to a knowledge of their source, not to mention the coarse tobacco that no peasant would be seen dead smoking.

"What the English do with it, I daren't think," one of them said to her.

"Probably shove it up their arses," said his neighbour, "knowing those English."

Jane had made herself useful in the village by helping to care for some of the young children while their fathers were out at sea fishing, and their mothers were working in the family field, or tending to the animals. She had never had anything to do with children before, but it seemed that this was the only work that she could do that would be useful and bring about a sense of gratitude from the villagers. She knew instinctively that she would be unable to work with the farm animals. Dogs shrank from her, cats hissed their disapproval, and even chickens seemed to run from her. Children, on the other hand, seemed to adore her, even when she was not consciously attempting to charm them.

In the evenings, she was often invited to share an evening meal with the family of one of the children for whom she had been caring earlier in the day. Sometimes she would perform one of the conjuring tricks which she and Otto had practised together, but without using any of her special powers. She still managed to produce "Oohs" and "Aahs" of astonishment when she managed to make a coin disappear from her hand and magically re-appear in a child's ear, or to produce an apple from under an upturned cider tankard. Her playing on her recorder, which she had discovered she was still gripping in her hand when she had fled the Paris house, also charmed the villagers, especially when she learned some of their tunes and accompanied their singing.

She was lucky, she supposed, to have arrived in such a community, which appeared to have little interest in any persons or events outside its own boundaries, but it was still a relief when one of the fishermen told her to "Get your things ready. We're off tonight."

She had already agreed a fare for her passage, and she'd come to know these men well enough to trust them not to cheat or rob her. But the English? She mentioned her fears to Jean-Paul.

"They may be English, but they're good lads. I'll make sure they take you there safely for the same money that you're paying us. Tell you what, give me our money and the money you're going to give them. Then I can pay them, and tell them you haven't got no more, so that's it. And if they hurt you in any way, then us lads won't do no more business with them. And I'll know if they do. I've got a nose for this sort of thing."

She reluctantly agreed, and handed over some of her gold – real coins, rather than her fairy gold that might turn into something else at an inconvenient moment.

"You'll be all right, lass," he told her. "I know you can take care of yourself, but I'll make sure you don't have to bother. See you here with your things at six this evening."

And so she set sail for England after more than ten years away.

PART FOUR

THE REVELLERS OF THOTH
(1793)

XIV

The House

SHE WAS BACK IN ENGLAND. It smelled different. Not just that the smell of the food being cooked in the cottages of the lonely Dorset villages through which she was now walking was different, or that the air seemed fresher and cleaner than she had experienced in France, but there was a strange, somewhat unpleasant undercurrent to the sensation in her nostrils.

With a start, she recognised it as the scent of Them, faint, but now that she recognised it, unmistakable. She was back in Their country. While previously, she and her father had met on almost equal terms, now she was in what was to her by now a foreign country, and he was comfortably at home. Would she still be able to conjure up Elementals here? Now was not the time to try, though.

She had landed a little before dawn, having spent a restless and seasick night, first in the French fishing boat, where Jean-Paul had solicitously watched over her, and then transferred to the English smugglers, along with the bales of silk and tobacco, and barrels of spirits. Jean-Paul had talked to the English skipper in low tones, and she saw something pass from him to the Englishman, and heard the chink of coins, presumably her passage money. Jean-Paul's finger was wagged in the English skipper's face, and she could hear low growls of warning – presumably he was telling the other that she was to remain unmolested, with suitable threats if the orders were ignored.

She need not have feared for her safety, at least as far as the attentions of the English crew were concerned. She sat huddled on one of the thwarts in the bows of the boat, where the Channel spray occasionally dashed into her face, but ignored, even shunned, by the Dorset smugglers. She wondered what exactly Jean-Paul had said to them to make them keep their distance in this way.

Even when they beached the boat on a pebbled shore, it seemed that they wished to avoid her. They carefully unloaded her few belongings, almost entirely consisting of her recorder and some cast-off clothes bestowed on her by her French hosts, placing them at some distance from their bales of contraband, but seemed to carefully avoid contact with Jane herself.

She picked up her things, and turned to the captain. "Thank you," she said.

"That's all right," he said. "Remember that you've never seen us, and we'll remember that we've never seen you."

It seemed a fair bargain. "Where am I?"

"A few miles outside Weymouth. Less than an hour's walk or two for a young lass like you. Just take that road there," pointing, "and keep going."

"And how would I get to Birmingham from there?"

The question appeared to puzzle him. "Wouldn't know. Ask

the folks in Weymouth. They'll know about them foreign places more than I do."

She walked on, smelling the air, with its undercurrent of Them, and listening to the birdsong. Even that seemed to be different to that of France, let alone Switzerland or Germany. She strained her ears to detect any trace of Them in the sounds she could hear, but stopped when she wondered whether such curiosity might in fact bring Them out of hiding to confront her.

There were few people around at this hour of the morning, and the ones whom she did encounter seemed to be too intent on their own business to notice a young woman, dressed in a rather different style to themselves and carrying a small bundle, earnestly walking fast.

In Weymouth, she made enquiries, and was informed that a stagecoach the next day might take her to Southampton, whence she could proceed via Winchester and Oxford to Birmingham.

"It'll cost you, though," she was warned.

Jane hesitated, wondering whether to wait until nightfall when no one was around to see her, and then take to the air again as she had done in France. She had no map or means of navigation, though, as she had used when following the Seine down to the sea. Even so, it would be easy for her to ask directions if at daybreak she found herself in an unexpected part of the country, and it would be quicker, not to mention cheaper, than taking the coach. Accordingly, she strolled around Weymouth, purchasing a few garments, a few from each shop, and paying with her "fairy gold", which she knew would turn to dead leaves or flower petals within twenty-four hours. But by that time, she'd be a long way away. And who would recognise her, once she had cut her hair short and thereby changed her apparent sex, as she had every intention of doing when she arrived at her destination? By spreading her purchases between different shops, she made sure that no single establishment would lose too much money, and the incentive to seek her out would be less.

By the time nightfall had come, she felt herself ready. She slipped out of the town to a seemingly deserted copse, and changed into her new garments, bundling the French castoffs together to take with her.

Now it was time to fly. Summoning all her energy, she willed herself into the air, but her feet remained obstinately rooted to the ground. Why? Why? Why? Furious with her failure, she found herself physically straining and even sweating. Worse than the failure was the nagging voice, just within earshot, which appeared to be mocking her failure. It was hard to make out the words, but the tone of voice, and the voice itself, appeared to be those of her father.

"No!" she screamed, careless of who might hear her, and made one more desperate effort, closing her eyes tight shut with the exertion. She could feel the physical strain as she willed herself to rise off the ground, and was sure that this time, she had succeeded, only to be bitterly disappointed when she opened her eyes, and found herself still earthbound.

With a helpless moan, she sank to the ground, exhausted. She must get away from this place, she knew that. Once the shopkeepers discovered the leaves and flowers of her fairy gold, she would be searched for, discovered, and brought to trial. In France, she would be guillotined for theft. Here, she was sure that she would be hanged as a witch.

She began to sob, and the voice of her father seemed to become louder and more distinct. She could feel him closing in on her. She curled into a whimpering ball, crouched on the earth, despairing of her future.

Without warning, a blast of pain hit her, and she knew her

father was very close. There must be some way of defending herself. And then it came to her…

She stood, newly confident, and placed the recorder to her lips. From it came a tune which seemed fresh and new, but yet was, if she had known it, older than humanity, from a time when Those from the other side of the sky had walked the earth alone except for the presence of the Elementals.

Within seconds, two Sylphs appeared and bowed before her. Though they appeared to be the same as those who had recovered FitzAlan's body and head, it was impossible for her to tell with certainty whether that was the case or not.

The taller of the two Elementals bowed low. "Your wish, Mistress?"

"Take me from here, and away from Him." She had no need to specify the entity from which she wished to flee.

"Certainly, Mistress. Where do you wish to be transported?"

"Shawborough Hall," she told them. She did not fully understand why she had given the name of FitzAlan's family home as her destination, but she had a vague feeling that she would be safe there.

THE SYLPHS LIFTED HER, together with her bundle of clothes, off the ground, one on her left side, and one on her right, and sped off in a direction she knew to be northwards.

"He cannot come near us while you are with us," one of the Sylphs told Jane. This was news to her, that she was in some way protection for the Elementals, as well as them being protection for her.

"And afterwards? When you leave me?" she asked. "Will He not punish you for helping me?"

There was a sound as of leaves rustling. Jane realised that it was the other Sylph laughing quietly.

"He would, if we were to leave you," it said.

"But you cannot stay with me for ever," Jane objected.

"Why not? We would remain invisible, of course, unless you wished to see us."

"And we would take care not to become any kind of... shall we say 'embarrassment'," added the other.

"We haven't been a nuisance since you asked us to help you in Paris, have we?"

"You mean, you have been with me all the time since then?"

"Of course. Weren't you surprised that you weren't tired after flying all the way to the coast along the river?"

"You were helping me? Jane asked, thoroughly astonished.

"A little," said one Sylph.

"More than a little, actually," said the other. "You can fly, of course, but we thought you needed some help."

"Well... thank you. Tell me," she went on after a pause. "Could you have taken me across the Channel to England?" There was no answer. "So you could? Why didn't you?"

"You never even thought of asking us, and we could see that you were safe."

"If we had seen that you were in danger, though," came the voice from the other side, "you may be sure that we would have helped you."

"Well, thank you," Jane repeated. "And what of the others? Salamanders, Gnomes, Undines?"

"We are unable to answer that question. We don't have anything to do with them."

They flew on in silence for a while, the fields and hedgerows passing underneath them even faster than she remembered them doing on her flight over France.

"Why couldn't I fly just now?" she asked the Sylphs.

She felt a sensation that might have been a shrug (did Sylphs shrug?). "Hard to explain now," said one of her companions.

"We'll show you later," said the other.

By now, she was feeling tired. The unsuccessful effort to fly on her own had exhausted her, and she closed her eyes and slept.

SHE AWOKE WITH A START to find her feet firmly on the ground, and the two Sylphs standing one on each side of her. They were clearly in the park of a great house. Deer were feeding some way off, and the sun appeared to have just risen. She looked to see a large mansion to her left, the golden stone of the house glowing in the morning light.

"We will vanish now," said one of the Sylphs, "but we'll be near you when you need us."

"The music you played last night was wonderful," said the other. "It reminded us of home."

"But you don't need to play if you don't want to. Just want us badly enough and we'll help you."

"You've helped me a lot already," Jane said. "Thank you so much." She reached for the recorder, and started to play. This time the tune was a lively jig, and the two Sylphs broke into smiles, and then started to whirl in a fantastical dance. As Jane speeded up the tempo of the music, so the Sylphs' dance became faster and faster until they were whirling so fast that they were lost to sight.

Jane sighed, placed the recorder back in the placket of her skirt, and wondered what to do with her old clothes from France. In the end, she decided to make a detour into the woods and hide them under a pile of branches and leaves before making her way to the house.

She hesitated before approaching the main door of the house. Would it not be more appropriate, she asked herself, to go to the servants' entrance at the back? No, she decided firmly, she had come to see Thomas's elder brother, whom Thomas had named to her as George, and when visiting the family, one should use the family entrance.

There was a bell-pull near the door, and she pulled at it, hearing the sonorous clanging of a bell somewhere inside the house. After a few minutes, she heard footsteps, the drawing of bolts, and the door swung open to reveal a liveried footman, who simply stared at her expectantly.

"I am here to visit Sir George FitzAlan," she announced.

"Is he expecting you?"

"No," she confessed. "I am a friend of his brother, Captain Thomas FitzAlan, and I have news of him."

"I see, madam." The servant's manner was a touch more deferential at the mention of the family name.

"Sir George is breaking his fast. I will ask him if he wishes to meet you. What name should I give?"

"Machin. Jane Machin."

"Very good. Please wait here." He turned as if to leave her, but she called after him.

"Do you leave all your guests to cool their heels on the doorstep?"

He turned back, blushing. "I apologise. Please enter, and wait here." He gestured to a seat in the entrance hall, and left her.

While she was waiting, Jane took in the splendours, such as they were, of Shawborough Hall. Compared to the rather spartan draughty atmosphere of Tiengen and the Landgrave's castle, it was lavishly furnished, and some of the porcelain displayed in cabinets along the walls was exquisite.

There were some portraits on the walls, and with a pang she recognised a family likeness to Thomas in many of them.

She was on the point of getting up and examining one of them more closely, when a door opened, and Thomas FitzAlan entered the hall.

FOR AT LEAST A MINUTE she sat, stunned, while he looked down on her quizzically. At last she recovered her composure a little.

"Thomas?" she gasped.

He smiled. "No, I am George. I was told you are a friend of Thomas's, and I can see that you are telling the truth, since you have mistaken me for my younger twin brother."

By now she was on her feet, and she made him a curtsey. "I beg your pardon, Sir George," she said. "Thomas had told me that he had an elder brother, but not that he was his twin."

"Elder by a mere twenty minutes, Miss Machin. Like as two peas in a pod we are. Such fun we had as boys, confusing everyone. My dear, have you eaten?" he asked with a burst of solicitude. "Pray, join me at table. James," he called to the footman. "Make sure Miss Machin is refreshed after her journey. Send Lucy or one of the other maids to assist her if she needs it, and then bring her to me in the dining-room. I will see you in a few minutes, I trust," he smiled at her as the footman led her away.

She washed her hands and made herself more comfortable before allowing herself to be escorted to meet Sir George.

"Excellent," he said when he saw her. "James, pour Miss Machin some coffee. And bring her an egg and some bread and whatever else takes her fancy. Now then," he said to her. "You have news of my brother."

"Yes," she said, and began to weep.

He watched her, seemingly helplessly, and waited for words.

"He is dead," she sobbed.

He reeled a little, but recovered to ask. "Where? When? How?"

"In Paris about two weeks ago. He was betrayed by a group of evil men. Betrayed to the Jacobins, and he was guillotined."

"Lord save us!" Sir George was visibly shaken. He paused a while. "I hate to pry, but I feel I must. Excuse me, but what relationship did you have with Thomas? Were you..? Are you..?" He left the questions open, seemingly embarrassed to ask any more.

Now feeling a little bolder, Jane took a sip of the coffee before her. "Thomas was my friend. My colleague in the business we were pursuing together." Sir George raised his eyebrows, clearly expecting more. "And we were never lovers," she told Sir George frankly.

"The business being that on which he was engaged for the government, I take it?"

She nodded.

"The business about which he told you, and about which you were supposed to know nothing?" he smiled.

Another nod, and a pause.

"How did you come here?" he asked.

"I made my way to the coast from Paris, and then crossed the sea with the help of French fishermen and English smugglers. And from Weymouth I made my way here." She felt that nothing would be gained by telling the exact truth here.

"I see," he said, striking the same pose with the same expression on his face as Thomas had done when he was thinking, and thereby unconsciously twisting the knife in her heart. "I am so sorry, Miss Machin," he said to her. "It appears that you have suffered a loss with Thomas's death. As have I, of course." Another pause. "Please, do take one of these eggs. And some bread. Perhaps a little ham? Good."

They ate together in silence, digesting the fact of the death of a friend and a brother.

"They say that twins have an invisible link," he suddenly burst out. "On what day and at what time did he die?"

It was the Thursday before last. I am unsure of the exact time, but it was late afternoon."

"I knew it. At four thirty-two on that day – I know because I made a memorandum of it – I experienced a sudden pain here." He pointed to his neck. "Poor Thomas. At least the guillotine provides a quick death."

"Florella told me that," she agreed.

"Florella?" he asked, seemingly astonished. "How did you come to know her? Did you know the old man she calls her great-grandfather? And their friend, who calls himself Montalba?"

"They were the ones who betrayed him," she said, tears in her eyes. "Not Florella, but Montalba and the other."

There was a loud crash as Sir George smashed his fist on the table, causing the plates to rattle, and his coffee cup to jump off the table onto the floor. "The snakes! The poisonous snakes! Make no mistake, Thomas will be avenged."

"He has been," Jane said simply.

"What? How?"

"I procured their deaths," she told him, and held up a hand. "Pray, do not ask me what means I used. Simply rest assured that they died, and not as quickly or painlessly as your brother."

"And Florella?"

"She died at the hands of the man who called himself her great-grandfather."

A groan.

"You knew her?" she asked him.

"I was… fond of her. It was I who was at least in part responsible for her introduction to Montalba and the other in the belief that with her youth and her beauty, she could go to places and achieve results which would be impossible for a pair of elderly men. And it was I who also asked Thomas to work with them. So his death is upon my head."

"Do not blame yourself," Jane told him. "He was living a life full of danger. From the stories he told me, he was lucky to return from America alive."

"I suppose you are right." He paused and looked at Jane intently, reminding her of Thomas in his pose and expression. "Where are you staying?" he asked her.

"Nowhere," she confessed. "I was going to go to Lichfield, and see if any of my old friends whom I knew before I left there are still alive."

"I hardly know you, Miss Machin, but I believe you to have been a true friend to poor Thomas, God rest his soul, and your presence here would be some comfort to me. Might I prevail upon you to stay here for at least a few days?"

"I would be delighted, but…" She hesitated. "The truth is that I have no clothes other than the ones in which I stand before you now. As you may imagine, I was forced to leave France in somewhat rushed circumstances, and—"

He interrupted her. "Have you any money?"

"A little."

"No matter. I will arrange for the dressmaker to come here from the nearest town as soon as possible. It is no great metropolis, but you will be able to order what you require from her, I believe. Being a bachelor myself, I have no great knowledge of such things, but my neighbours' wives and daughters all speak very highly of Mrs Loseley. Pray feel free to order whatever you care to, and the bill will naturally be sent to me. For now, I am sure that Mrs Mallabar, the housekeeper, can provide you with—" he coughed in an embarrassed tone, "such garments as are necessary for female mysteries."

"You are too good to me, sir."

"Nonsense. It is no more than you deserve. Now finish your breakfast while I make the necessary arrangements."

THAT EVENING, Jane sat with Sir George after their dinner which they had eaten together. She had spent a few happy hours with the seamstress, ordering some garments which, while not the most fashionable that might be obtained, would represented an improvement on those she had been wearing when she arrived. For the moment, she was dressed in clothes borrowed from Sir George's housekeeper, which hung somewhat loosely on her slender frame.

Their conversation over the evening meal had been largely composed of formalities. It was clear to each of them that the other had questions to ask regarding Thomas, but it had not seemed appropriate to ask them during the meal.

"This may be painful for you to remember, Miss Machin," Sir George said to Jane, "but I would be much obliged if you could tell me some more about my brother's death. Indeed, if you could tell me some more about how you came to know him and the nature of your business with him, though I realise that this may be intruding on your privacy to an unwarrantable degree."

Jane considered for a moment how much she could tell this man. She had to remind herself that although he reminded her strongly of her deceased friend, a man in whom she had come to repose a great deal of trust, he was not that man, and might react unfavourably to her account of Them and her father. On the other hand, he had expressed knowledge of Montalba and Florella and Ortolanus. He must have some knowledge of what they were about, she realised.

"I met him at an inn in Hasselt in Belgium," she began.

Sir George raised his eyebrows in a gesture that reminded her strongly of his brother. "Not in France, then? You intrigue me, Miss Machin."

"I was travelling from Germany," she explained. Again the raised eyebrows.

Jane sighed. It might be necessary for her to say more than she had originally intended. Like his brother, Sir George did not give the impression of being content with partial explanations.

"I suppose I should give you a little more information about myself," she explained.

"I was born quite close to here, in Soho, near Birmingham," she went on. "The man I knew as my father worked for Matthew Boulton, the industrialist. My mother died when I was young, and I was sent to live with a kindly family in Lichfield, where I became acquainted with Dr Erasmus Darwin and some of his friends." Sir George appeared to start somewhat at the name of Darwin, but made no comment, and she continued. "However, for reasons that I may explain later, it was considered necessary for me to leave the country, and I was sent to live in Zürich through friends of Dr Darwin at the age of nine. After about ten years, I met a mesmerist and alchemist who went by the names of Hermecritus and Philomentor among others – his real name does not matter – and we travelled to Germany and stayed as guests of a Landgrave in Tiengen for a while." She paused, somehow conscious from Sir George's expression of the fact that she was informing him of events of which he was seemingly already aware. "We then went on, he to Heidelberg where he wished to become a professor at the University, and I to France, where I wished to learn more about the Revolution." Her voice broke at this point. "I learned more about the Revolution than I had expected, didn't I?"

There was near silence in the room for a minute or so while Sir George waited for Jane to collect herself. "As I was travelling from Germany to France, I stayed at an inn, as I said earlier, and the landlord there suggested that I meet another Englishman, your brother Thomas." She paused, wondering whether to go on. Decision made, she continued. "At the time, I considered it to be purely coincidence that he and I should be staying at the same inn. However, in Paris, Montalba told me that he and Ortolanus had been keeping watch over my companion Hermecritus and me since the time that we were in Germany, and had ordered your brother to make my acquaintance." She looked at Sir George, expecting some reaction, but he merely nodded, which she found infuriating. She raised her voice. "Sir, you informed me this morning that you had sent your brother to work with these men, for reasons I am unable to comprehend. Did you also instruct him or them to make contact with me?" Her tone had become shrill by the time she had finished speaking.

FitzAlan held up a hand. "Please, Miss Machin, listen to me. I will explain to you shortly why I employed the two men you mention, and why I sent the woman you knew as Florella and my brother to be with them. For now, however, please accept my assurances that I had no knowledge of this aspect of their operations. Indeed, your very existence was unknown to me until two days ago, when a letter arrived from my brother, sent from Paris three weeks ago, presumably a short time before his death. I believe that the letter may have arrived in this country using the same method as you employed." Jane smiled to herself, remembering how much she had relied on the Sylphs' assistance. "That is to say, with the aid of fisher-men and smugglers."

"A letter?" She wondered when he might have sent it. "What did he have to say about me?"

He chuckled. "We all wish to know what others have to say about us, do we not? He was extremely complimentary about you, I must say. If it will not embarrass you too much, with your permission I will read what he had to say about you, eh?" She nodded. "Very well, then." He pulled a paper from his pocket and peered at it. "Here we are, yes. 'I am in Paris with a most agreeable young Englishwoman, Miss Jane Machin. I know next to nothing of her antecedents, but what I know of her character and intelligence gives me confidence to expect that, should our acquaintance continue, she is in a fair way of being asked to be Mrs FitzAlan'. My dear Miss Machin," breaking off. Jane was now openly sobbing.

"He never told me anything of this," Jane said. "If he had asked me…"

To her intense relief, Sir George said nothing, but refolded the paper and replaced it in his pocket before rising. "Perhaps I should leave you alone?" he suggested.

Jane shook her head emphatically. "No, no, do not leave me," she said. "I do not wish to be alone. I will tell you more."

She forced herself to be calm as she recounted the events of the day when Thomas FitzAlan had met his end, starting with the scuffle with the *sans-culottes*, and moving through the catacombs.

Sir George listened in silence until she came to the point in her story when she had discovered that her brother had been betrayed, and Florella's subsequent murder.

"Poor Thomas, and poor Florella," he remarked. "And you as well," he added. "It is abundantly clear to me from what you have told me, and the way in which you have told me of these events, that you were genuinely attached to poor Thomas.

May I ask how you escaped? You said that you procured the deaths of those who were responsible for his death?"

"I did say that, but forgive me if I do not tell you at this time. That is, until I know a little more about your dealings with those people." Again her feelings threatened to overwhelm her, and her eyes filled with tears.

AT LENGTH she regained a little of her self-control, and looked at Sir George with eyes which had been recently dried with her hand-kerchief. "May I now know about your dealings with... with those men?"

He regarded her seriously for some moments before replying. "I will tell you, and though I believe that what I am about to say might prove a source of distress to some, my feeling is that this will not upset you. Indeed, some of it may already be familiar to you." He cleared his throat. "What I am about to say to you is in confidence, and I have every expectation that you will not repeat it to anyone." She nodded in silence. "Very well, then. I may appear to others to be no more than a simple member of the minor provincial nobility, with an interest in little more than the pheasants in my woods, and the cattle out there." He swept an arm towards the windows of the room through which it was indeed possible to see a herd of cows contentedly grazing in the park beyond the ha-ha.

"Indeed, Thomas described you as such at one time," Jane told him.

"Did he, by Jove? But no matter. I am involved with a group who are concerned with some very dark matters. No, not politics, but those things which are invisible to the majority. Indeed, their very existence is unknown to most. In short, beings that those few who suspect their existence might describe as Faeries." He stopped, and peered at Jane. "You are not laughing? A grown man who believes in fairies?"

"By no means, Sir," Jane assured him. "Pray continue."

"Very well. A small group of us, some of us personally known to the Prime Minister and appointed by him, is now engaged in the investigation of these beings, whom we refer to as the Fae. We believe that they may be plotting to take over this world, and to force us – that is to say, human beings – into some sort of subjected state. You no doubt think by now that I am deranged, and you wish to remove yourself from my presence before I turn into a raving monster?"

"By no means," she repeated. "Indeed, I believe that I should tell you more about myself when you have told me a little more about your group. Are you followers of the Rosy Cross? Perhaps you are Freemasons?"

FitzAlan laughed easily. "Not at all, nothing of that kind. There is, of course, some link between these people and our beliefs, and some of us are Freemasons, but no, we do not subscribe unthinkingly to their doctrines. We call our group the Revellers of Thoth."

"Thoth?" she queried him. "The Egyptian god of the underworld and judge of the dead?"

He nodded in assent. "The same. Also science and magic."

"And you are revellers? Am I to assume that you participate in wild uninhibited activities?"

"No, no. We merely revel in knowledge."

"And those men in Paris, and Florella? Are they – were they – fellow Revellers?"

"No, they were not. Those who work within our group are by no means all adepts in these matters. To be sure we have a sound theoretical knowledge, and between us, our libraries on the subject may be accounted as being the foremost in Europe. But we required the services of those who could bring practical experience to our quest. The one known as Montalba represented himself to one of our number as being such an individual, as did his companion."

"Ha!" Jane exclaimed involuntarily. "Indeed?"

Sir George regarded her sharply. "You have reasons for doubt? I may enquire further about those reasons later. But yes, I, too, shared your doubts to some degree. So I sent the woman you knew as Florella to join them and to report back to me. She was recommended to us as a wise woman, who had knowledge of these matters. She was also possessed, as you may have noticed, of an extraordinary, almost unearthly beauty. Sadly, her knowledge was not what I had been led to believe, and her reports neither confirmed nor denied the abilities of the others.

"I was therefore forced to send Thomas to meet them. He was, as I am sure you observed, of a more reflective turn of mind than the average Army officer. Though he lacked much of the theoretical knowledge that we Revellers possess, he nonetheless studied enough to be able to protect himself against any attack from the other side— What is it?" he asked. "You started just now."

"You used that phrase 'the other side'. What do you mean by it?"

"Those beings – the Fae. We believe that they somehow come from the other side of our reality. I find it difficult to explain simply. It is one of those things that one either understands instinctively, as I perceive you do, or dismisses as nonsense."

"Your brother used his knowledge at one time to protect me," Jane said. "Garlic, crucifixes, and Hebrew characters."

"You were under attack?" Jane nodded. "I must know more."

"Later, if you would, sir."

"It strikes me, Miss Machin, that you know much more

about these matters than you have told me so far." He smiled, but his voice was firm.

"I do, but I would like to tell not just you, but the other Revellers, as you call them. Without any disrespect to you, sir, I feel that my situation demands the attention of more than one man."

"I trust that what you have to say will be worthwhile?"

"Depend upon it, sir, it will."

Very well. It will take a few days to have them assemble here. In the meantime, naturally you are welcome to stay here, and take your meals with me. Should you wish to avail yourself of my library, you are free to do so."

JANE ENJOYED HERSELF in Sir George's library. As he had said, it was splendidly stocked, with many volumes that she had never seen before.

"Do you read Arabic?" she asked him one evening over their meal together. "And Hebrew?"

"A little Hebrew, yes, but sadly no Arabic. I suppose you…?"

She shook her head. "I fear not. French, German and Latin with a little Greek is the best I can muster."

"A good solid grounding," he agreed.

Unlike the library at Tiengen, the books seemed to be arranged in some sort of order, and the books which appeared to deal with various aspects of Them, or the Fae as she had now decided to call them, adopting the name that the Revellers had bestowed on them, were all on one shelf together. Some of them she had already seen in the Landgrave's library at Tiengen, but many of them, in English, were new to her. As she had been told, many of the books, especially those written in English, appeared to identify Them with the Good Folk or Fae, especially those written in the paſt hundred years.

There were several books written in earlier times who deſcribed them as similar to demons.

But there was one book of natural hiſtory, printed in the city of York in 1547, which gave a brief description, between an account of the Indians of the newly-discovered continent of America, and a description of the African Unicorne, supposedly quoting from an earlier unnamed text, which seemed to describe what Jane knew of Them all too well.

"Of Faerie and their Properties

"This Claſſe of Being ſome term the *Goode Folke*, though in truth they doe lacke moſt of thoſe Qualities of Chriſtian Men and Women. Others do call them *Sith* or in the Tongue of the Scots, *Daoine Sidhe*. Some term them as Demones or Fallen Angels, and ſome ſee them as the Survivors of an older and brutiſh Race of Men, who hyde from us through Feare. Still otheres term them *Fae*. The Doctors of our Schools for the moſt part do believe them to be a Race older than ours, neither Human nor Divine nor Helliſh, with Powers ſuch as we do not poſſeſs.

"Faerie may make for themſelves Dwellynges, the whych they term Palaces or *Brugh*, though they be no more than Holes in the Earthe. They are ruled by One they term their Kynge, who nonetheleſs appears to be poſſeſſed of no Majeſtie or Dygnitie, his Quality being the Poſſeſſor of a greater Strength than the others, whom he ſubjugates by Force. It is alſo ſaid by ſome that this Kynge may poſſeſs the Qualities and Attributes of all his Subjects, the latter only poſſeſſing a ſmalle Portion of the ſame.

"Certes, they do lack the Power to diſtinguiſh Goode and Eville, and may often ſteale away ſmall Infantes, claiming theſe unfortunates as their own. Some fooliſh Women have claim'd congreſs with theſe, even to their Kynge, and borne children. Such children are held by the fooliſh to have Powers like thoſe of the Elementals.

"As to the home Landes of the Sith, though they inhabyt their Moundes and Holes in wylde and rugged places such as the Northern Mountaignes and Laykes, and the Hylles of Derby Shire, their true Home is held to be in the sixth Sphere above the Hevennes, that is to say the primal Chaos. Thus some do name them as the People of the Other Side of the Skye."

"These others, that is, the Subjectes of the Faerie, may be divided into four Classes or Categories, each Categorie in correspondence with the four Elements, thus:

"Primus: *Earthe*, represented by the *Gnomes*, of a squat and brutish Forme, who have Power to move through solid Grounde and Walls of buildings.

"Secondus: *Water*, inhabited by the *Undines*, of a smoothe and shining Appearance, who like Fysshe may exist and take their nourishment from beneath the Waves of Pondes, Rivers, and Oceans.

"Tertius: *Ayre*, in which dwelle the *Sylphes*, of a tall and pleasing Forme, who may travel through the Ayre, though not as do Byrdes.

"Quartus: *Fyre*, wherein the *Salamandres* have their being. In their human Forme, they are possess'd of great Beauty, but more commonly take the Shape of a loathsome Reptile.

"These four Classes we may term *Elementals*, in reference to their attachment to the Elements. They bear little Relation to the Faerie, being Natives of our Worlde, but now unwillingly serve as Slaves of the Faerie."

Jane closed the book and stared at it thoughtfully. Much of what the book described as myth or superstition, she knew inside herself to be no less than fact.

She glanced at the title: *De philosophia contra naturam Mundi* by a Hugo Lombardi – "Of the unnatural philosophy of the world". Did the gentlemen – these Revellers of Thoth – know of this book? If they did, would they believe it, or would they have more modern views about the Fae? And if she really was one of the Fae, or at least half of her was Fae, she did have these powers, and the respect of the Elementals whom she had summoned. She could prove that she had the power to summon Elementals, and to use their powers to fly, to walk through walls, possibly even (though she was reluctant to do this) to live underwater or walk though fire.

XV

The Gathering

THE DAY CAME WHEN THE REVELLERS OF THOTH were to assemble in the evening. Jane's new clothes had been delivered that morning, and she delighted in the sense of well-being that they gave her.

"You look very well in them," Sir George had said to her when she presented herself wearing the new garments to him.

"Thank you, sir," she answered, sketching a half-curtsey to him. "You are most kind."

"Nonsense," he said, clearly embarrassed. "It is the least I could do for a friend of poor Thomas. The Revellers will be here this evening. May I suggest that you dine apart from us tonight? I would like to take the opportunity to tell my friends – and I trust that they will become your friends, too – a little about Thomas, based on what you have told me, and a very little about what I know of you. Indeed, I know remarkably little. I feel it will be easier for me to do this when you are

279

not present. Have no fear, I intend to say nothing derogatory or that might embarrass you."

"Very well, sir."

"I will send someone to fetch you when the time is right. Probably about half past eight? Good. I will have dinner sent to your room at about seven."

In her room, as she waited for her meal, Jane rehearsed in her head how she would explain herself, and how she could give a coherent account of the Fae. She had brought the book from the library, and it gave her some comfort to realise that the things she had learned about these beings were seemingly accepted by at least some others whose work was considered to be of sufficient significance to be included in a library of such matters.

Who would these men be? she asked herself. If they were all of the same quality as Sir George, who seemed to be honest and straightforward enough, and of a pleasing nature, then she should find it easy enough to provide them with her story.

She ate, and sat in front of the mirror, waiting for the summons. As she sat, she became aware of her father, outside the window, and furiously making repeated attempts to enter.

"Go away!" she shouted aloud, not caring if she could be overhead or not.

To her horror, the familiar oily sticky feeling swept over her, and she could hear his voice in her head.

"This is your last chance to join us, and to claim back that which is rightfully ours," He hissed.

"And if I do not?" she asked.

"Need you ask? You and those who claim to be your friends will be destroyed."

"When do you want my answer?" she asked, playing for time, and instantly realised that He knew she was stalling.

"Now. But you have already made up your mind, have you not?"

"I have," she said. "I will not join you."

"Weak. Weak like your mother," He told her. "Very well, then. I shall leave. But rest assured, I will return."

There was a sound from outside the house of a mighty wind sweeping past, rattling window-panes, and slamming shut the door of an outbuilding which had been left ajar. The force of the gale seemed to be centred on Jane's window, and the wind howled its rage for minutes on end. Then, as abruptly as it had started, it ceased, and there was silence in the room, broken only by the sound of a knock at the door.

"Excuse me, Miss, but Sir George says to come down and meet the gentlemen now, if you're ready, that is," came a voice she seemed to recognise as belonging to one of the maids.

"I'm coming," she answered, and opened the door, to a being that was definitely not a servant of Sir George's. A tall dark figure, with almost shining black hair, and burning eyes stood, an evil smile on its face.

"You thought I'd gone, daughter of mine, didn't you?" he asked. There was little malice in his tone, but there was a certain triumph.

"I did," she confessed. She fumbled in the placket of her new dress. Surely she had remembered to put it in. She had. She remembered putting it there. But there was nothing.

"Sylphs of mine. Help me. *M'aidez!*" she called out.

"*Your* Sylphs, daughter? Mine, surely?" he mocked, but the gloating smile faded as the two Sylphs who had carried her across France and England appeared. "I command you both, return to my power, or it will be the worse for you."

The taller Sylph spoke. "It will be the worse for us if we are in your power. Mistress Jane here has done nothing to damage or hurt us."

"Unlike others," added the other. "Others who are now here."

"Silence!" he flashed, and levelled a finger at the second Sylph, who shrank back involuntarily.

While this exchange had been going on, Jane had remembered that the new dress had its placket on the other side, and had been searching in it. At last her fingers closed on it.

She drew out one of the silver crosses that Thomas FitzAlan had placed in her room in Paris only a few weeks previously, which she had taken on an impulse and carried with her ever since then, and held it in front of her, thrusting it towards the face of her adversary.

He snarled, beast-like, and took a step backwards. Jane and the two Sylphs stepped forwards, causing her father to retreat further.

"I see now what you are," he said. "I will remember this." And with a loud pop, as of an inflated bladder bursting, and a puff of dirty grey smoke, he was gone.

"Thank you, my friends," said Jane to the Sylphs. "You are free to leave me."

"Oh no," said the taller one. "We will stay close to you, though you will not see us."

"Unless you wish it," said the other.

"As you will," said Jane.

The two Sylphs vanished from her sight, as a maid came towards her through a door at the end of the passage.

"I'm sorry, Miss," she said. "I'm a little late on account of that wind just now. Dreadful shocking it's been. Stable door near off its hinges, Jesse says, and two of Sir George's carriage horses gone galloping off the Lord knows where, and all in a mess and a pig's ear. Sorry, Miss," she repeated, and seemed to pull herself together a bit. "Sir George's compliments and would you care to join him and the gentlemen downstairs when you're ready."

I'm ready now," Jane said, and followed the girl down the stairs.

"Are you feeling well?" were Sir George's first words to her as she entered the drawing-room and he stood to greet her.

"Of course," said Jane. "Why do you ask?"

"You appear pale and shaken. Has that sudden wind upset you? I am told that two of my horses have bolted and cannot be seen."

"He will never see them again," came the voice of one of the Sylphs in her ear. "Tell him."

"I believe, Sir George, that those horses are lost to you for ever."

He started at that, but recovered himself quickly. "A glass of something strengthening for you, Miss Machin?" he suggested. "There is an excellent port if your tastes happen to fall that way, or some sherry-wine."

"A small glass of sherry-wine sounds ideal," Jane smiled.

She accepted the glass that the footman held out to her, and Sir George allowed her to take a few sips before escorting her to the other side of the room where half a dozen or so men were standing or sitting talking, ostentatiously not taking any notice of Jane, presumably under orders not to embarrass her. Sir George called them over to Jane and himself and made the introductions.

"Lord Grenfell," he said of a tall thin man who looked to be little more than a handsome schoolboy. "His Lordship is studying at Christ's College in Cambridge."

Jane made him a curtsey, he returned to the group, and next Sir George introduced Professor Marlowe of Oxford who appeared to be, Jane thought, everything that an Oxford professor should be, with a mane of silver hair and a round face in the centre of which was a red nose decorated with broken veins.

Next was Sir Richard Willington, of Heathfield, near Nantwich. A middle-aged, corpulent and well turned-out man, who bowed low to Jane as she acknowledged his presence.

White-bearded Herr Professor Wolfgang Parseval from Heidelberg University in Germany came next. "Do you know Professor Otto—" Jane broke off, realising that she had, for the moment, forgotten Otto's name. "He called himself Philomentor at times…?" she finished, a little embarrassed.

"Of course I know Otto!" he exclaimed in accented English. "He joined us only recently, but he has given us all inspiration and new ideas." He stopped and looked at Jane. "You must be the one."

"The one?" asked Sir Richard.

"Yes, the girl who travelled with Otto and worked marvels. Delighted to see you, and I look forward to hearing your story."

Next to be called to meet Jane was the Bishop of Chester, the Right Reverend Doctor Solomon Juspitt, who regarded Jane with a suspicious air as he offered her his limp hand, though whether to kiss or to shake she was unsure. She ended up shaking it.

Last was a heavy-set man, scarred by smallpox, who walked heavily towards Jane, his eyes fixed on hers.

"And this is—"

"Uncle 'Rasmus!" exclaimed Jane in delight. "I mean, Doctor Erasmus Darwin!" For a moment she was nine years old again, with the man whom she had adored, and who she had believed had adored her, until the time when he had arranged to send her to Switzerland.

"My dear Jane," he replied, the large stupid-looking face breaking into a smile. "I am so very very happy to see you again."

"And I you," she said to him, her happy memories of Lichfield driving out the faint traces of her resentment.

"You are too old now for me to take you in my arms as I used to do," he said, smiling.

"Nonsense!" she exclaimed, and threw her arms around him, taking in the scent of the medicines and lotions which clung to him. "Are you still living in the Close?"

"No, no, I now live in Derby. I will tell you all about it in time."

Sir George had been watching, as had the others, at this exchange. "I am delighted to have brought about this reunion," he said.

WHILE THE OTHER SO-CALLED REVELLERS were exchanging comments, most of which Jane guessed were concerning her, from the looks she observed being cast in her direction, she cornered Darwin. They moved into a corner of the room and spoke in low tones.

"It is a long time since we met, is it not?" he said. "I hope you can forgive me for wrenching you from Lichfield. Believe me, it seemed to be the best thing at the time."

"Later, later," she answered him. "For now, please tell me about the others whom I have just met. Who are they, and why has this assembly been constituted?"

"Let me answer your last question first. Sir George

FitzAlan has the ear of the Prime Minister. He may appear to be little more than an idle provincial landowner, but he is extremely well-read on the various subjects, such as alchemy and the Rosicrucians, as well as some Jewish mystical traditions known collectively as Kabbala. He became convinced that there was a danger to the nation posed by the beings such as the one who calls himself your father. He talked to the Prime Minister, and was allowed to form this group, which reports directly to London through Sir George."

"Is he to be trusted?"

"The Prime Minister?" Darwin laughed. "Perhaps. Sir George? Absolutely. In matters of honesty and probity, that is. Perhaps I do not trust his judgement and understanding of certain matters. Which is why he has collected differing points of view."

"The bishop, for example?"

"Indeed. A dear man, devout in his own way, and certainly able to give us some guidance from a more conventional view of these matters."

"And Lord Grenfell? Is he not rather young compared to the rest of you all?"

"He has money, which is always useful. Also, unlike many of those with money, he has curiosity and intelligence. He has come on remarkably in the past six months or so in his understanding of these esoteric matters."

"Sir Richard?"

"Admirably educated in these affairs. He has pursued certain lines of enquiry further than anyone else in our little group. A valuable asset in that regard, and he has made several practical contributions as well."

"The professor from Oxford?"

"A most delightful companion, and possessed of a valuable library of his own, rivalling that of Sir George, as well as providing us with access to the locked shelves of the Bodleian Library."

"And the German?"

"It was felt that the group required a member with a knowledge of the German language, as well as a knowledge of the hermetic sciences, including the Continental and Jewish traditions. Had your friend Otto been a member of the faculty at Heidelberg at that time, he would have been our first choice, but as it is, Professor Parseval has been most useful."

"And yourself? I am delighted to see you here, but from what I know of your beliefs, you would seem to be the odd man out in this company."

Darwin sighed. "It is true that in the past my thoughts and beliefs have been almost exclusively based around empirical science and natural philosophy – those things that one can perceive with the senses. However, talking to Kate Perkins, and experiencing some of the events surrounding you and her – including your performance at Matthew Boulton's house that evening so long ago – I am forced to the conclusion that there may be more to these matters than I had originally considered was the case. However, I do not accept everything unquestioningly, and hence I am looked upon as the group's sceptic."

"I see. You mentioned Kate Perkins. How is she?"

Darwin's face lengthened, and he appeared to be about to reply, but was forestalled by Sir George, who moved towards them.

"Leave us," Sir George commanded the servants, and waited until they had all gone out of the room. "There is no need for them or anyone else to hear what is to be said tonight – at least, not at this stage of the proceedings. Now, if the gentlemen would please take their seats as previously discussed, and if Miss Machin would take this seat here…"

The company were soon arranged in a crescent shape, facing Jane, who sat alone facing them.

"There is no need to be nervous," Sir George told Jane. "Indeed, perhaps we are all more nervous than are you, as we wait to hear what you have to say to us."

JANE CLEARED HER THROAT and began, her eyes cast down. "I know from Sir George, who has been a most gracious host, that you are all concerned with the Others. Those whom I have known as Those from the other side of the sky. I know that They have been given other names by some, but up to now, I have simply referred to these beings as Them." She pronounced the last word in a singular way, which seemed to imply a capital letter. "But thanks to you, I now have a name for them – the Fae." She looked up to see some nods of approval, and all eyes fixed upon her.

"First of all, I want to tell you— I do not use the word 'confess' because this is none of my doing and therefore does not count as a confession — that I am half one of Them – that is to say, those whom you term the Fae." A stir. "My father, somehow, is one of the Fae. Indeed, he seems to be the chief or king of Them."

"How do you know this?" This from Bishop Juspitt.

"I have seen him, and I have heard his voice on enough occasions to believe him. Indeed, the small tempest earlier this evening was of his doing. He was attempting to persuade me, as he has done on several occasions in the past, to join him to drive the race of men into servitude so he and his race may take over the earth."

"This is not delusion on your part?" asked the bishop.

"Is this delusion?" asked Jane, standing up, and calmly

walking through the wall of the room into the next room. She returned the same way, to find the men talking excitedly among themselves.

"Is this delusion?" she repeated, willing the two Sylphs to make themselves visible.

A stir, as the bishop shrank away from the Elementals standing before him and crossed himself. "Sylphs?" he croaked.

"Indeed," Jane affirmed. "You may go," she told the pair of Elementals.

She made as if to continue, but Sir George held up his hand. "My dear Miss Machin, pray do not give us any more shocks of that nature. Despite the fact that we have England's finest doctor in this room with us (cries of "No!" from Erasmus Darwin), some of us have weaker constitutions than others, and any further demonstrations without warning…" He tailed off. "Do any of you require brandy?" The bishop raised his hand, and Sir George poured and brought a glass to him, which he accepted and drank off with alacrity.

"How did you manage to persuade your father, as you call him, to leave?" asked Professor Marlowe.

"With the aid of my Sylphs," Jane answered, "and with this," displaying the silver cross.

"Then you are, after all, a Christian?" said the bishop.

Jane was at a loss how to answer him, but Erasmus Darwin answered on her behalf. "It matters not one jot or tittle," he said firmly. "Some of us here might not qualify for that distinction according to your standards, my Lord Bishop."

"Oh, very well," muttered Juspitt.

Jane realised that these men would not be fobbed off by easy answers from her. They were men who were accustomed to asking questions, and attempting to prove by query and logic what they could not readily experience for themselves.

"As to how this man came to be my father, I do not know.

My mother died when I was young – I have reason to believe that my father was the ultimate cause of her death – and her husband – my human father, if you will—" she shrugged. "I have not seen in years."

Again it was Erasmus Darwin who spoke. "I had word that he died in Cornwall some three years ago," he said. "I am sorry."

"I am not," said Jane. "I hardly knew him. If he were to walk into this room, I would not know him. He would be a stranger to me."

A silence descended over the room for the space of about a minute.

"Very well, Miss Machin," said Sir George, breaking the silence. "Could you please tell us something of your experiences in Paris, if it would not be too painful for you. I have already informed the company of my brother's sad demise, but not of the circumstances surrounding it."

Jane proceeded to relate her adventures since she had met Thomas FitzAlan at the Belgian inn. When she came to describe the nocturnal visit of her father in Paris and the entreaty to join the Fae, there was a buzz of conversation.

"Excuse me, Miss Machin," Professor Marlowe said to her. "Are we to understand that the Fae are in favour of the French Revolution? That they desire to see the Jacobins in power?"

Jane considered for a moment before answering. "I do not believe that They care very much for the details who is in power. I believe that all that the one who calls himself my father wants is chaos and destruction, which weaken the power of humanity to stand against him and his forces."

"I was of the opinion, as I informed you, that this might be the case, Professor," said the young Lord Grenfell.

"So you did, so you did," the Professor acknowledged. "My apologies, Miss Machin. Pray continue."

Jane described the defences that she had found in her room and which had been chalked on the floor, which Thomas FitzAlan had later admitted to providing. "The silver cross that I showed earlier was one of those," she explained.

"You taught him well," Sir George said to Professor Parseval, who shook his head.

"Not I," he replied. "Naturally I am aware of the power of garlic and of the silver cross, but a deep knowledge of Kabbala is outside my sphere of understanding."

"Could it be," suggested Professor Marlowe, "that the man who called himself Montalba was the one who taught him?" He stopped and looked at Jane. "The name means something to you?"

"Unfortunately, sir, it does," she answered him. "If I may continue?"

"Of course."

Jane proceeded to tell them of the time when she and Thomas had confronted the *sans-culottes*, before she had met Montalba and been led down the stairs to the catacombs, where she had met Florella and Ortolanus.

She described how Ortolanus and Florella had been playing with the Tarot cards and their links to the Sephirod and the Tree of Life, at which the bishop let out a most unepiscopal snort. "The devil's picture-book," he exclaimed dismissively.

"Nonetheless," began Professor Parseval, who appeared to take exception to this description of the Tarot, but he stopped on noticing Erasmus Darwin holding up a warning hand.

Jane continued with the description of the long wait for Thomas FitzAlan, and the reluctant decision to move on to the house near the guillotine.

Tears came to her eyes as she described the sounds of the blade falling on the neck of its victims, the last of which was Thomas, and the cheers that accompanied each decapitation.

The tears vanished as she described the way in which the Sylphs had brought Thomas's head and body to the house, and anger filled her voice as she told the company of what Florella had said, describing the treachery of Montalba and Ortolanus and their betrayal of the British cause.

She then proceeded how she had lured the two men to their deaths at the hands of the Salamanders, using the promise of the knowledge of life and death as the bait to entrap them. There was a gasp as she concluded with, "And so I avenged the death of my friend – my friends, for Florella in her last hours had become my friend." She saw Erasmus Darwin turn away and dab at his eyes with his hand-kerchief.

All eyes turned to Sir Richard Willington, and it was Sir George FitzAlan who spoke.

"Sir Richard, it was you, was it not, who proposed the recruiting of these two men?"

"It was."

"And was it not you who proposed that the woman Florella be sent to be with them, and also my own brother?"

"Indeed it was, but I had no idea of the state of affairs that has just been related to us by Miss Machin here. That is, of course, if Miss Machin's story is to be believed." Sir Richard's face was red, and he appeared almost ready to explode as he faced Sir George.

"Upon my word," expostulated Lord Grenfell. "If it were not for the common cause that unites us, Sir Richard, I would have no hesitation, sir, in calling you out for your lack of courtesy to a lady."

Sir Richard was clearly not to be put down. "And I, sir, would have no hesitation in accepting a challenge from an insolent young puffjockey such as yourself."

It appeared that matters were about to become dangerously overheated, but Sir George intervened.

"Your Lordship, Sir Richard, let us have some peace in this room. I would remind you that Miss Machin is not only a guest in this room, but has, it seems, a long-established friendship with Dr Darwin."

"Nonetheless," said Sir Richard, still plainly unmollified, "I would remind the company of two things. Imprimis, Miss Machin, no matter how charming and intimate with our friend she may have been all those years ago, would appear to have vanished from the sight of Englishmen for a number of years. Who knows what changes in her temperament she may have undergone in that time?" There was a general murmur, but whether of approval or disapproval it was difficult to judge. "Secundus, we have seen for ourselves her powers, which would seem to include the summoning, and therefore, the control, of Elementals. How are we to know her true sympathies in this matter?"

There was a general uproar at this, lasting for what seemed to Jane to be an eternity. From what she could make out, the general opinion seemed to be in her favour, but there was also an opposing point of view, led by Sir Richard, that she was not wholly to be trusted.

Sir George rose to his feet, and with a roar that might have been heard in the next county, called for silence. The voices stilled, as he withdrew a paper from his breast pocket.

"You all knew my brother, Thomas," he said. There were nods of agreement. "You knew him to be an honest and capable man, who had served his country well." More nods. "Then let me read to you the words of this honest and capable man, who had knowledge of Miss Machin and her character at a much more recent date than Dr Darwin, and also was aware of her powers and capabilities. This is a letter written in my brother's last hours, following the clash between him and the bravos of which we have just heard, following his detention and before his execution by the Revolutionary authorities. Somehow he was able to pass it to a trusted colleague, who ensured that it would eventually be in my hands, albeit that it only reached me this morning. Do I have your permission to read it, Miss Machin? Parts of it concern you."

She nodded, and Sir George began.

"'MY DEAR BROTHER'," he started. "'I have no surety that this letter will ever reach you. I am permitted pen and paper by my gaoler, for I am now awaiting trial – which will be brief, and the verdict pre-ordained – and almost certain death.'" Here Sir George paused, visibly affected by what he had just read.

"'Briefly, for I have little time, I must tell you that I was betrayed by the men known as Montalba and Ortolanus. I was forced into a scuffle with some of the riff-raff who infest this town, and then sent to settle the unfinished business, with the certain knowledge that I would be killed outright or captured. I was assured of this by my captors, and with the benefit of hindsight, I have no reason to disbelieve them.'"

"How has this letter arrived with you?" asked the bishop, curiously.

"Pray have a little patience, my Lord Bishop. This is partly explained later in the letter, and was partly explained by the messenger who delivered it to me. To continue. 'I confess that I had had my suspicions of the two men for some time, that they were working for their own ends and were willing to form an alliance with the Fae. It seemed to me, though she would never admit that it was so, that poor Mary—'This was the young woman known to you as Florella," Sir George helpfully explained to Jane, "'was brutally treated by these two.'" He paused, and there was an intake of breath from several of the assembled company.

"It would seem that at least some of Miss Machin's statements are corroborated here, then," said Professor Parseval in his heavily accented English.

"Indeed they are. Let me read on. 'As to Miss Machin, there is much to say that I fear I have been negligent to report. First, she possesses vast powers – beyond the scope of our imagination. She would appear to be half-Fae, and to be possessed of their powers, but also of a human conscience and sensibility. As I mentioned in an earlier letter to you, I find her to be most agreeable company. She seems to be of an honest disposition, to be genuine in her dislike of the Fae and her willingness to work against them, and it is a sadness to me that I will never, other than by the power of a miracle, see her again. Should you by chance ever have the good fortune to encounter her, please pass on my most affectionate regards, though they will necessarily be from beyond the grave.

"'This letter will be smuggled out (for an outrageous fee in gold pieces) by my gaoler, who swears that he knows how to have this letter conveyed by trusty hands to England. He is a surly brute, but possessed of some intelligence, and I have no alternative but to trust him.

"'Farewell, your affectionate brother, Thomas.' And so it ends. This was brought to this house this morning, apparently by an unknown man, and handed to my butler." Sir George folded the letter and replaced it in his pocket before withdrawing a hand-kerchief and offering it to Jane, whose face was covered by silent tears.

She thanked him, and turned to face the company, all of whom, with the possible exception of Sir Richard Willington, regarded her with expressions of the utmost sympathy.

"Your brother was a good man," the bishop remarked to Sir

George. "A little fanciful in some of his imaginings, perhaps, but sound judgement in most things."

"I must agree with His Grace," said young Lord Grenfell. "His ability to perceive the qualities of others was remarkable."

Sir Richard Willington appeared to be unconvinced by this. "Your brother, though a good man, Sir George was, at times…" He appeared to be picking his words carefully. "Shall we simply say that his relationships with the fair sex were, at times…" He stopped, seemingly unable to finish his sentence.

Jane had a fair idea of what he was about to imply. Silently she mouthed to herself, "Sylphs, help me, please. Do not show yourselves, but help to lift me and carry me towards that man."

She stood, and rose in the air until her feet were at least six inches above the carpet, and glided over to Sir Richard.

"Allow me to complete your thoughts, Sir Richard. You were about to say, were you not, that in your experience Thomas FitzAlan was overly susceptible to the charms of women. And in this particular instance, you were probably going to say, he was over-fond of me, and was thereby blinded to my defects and my true intentions. Is that the case?"

There was no answer. Jane, angry, could be frightening enough. Towering over him, seemingly suspended in mid-air, she was terrifying. Sir Richard gasped and gargled, but no words emerged from his lips.

"You do not choose to answer?"

"No. I mean, yes. I mean that what I was about to say had the same meaning as your words, though I would not have used such blunt language."

"Of course not," Jane answered sweetly. "Let me make some things perfectly clear to you, Sir Richard, and to the rest of you. I was fond of Thomas FitzAlan. Had he ever asked me to be his wife, as it seems that he might have done, I would have considered his offer. However, at no time did he ever declare any such interest in me and my person, nor I to him. It was clear to me that he enjoyed my company, and I hope it was clear to him that I enjoyed his. However, under no circumstances could we ever have been described as lovers. Is that clear to you, Sir Richard?" While she had been speaking, she had slowly drifted down so that her feet were now on the ground. She extended her hand, forefinger outstretched, to touch the baronet on his forehead, at which he started back, rubbing the spot ruefully. "I warn you," she said, "that as Thomas FitzAlan said, I possess great powers. I have killed with them, and I will do so again, should it become necessary to do so. Please remember also that although I am part-Fae, I am also part-human, with all of a woman's moods and emotions. You have all heard of the impenetrable mysteries that are women's emotions, and I am sure you are all familiar with the phrase 'Hell hath no fury like a woman scorn'd'. Need I say more?" She smiled as she looked around the room at the faces, all of whom, including her old friend Doctor Darwin, were looking at her with a mixture of fear and respect, with the fear uppermost. "Do not worry too much. You are safe from me, as long as I am not crossed. Rest assured that I wish to banish the Fae from this world as much, if not more, than do you. I have suffered as a result of their actions, and I fear what is coming next. The Fae in me can comprehend their wishes and their methods."

There was a series of embarrassed coughs and shuffles as the assembled company took in her words. It was left to Sir George to speak. "Miss Machin, I think I can speak for all of us here," with a meaningful glance towards Sir Richard, who was still ruefully rubbing his forehead and muttering "Burned, by God!" to himself, "when I say that we would welcome you as the seventh member of the Revellers of Thoth, sworn to rid our world of the Fae."

There was a chorus of "Ayes" from the other members, including one seemingly reluctant one from Sir Richard.

"Miss Jane Machin. As a result of what you have done for us as a group, and me personally, with regard to my brother, and also on account of what you have told us you will do to assist us, I am honoured to invite you to become the seventh Reveller of Thoth. Seven is a lucky, indeed, a sacred number, and we welcome you as the seventh Reveller. Pray, accept this invitation and help us to defeat the Fae."

"On behalf of myself, and also of those who cannot be with us tonight, your brother Thomas, and Florella, I am happy to accept, Sir George. Thank you for the trust you have placed in me. I shall do my best to justify it." She curtseyed.

NOW THAT SHE HAD BEEN ACCEPTED as one of the group, Jane felt that much of the tension that she had experienced earlier had now dissipated. Only Sir Richard now seemed to be somewhat aloof and distant, but she put that down to the way in which her finger had caused him to experience the burning sensation that had annoyed him.

The others were keen to know of her dealings with the Elementals.

"Is it true that you can summon Salamanders?" asked young Lord Grenfell. "And are they as beautiful as they are rumoured to be?"

Jane could hear quiet sniggers from others, and could not resist a faint smile herself. "Yes, it is true that I have, sometimes without consciously meaning to do so, brought Salamanders into our world. And yes, they are beautiful beyond imagining. However, you should know that they are dangerous. Of all the Salamanders of which I have experience, that is to say, four, death has come to their lovers or would-be lovers in every case. If you had ideas of a Salamander for a companion, my lord, I would abandon them now."

The young peer blushed a little as he stammered out a denial that nothing could have been further from his mind.

The next question came from Professor Marlowe. "How do you walk through walls, and so on as the Gnomes are said to do? Does your body transmute into some sort of airy element, or do the walls become porous like a sponge? I can think of nothing in natural philosophy that can come close."

Jane shrugged. "How do I do it? I confess that I do not know, any more than I know how I fall asleep or wake up. It is just something that I do. However, I can tell you that it can at times be a somewhat tiring action – if you can imagine yourself swimming through thick mud, you may have some idea of what I mean. The sensation as I go through a solid obstacle – and it is not something that I do very often – is strange. I can only describe it as being stabbed with cold flaming knives." She laughed. "It sounds ridiculous, does it not? However, it is the closest I can come to describing the feeling."

The German, Professor Parseval, expressed an interest in the events at Tiengen. Jane recounted some of what she and Otto had experienced, and the company listened attentively. There were chuckles from Parseval when she described the way in which Otto had "made" gold. "But," she added, "it soon became clear to me that his interest was not in the physical alchemy whereby lead transmutes to gold, but in the spiritual side of the science." At the word "science", there was a "Harumph!" from Doctor Darwin, at which Jane smiled inwardly.

There was a universal shudder at the description of the nephew Ludwig's death at the hands of "his" Salamander, and

Lord Gresham once again blushed prettily at the description of the Elementals.

"Tell me," said the bishop, when her recital of the events at the Landgrave's castle was ended, "about the Sylphs that we saw earlier and your relation to them. Are they your servants?"

Jane smiled. "I hardly know the answer to that myself. Perhaps you should ask them, my lord bishop." Wordlessly, she requested the Sylphs to make themselves visible, and there were gasps as they appeared. "This gentleman," she told them, indicating the bishop, "would like to ask some questions of you. If you would be kind enough to answer him…"

The bishop thanked her, and addressed the Sylphs. "May I have the honour of knowing your names?"

"Most courteously requested," said the taller Sylph.

"But unfortunately, we prefer not to give our names."

"You should understand," said the first, "that to know the names of Elementals is to have power over them. When the time is right, that power could be used to destroy them."

"But Miss Machin knows your names?" asked the bishop.

It was Jane who answered. "I do not," she said simply.

"She tells the truth," the Sylphs confirmed.

"So she has no power over you?"

"That is correct."

"But you serve her? You help her to fly and to travel," pointed out Sir Richard. "Why do you do that?"

"Because we know that she wants to set us free from Him. The one who calls himself her father."

"He commands us."

"He knows our names."

"We are powerless against him."

"She gives us strength to resist him."

"She wishes to see him gone."

"As do we."

"She does not hurt us."

"She is strong."

"We trust her."

The Sylphs spoke in antiphony and the listeners' heads turned from one to the other as they spoke.

"I see," said the bishop at length. "Thank you both for your explanation. From what you say, you do not know the name of Him – her father."

"That is correct."

"No one knows his name, except He Himself."

"If you were to discover his name…"

"Impossible though it might be…"

"She could defeat him."

"And we would be truly free."

There was a pause, and the taller Sylph addressed Jane directly. "Do we have your permission to take ourselves from your sight?"

"Of course," Jane said without a pause, and the Sylphs vanished.

"What agreeable Elementals," said Darwin. "The reports make them out to be proud and independent creatures of the air."

"As you heard, they are not independent at present. They are subject to Him. And He wishes to replace humanity with His kind."

"Including you?" from Sir Richard.

"Yes, as I have said, He has asked me several times, the most recent being this evening, to join Him. I have refused every time."

Darwin spoke again. "Jane – or should I call you Miss Machin?"

"Jane, if you would, Uncle 'Rasmus," she smiled.

The heavy pockmarked face broke into a smile of its own. "Jane, if we were to learn the name of Him, and if you were thereby enabled to defeat him and expel him from our world, what would become of the Elementals?"

"This is my belief only, but I believe that those few Elementals who follow Him, such as the Sylphs who caused tonight's tempest and purloined Sir George's horses, would likewise be banished. The majority of the Elementals would remain in this world, invisible and unnoticed by mankind."

"Then we must discover the name by which he calls himself."

"Beelzebub," muttered the bishop. "The Lord of the Flies."

"If it were only that simple," said Sir George. "That name has been known for centuries, and it has no effect. It will not be the name of one which has been known and bandied about like that."

"Alchemy," said Professor Parseval. "That and Kabbala. You may laugh, Sir Richard and Doctor Darwin, but I tell you that alchemy has much to tell you modern chemists or whatever you choose to call yourselves, yes, even the greatest of you, such as Priestley or de Lavoisier."

"We need the services of your friend Otto, it seems," said Sir George to Jane. "Professor Parseval, do you consider it possible that he might come here from Heidelberg?"

"More than likely, I would say."

"Is it the will of the Revellers of Thoth that the man once known as Hermecritus should be admitted to our ranks? Would those in favour please indicate their intention by raising their hand? I myself will not vote, unless a casting vote be required." Three hands went up, among them Jane's.

"Those against?" Sir Richard's hand was raised.

"Doctor Darwin? Your Grace?"

"I abstain. I am not in favour, neither am I against. I reserve judgement."

"And as for me, I am against meddling in such practices,"

said the bishop, "though I recognise that there may be a need for this man's strange skills."

"I understand. Professor," Sir George addressed the German. "Would you be kind enough to issue the invitation?"

"With pleasure. I shall create a draft at my earliest convenience."

Sir Richard's face had turned an alarming shade of dark red. "You said earlier this evening, Sir George, that seven was an auspicious number. Admitting this man would make the number eight."

"Indeed," Sir George agreed.

"However, the number shall stay at seven. If this man is admitted as a Reveller of Thoth, I will resign my place."

"Now, now, no need for hastiness," said Lord Gresham. "There is room for us all in this group. Pray do not be prejudiced against this man simply because his views on certain topics may differ from yours."

"How dare you lecture me, you young whipper-snapper?" This is the second time tonight you have crossed me."

"Gentlemen, gentlemen," pleaded Sir George. The hour is late, and we are tired. Peace for now, if you would. Let us all retire, and the morrow will help us see things in a new light."

XVI

The Search

DESPITE BEING TIRED by the events of the evening, including the visit by Him, Jane found it difficult to sleep. When she had risen, and been helped to dress and prepare herself for the day by the maid who had been appointed to serve her, she was already tired.

She forced herself to enter the dining-room where Sir George and Erasmus Darwin were already breaking their fast. There appeared to be no sign of any of the others.

"My dear Jane," Darwin exclaimed. "How glad I am to see you again. I hope you do not mind, but I have been explaining to our friend here some of the circumstances that led to your removal to Switzerland. I realise that at the time it must have seemed like an unimaginable cruelty to you, but believe me, I am sure it was for the best."

Tears started to Jane's eyes. "I missed you very much, and Kate Perkins and Will and Mary. How are they?" She sat and accepted the coffee that had been placed in front of her.

Darwin's face grew grave. "Mrs Perkins died the year after you left."

"Dead?" Jane exclaimed in horror. "She seemed so well and full of energy. An illness?"

"Some would term it so," he answered her. "I believe it to be murder."

Jane's hand flew to her mouth, and the coffee cup that she had been holding in her other hand crashed to the table, spilling its contents over the mahogany. Her apologies were swiftly waved away by Sir George. "Murder? Who?" was all she could say.

"By Them. Those whom I have learned to call the Fae. Kate Perkins told me that the one who calls himself your father was constantly visiting the house in Dam Street, shrieking and screaming that He had been betrayed and that you were his, and that she had no right to let you leave England."

"You believed her?" asked Sir George, clearly hearing these details for the first time.

"I did indeed. I had seen little Jane, as she was then, and what she was capable of attracting through no fault of her own. Also, I had seen some of her powers, which I realised might be perverted for evil ends by Them. Somehow Kate Perkins knew that these entities could not travel outside England at that time, though it seems that they have at least crossed the Channel to join in the Revolution there."

"So it was Zürich for me," said Jane, ruefully. "But poor Mrs Perkins. What happened?"

"She became weaker and weaker, as though the life was being sucked out of her. She complained to me of head-aches and other such infirmities. I examined her, of course, but could find nothing in her constitution that might explain such a condition."

"Did she have any explanation for this?" Sir George enquired.

Darwin nodded sadly. "She reported that the one who calls himself Miss Machin's father had been visiting her."

Jane wiped her eyes. "Poor Mrs Perkins. I would not for the world have brought such a fate upon her."

"I do not think you were aware, Jane, that Kate Perkins was herself part-Fae. Not as you are, but at least partly – she told me that her great-grandfather was Fae – and possibly even the same being as He who calls himself your father!"

Jane let out a gasp of horrified surprise. "You mean that Kate Perkins is— was my sister, or half-sister?"

"It is possible," Darwin admitted. "In any case, as in your case, this circumstance makes it easier for them to visit, speak and torment those who must be regarded as their kin."

"This is monstrous!" exclaimed Sir George. "How many such are there living in England, do you think?"

"We cannot tell," Darwin replied. "It is clear that even those who are themselves part-Fae may not instantly recognise their fellows, as can be evidenced by the fact that Jane here was unaware of Kate Perkins' ancestry. Mrs Perkins herself was only certain of Jane's parentage from the events surrounding her, rather than by any inherent qualities of Jane herself. There is one thing of which I have a strong suspicion, and that is that the Fae's gateway to this world is centred here."

"In England?" asked Sir George.

"Here in the Midlands. To be precise, in Derbyshire, not some fifty miles from here. Not for nothing is one of the caverns there known as the Devil's—" Here Darwin checked himself. "My apologies, Jane. The full name is one which should not be uttered by a gentleman in the presence of a lady."

Jane smiled wryly. "I am flattered that you consider me to

be a lady, my dear uncle. In any case, I have indeed heard of the Devil's Arse. Indeed, I have heard of no other name for this cavern near Castleton, and I have read that its name was given as the result of the noises that emanate from it following heavy rain."

Sir George chuckled. "That's telling you, Darwin. It seems that Miss Machin here is a lady of true quality. One who was not possessed of ladylike qualities, but merely affected such airs and graces, would profess herself to be shocked, and fall to the ground in a fit of the vapours, but our friend here merely accepts this fine old English word for what it is, in the fashion of a true aristocrat."

Jane made no answer to this, but blushed a little.

"Very well, then," said Darwin. "I made an expedition to Castleton to visit the caverns there. They are indeed a most impressive sight. However, as I was saying, the cavern whose name we have just been discussing made me feel uneasy."

"Who would not feel so?" asked Sir George. "I have never visited there, but I can imagine that the feeling caused by the knowledge that a mountain is above one's head is one which would induce a feeling of unease."

"There is that, to be sure," admitted Darwin, "but there was also the feeling that there was something there. A sensation that I have only experienced a few times previously. A presence of something intelligent, non-human, and not entirely well-disposed."

"The Fae?"

Darwin nodded. "Though, of course, I did not know them by that name at that time. I only knew them as those from the other side of the sky, as the folk in Lichfield and thereabouts refer to them."

"Poor Mrs Perkins," said Jane. "I had no idea that she was as close to Them as that."

At that moment, young Lord Grenfell entered and greeted them.

"After you retired last night," he told them, "I stayed up talking to Professor Parseval for an hour or so. I am intrigued by this Otto, or whatever he chooses to call himself now, who appears to be a most interesting character. Would you mind giving us a few more details about him, Miss Machin? How did you meet him?"

Jane obliged by recounting more details of the history of her meeting and subsequent adventures. While she was telling her stories, the room slowly filled with the other Revellers, who took their places quietly, and sat in silence, broken only by an appreciative chuckle at times, or sometimes gasps of what sounded like horror at some of the incidents she described.

At the end of her recitation, there was a stir as the listeners, who had clearly been staying still in order not to miss a word of the story, relaxed and coughed.

"I must ask you, Miss Machin, do you trust this man? Should we trust him? Your stories of Otto's trickery and alchemy are, quite frankly, quite disturbing to me as a man of the Church." It was the bishop, predictably, who spoke these words.

"I will tell you frankly that, regarding him merely as a mesmerist or as a magician, or a mere prestidigitator, I would have no faith whatsoever in his qualities. However, as a man, he was a good friend to me, he never tried to take advantage of me in any way, and he displayed good honest feeling and sensibility. I have entrusted him with my life on occasion, and he never failed me. I believe that we should make use of the talents that he possesses, and discount those aspects of his character that we may find objectionable."

"In any case," interjected Professor Parseval, "the man

whom I know as a fellow-professor at Heidelberg is far from the wandering mountebank that Miss Machin first encountered. She has told us herself that he made good use of his access to the library at Tiengen, and thereby improved his mind."

There was a cough from Sir Richard Willington. "If I may be permitted to raise a practical matter?"

"By all means, my dear fellow," Sir George answered him. "We are all practical men – and women – here, after all. And though you announced your intention to leave this group, I cannot help but remark your presence with us here this morning."

"I have my doubts regarding your all being practical," Sir Richard answered acidly. "As you know, I am against this man's being invited into the country. But, as you may have noticed, there is chaos in France. War, if not actually declared, is taking place there and in surrounding areas. Even assuming that a message can be sent to Heidelberg, and that he deigns to agree, how is he to make his way here, eh?" There was silence. "Well?"

"I am at a loss, Sir Richard, as to whether you still regard yourself as a member of the Revellers of Thoth. If so, then your point is a good one. Otherwise, I must ask you, with the greatest respect, what you are doing interfering in matters which are none of your business." Erasmus Darwin spoke with a quiet voice, but the anger there was plainly perceptible.

"Last night I considered my earlier words, and determined that I wish to remain as a member of the group—"

"Excellent," said Sir George, but looking round at the other faces in the room, it was clear to Jane that this was not a universal opinion.

"—and therefore my question is, according to Doctor Darwin's definition, a valid and a good one."

There was silence in the room for the space of about half a minute, broken eventually by Jane.

"I think that my Sylphs will be able to pass the invitation to him, and even to transport him here, should he accept the invitation," Jane told the room.

The bishop seemed about to object to this solution, but a whispered word from Erasmus Darwin seemed to cause him to relax, and he sank back, though with a frown still on his face.

"Excellent," said Sir George. "Professor Parseval, when you have written your invitation to Professor Hermecritus, or whatever we must call this man, please pass it to Miss Machin here, and she will ensure that it reaches its destination."

THE DISCUSSION CONTINUED, with the table still providing the later arrivals with the wherewithal to break their fast.

The subject turned to the possible geographical origins of the Fae, with Darwin repeating his idea that they came to our world ("though whence they come, I confess that I know not," he admitted) through the Devil's Arse in Derbyshire.

"But yet you say they were in France? And you were able to summon Elementals there, and in Germany, were you not?" Sir George enquired of Jane.

"That is so, sir," Jane answered him. "However, based on what I have read, and what I have experienced... I confess that I am unwilling to express myself in front of those of you who have spent so long and delved so deep into these mysteries." She hesitated.

"Yes? Go on," Darwin encouraged her. "For my part, and I am, sure that I also speak for Sir George and the rest of us here, I am ready to learn from any source."

"As regards the Fae, I have no proof as such, but my impressions are that you are correct," she replied, with a nod to Darwin. "I too believe that the Fae are from somewhere outside our world. Maybe, as you say, they appear here from the Devil's Arse," smiling, "or some other place. The Elementals, however, are part of our world, as much as you and I. However, we can only, under very rare conditions, be aware of their presence. The Fae, and those who are part-Fae, such as myself, are able to see and converse with them, however. Some say that these Elementals have no souls, and while they are not actually immortal, in our terms they are so."

"I have read this about the Elementals in some books," agreed Sir George, "and I believe that you will find some others of our group in agreement with you. But the relationship between the Elementals and the Fae?"

Jane seemed lost in reflection for a moment. "I am trying to imagine how to describe it best," she said. "The best I can achieve is perhaps to compare our world to America, the Fae to the English, French, and Spanish who have gone there, and the Elementals of our world as the natives of America who have been enslaved for the pleasure and profit of their new masters."

"I wonder what poor Thomas would make of that analogy," said Sir George. "He spent some time in America, as I am sure you are aware."

"Indeed, most ingenious," Darwin said, removing his wig and scratching his head before replacing the wig. "And we humans? Did you not say that the one who calls himself your father was in France, attracted by the Revolution? How is it that he has roamed so far from what I believe are his origins here in the Midlands, and what is the attraction of the Revolution to him?"

"It does seem to me that the Fae thrive on disorder," Jane

said. "By encouraging such disorder among mankind, I believe they hope to weaken us, and thereby bring about their own dominance in this world. Such chaos may also strengthen them, at the same time that it weakens us."

"Most unfortunate," muttered Darwin.

"What do you mean?" Jane asked.

"Well, I, along with other members of the Lunar Society, were very much in sympathy with many of the ideals of the French Revolution, as well as supporting the American rebels— My apologies, Sir George. I have no wish to denigrate the courage and patriotism of your brother who went to America. We merely felt that Lord North had committed numerous blunders in his treatment of the Americans, and that the more reasonable of them, as exemplified in our friend Mr Benjamin Franklin, were justified in distancing themselves from London. I apologise if I have given offence."

Sir George waved a negligent hand. "We are all men of reason," he said. "I may not agree with you, but I respect your reasons for holding that belief."

"Would that mean," the bishop enquired sweetly, "that your meetings of the Lunar Society, the which, I may add, I have always regarded with the utmost suspicion as being impertinent scrutiny into the mysteries of the Almighty, were in fact a way of attracting the Fae to our world?"

"May I speak?" asked Jane. Receiving a nod of approval from her host, she addressed the bishop. "Your Grace, with all due respect, I cannot believe that the members of the Lunar Society to whom I had the honour to be introduced when I was but a child, could ever be engaged in the sort of activity that would attract these beings."

"Is it perhaps possible," asked Lord Grenfell, "that the two men whom you, er, eliminated with the help of your Salamanders, were in some way responsible for the Fae visiting Paris? In other words, were Montalba and Ortolanus capable of summoning them?"

"Inconceivable!" exclaimed Professor Parseval. "But yet I always maintained that those two were mountebanks, did I not?" appealing to the assembled company, "and that it was a mistake to employ them."

"You did indeed," confirmed Professor Marlowe. "I believe that some of us at the time were in full agreement with you. However," and his brow furrowed as he appeared to remember something, "was it not you, Sir Richard, who originally suggested that we employ them as agents in Paris, to determine if the Fae were in some way behind the unrest there, informing us that Montalba was well known for his study of the Fae and ancient alchemical texts, and that Ortolanus was an adept in many of the esoteric sciences?"

Sir Richard nodded. "It may be that my sources were mistaken."

"Who exactly were those sources?" asked Erasmus Darwin.

"It is some time ago. I cannot remember clearly now."

"No matter. In any case, Miss Machin, his Lordship enquired as to whether you considered it possible that these two men could have summoned the Fae to Paris. Have you any opinion on this?"

"I quite honestly do not know. All I know is that they lacked the power to summon Elementals – so much was obvious from the surprise on their faces when the Sylphs and Salamanders appeared. I suppose that it may be possible to be in contact with the Fae without having the knowledge of how to summon Elementals."

"What would be the reason for them to do that, in any case?" asked Lord Grenfell.

Darwin stirred his bulk and coughed.

"Doctor Darwin?" asked Sir George.

"Let us assume that somehow these men have been able to communicate with the Fae. Sir Richard, I seem to remember that you reported that they had been vouched for by some gentlemen from a learned society near Nantwich of which you are also a member? Does that correspond in any way to your recollections?"

"It does seem to strike a chord, yes," Sir Richard grudgingly admitted.

"And did those gentlemen mention where they had met those two? Was it in France, Germany, or the Low Countries? Can you remember?"

"I admit, I cannot. It was some time ago."

"A mere year and a half, to be precise. Happily, I do have a good memory, and I also write notes. Let me see." He drew a thick memorandum book from the inside pocket of his coat. "Ah, yes. 'Sir Richard reported that the Philosophical Society of Nantwich declared that although they had not known Messrs Ortolanus and Montalba for long, they had been impressed by the speech of these two gentlemen when the Society encountered them on an expedition mounted by the Society to...'" Darwin stopped and looked around the room. "I will offer you the chance to guess where the Society encountered the two men recommended by Sir Richard. No? No one? I will tell you, then. It was at Castleton in Derbyshire, the town closest to the Devil's Arse."

"Of what, sir, are you accusing me?" Sir Richard had sprung angrily to his feet and stood over Erasmus Darwin, who, however, seemed to be unperturbed by this.

"Why, nothing, sir. I make no accusations. I merely point out facts. If you choose to interpret those facts in such a way as to construe them as an accusation..." Darwin shrugged.

"Might we be justified in assuming that these two men, Montalba and Ortolanus, were in fact in Castleton for the express purpose of attempting to communicate with the Fae?" asked Professor Marlowe. "And if so, and if they had established communication, and – this is almost too horrible to conceive – if they had made an agreement to assist the Fae in ways unknown to us—"

"Or if one or both of them was in fact part-Fae," interrupted Jane, "with the ability to communicate with Fae, but without the ability to summon Elementals?" She stopped and blushed. "Pardon me, Professor, for speaking out of turn."

"Not at all, my dear Miss Machin," he answered. "I do like to see younger people expressing their own opinions, and in this case, I find this to be a perfectly valid assumption. Now, where was I? Oh yes, perhaps they had made a bargain that should they assist the Fae in gaining power in this world, they would be rewarded with power and riches."

There was an instant hubbub.

"Inconceivable treachery."

"Horrible to think of."

"We have been tricked and betrayed."

"What do you have to say to this, Sir Richard?"

There was silence. After they had looked around, it was clear that he was not in the room. An open door to the hallway marked his probable route.

"We may be thankful that he did not walk through the wall to leave us, unlike some young ladies I could mention," Darwin said, not without some amusement in his voice. It was not the most witty of jests, but it raised a nervous laugh from some.

SIR GEORGE SENT SERVANTS to discover Sir Richard and request him to rejoin the company, but it appeared that he had gone straight to the stables, had his horse saddled, and had mounted and galloped off almost before the party had remarked his absence.

"We need your alchemist now," Darwin said to Jane. "Professor Parseval, have you written your invitation to him?"

"One moment," the German replied, scribbling on a piece of paper. "Here," handing it to Jane, who looked over it.

"That will do very well," she said to Parseval.

"You read German? Of course, I had almost forgotten the time you spent in Switzerland and Germany."

"If I may add a little sentence of my own?" Jane asked. Parseval nodded, and Jane added a few lines to the message.

"And now," she said, "for the delivery." Silently, she willed her Sylphs to make themselves visible. Again, there were gasps from the assembled group, as they appeared, seemingly from nowhere.

"Take this, please, and deliver it to Professor Otto Esquibel-Schultz whom you will find in the University in Heidelberg. Tell him that I urgently require him to be here to help us rid this world of Them."

"With pleasure," said the taller Sylph. "At once."

"Stop! Wait!" Jane called, frightened that they would go too soon before she had finished giving them their instructions.

"Mistress?"

"When you have delivered the message, add that I particularly desire his presence. If he agrees to come, assist him as you did me when I arrived here."

"Can he soar in the air as do you, Mistress?"

Jane smiled. "I do not believe he has that power."

"We will require assistance in the form of others of our kind."

"Will you be able to obtain that assistance?"

"If you can truly promise that we will be free when all this is over."

"I make that promise," Jane told them. "Now you may go."

Rather than vanishing, the Sylphs remained. "Well?" Jane asked.

"Mistress, what if he does not wish to come?"

"Then you must bring him anyway, whatever he says. Is that clear?"

"Yes, Mistress," the two Sylphs said in unison, and vanished.

"Remarkable," said Professor Marlowe.

"Indeed, I have never seen the like," said Lord Grenfell. "Come to that, has any man?"

"I believe that these Elementals are usually hidden from our sight," said Darwin. "How is it that we can see them now?"

"I do not pretend to understand the mechanism by which they can become visible and invisible at will. I leave that to natural philosophers, such as yourself," Jane told him. "It is not a property of the perceiver that makes them visible, it is a property of the perceived, or the unperceived, as their will dictates."

"How long will we have to wait?" asked the bishop, who was looking slightly shaken by the vision of the Sylphs. Perhaps they reminded him of angels, Jane thought to herself, and he believes he has seen a vision.

Aloud, "I do not know. If Otto wishes to come, he may take a little time to collect such books and apparatus as he considers necessary. A few hours, at most."

IN THE EVENT it was the next day before Otto arrived. He was preceded by Jane's Sylphs, who informed her that Otto would follow in an hour or so.

He arrived, somewhat out of breath, but beaming radiantly, supported by two Sylphs, both of whom were unknown to Jane. He was smartly dressed in a scholar's robe, his beard and hair were clean, and he seemed to Jane to be prospering, if his general appearance was to be believed.

"I had no idea…" he exclaimed. "I can hardly believe that this has happened to me." He moved over to Jane, and impulsively threw out his arms to embrace her.

She stepped away, but she was smiling. "No, no, Herr Professor," she said. "Consider your dignity."

"My dignity? What of it?"

She submitted to his embrace, remarking inwardly that he was a good deal cleaner than when she had first known him.

"And so," he said when he had released her from his embrace, "you feel you need my help? But first, where am I? And what has happened since we parted?"

Jane swiftly outlined the events from the time when she and Otto had parted ways, and explained how The Revellers of Thoth were largely of the opinion (she omitted the circumstances surrounding Sir Richard's departure) that Otto's alchemical and hermetic knowledge might assist in determining the name of the Fae who called himself her father.

Otto heard her in silence, his eyes closed much of the time, but it was clear that he was far from asleep, but was in fact deep in thought.

"I see," said Otto, stroking his beard thoughtfully. "Tell me more of the members of this group who have set themselves against the Fae, as you call them – a good name for them."

Jane listed them and Otto nodded slowly as she gave details of each.

"Of course, I know Parseval," he said. "A man with an open mind and not afraid to state his views. A bishop, though, and a Protestant at that – can we really believe that he will be of use? And Doctor Darwin? A natural philosopher of the first order, to be sure, but is he the man we need to defeat these Fae?"

"I believe he is. He is not one of those who believe that the universe is composed solely of those things that we can touch and feel."

"As to the others, I am afraid I have never heard of them, but I will reserve judgement until I have made their acquaintance."

As IT TURNED OUT, Otto appeared to be suitably impressed by the Revellers. He greeted Parseval as an old friend, and was duly deferential to Erasmus Darwin, even quoting some of Darwin's own poetry to him.

"But," he said as he sat at the table with the others, "it's very pleasant to be here, and I am delighted to see my friend Fräulein Machin again, but as for the precise task for which I have been summoned," he shrugged, "I believe I am unable to help you at present."

All eyes turned to Jane. "You told us that our friend here would be able to help us." Sir George sounded saddened rather than angry. "Of course, the pleasure is ours to be able to meet such a distinguished guest, but it seems to me that we are no further forward."

Otto held up a finger. "One moment, please. Let me explain further. From what I know already, and what Miss Machin has told me just now, we are contending with an adversary which is older than us."

"Even myself?" asked the bishop. "At the age of eighty-six, I believe myself to be the oldest here."

"Your pardon. I expressed myself poorly," Otto answered

him. "When I used the word 'us', I was referring not to the present company, but to the whole of humanity. I believe that the Fae pre-date humanity, like the Elementals. However, unlike the Elementals, they are not of this world. There are stories which tell of other worlds, made and discarded by the Creator of this world as being unsatisfactory. It may well be that the Fae are now homeless, living beyond our skies – that was the phrase that you used, was it not, Jane? – and seeking a place to live."

"Where are these stories?" asked Sir George. "In all my reading I have never read of such a thing. Have any of you?" he asked the others. All shook their heads.

"These are Jewish legends," explained Otto. "They are not part of the Christian tradition."

"Ah." The bishop sat back in his chair.

Darwin looked as though he was about to say something, leaning forward, but then abruptly sat back.

"I know, Doctor Darwin," Otto said. "You have another belief as to how the world was created, do you not? *E conchis omnia*? From shells, all things?"

Darwin smiled. "You know my writings well. I am flattered. Yes, I do have other ideas regarding the formation of this world. But I am willing to believe that there may be a sense in which we are both correct."

"Most generous of you, sir." Otto bowed slightly.

"But if you know of these legends, can you not discover the name of our enemy?"

"I know of these legends, sir. I have not studied them. What we will require is a man who has dedicated his life to these things, and has spent many decades meditating on them, and the writings that surround them."

Sir George spread his hands in a gesture of hopelessness. "And are such men actually in existence?"

"To be sure they are," Otto replied calmly. "I have the honour to be acquainted with one of them who may be regarded as the foremost in this field."

"Who would that be?" asked Professor Parseval. "Am I acquainted with the gentleman? Is he at Heidelberg, a colleague of ours?"

Otto shook his head. "No, I have known him since long before I arrived at Heidelberg. Most of our friendship has been conducted by means of letters."

"He is a Jew?" from the bishop.

"Emphatically so. His name is Rabbi Baruch ben Chaim. He lives in the city of Brno, in Moravia." Jane remembered that while they had been living in Tiengen, Otto had received several letters from that city.

Sir George sighed. "So we are no better off. How long will it take for a letter from us to reach Moravia, and if he deigns to respond, how long will it take for his reply to reach is? We do not have much time, I fear."

Otto said nothing, but simply looked at Jane.

"I might be able to prevail on the Sylphs once more to bring him here," Jane told the assembled company after a pause. "That is, if he feels sufficiently persuaded to leave his home and travel here." It was her turn to turn a wordless look in Otto's direction.

"Why do you look at me in that way?" Otto asked. His face cleared in understanding. "You wish me to travel to Brno and persuade him?"

Jane nodded. "That is, if the Sylphs are willing to transport you and him."

Otto sighed. "I suppose one could get accustomed to this mode of travel. I pray that I experience it so infrequently that I never become so accustomed."

321

TWO DAYS LATER, four Sylphs appeared, two with an exhausted looking Otto between then, and a further pair on either side of an elderly man dressed in black, who was clutching a pile of books under his arm.

"That is the last time I journey that way," said Otto. "Exhilarating and exotic it may be, but quite frankly, it terrifies me. How are you, my friend?" turning to the other, whom Jane presumed to be the rabbi.

To Jane's surprise, the rabbi, for such she took him to be, was smiling broadly through his bushy beard.

"Amazing!" he exclaimed in German. "I have been carried to the ends of the earth by angels!"

"I think that Sir George FitzAlan would not like to hear his house described as being 'the ends of the earth'," Jane laughed.

"Where am I, then?"

"You are in the Midlands of England. Staffordshire. Shawborough Hall, to be precise."

"Ah. England? Close enough to the ends of the earth, surely?" He chuckled. Clearly he was not being altogether serious in his condemnation. He peered closely in Jane's direction, squinting. "So you are the one?" he asked.

"Sorry?"

"You are the one whom Otto spoke about in his letters? You can summon angels and make them do your bidding?"

"Elementals, not angels," Jane answered him. "I believe there is a difference."

"Excellent. If you had told me that you could command angels, or that your Elementals were the same as angels, I could not work with you. By your denial, you show me that you have discernment. Maybe even wisdom. Perhaps too early for me to be sure, though."

"Thank you, sir."

"Oh, I am not 'sir' to you, my dear. Call me 'rabbi', if you choose to give me a title. It is the Hebrew for 'master', as I am sure you are aware. Now, Otto tells me that you require a name."

"That we do. The name of the one who calls himself my father."

"He is your father, or He merely describes himself as such?"

"I have reason to believe that he is indeed my father, and I have inherited some of his powers."

"Tell me more about him. Your experiences with him. I wish to know more." He sank into a chair facing Jane. "Come, sit. We may as well be comfortable. Otto, make yourself useful. Arrange for some refreshment to be brought to us. Wine, cake. Something of that order."

"He frightens me," Jane began. "He wishes me to join him, in his wish to become ruler of this earth."

"You say, 'of this earth'. Do you believe that there is another earth besides this one?"

"Perhaps. I do not know. I know that he and the others of his kind are often described as coming from the other side of the sky. Does that not imply another earth from which he may originate?"

"Maybe."

"Can you believe in another earth?" Jane asked curiously.

"I can believe in many things, my dear. The question is how strongly I believe in them. But yes, there may well be other worlds, or perhaps there have been other worlds in the past before this one. I think our friend Otto believes something of the sort. Now, your father, if we may call him that. How does he appear to you?"

"I find it difficult to describe his appearance. He usually appears to me at night, and it is hard to describe him clearly. If I described him as being 'luminous black', would that make sense to you? Although he is nearly invisible in the dark, he seems to glow. With an unholy light." She shook her head. "I am not making much sense, am I?"

"On the contrary, my dear, this is all most valuable. Ah, thank you," he broke off as a servant appeared, bearing the requested refreshments. He sipped at his wine. "Ah, excellent. I had no idea that the English had such good taste in these matters. Pray, continue."

"When he visits me and attempts to persuade me to join him, I have the sensation of being trapped in something dark and sticky. It is like trying to wade through a bath of treacle. At least," she smiled, "I can imagine it is like that. I have never actually tried to wade through treacle."

"A pastime that few of us have actually experienced, I am sure. Interesting, though." Another sip of the wine. "I assume he is offering you infinite power. The power to rule the world. All creation at your feet. That sort of thing?"

"Essentially, yes."

"And you are not tempted?"

"Of course. Who would not be? However, even if I were to genuinely desire what he is offering, I do not feel that I could trust his word." She paused.

"Go on."

"I know – do not ask me how I know, because I cannot tell you how I know – that he killed my mother by deceit. I am convinced that he would do the same to me. I believe, on the word of Doctor Darwin, that he was also responsible for the death of another woman, who became my foster mother, and whom I also learned to love as my mother."

"Your voice tells me that you are angry. That is good. Your anger will carry you far in your fight against this being you call your father. But take care. You must be the master of your anger. Do not let your anger master you." He sat back, and took a bite out of the cake that lay before him on his plate.

"But how do we discover his name?"

Ben Chaim produced a half-smile. "Leave that to me. I think I may be able to discover it from what you have just told me. Leave me with my books for a few hours. I will then tell you Revellers of Thoth – I do not like that name, but let it stand – what I have been able to discover."

THE REVELLERS OF THOTH assembled around the table, at the head of which sat the rabbi Baruch ben Chaim. He spoke enough English to make his general ideas known, but dropped into German or Yiddish at times when he became more excited about the subjects he was describing. Otto and Jane could interpret his German for the English-speakers, but Otto alone could make sense of the Yiddish.

The rabbi started by producing a piece of paper on which the following was drawn.

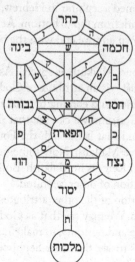

"Does this look familiar to any of you?" he asked.

"Of course," replied Otto.

"Not you, Herr Philomentor or whatever name you go by these days. The others. You?" appealing to the bishop, who shook his head.

"Beyond the fact that the characters are in Hebrew, a language which I studied, but in which I confess that I had little proficiency as a student, I cannot say."

"Professor?"

"Likewise. I recognise the fact that it is the Tree of Life in Hebrew, but little else."

Jane spoke up. "When the Fae whose name we seek attempted to visit me in Paris, your brother," turning to Sir George, "wrote some Hebrew characters on the floor using chalk. I seem to remember that one," pointing at one.

"Ah, yes. Netzach, Victory. Let me explain. This diagram of the Sephirod may be seen as the Tree of Life. Each circle, each being termed a sephirar in Hebrew, is an attribute of the Divine. We work from top to bottom. At the very top we have Keter, the Crown and we end with the bottom, Malkuth, the Kingdom.

"Now, this one, Malkuth, is special. As I said, each of these – except this last – is an attribute of God. This last is attained through following and coming to a full understanding of the attributes of God, and we can see that there is only one way to Malkuth, and that is through the Foundation, Yesod, immediately above Malkuth. Now some may say that Malkuth is in Keter, and Keter is in Malkuth. Both show a completion or a manifestation of other Sephirod."

"The realisation of the other attributes?" asked the bishop.

"Precisely so. We may say that as God's human creation, it is our privilege and our duty, to make manifest the attributes of God, that is to say, the other Sephirod, and bring them to physical reality in Malkuth. Is all clear to you?" There were nods all round.

"In addition, there are those, myself among them, who say that it is also necessary to ascend the tree, in other words, to return the divine energy to the Divine Presence."

"This corresponds to what many of the true alchemists have proclaimed," Otto added. "That we do not seek gold as a metal, or the philosopher's stone as a stone, but the pure spiritual gold and stone that come from a knowledge of the divine and thereby to unite ourselves with the divine."

"Quite so. Even you Gentile alchemists," aiming what might be described as a wicked smile at Otto, "hit upon something of the truth sometimes," agreed the rabbi. "Now, without Yesod, the Foundation, it is impossible to reach the Kingdom, in other words, unity with God."

The bishop seemed to be following this with great attention. "This is new to me, but it is most interesting. Pray continue."

"Thank you. Attaining the Kingdom can be done through several paths, as you can see." He used his finger to trace various routes between the circles from the top to the bottom of the diagram. "All, as you can see, go through the Foundation. Without the Foundation, there is no path to the Kingdom. This is important. Now," he continued, producing another paper which he spread on the table, "be so good as to look at this."

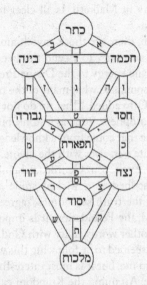

"I see it," said Lord Grenfell. "There is more than one path to the Kingdom, and that central circle is missing."

"*Mazel tov* – congratulations, young man! You have seen instantly what it is about what we may term the Unholy Sephirod that leads us to name it thus. It is possible to come to the Kingdom through other paths.

"Now, as you can see, as well as the central path, there are two paths, one on each side, which lead to Malkuth. The right is known as the Pillar of Mercy, Jachin, passing through Chokmah, Chesed and Netzrach, that is, Wisdom, Mercy, and Victory. But of course, it should also pass through Yesod, the Foundation."

Grenfell traced the path on the diagram with an elegant forefinger.

"Precisely," said the rabbi. "But here, look." His finger went down the three Sephirod at the left, and avoided Yesod to arrive directly at Malkuth. "This is Boaz, the Pillar of Severity, passing through Binah, Geburah and Hod. Understanding, Severity, and Glory. This is wrong. UnGodly, and wrong. Wisdom, Mercy, Beauty, and the Foundation – all of these are omitted."

"I understand what you are saying," said the bishop, "but I fail to see how this is of any help to us."

A broad smile spread over the rabbi's face. "You are seeking the name of one who is not of this world, are you not? One who wishes to control this world? An enemy of the human race?"

It was Darwin who nodded agreement.

"Such a one would not choose Jachin as the path for his manifestation. Rather, he would use the Pillar of Boaz to reach Malkuth."

"I comprehend your words, and it seems logical, given everything else that you have told us. But it is his name that we need, if we are to defeat him, not the path that he has taken to manifest himself."

Again the broad smile. "It is written here, in front of you." He tapped the second piece of paper, the 'Unholy Sephirod'.

"With the greatest respect, I do not understand what you are saying," complained Lord Grenfell. "I do not read Hebrew, and even if I did, I would not know how to discern a name in this pattern."

"Look closely, my friends," replied ben Chaim. "Here in the lines connecting the Sephirod."

"Hebrew letters," said Jane.

"And they are different in the two versions that you show us," Grenfell said. "The paths in one are labelled differently to those in the other."

"Indeed. Let us follow the path in the Unholy Sephirod that we may assume your adversary will take as he descends the Pillar of Boaz. Bet, Chet, Men, Shin. That is B, Kh, M, S." He wrote the four Hebrew letters on a scrap of paper and showed it to them. "He takes his name from the path he treads."

"So his name is Bakh—"

"Silence!" ben Chaim's word shocked Grenfell into a shocked stillness. "Never, never, never say that name out loud unless you are sure you know the consequences of saying it. Names have power. You now have that power, thanks to me. Use it wisely. Remember what I have just told you." He picked up the piece of paper on which he had written the four Hebrew letters comprising the name of Jane's father, and placed it in the flame of the candle standing on the table. A foul-smelling green smoke arose as the paper turned to blackened ashes in the flame. "You see, even the written name contains within itself the potential for evil, and has power. The spoken name…" He shrugged. "Use it only when you know what you are doing and what will happen as a consequence. And even then, prepare for the worst."

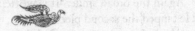

XVII

The Killer

THE RABBI SOON MADE HIMSELF AT HOME, and despite his reservations regarding the name of the group, was soon accepted as a full Reveller of Thoth. Once he had had an opportunity to view the grounds and park of Shawborough, ben Chaim expressed his pleasure at being in England, and declared that if he had known of the beauty of the countryside and the friendliness of its people, he would have removed himself from Brno and settled in Staffordshire long ago. No one really believed him.

He and Otto spent much of their time in the library talking together in a mixture of German, Yiddish and Latin as they pored over some of the volumes in Sir George's collection.

The name of Sir Richard Willington was hardly mentioned, but one day Erasmus Darwin encountered Jane as she was walking in the orangery, and requested her company for a few minutes.

"Of course," she answered him, offering him her arm, which he took.

"I want to ask you a few questions about Paris, if the subject is not too painful for you. Do you still miss Thomas FitzAlan?"

"I am sorry to say that I do. He was a good man, and I am sure that I owe my life, or at least my sanity, to him, for what he did that night when my father visited."

"He was indeed a good man. I did not have the privilege of knowing him well, but I had the pleasure of meeting him on one or two occasions when he was visiting his brother here. What interests me, though, are the two mountebanks whom you met, Montalba and Ortolanus. What did you discover about them?"

"Very little, other than what I told you."

"And Florella?"

"I was under the impression at first that she was in league with the other two. Later, she confessed that she was nothing to do with them. The two old men both spoke English, though with an accent. She also spoke English, but with no foreign accent." She reflected. "Her voice, or rather, the rhythm of her speech, seemed strangely familiar to me."

Darwin sighed. "I must tell you. She was indeed familiar to you. She was Kate Perkins' daughter, little Mary."

Jane released Darwin's arm and stepped back in shock. "Mary? But Florella was... She was beautiful. Little Mary, I can remember her only as a little round pudding of a child. Pretty enough, to be sure, but... Florella?"

"Come, sit by me on this bench. Let me explain this to you. When Kate Perkins died, as I explained to you, her children were left motherless and without support. I would gladly have taken them in myself, but," he smiled, "I suffered, if that is the term, from a surfeit of children. I therefore arranged for Will to live with a family of farmers near Wychnor, and for

Mary to be lodged with my friend Sir Richard Willington in Cheshire, with the eventual aim of her employment in his household as a servant. Sir Richard seemed happy enough with this idea. His wife had died in childbirth the previous year, and I think he was finding a solitary life to be uncongenial. A young child in the house, even of a different class, would seem to be a welcome distraction, or so I as his physician judged it to be."

"So it was Sir Richard who sent her to Paris?"

"Eventually, yes. But let me explain a little more. When Mary was sixteen or so, Sir Richard arrived here to attend a meeting of this group, bringing her with him. I was astonished at the change in her. While before she had been – well, perhaps I will not use your exact words, but I agree with their meaning, she was now ravishingly beautiful in a fashion which would have delighted Mr Gainsborough or Sir Joshua Reynolds, had they been privileged enough to behold her. It was almost inconceivable that the infant I had known years earlier had matured into this beauty."

"Some children do change their appearance as they grow older," Jane pointed out.

"My dear Jane, I am well aware of the fact, having observed many children, mine and others, in my lifetime," Darwin replied tartly. "This, however, went beyond anything I had seen before. Furthermore, she spoke in a fashion that showed that her mind had not been neglected. She could easily have passed for a lady of fashion."

"And you were sure that this was little Mary?"

"I was positive. There was a birthmark on her arm that was in the exact location and shape that I remembered from the infant Mary."

"And this— my little playmate became the beautiful Florella, who was cruelly murdered before my eyes?" Jane was weeping silently, and Darwin passed her a hand-kerchief. They sat silently as Jane reached out her hand to Darwin, who rested it in the palm of his own. At length, her tears stopped.

"How did all this come to be? And how did she then become Florella?"

"Let me answer the second question first. At the meeting where Sir Richard introduced the transformed Mary to us, it was proposed that one or two adepts be recruited to observe the goings-on in France. Sir George already had suspicions that the Fae would be interested in the chaos there. Once more I remind you not to underestimate him, by the way. He has read and understood many of the books in his library – not a thing I can say of many landowners of my acquaintance."

"And the two old men whom I met in Paris, Montalba and Ortolanus, were Sir Richard's choices?"

"They were indeed. At the same meeting, he also proposed that Mary be sent over in a few months' time to report on their doings. He explained that she had been educated to speak French fluently, and had a good understanding of the esoteric arts. I protested at this. I considered that it was sending her into danger, and none of us, other than Sir Richard, had ever met the two men who had been sent to Paris. As far as I, and the others here, were concerned, this was sending her to her death."

"As it turned out, you were correct."

"I should have been firmer in my protestations. I feel responsible for what happened."

Jane turned to look at him. Erasmus Darwin appeared to be weeping in his turn, and she turned away in order to avoid embarrassing him.

He resumed his speech after a few minutes. As to your first

question, I suspect the worst, especially since Sir Richard has left us in such a dramatic fashion."

"The worst being what?"

"That Sir Richard Willington is, and has been for some time, an agent of the Fae. I believe that he made a bargain with them to change Mary into the creature you saw as Florella. Why, I know not, but we may suspect the worst. Remember that Kate Perkins was partly Fae, and that Fae blood therefore ran in Mary's veins. The Fae might have been willing to do this for one of their own."

"And what would he give the Fae in return?"

"All the knowledge that he acquired as a member of the Revellers. That would include their knowledge of your meeting with Thomas, and all other events connected with this."

"This explains how my father came to find me in Paris."

"Indeed it does."

"But why, when we are so close to confronting the Fae, did Sir Richard decide to leave us?"

"Can you not guess?"

"I cannot."

"The reason is you, my dear," Darwin said softly. "You saw how terrified of you he was at your first meeting. Together with your friend Otto, whom he no doubt knows by repute, you would almost certainly unmask him. I can assure you that in that event, no mercy would have been shown to him by us. You are dangerous to the Fae and their servants. You have more power in you than they can withstand. Your powers, and the knowledge of both Otto and the rabbi, have given us what we need to send the Fae back where they belong. Homeless, on the other side of the sky." After pausing a while, he added. "Wherever that might be."

JANE COULD NOT HELP BUT GRIEVE for the loss of her childhood friend and playmate – almost her sister. Mixed with that grief was a burning anger, partly directed towards Sir Richard Willington the traitor (for so she considered him to be), but principally towards the Fae's leader, her father.

She sought out Otto, finding him dozing in an armchair in one of the smaller rooms in the Hall.

"Have you nothing better to do?" she asked him as he shook himself awake.

"My dear Miss Machin, I have been listening to our friend Baruch expound his theories of the beginning of our world for hours on end. Do you wish to hear my brief summary of his beliefs? The Breaking of the Vessels is a complex concept, but it does provide some explanation of the origin of the Fae. My simplified précis should not occupy more than an hour and a half of your time. No? Then allow an old man his rest." He sat back in his chair and closed his eyes again.

"Otto, do please wake up and listen."

She related to Otto all that Darwin had told her.

"And what do you want me to do about it?" Otto asked. "I cannot bring this Mary or Florella back to life."

"Let us at the very least find and destroy this Sir Richard."

"My my, you are bloodthirsty, are you not?"

"As was he. As are the Fae."

Otto groaned. "Oh, very well. Let me know how you think I can help you where one of the greatest men of our age cannot."

"Do you know a way to find where Sir Richard might be at this moment?"

"I have read of such methods, but they typically involve some article owned by the one who is being sought."

"We did not use such when the Sylphs brought you here, or the rabbi."

"Very true, but you knew that I was in Heidelberg, and that Baruch was in Brno. It was a great help to them, I am sure. But you are almost certainly correct, I feel. The Sylphs may well be the answer here."

"Let us proceed, then, on the assumption that Sir Richard has made his way back to Cheshire."

"Very well."

After a few minutes, the Sylphs appeared.

"I do not wish you to bring anyone here," she told them. "I simply wish to know the location of a certain individual."

"Can you describe him to us, Mistress?"

"Listen to my thoughts," she told them, and closed her eyes to concentrate on an image of Sir Richard drawn from her memories of him.

"But where should we start to look for him, Mistress?" asked the Elemental.

"North of here. In the part of this country known as Cheshire. Near the town of Nantwich."

"Very well, Mistress," said the Sylph, and both Elementals vanished from sight.

"I am not going with the Sylphs when they have found him," said Otto.

"You are coming with me?" asked Jane, surprised.

"Do you doubt me?" replied Otto. "Of course I will come with you. Just not by Sylph. You're going to need me, I am sure."

THEY WAITED for the Sylphs' return. Otto explained that the method for locating another person which did not involve the Sylphs would require a mirror or some kind of reflective surface.

"Is this anything like your crystal globe that you promised to the Landgrave? Will it take several years before the mirror is prepared to the exact standard required?"

"I am assured that is not the case. I say 'Mirror', though I believe an ordinary metal bowl filled with water will serve."

"So you believe this is possible?"

Otto merely nodded.

"I see. You don't want me to say later, 'You told me that this would work'. Just nodding doesn't commit you to anything."

Otto said nothing, but merely smiled.

"Oh, very well, Sir Alchemist."

At that moment the Sylphs returned, bowing low to Jane.

"Mistress, do not be angry with us, but—"

"You have been unable to locate him?"

"We are sorry. We searched the whole area, but he is not above the earth."

"I am not angry. You did what you were bidden to do, and it is not your fault if the task turned out to be impossible. You may leave us."

The Sylphs vanished, and Jane turned to Otto.

"Well?"

"We need a metal basin full of water, don't we? Our Mirror."

"But did you not say that we need some object connected to Sir Richard?"

"Was he not residing at this house before he left so abruptly?" asked Otto. "Is it not possible that he left some personal articles behind him in his haste to escape?"

"Of course. We will ask the housekeeper, Mrs Mallabar."

It was quickly ascertained that several of Sir Richard's articles of clothing were still in the room that he had occupied.

"A few of his hand-kerchiefs, and a neck-cloth, if you would be so kind, Mrs Mallabar," Jane requested.

"And if one of the footmen could bring to us a metal basin,

as shining as possible, filled with water, we would be most grateful," added Otto.

A few minutes later, a footman arrived bearing a large silver vessel. "It was Sir George's father's punch-bowl," he informed them. "Won at the Uttoxeter races by his filly Longthorpe."

"We'll take good care of it," Otto assured him.

"And filled, as you asked, with water." The footman's tone suggested that the bowl would be better filled with some other liquid, such as punch.

"Thank you," Jane told him as he placed the bowl carefully on a side-table before leaving the room.

Mrs Mallabar entered with a selection of hand-kerchiefs and two neck-cloths. "Just as he left them when he left the house," she assured Jane and Otto. "No one's touched them other than me just now."

"Excellent," said Otto.

Alone in the room, Jane and Otto contemplated the bowl and the cloths.

"Now what?" asked Jane.

For answer, Otto arranged the cloths around the bowl, so that they formed a ring around the water. "There," he said, surveying his work with an air of satisfaction before standing back.

"And now what are you going to do?" Jane asked him.

"Why, I will write down what you see in the Mirror," he replied.

"Me? I thought it was you who was going to perform some kind of miracle."

He shook his head. "No, no, no. I am not Fae. You, my dear, are part Fae. This is a Fae gift, not given to us mere humans."

"Ha!" Jane was angry. "I suppose I can say that you never deceived me with the words you spoke. But you definitely misled me with the words that you did not speak."

"Quiet. You will need a calm mind for this."

Jane took several deep breaths, attempting to clear her thoughts of all annoyance at Otto's deception, and her anger towards Sir Richard.

"I am ready," she said at length. "Now what must I do?"

"As you did with the Sylphs," Otto told her. "Hold the image of Sir Richard firmly in your mind, while gazing at the reflection in the water."

"It's no good," she said after several minutes had passed. "All I can see is my own stupid face and the moulding of the ceiling above."

"Keep trying," Otto told her.

A few minutes passed.

"What did the Sylphs say to us when they returned?" she asked suddenly.

"That they could not find Sir Richard, of course."

"No, what were their words?"

"If I remember rightly, they said he was not above the earth."

"That was it. And they were right."

"What? He's dead and buried?"

"No, nothing like that. He's underground in a cave or a mine, or something like that."

"That cave you call The Devil's Arse?" asked Otto.

"No, no. It's earth, not rock. And it is in Cheshire. Wait. He is living under the ground." A long pause. "I can just make out the way he has taken to come here. Wait again." She stood for a few minutes, motionless, other than for her fingers flicking over the surface of the water. At length she let out a great sigh, and collapsed into a chair.

"Otto," she told him. "That was amazing."

"What happened?" he asked.

"After a while my reflection vanished and I could see him

– Sir Richard – take my place. He didn't seem to be aware of the fact that he was being watched. And then, the most amazing thing. I was actually there – and I could move around the place where he was. I just had to point with my finger, and I went in that direction."

"And?"

"I followed the tunnel by which he had entered the chamber to the surface. He is in Marston Rock-Salt Mine. Write that down." She seized the notebook and pencil from Otto. "This is the route we must follow from the entrance to the mine to the chamber where Sir Richard is at present." She scrawled a rough map on the page below the words Otto had written. "Good enough to follow?"

"As long as it corresponds to the real thing, yes."

"Then we will go there."

"By Sylph?"

"Yes."

Otto groaned.

"I DON'T LIKE THIS," Otto said to her as they inched along the dark passage in the salt mine. "I still feel dizzy from the Sylphs. It's not my favourite way to travel, as I said. And now this passage."

"Do you think I'm enjoying it?" she snapped back at him. "This reminds me of Paris and Montalba and Ortolanus. Ugh!"

"Not my choice to go this way," said Otto. "Yours, or perhaps the Mirror's."

"Oh, please. For— Oh, never mind. How much further do we have to go?"

He pulled a little vial from beneath his cloak, which gave

off a faint green glow, with the aid of which he consulted a piece of paper torn from his notebook.

"I wish you'd brought a proper lantern with you, instead of that stupid pissphorus."

"Phosphorus," he corrected her. "From the Greek for light—"

"Oh, just be quiet, would you?" she told him.

"Temper, temper."

She stopped and looked at him. "I'm sorry, Otto. We're both worried, and I'm not myself – I mean, I'm not sure what I am right now. Am I Fae or am I human or what am I? You're one of my best friends, and I shouldn't be angry with you. Sorry." Hardly aware of what was happening, she began to cry.

"Listen." His voice was firm. "You're not a child. Not a silly girl. If what Baruch says about you is true, you may be the only thing standing between us and these Fae." His voice sharpened. "Now act like it! Be angry if you want, but not at me. At Them."

Her tears stopped, and she wiped her eyes. "I suppose you're right," she said and thought for a moment. "What did Baruch have to say about me, anyway?"

"You wouldn't understand."

"Why wouldn't I understand? I'm not stupid or ignorant."

He sighed. "Neither am I, and I didn't understand it either. It's all to do with something very mystical and Jewish, according to him. You can ask him yourself when we get back."

"*If* we get back," she corrected him. "This is dangerous enough without dragging your Kabbala into it."

"It's not mine. It's Baruch's."

"It might as well be yours, the amount of time you spend reading that nonsense when you might be doing something useful."

"Oh, for God's sake, stop snapping at me."

"Sorry," she said again. "Something is coming between us – or rather someone."

"And I think we both know who that is, don't we?"

"*Arschloch!*" she spat out. "Him, not you."

Otto chuckled. "I do speak German, you know."

She laughed back. "At least we both seem to have kept our sense of humour."

"Do you want me to go in front? According to what you saw in the Mirror this morning and what you drew for us, we're quite close."

"But that's putting yourself into danger."

"And shielding you from the first blow. I'm not a hero. I like my life and what happens to me in it, but it's not me who's going to be saving the world, is it? If anyone is disposable, it's me. Logic?"

"Logic, damn it."

"I go in front."

They continued to creep through the passage. Otto bumped his head on the low ceiling a couple of times. Jane, following, had advance warning of these low points, thanks to Otto's swearing in what Jane assumed was Basque. At least, it wasn't a language she recognised.

At length they found themselves able to stand upright. Otto produced his vial of phosphorus, and by its dim light, they were able to make out that they were now in a large roughly circular chamber about ten yards in diameter, with earthen walls, and a ceiling twice the height of a man. There were two tunnels leading from the chamber, other than the one by which they had entered.

"Have we any light other than your pissphorus?" Jane asked.

"You could try summoning a Salamander," Otto suggested.

Jane closed her eyes and concentrated. "I'm trying." She opened her eyes again. "I can't reach any Salamanders."

"A Gnome, perhaps?"

She closed her eyes again. After about a minute, a small figure emerged from one of the other tunnels.

"Mistress?"

"Can you bring light?" she asked him.

"I can."

"And will you?"

"If you can free us from our bondage to those who have come from the other side of the sky, yes."

"I can promise only to do my best to make this happen."

"Good." The Gnome turned, and rather than re-entering the tunnel from which he had emerged, walked straight through one of the earthen walls.

Otto shuddered. "It's not natural, that walking through walls."

"I can do it," Jane reminded him.

"I know. And I still say that it's not natural."

"Quiet," Jane commanded. "Can you hear something? A sort of rumbling noise?"

Otto listened. "Yes, you're right. It's getting louder."

With an almost explosive noise, a dozen or so Gnomes burst through the walls, each bearing a lantern. Jane and Otto were dazzled by the relative brightness, as the Gnomes saluted Jane and hailed her as their mistress who had come to save them.

"This doesn't help us very much, does it?" said Otto.

"It's more comfortable, though. And I think that my father hates light like this." She looked down at the Gnomes. "They're rather endearing, aren't they?" she said to Otto quietly. "I keep wanting to reach down and pat their heads, like a dog. But I don't think that would be a good idea."

"Certainly not," said Otto. "What's that on the wall?" He

pointed to some marks scratched into the earth wall of the chamber.

"It's Hebrew," said Jane.

"I can see that. It says 'Geburah'."

"Meaning?"

"It means severity," Otto told her. It's one of the Sephirod. The middle one in the Pillar of Boaz."

"Oh. And what do you make of that?"

"That we are close to your father. Any moment now, I expect him to come out of one of those tunnels," pointing to the tunnels in front of them.

"Or perhaps this one," came a familiar hated voice from behind them.

Jane spun round to face her father. "You?"

"Who else?" He looked down at the assembled Gnomes. "Ah, my little pretty ones. How sweetly you sing your hymns to your new mistress." His voice rose as he continued. "Or rather, the one you call your new mistress. Remember, if you would, that I am still your master." He pointed his long finger at one of the Gnomes. A flash of electrical fire, as if from a Leyden jar, shot out towards the unfortunate Elemental, who screamed briefly as his body disappeared, leaving only a small pile of smoking black ashes on the ground. "Now leave!" he shrieked at the terrified Elementals. "I have private business with these two."

Jane and Otto watched, paralysed with fear, as the surviving Gnomes scuttled through the walls of the chamber, squeaking in terror as they went.

"Why did you do that?" Jane asked.

"Why didn't you stop me?" her father answered.

"How?"

"By putting protection over them all, of course."

"How would I do that?"

A slow smile, exposing long teeth. "You mean you don't know?"

Jane shook her head.

"This one," pointing at Otto with the same finger that had shot the fatal flame, "is not protected. Is he?"

Jane said nothing, but shook her head silently.

"You won't tell me? Perhaps I'd better find out."

"No!" Jane screamed. Otto had gone white, and he was shaking with fear as Jane's father fixed him with his gaze and the finger continued to point steadily at his heart.

"Give me a good reason why I shouldn't. I might take note. I'm listening. Come on," her father urged Jane.

"He's… he's my friend. He's helped me in the past."

"Who can help you more in the future? Him? Me? No, don't answer. You'll upset one of us, however you answer. Difficult choice, isn't it?" The smile returned. "I'll make it easy for you."

Again the flame shot out. Otto writhed in agony for a second or two, and let out a single scream before he, too, became a pile of ashes beside that of the Gnome.

"You… you…"

"Killed him? Yes. Of course, like us and unlike the Elementals, he has an immortal soul. There's a new beginning for him somewhere."

"You are a…" Words were not enough.

"You should learn the arts of protection," she heard her father's voice say to her.

Angrily, she jerked her head up, her eyes snapping wide open – to find herself alone. Somehow, Otto's vial of phosphorus had survived intact in the dark pile that was all that remained of her friend, and was still glowing faintly, as if mocking her.

She wept bitterly for the loss of her friend. The memories

of the first time she had met him, Swiss and German inns, the hours in the Landgrave's library, the ride towards Paris, and the times here in England, all came flashing back as the tears rolled down her cheeks.

Her tears hissing on the hot ashes as she bent over, she retrieved the vial before retracing her lonely steps along the tunnel through which she and Otto had entered the chamber, weeping silently as she walked.

JANE WAS DISTRAUGHT at the loss of Otto, who she realised had meant more to her than she had recognised. In addition, she had found it difficult to come to terms with what Darwin had told her regarding the death of her foster-sister.

She desperately needed to talk to someone, but there were reasons why each one of them was not the right person. Darwin himself was in some ways the cause of her distress. Much as she admired and even loved him, it would be impossible for her to talk to him.

Sir George was certainly pleasant and intelligent enough, but every time she saw him, he reminded her uncomfortably of his dead twin, and it brought forward memories she would sooner have kept buried.

Lord Grenfell was a delightful companion, but he seemed too young to offer any constructive help or advice regarding her situation. In addition, Jane had a suspicion that he harboured feelings for her – perfectly honourable feelings, but ones which would only add further complications.

She felt that the bishop would only offer sugar-coated platitudes, and besides, she found it difficult to converse with him, since he was at least partially deaf.

Professor Parseval had also been Otto's friend, and had

347

wept copiously when she had announced his friend's demise to the assembled company. It would be her, she was sure, who would be attempting to console him rather than his consoling her.

She had no real dislike of Professor Marlowe, but he seemed to be unaware of her age at times, even going so far as to pat her on the head and call her "my dear", neither of which pleased her.

Which left the rabbi. She had not had much chance to talk to him, but the fact that Otto had said that he was both wise and compassionate would have made him her choice as a shoulder on which to cry, even if the perceived deficiencies of the others had been absent.

Finding Baruch ben Chaim alone in the library, she told him of her recent conversation with Darwin and all the details of how she and Otto had squabbled and bickered just before his extinction at the hands of her father. She also remembered how Thomas FitzAlan had died, and how she had witnessed the death of the girl with whom she had grown up, while ignorant of her identity.

"I wish I had been kinder towards him. If only..." she sobbed. "And Florella – Mary – if only I had known."

He heard her in silence. All this must be hard for you to bear. But why have you sought my counsel? You are no Jew. Why do you think that an elderly rabbi such as myself can be of assistance?"

"I feel you are better able to give me advice to protect me. The words you spoke about the Tree of Life, and before that, the advice you have given me, seem to me to be valuable."

"You mean what I said about your being in charge of your anger, rather than your anger mastering you?"

"Yes, among other things."

"Anger is a powerful force. Control it. Direct it against

those who deserve it. But do not turn it against yourself. Neither should you let it build up inside you like steam within a pot. The result will not be pleasant when the pot bursts. Grief, on the other hand, is natural and healing. Your weeping now is a gift from God, if you choose to make it so."

"Did you weep at the news of Otto's death?"

"Of course I did. I also said Kaddish for him, though we do not have a minyan – that is, ten Jews – to say it together."

"Kaddish?"

"This is the prayer that we offer to God when one we love has gone from us. You have no Hebrew?" Jane shook her head. "Then I will tell you. It is a prayer for peace and a blessing of His name. This is how it starts. 'Exalted and hallowed be His great Name. Amen.

"'In the world which He will create anew, where He will revive the dead, construct His temple, deliver life, and rebuild the city of Jerusalem, and uproot foreign idol worship from His land, and restore the holy service of Heaven to its place, along with His radiance, splendour and Shechinah, and may He bring forth His redemption and hasten the coming of His Moshiach. Amen.'

"And it ends thus, 'May there be abundant peace from heaven, and a good life for us and for all Israel; and say, Amen. Amen.

"'He Who makes peace in His heavens, may He make peace for us and for all Israel; and say, Amen.'"

"Amen," Jane echoed automatically. "That is beautiful. And thank you so much for remembering our friend Otto in this way."

Ben Chaim bowed his head. "What else could I do?"

"But what should I do? What can I do to help myself? Are you able to help me?"

"Take this," he said, reaching inside his robe and producing two small boxes with straps attached to them. "These are tefillin. One on your right arm, above the elbow," he pointed to his own arm, "and the other on your forehead."

"What is in the boxes?" Jane asked. "Magic spells?"

"Oh no. Not magic. Words from the Torah which will dispel demons. Let me show you how to put them on."

He produced two more similar boxes, and while standing, recited some words in Hebrew while binding the straps of one box in a complex pattern around his arm, and the straps of the other around his forehead.

"I will never remember how to do that," Jane complained. "In any case, I'm not Jewish. Will they protect me?"

"It is not they who protect you, but God who protects you. These are a sign that He protects all they who love and serve Him. I believe you to be one of those. But if you find these too complicated to wear in this way, you may simply wear them as an amulet around your neck."

"Thank you," Jane said.

After a period of silence, ben Chaim suddenly said to Jane, "You could not have saved any of them, you know. Thomas FitzAlan, Florella, Otto. These things were outside your control. I say again to you, do not be angry with yourself. Turn your anger against those responsible for the destruction of those you have loved."

"I am powerless, though, even if I am protected, thanks to you."

The old rabbi sat for a while, stroking his beard thoughtfully. "I have the beginnings of an idea how you may achieve this," he said at length. "Give me a day or so to prepare. I will let you know when we may speak again. Now, go, prepare yourself. Mourn for those you have lost. Pray for strength for yourself." He stretched out his hand and said a few words in Hebrew.

"What is that?"

"Blessed are You, Lord our God, King of the Universe, Who bestows good things upon the unworthy, and has bestowed upon me every goodness," he replied. "Keep these words in your heart as you pray."

FOLLOWING THIS CONVERSATION, Jane attempted to follow ben Chaim's advice. She kept reminding herself that her anger was not to be directed against herself, and repeating as much of the rabbi's prayers as she could remember.

She walked in the park, attempting to find peace and happiness in the trees and greenery. Young Lord Grenfell joined her on more than one occasion, and though it was clear to Jane that he possessed affectionate feelings towards her, he was also in possession of sufficient intelligence and manners to keep these to himself. Together they walked in a silence which she found companionable. Even though few words were spoken between them, and these few of a formal kind, she had the sense that if she were to pour out her feelings to him, he was possessed of sufficient sensibility as to respond appropriately.

After three days of this, a servant brought word to Jane that the rabbi wished to speak to her in the library. He greeted her, beaming.

"I believe I have the answer," he said. "Let me tell you a story. Sit down."

Jane settled herself, and the rabbi began. "You remember this," he said, producing the paper on which he had drawn the 'Unholy Tree of Life'. "Do you remember? Our enemy – your father, that is – has reached Malkuth without passing through the foundation, Yesod. Your task will be to remove him from Malkuth and return him to a state of non-completion and hence non-being, by exposing him to the previous Sephirod that he passed through on the way to Malkuth." He pointed to these on the paper. "If he is exposed to the full force of Hod, that is to say, the splendour and glory of God, and then to Gevurah, the principle of God's judgement, I believe he will perish."

"You speak of these attributes as if they were real physical substances, like the airs that the natural philosophers talk about."

"They are indeed real. They are with us at all times. Maybe we cannot see them or experience them with our senses, but trust me, they are with us, sustaining and supporting us."

Jane frowned.

"Let me explain." From under the table, he produced three earthenware jars, undecorated other than by a few Hebrew letters on each, with oilcloth tied to cover the neck, and sealed with wax. "These represent the Vessels which were broken at the beginning of all things. I see you are still puzzled. According to some of my co-religionists, at the beginning of the world, at one stage all the attributes of God were contained in fragile vessels which broke. These here," indicating the three vessels, "contain the attributes that will take him back to a state of non-being."

"He will die?"

"No. He will cease to be. There is a difference. Think on it."

"I see what you mean. But how is this to be achieved?"

"You must break these vessels in order. First, call his name, and then break this one, Malkuth. Next, Hod, again calling his name before the vessel is broken. He will weaken with each breaking. And lastly, shout his name so that the Lord will hear it, and smash this one, Gevurah, so that he may experience the full measure of God's justice. And that," he concluded with an air of satisfaction, "will be the end of him."

"And what will happen to me?" Jane asked. "Will it be safe for me, half-Fae as I am?"

The rabbi sat in silence looking at her for some time before answering. "I cannot give you any assurance there," he said at length. "My fear is that you will also cease to be."

"You are not sure of this?"

He spread his hands in a gesture of hopelessness. "How can a man be sure of anything that God governs? My hope is, naturally enough, that you will come through this ordeal unharmed. But I cannot be sure that you will."

"And if I refuse to meet him? Or, when I have met him, I cannot break these vessels, and will spare him in order to save myself?"

"Now, my child, you are talking nonsense," the rabbi told her. "I may not know what will be the result of your breaking of these vessels, but I know that you will indeed break them and destroy the one who calls himself your father. If that were not so, the power in them would not be there now."

"Are you sure of this?" Jane asked, reaching out and gingerly touching one of the earthenware pots. It felt somehow alive. She was sure that it was humming silently to itself, and she felt a sense of what might almost be described as exhilaration as her fingers made contact with the vessel.

"I am sure. Leave your fingers there," for Jane was withdrawing her hand from the pot. "What do you feel?"

"Power," said Jane instantly. "But it's good power. Not the sort of power He – my father – brings with him."

"You will prevail. It is willed. What happens after you prevail..." He shrugged. "Now go. Take those pots with you. And take my blessing and prayers with them."

It was a clear dismissal, and Jane did as she had been ordered.

Now she had to make her way back to face her father. For

a brief moment she considered the idea of inviting Lord Grenfell to accompany her. He was certainly happy enough to be in her company, but she had a sickening feeling that such an invitation would result in his death.

Her eyes filled with tears as she took the punch-bowl which she had previously used with Otto, and placed it in the centre of the table, surrounding it with Sir Richard's discarded kerchiefs. Then it struck her that Sir Richard was not the ultimate object of her search – her father. Of course, it was quite possible that her father was with Sir Richard. On the other hand, it was quite possible that he was not. Even so, Sir Richard was probably the only way through which she could reach her father.

She concentrated on finding Sir Richard, and soon enough it was possible for her to see him in the water in front of her. As before, she was able to enter the space where he was. No longer a salt mine, but a huge rocky cavern. Daylight was just visible, and she followed it to the entrance of the cave, which she recognised from engravings she had seen in books as the Derbyshire cave known as "The Devil's Arse".

Once again, she called to her Sylphs, who appeared in front of her. When she explained her destination, it was possible to detect a tremor in their voices.

"As you wish, Mistress," said the taller Sylph. "But forgive us if we do not stay with you."

"I will be safe," she said, thinking of the protection that ben Chaim had given her. She hoped that the doubts she felt regarding this protection were not perceptible in her voice.

THE SYLPHS TOOK HER to the entrance to the cave, and she made her way through the first chamber, past the cottages of the rope-makers who lived there, to the pool formed by the stream that led to the Great Cavern. Ignoring the boat that was tied to the shore, she used her own powers to raise herself off the ground, and made her way to the other side.

To her surprise, she could clearly see the details of the Great Cavern's walls, though only a faint light from the entrance was immediately visible.

Against the backdrop of the rock walls, she could make out a shape moving, which resolved itself into a human form. The warm sticky feeling that she usually associated with her father's presence began to make itself noticeable, as the figure, now recognisable as Sir Richard Willington, dressed immaculately and incongruously in the height of fashion, became clearer.

He extended a hand towards her as he approached, and swept a low bow.

"Good evening, daughter." Though there were no sibilants in the greeting, nonetheless his voice had a hissing quality to it.

"You are…"

"Yes, I am your father."

"How are you…?" She gestured towards him.

"How am I now in this human's body?" He shrugged. "He had no further use for it."

"How is that so?"

"He was a fool. Like others in the past, he believed he could control me, and through that, control all of us, and thereby make himself master of this world, and those worlds on the other side of the sky." He shook his head, a look of sardonic amusement on his, or to be more precise, Sir Richard's, face. "He was mistaken in his belief."

"And?"

"And so I decided it would be amusing to take his form for

a while. Do you not agree? Amusing?" He bent forward in a parody of a courtly bow.

"Amusing to inhabit a corpse? I do not find it so," Jane replied with a shudder.

"Daughter of mine, you lack our sense of humour," he chuckled. "You will learn when you come to join us."

"I will never join you. You may be my father, but I am not your daughter, Bakhamas," said Jane, calling him by the name spelled out the Hebrew letters that the rabbi had denoted on the Tree of Life to form the name of the being in front of her.

The effect on the other was dramatic. His face, formerly the fashionable pale skin of Sir Richard, turned a dark red, almost black, and his eyes glowed.

"How do you know my name?"

Jane faced her father, ignoring the question. "How long do you imagine that you can continue here? We know enough of you and your kind to expel you from this world for ever."

He laughed bitterly. "You speak of 'we'. Who are you? Are you not as much a part of us as you are of them?"

"In my blood, perhaps. In my heart I am of this earth. And you? You are of nowhere. Your world was destroyed long ago, and all you have left is the nothingness on the other side of the sky."

"We have this world now. We control the Elementals." A pause. "At least, we did. Now it appears that you do." His tone changed to one of pleading. "We need you, my daughter."

"For what? To enslave and kill my friends, as you killed my mother and the one who replaced her in my affections?"

"The killings were necessary."

"Explain."

"You cannot understand. Not as you are now."

"How do you mean?"

"You are too bound by the chains of humanity. Cast them off, and you will understand."

"And what of the Elementals to whom I have made promises?"

"What of them? Promises are made to be broken. In any event, the Elementals have no souls like you or I, or humans. If they perish, will they be missed?"

"Your morality is not mine. I may have your blood in me, but I lack your heartlessness and cruelty."

He laughed again. "The Landgrave's nephew? The boatman on the river? Those who sought to rob you on the road to Paris? The poor deluded fools in Paris who thought they could best me? You too have blood on your hands."

"They deserved to die."

"And who are you to judge them?"

She had no immediate answer to that. They faced each other for what seemed to be an eternity.

"You see, you really are one of us," he said. There was a note of triumph in his voice.

"I am something else. Something more than you."

"You are nothing." He raised his finger and pointed it at her in the same fashion that he had pointed it at Otto.

Flame shot from the finger towards Jane, and stopped, a foot or more from her body.

"So you have learned the secret of protection? Congratulations." His voice dripped irony. "Perhaps..?" Without warning, about twenty Gnomes appeared through the walls. "Seize her and bind her," commanded the Fae. Not a Gnome moved. "Why do you not obey me?" he screamed. His finger shot flame at the nearest Gnome, who disappeared in a flash of light, leaving the now-familiar pile of ash. "Now you will obey me!" he yelled at... nothing. The Gnomes were no longer there.

"How did they move so fast?" he asked, more to himself than to Jane, who stood there placidly, a faint smile on her lips. "You…? What did you do?"

"That is for me to know. Not you."

She removed the first vessel, Hod, from the placket of her dress.

"Bakhamas!" she screamed, and dashed the clay vessel to the stone floor.

THERE WAS A POWERFUL FLASH OF LIGHT as the vessel broke into tiny shards. The intensity was so great that Jane was forced to close her eyes against the searing brilliance, tensing herself against the forthcoming sound of what she was sure was going to be a powerful explosion.

Rather than a loud crash, all she could hear was a pitiful wail, amplified by the echoes of the chamber, and drowning out the faint tinkle of the pieces of the vessel falling to the floor of the cave.

She opened her eyes and blinked. The creature in front of her – Sir Richard? Bakhamas? – now had an almost ghostly quality. She was sure that she could now see through it to the walls of the cavern. It fell to its knees and looked her in the face.

"You… will… destroy… yourself… if… you… destroy… me." The voice was weak and tortured. Clearly the first vessel had produced the effect that ben Chaim had predicted. But, she asked herself, what about the part that he felt unable to predict? Would be that she would cease to be? Her fears increased, but she forced herself to answer her father. "And what if I do? Will this world not be better without the Fae? Even the half-Fae, such as myself?"

There was no answer as she drew the second vessel, Hod, from her placket.

"Bakhamas!" she shrieked, throwing the vessel at the floor directly before her adversary. Again the blinding flash, but this time accompanied by what sounded to her ears to be the sound of a lone trumpet sounding a mournful note, reverberating from the walls of the cavern.

She opened her eyes and blinked. The kneeling figure was now almost transparent, and she had to strain her eyes to discern its boundaries. A hoarse whisper came from it, so faint that she had to bend to make out what it was saying. She could just make out its words.

"You... do... not... understand... what... you... are... doing... to... yourself..."

Again, she paused for thought, but only for a moment, as she remembered her mother, Kate Perkins and her daughter whom she had known as Florella, Thomas FitzAlan, and Otto. Even Montalba, Ortolanus, and how many others had there been over the years? If she also was to die, would that one extra death have any significance? Would her death together with her father save lives in the future? She weighed the possible future of thousands in her mind, and weighed it against her own life. Tears in her eyes, she drew out the last vessel, Gevurah, Justice, and held it in her hand.

"You... little... fool...," were her father's last words to her as she hurled the vessel at him. It passed straight through him, and bounced once off the floor before landing on a sharp rock, where it shattered.

The flash this time was even more brilliant than the previous occasions, and was accompanied this time by the muffled sound of a solitary drum, which grew ever fainter as if the drummer was marching away from her.

She opened her eyes as the sound died away to behold

– nothing. There was no trace of the being that had been in front of her. What was clear, though, was the fact that she was still obviously alive. She pinched herself to make sure.

From the silent walls, she could hear the beginnings of a rustling and a buzzing, as of a mass of insects swarming and she could make out dozens of shapes that appeared to be similar to her father's true shape emerging from the walls into the cavern. With horror, she realised that she was now surrounded by the hosts of the Fae, who were no doubt bent on revenge for the destruction of their leader.

"I am here," she called. Her voice, thin as it was, bounced off the walls of the cavern, and transformed her words into a challenge.

One of the Fae stepped forward, and sank to one knee. "We are here, Highness. At your command. Speak what you will, and we shall obey you."

She realised with a shock that the Fae, once loyal to her father, had transferred their allegiance to her. Whether it was because she was his daughter, or she had shown herself to have a greater power than he had possessed, she was unsure. What mattered now was that the Fae were hers to command.

The whole world and all that was in it, humans and Elementals, were now hers for the taking if she chose, now she knew she was destined to live. It was an easy decision to make. She considered the matter for a few seconds at most before she knew what her answer must be.

She raised her voice. "My people," she cried out to them. "Return to the place whence you came. Return to the worlds on the other side of the sky. This world is not worth the struggle and pain that will be inflicted on you, believe me."

"Will you return with us?" asked the kneeling Fae.

She shook her head. "I cannot return. I was never there. But I command you all to leave. On the other side of the sky, you may choose for yourselves a new leader. But before you leave, you must, all of you, swear never to return to this world."

"I hear and obey you," said the kneeling Fae. He rose and turned to the others. "Do we all swear never to return to this world once we have left it?"

"We swear this," came the answer.

"You may depart this world now," Jane commanded them. "Go!"

Again the rustle of insect wings as the cavern emptied, and Jane was left in the semi-darkness.

She began to realise the enormity of what she had just done. She felt weak and faint, and slumped onto a stone, exhausted.

The Aftermath

S HE AWOKE, COLD AND HUNGRY, with no idea of how much time had passed. It was pitch black, and for a moment she had no idea of where she was.

Before she had started on her journey to the Devil's Arse from Shawborough she had taken a candle and a flint and steel, and she used these to provide her with light. As soon as she saw the rocky floor, and fragments of the shattered vessels, everything fell into place. Something felt wrong, though. She could not put her finger on what it was, but something appeared to be missing.

She could remember clearly what had just occurred, and how she had banished the Fae from the world. Exploring her memories, she could think of no gaps. She could even remember the colour of the walls in her Parisian room where she had stayed with Thomas FitzAlan.

Time to return to Shawborough. She attempted to summon her Sylphs and waited, but there was no answer to her summons. Perhaps the Sylphs could not be summoned from within a cavern such as this? Perhaps the Gnomes could answer this question? But no Gnomes responded to her summons.

In the flickering light of the candle, she made her way to the pool that blocked the route to the outside world, and willed herself into the air to cross it, as she had done when entering the cave. Her feet remained obstinately on the ground, despite her best efforts.

She had to leave the cave, so she hitched up her skirts, and holding them as high as she could with one hand, and holding the candle with the other, waded through the water. Despite her efforts, her clothes had become wet, and trailed behind her as she dragged herself out into the fresh air outside the cave. It was a calm cloudless night, and the cold chilled her to her bones. The cottages of the rope-makers within the cave appeared to be deserted, but there were some lights visible a few hundred yards away in the town of Castleton.

She dragged herself to one of these lights, a tavern, and knocked on the door as hard as she could.

"We're closed," a man's voice shouted through the door.

"Please let me in," she cried back.

"It's a woman, Jethro," she could hear a female voice saying. "For pity's sake, at least open the door."

There was a sound of bolts being drawn back, and the door swung open. A burly man stood in the doorway, a lantern in his hand, and a woman's shape stood behind him.

"Where's tha been?" he asked in amazement, as he took in Jane's dirty wet clothing. "Half clemmed with the cold, I reckon."

"Poor lass," said the woman. "Come in and sit by the fire."

Gratefully Jane entered the room and took the seat.

"We'll get thee a blanket, and help thee out of tha wet

clothes," said the landlord's wife. Jethro, don't stand their gawping like a dead sheep. Get the lass a blanket."

Soon Jane was wrapped up and warming by the fire, her clothes steaming beside her.

"Where's tha from?"

"Shawborough Hall. Staffordshire. My name's Jane Machin, by the way."

"I've heard of 'un," Jethro said. "How did tha come here from there, lass?"

Jane told a story of how she'd been part of a party of ladies and gentlemen who had come to visit the cavern, and how she'd been separated from them in the dark. Although she'd heard their voices searching for her, the voices had drifted away, and she'd been left alone in the cave.

"Have you seen any of them in the town?" Jane asked.

"Seen nowt. Have you, Becky?" Jethro asked his wife, who shook her head. "That's right bad of them to go away and leave you there." Somehow it didn't seem to be strange to her that a party of well-heeled adventurers would abandon one of their party in a dark damp cavern.

"Can someone get a message to Shawborough? Or can someone take me there?"

"Old Dickson might take thee in the morning. He'd charge a pretty penny for it, mind," Becky told her. "But I don't reckon that'd be a problem for thee," looking at Jane's clothes drying beside her. "Hungry?" she asked.

Jane nodded, and in a few minutes a slab of bread and a cup of milk was set before her. "I have no money to pay you," she said. "But if this Mr Dickson can take me to Shawborough, I will be able to pay him for his trouble, and give him money to take to you."

"We'll see about that in the morning. Now, the bed upstairs is ready for the. Follow me, me duck. I'll fetch the clothes to thee in the morning. And Jethro, no peeking as Miss Machin goes upstairs dressed in nowt but a blanket."

Dutifully, Jethro turned his back as Jane climbed the stairs behind her hostess, and was shown to a room containing a bed.

"Reckon thee'll be warm enough, duck," she said as she left the room. "I'll call thee in the morning and bring tha things upstairs for you. I'll get Old Dickson round here and you can speak to him then."

Jane climbed into bed, and, as promised, soon felt comfortably warm. Her sleep in the cavern meant that she was not tired, and her thoughts whirled around her head.

She had changed. First and foremost, she realised that a sense of fear that had always hung over her like a black cloud had vanished. Her father was no more. The Fae were no longer in this world.

But there was a sense of loss. Somehow she knew that she would never again see another Salamander. She would never again be able to summon Sylphs to carry her where she wished. And if she tried to walk through walls like a Gnome, she would probably break her nose. As for living underwater like an Undine…

It came to her in a flash that she was human. Purely human. For the first time in her life the word "we" fully included her.

She turned over in the warm soft bed and relaxed. Now she knew who she was, she could let her fancy freely roam where it wanted to go.

Her last thoughts, before she drifted off to sleep, were questions in her mind on what the future might hold for her if she allowed herself to become Lady Grenfell.

AFTERWORD

"No man but a blockhead ever wrote except for money."

I'VE ALWAYS BEEN FASCINATED by the idea that we are not alone as a sentient species. The "Others" may not always be little green men from outer space, though. There are many stories from around the world of beings coming from other worlds that are not physically part of our universe.

Borges, in one of his stories, talks about a Chinese legend whereby demons were imprisoned behind mirrors following a war with humans, and were condemned to mimic the actions of humans standing in front of the mirrors. One of these days, the demons will escape. In her wonderful book, *Jonathan Strange & Mr Norrell*, Susanna Clarke also sees mirrors as gateways into other worlds. I too make use of a mirror in this book at one point, as a means to aiding clairvoyance. I apologise to Ms Clarke if she feels I have taken some of the aspects of her Faerie for my Fae, but ultimately, I feel that she and I are both speaking of the same universal archetypes which are characterised by these creatures.

Lots of cultures describe the Little People, the Good Folk, the Faerie, or other such creatures, and they are not universally seen as friendly or well-disposed towards humanity. However, I don't see them as the prototype for demons, but as amoral creatures who are homeless and seek a refuge. Homeless because they are the products of a failed creation, as described in some Jewish legends.

There are also legends from other cultures of other non-human beings, be they Sylphs, Dryads, Naiads, Gnomes, Fauns, Salamanders, and so on. These were codified by the Rosicrucians and their predecessors, the spiritual alchemists, into the four types of Elemental listed here. These are (in my universe) native to our world, unlike the Fae, and lack souls, unlike humans or Fae.

The writing of this book occupied me, on and off, for just over a year. In the course of this, I found myself drifting into interesting byways of knowledge. The history of the Lunar Society and its members, focussing on the life of Erasmus Darwin, whose Lichfield house is less than ten minutes' walk away from where I am currently writing these lines, was obviously a subject of interest.

And then I found my course leading me into 17th century and earlier writings on alchemy, and the Rosicrucian experience, attempting to make sense of the deep nonsense that seemed to run like a thread through the genre. It was clear that the idea of making gold from lead, and all the other recipes were for many alchemists merely a symbol of something more, and this was obviously taken up by the Rosicrucians later on.

And then Kabbala – a subject of which I knew very little, and still do know very little, relatively. I become fascinated by the idea of the Tree of Life and the Sephirod, and looked at various aspects of the Jewish traditions regarding these. I am well aware that what I have written regarding Kabbala is not what many believe and I make no pretence that what I have written here is in any way an authentic representation of their beliefs or interpretations. From my reading, it does appear that the rabbinical traditions are extraordinarily diverse, and the interpretation I ascribe to ben Chaim may well correspond to some schools of thought.

I love the Jewish idea of the Breaking of the Vessels at the time of creation, and decided to use that as a metaphor of destruction as well as of creation. Knowing one's adversary's name, of course, corresponds to a long-held belief that knowledge of a name is power.

And the Revellers of Thoth? Why do they have such an extraordinary name? I don't know. It came to me in a semi-dream one night, lodged in my memory, and I loved the sound and feel on the words, so decided to use it.

HISTORICAL NOTES: The timeline I have employed is pretty accurate to a year or two. Most historical events mentioned are within or very close to the timeline here. The main exception is the painting of Joseph Wright of Derby's *An Experiment on a Bird in the Air Pump*, which was painted long before the events related here. I therefore had to invent a supernatural explanation for this.

All other inaccuracies are, I believe, minor ones. I have endeavoured to keep the characters of the real historical figures in the story as close to their reality, as far as possible, given what we know of them, and the constraints of fiction.

LOOKING BACK over what I have written, I enjoyed the story I created, but I have a sneaking suspicion that there's something more to these words than I first thought. Hope you enjoyed reading it.

ABOUT THE AUTHOR

HUGH ASHTON was born in the United Kingdom, and moved to Japan in 1988, where he lived until his return to the UK in 2016.

He is best known for his Sherlock Holmes stories, which have been hailed as some of the most authentic pastiches on the market, and have received favourable reviews from Sherlockians and non-Sherlockians alike.

He has also published other work in a number of genres, including alternative history, historical science fiction, and thrillers, based in Japan, the USA, and the UK.

He currently lives in the historic city of Lichfield with his wife, Yoshiko.

His ramblings may be found on Facebook, Twitter, and in various other places on the Internet. He may be contacted at: author@HughAshtonBooks.com

IF YOU ENJOYED THIS STORY…

PLEASE CONSIDER WRITING A REVIEW on a Web site such as Amazon or Goodreads.

You may also enjoy some adventures of Sherlock Holmes by Hugh Ashton, who has been described in *The District Messenger*, the newsletter of the Sherlock Holmes Society of London, as being "one of the best writers of new Sherlock Holmes stories, in both plotting and style".

Volumes published so far include:

Tales from the Deed Box of John H. Watson M.D.
More from the Deed Box of John H. Watson M.D.
Secrets from the Deed Box of John H. Watson M.D.
The Darlington Substitution (novel)
Notes from the Dispatch-Box of John H. Watson M.D.
Further Notes from the Dispatch-box of John H. Watson M.D.
The Death of Cardinal Tosca (novel)
The Last Notes from the Dispatch-box of John H. Watson, M.D.
The Trepoff Murder (ebook only)

1894

Without my Boswell
Some Singular Cases of Mr. Sherlock Holmes
The Lichfield Murder
The Adventure of the Bloody Steps
The Adventure of Vanaprastha (ebook only)

Children's detective stories, with beautiful illustrations by Andy Boerger, the first of which was nominated for the prestigious Caldecott Prize:

Sherlock Ferret and the Missing Necklace
Sherlock Ferret and The Multiplying Masterpieces
Sherlock Ferret and The Poisoned Pond

Sherlock Ferret and the Phantom Photographer

The Adventures of Sherlock Ferret

Short stories, thrillers, alternative history, and historical science fiction titles:

Tales of Old Japanese

At the Sharpe End

Balance of Powers

Beneath Gray Skies

Red Wheels Turning

Angels Unawares

The Untime

The Untime Revisited

Unknown Quantities

Mapp and Lucia stories in the style of E.F.Benson:

Mapp at Fifty

Mapp's Return

La Lucia

A Tilling New Year

Full details of all of these and more at:
https://HughAshtonBooks.com

CPSIA information can be obtained
at www.ICGtesting.com
Printed in the USA
LVHW040244161121
703395LV00004B/4